Midnight Scandals

CAROLYN JEWEL

COURTNEY MILAN

SHERRY THOMAS

This is a work of fiction. Names, characters, places, and incidents are the product of the author's imagination or are used fictitiously. Any resemblance to actual events, locales, or persons, living or dead, is purely coincidental, except where it is a matter of historical record.

"One Starlit Night," © 2012 by Carolyn Jewel.
"What Happened at Midnight," © 2012 by Courtney Milan.
"A Dance in Moonlight," © 2012 by Sherry Thomas.
Cover design © Courtney Milan.

Cover photography credits:
  © Zagorodnaya | Shutterstock.com
  © Yeko Photo Studio | Shutterstock.com

All rights reserved. Except as permitted under the U.S. Copyright Act of 1976, no part of this publication may be reproduced, distributed, or transmitted in any form or by any means, or stored in a database or retrieval system, without the prior written permission of the author.

Table of Contents

"One Starlit Night," by Carolyn Jewel 5
"What Happened at Midnight," by Courtney Milan 93
"A Dance in Moonlight," by Sherry Thomas 191

About Carolyn Jewel 262
About Courtney Milan 264
About Sherry Thomas 266

One Starlit Night

CAROLYN JEWEL

Chapter One

March 13, 1813, the rear lawn of Doyle's Grange, Somerset, near the Exmoor hills, England

CRISPIN HOPE, FOURTH VISCOUNT NORTHWORD, stood to one side of the lawn and prayed for a miracle. None arrived. He remained unable to summon a blessed word. He twitched with the need to do something besides stand mute. Words, any words, would be better than his damnable silence. Action, any action, would be better than inaction. He managed to force a smile. A minor miracle, then. Hallelujah.

Naturally, a woman was involved in his present difficulties. A particular and specific woman. Was any man's heart ever brought to its metaphorical knees except by a woman? Minor miracle or no, he needed to say or do something to convey how unmoved he was by her.

He tapped the side of his left leg with two fingers. Next, he cleared his throat. Portia sent a questioning look his way. Of course, words failed him. He affected what he hoped appeared to be mild interest in the proceedings; practically nonexistent. He coughed again and dug into his store of conversational inanities. "A fine day."

"Mm." She arched her eyebrows. "A touch cold for me." Her attention returned to the sapling that was the reason he was standing out here in the first place.

He'd known Portia Temple since he was a boy of eight and she a girl of six. Twenty-one years. For the first ten years he'd never thought of her as anything but a friend and companion who by a quirk of fate happened to be female. Pity for her when boys were so superior, and how annoying that she'd disagreed.

For the second ten years he'd managed to set her neatly into a box in which she was devoid of femininity yet continued to exist as his best friend's sister. A woman he avoided, but with whom he kept a friendly correspondence. Friendly. Nothing more.

He did his best not to think about the time between those bookends of decades. Silence reached out and set fire to his nerves. "It's spring," he said. Oh, Jesus. Had he really said that? "One ought not be cold in spring."

That got him another careless glance, and he was convinced that she, unlike him, had found a way to forget. But then, in all their years of friendship, he'd always been the one who felt more deeply.

She stared at the sapling, head tilted. "You've been away too long. You've forgotten our weather."

Resentment boiled in him, and he required a monumental amount of sang-froid to let that pass. Forgotten? He bit back a retort but could not quash the sentiment that came with the impulse. He'd not forgotten a damned thing. It was no accident that this was his first visit to Doyle's Grange in ten years. Nor that this was his first time socializing since his wife's passing nearly two years ago. Outside the circle of his most intimate friends and women of a certain reputation, that is. He straightened the lay of his coat and said with sharp intent, "I've not forgotten anything."

"We'll disagree on that." If he'd not been watching her so closely, he might have missed the distress that briefly replaced her pleasant smile. But he had been watching, and he did, and it ripped him to shreds.

Jesus. They'd made their peace in letters and it was all a lie, all those words they'd written to each other were now stripped of that fantasy pax now that he was here. Instead of the two of them moving on in person as they had in letters, they were mired in the past.

She put a hand on one of the slender branches of the sapling. One would think that in ten years she'd have changed more than she had. He had. Her brother Magnus had. She was remarkably unaltered. Smiling, too-tall-for-a-woman, auburn-haired, full of life. It was—almost—as if those second ten years had never been.

While he watched her, she lifted the hem of her muslin skirt and tamped down the last shovelful of dirt around the tree she'd just planted. She was wholly unconscious of his stare. No. He'd not forgotten anything.

Mud coated the bottom and sides of her plain leather half-boots. Spatters of dirt clung to her hem. She'd not been careful when she pinned her hair this morning, for there were curls, and not the fashionable sort. Hers came loose every which way. In daylight, there was no disguising that her hair was more red than brown, and of all things, that was what doomed him. That dark red hair.

To no avail, he reminded himself she was Magnus's younger sister. He had years of correspondence from her. He'd not realized how her spirit had stolen into the pages and words she'd written. Every time he'd read one of her letters, she'd filled a space in his heart he ought to have closed off. He'd not even known it was happening until now. Far too late.

"What do you think, Crispin?" She wore thick gloves of the sort ladies wore when they gardened, and when she swiped a wisp of hair out of her face the careless motion left dirt on her cheek. The breeze sent the curl free to dangle at the side of her face. An undeniably red wisp of hair. Most women with hair that color insisted it was brown. Hers was a deep, dark, secret red. Soft in a man's hands, a river of curling, mysterious color that glinted with strands of gold.

He had been careful, over the last two years, never to make love to a woman with red hair.

"Well? What do you think?"

"About?" His query came late enough that she laughed at him.

"You didn't have to come out here. I told you you'd be bored." She put her hands on her hips. "What do you think about my tree?"

One afternoon, one unforgettable day—God, they'd been so heartbreakingly young—she'd changed him forever, while she went on being Portia. She knew him better than anyone. Still did. For God's sake, she knew him better than the woman he'd married. She hadn't blamed him for his choice. Never a reproach for his decisions, never a hint that she understood he had been avoiding her these last ten years. She knew, of course. She was too intelligent not to know. When it came right down to it, he wasn't blameless either. Not entirely.

"Well." He pretended to study the tree, but he was really looking at her. Her gown was a striped muslin with no bows, no lace, no fancy trim to direct a man's attention to the curve of a breast or the column of a throat. Yet here he stood remembering his hand sliding down smooth skin, the bang of his heart against his ribs because he had never touched a naked woman before, and, Lord, how sinfully luscious she was. Had been. Still was.

He still wanted her. There was nothing so surprising about that. Men lusted after women all the time. But his lust and desire had got mixed up and confused with more powerful emotions.

"It's a tree, not a Venus in marble." She peeked at him, then returned to her study of the tree. "There is no meaning to divine other than God was right to make them like this."

"I like oak trees. An oak is a proper English tree." In London, her serviceable frock would have been thought plain two seasons ago. This season? The fact was, no woman of his set would be caught dead in such a gown. But Portia had never been farther from Doyle's Grange than the village of Aubry Sock, some twenty miles distant. He was guiltily aware that he'd never invited Magnus *and* Portia to London before or after he was married. The reasons were legion, and not all them were to his credit. He'd wanted to think of her here at Doyle's Grange. Safe. Unchanging. Here in sight of the Exmoor hills where she would always love him with a passion that moved better men to poetry.

"I'm glad you like oaks, but this isn't an oak. It's a rowan."

"What?" He could not stop staring. Before long Portia was going to take offense.

She rubbed at her cheek, frowned and pulled off one of her gloves. "Have I got dirt on my face?"

"Yes."

She handed her spade to Hob, the man who served as Doyle's Grange's general servant; footman, groundsman, groom, butler, and performer of any other work there might be. Hob stood several feet back, idly tapping the side of his boot against the bucket of water at his feet. The man had looked a weathered forty-five or a well-preserved sixty for as long as he could remember.

The servant came forward to take the spade from Portia. He retreated a respectful distance.

Portia made a few more swipes at her cheek and missed the dirt each time. So like her. Northword knew he ought not stand there like the sexually stunned lump that he was. She'd know something was wrong, and he didn't see how he could possibly tell her that absolutely nothing, and everything, had changed. He wanted nothing more than to take her to bed again, and to do it as a man, not a green boy who didn't know his way around a woman. He took a certain piquant satisfaction from imagining the results of his mastery of that.

Thank God Hob was here because the Lord only knew what he might say or do. He had made his peace with Portia in words, if not in his heart, and as he stood here, seeing her for the first time in ten years, his very soul resonated with all that had never been spoken or put to paper. Better, he thought, if they had done. They ought to have screamed and shouted and accused instead of burying everything beneath a veneer of pleasantness.

"Hold still." He pulled out his spare handkerchief and walked to her. He could, and would, control his base urges. He put one hand underneath her chin, turned her face to the side, and wiped at the dirt. The smudge proved more stubborn than was safe for him. Her lips were full, that bottom lip so tender. Yet another delicate curve. Once, he would he have stolen a kiss. Taken it. Shared it.

"Hurry," she said. "It's cold."

"It isn't."

"It is." She blinked while he worked at the smudge. He remembered the way her eyes had fluttered closed when he had somehow managed to bring her pleasure during their mutual discovery and clumsiness. Too quick the first time. But slow and tender the next. Oh, the enthusiasm and quick recovery of youth during those weeks that he thought, stupidly, they would continue to escape consequences. All that against the deep, wide landscape of loving her.

"What do you think, Hob?" She seemed oblivious to Northword's stare and his memories.

"Well and good, Miss Temple." The man's Exmoor accent was as thick as ever, but, as it happened, Northword had not unlearned how to listen to that accent and make sense of it. "Well and good."

The smudge yielded to him. He held her chin a moment longer than he ought to have. He knew, now, how to conduct an affair—never outside his marriage, he'd kept those vows. "There. As tidy as I can make you."

"Thank you." She pulled off her other glove and shoved it in her pocket with the first one and made an even bigger lump to spoil the line of her gown. They did not have between them the safety imposed by the formality of titles. She'd always been Portia to him, never Miss Temple. He'd always been Crispin to her. It was only the direction of her letters that styled him according to his title.

Crispin. There were nights when he lay awake remembering the sound of his name on her lips as she came to pleasure. His body came alive at those moments.

"Will the lavender be all right there?" She pointed at the plants in question. Again, she was talking to Hob. "Or do you think it will be in too much shade? Too late now, of course."

"It'll be years before the tree's big enough for that." Of course he said *avore* not *before*. Remarkable, really, how easily one slid into understanding that accent. Hob leaned a forearm on the shovel. "Thee and me'll be long gone by then."

With the toe of her boot, she knocked away a clod of dirt. A smile flashed on her face, and Northword thought of the kind of sex that made lovers laugh. "Perhaps one day relations of mine will stand by this tree." She used both arms to describe a tree of immense size.

While she did that, his eye was drawn, inexorably, to her bosom, and he felt an absolute dog for it. She remained lush in her curves, more than a good many women, less than others. They'd be as good together as ever. Better. He knew it down to his marrow, that thrill of animal attraction.

She lowered her arms. "They'll curse whoever planted the tree so close to the lavender."

"Surely," he said from the safety of his London drawl, "they'll wonder what bumblehead planted the lavender so close to the tree."

Portia laughed, and his heart eased, to be followed immediately by guilt at his reaction. Just once, when he and his wife lay beside each other, her hand on his chest in a moment of perilous intimacy, she'd asked him whether he had ever loved someone else. His denial hadn't come quickly enough. She never asked again.

"I hope you're right." She tapped the ground again with her boot. The view of her ankle damn near brought him low. Was he not a better man than this? Well. No. He wasn't. She crossed her arms underneath her bosom, and the flesh above her neckline shifted in the most beguiling manner. "Done, then, Hob? Well planted?"

"Aye." Hob came forward with his bucket and, after a glance at him—was that suspicion in the man's eyes?—slowly poured the contents around the base of the rowan tree destined to be gigantic in a future that would not include him.

"I should like to know what this tree will look like in a hundred years." She eyed the tree, but shot him a sideways look, a smile on her lips. "Don't you?"

He shoved his hands in his pockets. "Strong and tall, I should think."

"Yes. Yes, my rowan tree will be strong and tall."

Quite deliberately, he closed his eyes and imagined a hundred-year-old tree, thick trunk, branches spreading over the house and shading this corner of the garden. In a hundred years, the world would be a vastly different place, and yet, there would be this tree, which Portia, the sublimely sexual creature inhabiting his senses, had planted with her own hands in honor of her upcoming marriage. She wanted, she'd told him, to know she'd left something of herself behind at Doyle's Grange. As if she could help doing that.

When he opened his eyes, the first thing he saw was not Portia, but an auburn-haired woman with a delicious mouth and a ripe figure. He saw a woman with a lover's mouth and hands. He blinked and forced himself to see her as Portia, his friend. Sister of his friend and a woman he'd allowed no claim to a difference in gender.

In the main, he failed.

Hob backed away from the rowan tree and sent a dark look in his direction. "Don't worry, Miss, if the sapling looks ill for a bit. Root shock, you know." He nodded sagely but, to Northword's eye, his look was tainted with distrust. Hob knew men weren't to be trusted. "Give her time. Don't overwater."

"I shan't, then."

"I'll watch over the tree, Miss. Even after thee's away."

"I know you will." She focused on Hob. He, Northword, might as well not be anywhere near. "Thank you. That would be a great comfort."

"Ah," said another woman. They all turned, him, Portia, and Hob. Mrs. Magnus Temple walked toward them.

Portia's brother had married eight months ago. Magnus, it turned out, had met his wife during one of his visits to Northword's London home and had been waiting ever since to have a Church living that would support a wife. As it happened, the living at West Aubry had always been Viscount Northword's to give, which he had done as soon as practical after the previous possessor passed away. Within weeks, Magnus was married. Think of that. Waiting years to marry the woman you loved. Until the time was right and not a moment past then.

Northword had stood up for Magnus at the wedding, which took place by special license at Northword House in London. He'd offered them the chapel here, not even half a mile up the slope at Northword Hill and been refused. They would be married now, please, not in the time it would take to open up the house. And so it was done. Had been done, without Portia knowing about the marriage until Magnus had written to her. The couple had honeymooned in Bath, where Northword had a house he'd offered to them for a month.

"There you are, Portia." Mrs. Temple arrived at the site of the tree planting and pursed her lips. She pointed at the undisturbed ground between the tree and the lavender. "What are those?"

"It's spring," Portia said. "Crocuses grow here every spring. You cannot hope to obliterate them all."

"I can and I shall do so." Mrs. Temple gestured at Hob and stepped around the patch of ground where the flowers were opening to the sun. "Dig them up, please." She curtseyed to Northword and went so far as to bow her head. Her pretty blonde head. "Lord Northword."

He bowed. "Mrs. Temple. Good morning to you."

The woman had the most angelic smile he'd ever seen. "Portia, my dear. Might I have a word?"

Chapter Two

IN THE FRONT PARLOR, PORTIA STOOD with her back to the fireplace and smiled at her sister-in-law. Until recently, she'd not needed the ability to feign a smile or good cheer or any other mood. She was learning that most useful skill, though at times she feared the effort would turn her into a completely different person. Alone, she was Portia. Around Eleanor, she was another woman entirely. A false Portia. A Portia without truth.

Eleanor had stopped by the desk where Portia used to sit when she did the household accounts. The household accounts were now Eleanor's domain. Her sister-in-law perched on the edge of the chair and, one hand on her lap, tapped a finger on the blotter. She gazed at Portia with an open, guileless concern that made her heart break.

"Yes?" Portia looked at the chair nearest the desk and decided she didn't dare sit. She wasn't good at interpreting Eleanor's sighs and silences, though it was safe to assume Eleanor would be heartbreakingly disappointed when Portia failed to divine what was expected of her from all the things she did not say.

Her brother's wife was generous and kind and assiduous in managing Magnus's household, and she loved Magnus. She lived for Magnus, and Portia adored Eleanor for loving her brother with such honesty. And yet, other than Magnus, they had nothing in common. Their minds, their interests, did not intersect at any point, and she felt guilty for her failure to genuinely like Eleanor.

The finger tapping continued. "Dear, dear Portia."

She smiled despite her dread of the conversation to come.

"What *are* we to do about you?"

"Nothing." She managed, she hoped, to keep a pleasant expression. Her stomach contracted into a painful lump. "I am content as I am, you know."

"But, Portia, my dear." Eleanor tapped the lump that was Portia's gardening gloves. "You might be brilliant, you know."

She maintained her smile for, alas, Eleanor meant socially brilliant. Brilliant in fashion.

"You've led a sheltered life here at Doyle's Grange. You do not see things as I do." She cocked her head. "If only Magnus had brought you to London. In time, you would have sparkled. I am convinced you would have had a dozen beaus. Some gentlemen prefer a quiet woman such as you are, though I think if you had ever been to London, you would have come out of your shell. I've seen you smile, my dearest sister, and I cannot believe there is not a young gentleman of exemplary manners and family who would not see you smile and fall instantly in love."

"I do not wish to have a dozen beaus or to dance away the night."

"You are not too old to marry well. Imagine the good you would do your brother if you did." She bent toward Portia, so earnest and mistaken. "Our connection to Lord Northword might be of great assistance in that."

"Magnus cannot afford to send me to London so that I may dance with gentlemen who do not suit me. Particularly when I have already found a man who does." She folded her hands together and struggled to match Eleanor's cheerful concern. "I'm sure you did not bring me here to talk of this." She smiled brightly. "Is there something I may assist you with? The household accounts, perhaps?"

Eleanor blinked rapidly and Portia felt horrible for her relief at diverting the conversation from the subject of suitable husbands. "What good fortune it is to have you for my sister. Without your kindness, I'd have a far more difficult time. Your brother, too, appreciates all that you do here."

"How may I be of help?" She was not safely off the shoal yet. The most innocent remark or expression might send Eleanor's mind reeling off toward ballrooms and dancing.

"If I may be honest—"

"Please."

"It's not so much what you may do, but what you ought not do and say. Especially if we are to engage Lord Northword's assistance."

"Oh?" This, too, was familiar territory.

Her sister-in-law's lips set in a grim line. "I should hate for anyone to take offense when I know you do not mean to offend."

"Indeed?"

"I know you will feel the same when I tell you this. I think that, living here as you have all your life, you are not aware of certain expectations."

"Indeed, I hope not to offend anyone. Have I?" She did not hide her surprise, nor her concern, for if Eleanor, who was made of all that was light and sweet, thought she might have offended anyone, she may well have done so.

Eleanor intertwined her fingers. By now, Portia knew better than to think her distress would last beyond the next twenty minutes, but it was impossible not to feel the cruelty of allowing anything to beset her. Her sister-in-law lived so deeply in her emotions that it was probably for the best they never lasted for long. "You mustn't be so familiar with Lord Northword."

Portia clasped her hands behind her back. "You think I am?"

"You know I adore you and think the world of you." Her puppy-eyes softened, and Portia's heart fell at the possibility that Eleanor was about to lose track of their conversation again. "You did wonders before I came here. Looking after Magnus and the house."

"Thank you."

The corner of Eleanor's mouth twitched down. "But, Portia, my dear, Lord Northword is a nobleman. A viscount." She leaned forward. "The head of an illustrious and very old family."

"I am aware." As if she didn't know.

"I thought my heart would stop when I overheard you call him by his Christian name." She patted her chest as if she suffered still. "The proper style, the dignified style, is either *my lord,* or *Lord Northword* or, so as not to repeat oneself too often, *sir.* You would know this if you had ever been to London as I have. If your circle of acquaintance included men such as Lord Northword. Men who, I assure you, would not be as tolerant as he. Was there ever a man so forgiving? Besides Magnus." Her mouth firmed. "I think not."

She mentally counted to five. "The mistake is mine, of course. It's just that I've always called him Crispin."

Eleanor gave a frustrated sigh. "But, my dearest. Portia. How can I explain this? All our plans depend upon Lord Northword wishing to do you a service."

"What plans do you mean?"

"He is your brother's patron." She wrung her hands, and even Portia, who wasn't inclined to think much of helpless women, felt that familiar tug on her emotions that made her wonder if Eleanor hadn't hit on precisely the behavior that ensured she would always come away with what she wanted.

How could anyone bear to see Eleanor unhappy? "If we are to succeed, you must show him the respect due a man of his rank and influence."

"You're quite right."

Eleanor straightened. "I am so glad you understand. He knows you do not *intend* to insult his dignity. He is a gentleman, after all. A nobleman. But I assure you, he feels it here." She touched the middle of her chest again. "Naturally, he's happy about your engagement, but he's here in support of Magnus as he steps more fully into his position in West Aubry. He'll want to see how the improvements at the church are progressing."

"Yes, Eleanor." It had been a shock when Crispin arrived at the Grange, despite her knowing he was to visit. No longer a married man. A widower. He'd walked in, and her heart had somersaulted in her chest with the same thrill as always. The years fell away to leave her with bare emotion despite knowing that aspect of their acquaintance was over. Over. Over and over. He was a man of the world now. He had been another woman's husband.

"In London, among the Ton, others will misunderstand your familiarity and think you uncouth. Nothing could be further from the truth. For all that you have red hair and make no effort to improve yourself, we will make a success of you. I promise you. Honestly, my dear sister, if only your hair were walnut brown, I am convinced you would have a dozen more admirers."

"I'm pleased with the one I have."

"If you won't do anything about your hair, you really ought to follow my advice as to your wardrobe. When I was in London, everyone wanted to know the name of my modiste. Everyone! Twice I had to intervene when other ladies tried to hire away Bridget."

"Thank you, but I do not wish to go to London." My God. They were back to London and the inadequacies of her dress, yet another familiar topic between them.

"Think what you may do there. *My* family, as you know, is easily as old as Lord Northword's. Why, Ryans have been in Kent since the days of William the Conqueror." Her smile made Portia wish she had the knack of looking so perfectly helpless. "While I love Magnus madly and think there can be no man finer, the fact is Temples are not so old a family as the Ryans."

"We Temples are a youthful lot." She nodded and nursed her faint hope that the conversation might be diverted again. "Not at all impetuous. Why, my grandfather took twenty years to decide whether he ought to move the hen house."

Eleanor frowned and waved a hand. "I ought to have spoken to you before Lord Northword arrived." She fluttered her eyes, and Portia suppressed the urge to comfort her. *There, there, you poor dear thing.* "I assure you, I did not anticipate your manner with him would be so familiar." A cloud of discontent floated in her cerulean eyes. "If I'd known…

"I am Magnus's wife and *I* should never call Lord Northword anything but that, unless it is *my lord,* or *sir* and therefore, you mayn't either. You'll surely meet other men of his rank, and higher, even, and with them you must be scrupulous."

Portia nodded, and it was killing her, it really was, to speak of anything even tangentially to do with Crispin. "I do see. Thank you. You would have warned me. I understand. I'm sure you ought to have."

Eleanor nodded as if Portia had given voice to the obvious. "Everything depends upon your appearance and your connections. Everything." You'd think she was a surgeon discussing treatments for a dread disorder. "You have not my family's standing, but I shall be there at your side to remind everyone. If we have Lord Northword's support, why, you might marry very well indeed."

"Yes, thank you. I believe I will, of course." There were times she was convinced her sister-in-law was clever and possibly even diabolical. Such as now. "But I am not going to London."

"Of course you are. I understand you have an arrangement with Mr. Stewart, but such arrangements come to naught all the time. No woman ought to marry until she has met at least eleven gentlemen who would be suitable husbands."

"Eleven?" How odd. Her sister-in-law's mind often confounded her this way. "Why not thirteen? Or a hundred?"

Her eyes went wide and, oh, Lord, they sparkled with joy. Too late Portia realized the error of expressing curiosity over the number of suitors one ought to have. Eleanor reached for Portia's hand. "Thirteen would be unlucky, and a hundred is far too many. No, eleven is the perfect number. Never fear. I will guide and advise you."

Portia summoned a weak smile. Eleanor's fingers were soft and limp and milky white. Which fact brought home the shameful truth that, having removed her gardening gloves, she could see dirt under her fingernails. She drew away her hand and clasped them behind her back.

"I'm so glad we had this chat." Eleanor rose and took a step toward her. "You understand now how vitally important it is for you to be circumspect in everything?"

"Yes, thank you." Frustration threatened to burst from her in one long, terrible scream that dammed up in her throat. A vision of Eleanor in tears kept the impulse under control.

"I'll apologize to Lord Northword for you." The cloying scent of lilies floated between them when she stretched to press Portia's upper arm. "Please, don't feel you need say anything at all. I'll put everything right with Lord Northword, rely on it. I am happy to help you through this difficulty." She threw her arms around Portia and kissed her cheek. "You'll adore London just as I did."

When they parted, Eleanor checked the watch pinned to her bodice. "Goodness, we've hardly time to dress for luncheon. Do wear the pink frock we made for you. That's your best gown. Together we shall dazzle Lord Northword with our beauty."

"Yours perhaps."

She giggled. Good heavens, Eleanor giggled. "Men like pink on a woman."

Portia hated pink. She hated pink beyond anything. She especially hated that shade of pink in that thick satin. The gown was awful on her.

"I cannot wait for London!"

Chapter Three

AT A QUARTER TO TWELVE, Portia walked into the parlor a silent horror in a pink gown festooned with lace and bows. The very latest in London fashion, she had been assured. In order to accommodate her height, Eleanor had sewn frothy tulle over a five-inch layer of satin stitched to the bottom of the original hem. Though Portia did not entirely object to lace or bows, she objected to their combination almost as much as she objected to the unrelenting pink of…everything.

She was early to luncheon on purpose. God forbid she should make an entrance dressed like this. She sat and scooted her chair closer to the table while she exchanged a commiserating glance with Hob. One of Eleanor's early changes at Doyle's Grange was to put Hob into what amounted to livery when he served their meals. With Crispin here, the costume had been embellished beyond the bronze frock coat, breeches and heeled shoes with silver buckles. Now his costume included a powdered wig and a tricorn hat that refused to sit straight on his head. She found scant consolation in the knowledge that Hob looked as ridiculous as she did.

Two minutes before noon, Crispin strolled in with Eleanor on his arm and Magnus on his other side. "Portia." He lifted his free hand in greeting, and his gaze swept her up and down. His eyebrows shot up. She wanted to shoot him dead for that taken aback look. "Heavens, don't get up. Please."

He was dressed for the country, but you'd never mistake him for anything but a man of fashion. A man who was not from Exmoor. His toffee-colored hair was too perfectly cut. A grown man now. Not the young man she'd so desperately loved. With all that had happened between them, the awful strain of those last days, he'd moved on in his life. It was she who had been unable to move forward.

Crispin led Eleanor to the table and touched his fingers to the top of her chair while she sat. Magnus brought a chair closer to Eleanor but before he took his seat, he waved his arms in the air as if he were summoning food and refreshments by magical means.

This brought Hob away from guarding the door. He pushed a wheeled cart to Eleanor and then brought over, one plate or dish at a time, a selection of meat, cheeses, cakes, biscuits and various other comestibles. There was even a pot of coffee. Without a moment's hesitation, Crispin poured himself a cup, adding sugar and milk. So deftly done that one had to imagine he frequently sat down to coffee. It was a luxury here. And a rarity. This, too, was a habit of his of which she had no knowledge. She had herself never acquired a taste for coffee.

Conversation moved from politics to horses, to racing phaetons and the state of the poor who lived between Aubry Sock and West Aubry. Portia had little to contribute to the conversation. Every time she looked down or caught a glimpse of the frock Eleanor had so lovingly helped her make, she shuddered.

Hob brought over a plate of sliced duck and for a time there was no noise but that of silverware against the best china and teacups or coffee cups clicking against a porcelain saucer. She stared out the window. Clouds that promised rain all but blocked out the sky. She poked at her duck and set herself to mashing the remains of some cheddar. The thought of eating did not appeal. If this kept up, she'd waste away and become delicate through lack of appetite. She'd never look well in pink, though. Not with her hair. She didn't even want to look at Crispin for fear she'd see in his eyes a reflection of how unsuited she was to gowns with lace and frills. He unnerved her, to be honest.

Magnus gave a great harumph and took a large helping of duck. "Are we ready, do you think, Eleanor, for our journey to the seashore?"

Weeks before Crispin's arrival, Magnus and Eleanor had engaged to spend a fortnight in Brighton. They had rooms reserved at a favorite hotel, and Portia had been looking forward to several blessed days alone. She'd planned to stay up all hours, sleep away the mornings, and spend her afternoons transplanting crocuses to the rear lawns. That, alas, was not to be.

Once they had realized Crispin's visit would overlap with the Brighton trip, Magnus had suggested Portia ask Mr. Stewart to bring his mother to the Grange for a visit so as to avoid any hint of impropriety. This was done and the invitation accepted. As it turned out, however, Crispin had an appointment in West Aubry during the days that Magnus and Eleanor were to be away, discovered too late to even think of putting off the Stewarts' visit.

"Indeed we are." Eleanor put her hand over Magnus's and there was just no denying that when she looked at her husband, she glowed. "After Brighton, London. I hope, Lord Northword, that you will be in town then, for I know Portia is looking forward to seeing Northword House."

His expression smoothed out. "I don't know my schedule. I dare say it's possible." Crispin glanced at her, but Portia averted her eyes just in time. Having him here was much, much more difficult than she'd imagined. And that hint of distance in his voice? He did not want her in London any more than she wanted to go. The fact that Crispin and Jeremy must inevitably meet only deepened her tension and anxiety. "If I am not in town or at home, do please call. The housekeeper will give you a tour."

"You'll be in London for the sessions, I imagine," Eleanor said. "I know Mr. Temple would like to attend them while I show Portia the delights of Bond Street and my favorite shops."

Portia did her best imitation of one of Eleanor's helpless smiles. She hated herself for it, but she did it. "I have been thinking," she said for Eleanor's benefit, "that if your London excursion comes off, I'm sure Mr. Stewart and his mother would love to accompany us. Would that not be agreeable?"

Crispin returned a shallow grin. "I should be delighted to show all of you Northword House." He cut a slice of duck. "If I am in town."

"Portia dearest, are you certain Mrs. Stewart can withstand such a journey? It's such a long way for a frail woman."

Oh, how neatly her trap was sprung. "What a disappointment if she cannot. But let's not despair. I'll settle everything when they are here and write to you at Brighton."

"Have you been to Brighton, Portia?" Crispin pushed his cup forward so that Hob could refill it from the coffee pot. "Thank you."

"No. I've not been."

"You'd like it immensely. Seeing the ocean. Everyone ought to see the ocean at least once." He moved her untouched teacup out of his line of sight. Candlelight reflected off his hair and turned the darker streaks in his hair to bronze. He was astonishingly confident of himself and at ease with the sort of conversation that took no toll on anyone. "Tell me, ladies, have you bathing costumes?"

Eleanor fluttered her lashes. "I have, my lord. It's new, and I've been keeping it secret from Magnus."

Portia wished she were married already. She wished she were nowhere near Crispin or Doyle's Grange. The light in the room shifted with the gathering clouds and she seized on that as an excuse to stare out the window. She'd rather count cracks in the plaster than torture herself by watching Crispin bring Eleanor under his spell.

"And you, Portia? Have you a bathing costume?"

"I haven't." She looked away because she couldn't bear that there was so little left of the woman Crispin had once loved. Eleanor made a face at her, and, perhaps a shade too late, Portia understood why. She coughed and patted her upper chest. "Forgive me. My lord. I have no bathing costume, secret or otherwise. But I cannot go to Brighton in any event, sir. And while I should like to see London, sir, I expect that won't be possible. Not until after I am married."

Crispin leaned sideways against his chair. He'd dressed elegantly this afternoon, hadn't he? A far cry from the country clothes he'd worn when he'd lived at Wordless. His coat was the finest wool, his shirt a delicate lawn, and his waistcoat, well, that was heavy silk embroidered with tiny points of gold thread. "What's got into you?"

"I don't know what you mean."

"Nonsense to be so formal, and you know it." He rested his wrist on the edge of the table and his frown deepened. "I wish you would stop it."

Eleanor gave a gentle sigh. "But, Lord Northword. Good manners are never nonsense. She ought to show you the respect due from a woman of her position. Indeed, to all men of your standing." In tandem, Magnus and Crispin stared at Eleanor. She gazed back with that helpless gaze she'd so perfected. No one said anything for too long.

Crispin took a sip of his coffee. "Portia and I are old friends."

"What will people say when we are in London and she speaks of you with so little respect?" Her mouth trembled. "She will make entirely the wrong impression."

Crispin turned his head to her, and their eyes met. For a moment, it was as if they were lovers still, with none of their mistakes and missteps between them. Her heart stopped beating and did not start again until he looked away. *Thank God.* Thank God he had not acknowledged that moment.

"Eleanor," she said out of pure desperation for a change in subject. "Were you not telling me you have a list of improvements you'd like to make to the Grange? Is there anything I may do to assist with that while you and Magnus are in Brighton?"

Crispin gave every appearance of being fascinated by Eleanor as he was not by her. Watching him, Portia wondered if his late wife had been anything like Eleanor. She'd never been able to pry much information from Magnus on the subject of Lady Northword, other than to have him say she was the daughter of a duke and quite beautiful. Once, after one of his visits to London, he'd let slip that her health was delicate. Portia had understood that to mean she was in a way of giving Crispin his heir. But there was never any announcement and never any letter of congratulation to write.

"The Grange is perfect just as it is." Magnus helped himself to more cheddar.

"Darling man." Eleanor patted his arm. "That's because you have never known Doyle's Grange to be other than what it is. Of course you love your home. It would be unnatural if you did not."

"Quite right, my dear."

"Change is upsetting, I will never deny that." She smiled as she cut a slice of duck. From over Eleanor's shoulder, Portia watched raindrops hit the windows, pinpricks of water on the glass. "There are improvements to be made here. Am I not fortunate to have Portia to assist me?" She swept a hand in an arc. "I have such plans for this room."

Underneath the table, Crispin stuck out his leg and stepped on Portia's toes. "What do you think?"

"About what?" That earned her another puppy-eyed gaze from Eleanor. She stabbed her duck with her fork and wished she'd thought to feign illness and stay upstairs in her room. "What do I think about what, my lord?"

"The plans for redecorating, of course."

"Nothing." He was only trying to make conversation, and here she was turning into the sort of dismal drear no one liked at all.

He looked around the table. A diamond winked amid the lace of his neckcloth. The young man she'd known would never have worn a diamond or the fobs hanging from his watch chain. Nor the signet ring gleaming from the index finger of his right hand. "All I know is I've no taste in such things."

"I'm sure that's not so, Lord Northword." Eleanor returned him a brilliant smile. "Why, Northword House is all that is tasteful and elegant."

"My wife managed all that. I was happy to have her do so."

Magnus took Eleanor's hand in his and kissed her knuckles. "Everything I have is yours, as you well know. Do what you will with the place, though I don't see how it could be improved."

"But Magnus!" She went wide-eyed again. "The room is green, and green, my dearest Mr. Temple, is not a color I appreciate."

"No?" He kissed her knuckles again. "Away with it then."

Crispin looked to Portia. His expression was bland, but she was convinced he was taunting her. "What color would you do the room in?"

"Green, I fear." She had been a fortnight with the painters choosing that shade of green and another week before she was satisfied all the colors were exactly perfect for the room. It was six weeks before the room had been painted to her satisfaction. "If I had known Magnus was going to marry, I'd not have had the work done."

Eleanor gave one of her delightful laughs. "One acquires a certain sensibility when one has lived in society. I have seen, as you have not, Portia darling, some of the great houses of London. Northword House, for example. So inspiring, my lord. I am most anxious to see it again, and I do hope one day that Portia, too, will see the house so that she will understand precisely what I mean to do here at the Grange. After all, Lady Northword was a woman of exceptional taste, and one will never go wrong studying what she wrought at Northword House." She took a tiny bite of duck. "I will never forget how kind she was to give me a personal tour when I first called."

This fascinated her. "You met Lady Northword?"

"I like to think we became friends." Eleanor touched the strand of pearls around her throat. "I hope you don't think me presumptuous, Lord Northword, to speak of your wife. I know you mourn her still."

He nodded. "Not at all, Mrs. Temple."

"Your wife and I had a great many interests in common."

"Did you?"

Portia accepted the sting to her heart. She had nothing in common with Lady Northword. What had brought her and Crispin together was not what made a man settle on the woman he would marry. She shredded her duck until she had reduced it to a paste. Half an hour, she told herself. In half an hour, she could plead a headache and retire to her room. Which happened to be green.

"Oh, yes, my lord. We spoke at great length of how one ought to decorate and arrange one's home. To be sure, Doyle's Grange can never be on the scale of Northword House, or Northword Hill." Eleanor surveyed the room, eyes moving over the architectural features and, no doubt, totting up all that must be removed, repainted or destroyed in order to make Doyle's Grange over in the exquisite sensibilities of Lady Northword.

"The parlor, for example, might be made quite lovely. Lady Northword had the most exacting opinions about parlors. She had a particular horror of green, and ever since I have shared that opinion. Even so," Eleanor went on, "there is a charm here that can be brought out. A few of Magnus's best paintings might be hung on the walls, for example." She gazed at Magnus. He gazed back, besotted and beguiled by his wife, and Portia could only feel the hollow certainty that she would never, not in a hundred thousand years, gaze at her husband that way.

Eleanor continued. "Several rooms are in need of the attentions of someone with refined tastes. So as to bring out charms that currently are hidden. Imagine how much more easily this can be accomplished if Portia could see the homes that inspired me. My dear Mr. Temple, we simply must bring her to London!"

Portia shot to her feet. Crispin stood, napkin in one hand. Magnus, too, after a moment. "Do sit down, you two." She drew a breath and then found everyone staring at her as if she'd gone mad. Perhaps she had. The walls closed in on her, and she wanted nothing more than to be anywhere in the world but there. "Forgive me. I don't feel well at all."

"Of course, of course." Eleanor stood and pressed the back of her hand to Portia's cheek. "I'll send a tisane to you. You must rest, please."

"Thank you. You are too kind."

She did not go to her room. God, she'd suffocate in there with all that green that was so offensive a color to Lady Northword. Instead, she went out the front.

The heavy door slammed behind her.

Chapter Four

AFTER PORTIA LEFT THE PARLOR, Magnus sat again, but Northword stayed on his feet, in the grip of an understanding that cut to his core. Portia's life and his had diverged beyond hope of any reconciliation beyond the polite exchanges of their letters. It didn't matter that he found her more attractive than ever. It didn't matter that from time to time they fell into the old habits of their past intimacy. The woman he'd loved was gone.

"My lord?"

Mrs. Temple's overly sweet voice grated on his nerves, and he gazed at her, still lost in his thoughts. There was no reason to be concerned for Portia, Northword told himself. She was well looked after here, and before long she would be married and in the care of her husband.

"Lord Northword?"

The so-feminine lilt to the woman's voice snapped him back to the present. Could such naiveté be genuine? The moment the doubt entered his head, he felt guilty. She was a lovely, delicate woman who had never, at any time that he'd observed, said anything to deserve an unkindness from him. But good God, Portia must hate being spoken to as if she cared for nothing but the color of the damn walls.

"Hullo, there." Magnus rapped on the table. "Word, you great lump."

"I beg your pardon." He threw his napkin on the table and was in the act of sitting when the front door opened and then closed with more force than necessary. Uneasiness lodged in his gut and expanded to take up the whole of his chest. He did not care for the feeling. Out of the window, from the corner of his eye, he saw a flash of pink and then the unmistakable deep red of Portia's hair. What the devil was she doing outside when the skies looked ready to break open? She'd catch her death.

While he stared at that flash of receding pink, fat drops of rain hit the glass. She was out there, without a coat or cloak, and quite plainly, and to his mind, understandably upset. She had no one to talk to or rage at. He could not imagine her opening up to Mrs. Temple. Impossible, that.

"Excuse me, please." He forced himself to smile at Mrs. Temple. "I have just recalled a letter I must write immediately. I can't fathom how I could have forgotten to get it into the morning post."

Magnus took a sip of his tea. "Give it to Hob when you're done. He'll get it to Up Aubry for you. There's just time, I think, to make the afternoon post, if you're quick about it."

"Yes, thank you. I'll do that." He bowed and hurried out of the parlor. He hadn't even known his wife disliked the color green. Why had he not known that? By the time he'd fetched his greatcoat and hat and was himself outside and heading toward the rear of the house, rain fell steadily. Portia was long past the back gate and moving away from the Grange, her gown a splash of pink against the green of the field.

He started after her. He'd made up perhaps a quarter of the distance between them when, at last, she slowed, though she maintained a brisk pace and kept her head down. When she disappeared over the other side of the slope, he walked faster. Rain came down hard enough to pound on his hat and turn the surface of the path to mud. He lengthened his stride.

At the top of the slope, he caught sight of her again, moving rapidly toward the top of the hill that lead—eventually—to Wordless. And wasn't that a fine joke that he should call his own home by the name Portia had given it in her letters. Wordless, because he was familiarly called *Word* by certain intimate friends, and he was never at Northword Hill. He'd told Magnus about that, and they'd taken to calling all manner of things Wordless.

He cupped his hands to the sides of his mouth. "Portia!"

Wind whipped away the sound of her name, but she stopped. Then, without turning to look, she darted off, skirts in her hands. Wasn't that just like her, to be contrary and headstrong? He plunged down the hill and slid in the mud, though he managed to keep his feet. Once, she slipped, too, but as he had, she caught herself and kept going.

Water dripped from the brim of his hat onto his face and wherever the drops hit his cheeks his skin burned with cold. She slowed, and God knows she would have needed inhuman endurance to maintain her pace in these conditions.

He caught up at the stone fence that marked the border between the Grange and his property. From here, the side of Northword Hill rose up, turned a darker gray by the rain.

This time, he did not need to shout. "Portia."

She stopped walking but did not face him. Her hands hung at her sides. Water ran down the back of her neck, making rivers of the tendrils of hair that had escaped her hairpins.

Northword took a step closer. Even if he'd been close enough to touch her, he wasn't sure he'd dare. Never mind their difficulties, never mind the years and the chasm between them, he did not want to see her in distress. Not like this. "Portia."

She whirled on him, eyes ablaze. Rain dripped down her face, and she shivered once. Gooseflesh pimpled her exposed skin. "What could you possibly want from me? There's no need to humiliate me like this. Haven't I done enough to push you away?"

"I didn't come after you to humiliate you."

"Well, you have. Lord Northword." She walked away, keeping to the line of the fence, away from the Grange. The hem of her skirt was muddy for several inches, and the fabric was soaked halfway to her knees.

He followed and raised his voice to be heard over the rain and the distance she was putting between them. "Since when does my chasing after you to make sure you don't catch your death of sleet and rain count as humiliation, I'd like to know?"

The skies opened. Unbelievable as it seemed, it was actually raining harder, and cold enough now that there were tiny pellets of ice. He thought she meant to pretend she hadn't heard him, but then she made a rude gesture. And kept walking. This was the Portia he remembered. Passionate. Always passionate.

"Stop." He took three long steps and caught her arm, pulling her around to face him. Her mouth was rimmed with white but there was a telltale tremor around her jaws. "We can't stay in this downpour."

"I don't care." Rain plastered her awful pink gown to her body.

"I don't care much if you think I've humiliated you when I haven't."

She stared him down. He did not know this woman. She was not a girl. She'd lived ten years without him, and in ten years, people changed. They left behind fancies of love and passion. They married and went on to live dutiful lives.

"Thank you for telling me how I feel. Now that you are Lord Northword, of course you know all." She pulled away. He didn't let go of her arm, and a good thing, too, because she slipped, and it was only because he steadied her that she didn't fall.

He brought her close and raised his voice to be heard. "It's bloody hailing. We're going to freeze if we stay out here much longer."

"You needn't have come after me." Her chin tipped up in an expression so familiar to him he lost sight of those ten years.

"Yes, I did need."

"You didn't." She tugged on her arm. "Let go."

"You know me better than that."

"I don't think I do."

"You don't at all if you think I'd leave any lady outside in this weather, not one dressed as you are, and not when I know she's upset and unable to think as clearly as she ought."

Her eyes widened, and not in recognition of his good sense. She was magnificently furious. "Let me alone, Crispin Hope, you booby-headed jackass."

He kept his grip on her arm. "Use your intellect, if you haven't let it be worn to a blunt by listening to your sister-in-law prattle on about gowns and London and the proper forms of address. You know as well as I that you'll freeze out here." He pointed toward the dark gray stones of his childhood home. "Wordless is nearer than the Grange. Let's go there and wait out the rain." He brought her closer to him, and he forgot everything that had gone wrong between them, the wrongs they'd done each other. Whatever else had happened, he could not bear to see her unhappy. "You can tell me everything that's made you so miserable. Will you do that much? Please?"

Something of what he was feeling must have transferred to her, for she wiped water out of her face and nodded. "How long have you got?"

"As long as we need. You know that." He ached to touch her, to console her, but didn't dare. She was too angry. And he was too much on edge. "Out of the rain, if you please."

She nodded again.

"Thank you." He didn't give her time to change her mind or form an objection. He swung her into his arms and bodily lifted her over the fence. From the awkward way she reacted, he knew she hadn't expected to find herself in his arms. Nor had he anticipated doing so until it was done.

When she was safely down and steady on her feet, he stepped over the fence himself. He shrugged out of his greatcoat and put it around her shoulders. One did such things for ladies. As an afterthought, he clapped his hat on her head, too.

"Come along then." He managed a smile that at long last did not feel false. "Before we drown or are killed by hail."

He marched them toward the house and around to the front. He remembered the days when he had run up those twenty front stairs, often with Magnus and Portia in tow. He could see the house as it had been then—the servants, now long moved on to other positions, the interior of the house. How strange to think of those rooms as empty and dark. Rooms where his wife had never been and where she had left no mark.

No great surprise, the front door was locked. The groundskeeper lived in West Aubry and had no need for access to the house. His steward visited but twice a year to see to any interior maintenance that might be required.

Rain beat down while they tried every other entrance and found each door locked and barred, every shutter closed. Short of breaking a window or kicking in a door they weren't getting inside. In the abstract, he was pleased that Wordless was so well protected, but at the moment, he was inconvenienced at being denied entry to his own damn house. Both of them were shivering now, with no sign of the rain letting up and the cold getting sharper.

"The stables?" Portia said.

He nodded and took her hand while they dashed along the gravel drive that led to the stable block only to find the grooms' quarters locked up as tight as the house. They took refuge in the long stone archway of the stables, eight stalls on each side. The block emptied onto a courtyard with the carriage house at the far side. That was locked tight, too, he discovered.

Back in the archway between the two rows of stalls, they stood side-by-side, dripping water onto the paving stones. He stamped his feet and made a largely futile attempt to brush water off his coat and out of his hair. "At least we're out of the wet."

"Yes." She stared at the rain beating down on the courtyard and cascading from the gutters.

"Tell me why you're so unhappy?"

"I shan't. Not more than you've guessed." She shook her head. He'd give anything to have her look at him. "You'll only think less of me than you do already."

"She rubs my nerves raw, too, sometimes."

"Oh," she breathed. "Awful man."

"True." In the silence he stamped his feet some more and managed to dislodge some of the mud that clung to his boots. "It can't come down like this for much longer."

"Yes, it can."

He'd lived here long enough to know it could rain like this until tomorrow. "Listen to us." He rolled his eyes even though she wasn't looking at him. "Talking about the weather like two old ladies."

She shrugged, but halfway through the motion, she shivered. Without thinking, he put his arms around her. She didn't come close.

"Take pity on me," he said. "I'm cold."

After a moment of resistance, she leaned toward him. He eased closer and tightened his arms around her. "Better. Much better." He rubbed his hands up and down her back. She rested her head against his chest, and he slipped his hands underneath his greatcoat and rested them in the small of her back. He wanted to tell her he'd forgiven her, that he'd never forgotten a moment of their time as lovers, but that seemed…unwise.

After a moment or two of standing like this, she lifted her head and stared at the waterfall sluicing off the roof. The courtyard's central gutters overflowed. The noise was near deafening. "I don't think it's going to stop."

Like her, he stared at the water. "We can wait a while yet."

"Hob will worry," she said. "Magnus, too. They'll wonder where we've got to."

He continued to stroke her back. "Five minutes. Then we'll go even if it's no better."

With a sigh, she settled against him, tucking her hands between them. Five minutes later, the rain hadn't let up.

He forgot all about the cold and the damp as he brushed away a tendril of dark red hair that had stuck to her cheek. She pushed away, and he did the strangest, most contradictory, selfishly male thing imaginable. He brought her close instead of setting her back. She lifted her chin and gave him a quizzical look. The world dropped away. This was Portia. His Portia, and whatever had happened between them, no matter how they'd changed, nothing had changed at all.

He lowered his head to hers.

Chapter Five

FOR THE SPACE OF HALF A HEARTBEAT, he told himself he wasn't going kiss her. It would be stupid and wrong of him, and it would destroy the safety of the friendship they'd carved out for themselves during their years of letter writing.

His chest was so tight with tension, he could scarcely breathe. He was seventeen again, and his brain was overset with lust and desire and emotions too big to name. His cock was hard with the joy of holding this woman in his arms and at the prospect of being inside her. At long, long last.

Northword didn't move. Didn't breathe. Nor did she. In no way was that fact lost on him.

Her mouth brushed his. Barely there. For an instant, he didn't react. He couldn't. Surely, she had not meant that invitation. She was going to marry someone else, wasn't she? Except she didn't step away, and he didn't want her to. She relaxed against him and she made a sound that was not quite a moan yet was soft and edged with need.

Almost no contact between them, yet his blood pounded in his ears. Their first time had been like this. Needful. Soul shattering. He burned in the moment, in her, in the heat of having his arms around her again. Familiar. Blazingly alive. She felt good in his embrace. Right. For the first time in years, he was whole.

She rested a hand on his upper arm, light at first, then fingers gripping. It was sweet, the way she leaned against him, sweet in his arms, and he wanted her so badly he hurt. Jesus, she felt good, and he'd been too long without sexual satisfaction because he was imagining doing a good deal more than her practically chaste kiss.

That condition could not and did not last, a kiss that did not reflect the tension zinging between them. In the initial days of their relations, they'd kissed for hours, what seemed like hours, before he'd brought himself to touch a hand to more than her cheek. It wouldn't be the same now. Couldn't be. The soul-stealing pleasure of his first time was just that. First. And therefore memorable. He knew about women, now, thank you very much.

Even during that year between, he'd known how the world worked. So had Portia. They knew what it meant for her to be Portia and him to be the future Northword. He'd been to bed with her, they'd been lovers, and in his thoughts, he was already imagining sexual relations with her.

There was nothing innocent about his desire. Nothing at all. There never had been, not since that long ago day he'd realized his feelings for Portia were more than friendship. Not since the day he realized she felt the same.

She kissed him again, her lips parted this time, and he took what she offered. Somewhere in the back of his head he had the thought that she hadn't opened her mouth in order to invite more from him, but to draw breath. At the exact same time this was flitting through his thoughts, his mouth was open, too, and he was kissing her without restraint. Not in the least politely. Her mouth softened underneath his, matching, accepting him, answering him.

He knew a great deal more about kissing than he had ten years ago, but he was trembling just as he had then. They fit together, the two of them. He was taller since the last time she'd been in his arms, but she was still a good height for him, and she still made his heart too big for his chest.

The next thing he knew, the last of his restraint melted away, and he had her pressed against the stone wall of the archway, her head between his hands, his tongue in her mouth. Desperate for her. Desperately aroused. She kissed him back, her fingers gripping his upper arms in order to bring him closer. Familiar heat spiraled through him.

This.

He wanted *this*.

He rested his pelvis against her, and yes, he was hard and that seemed exactly how things ought to be. He filled his fingers with her wet hair and sent his hat tumbling to the flagstones. He pulled back so her head was at a better angle.

Lust rattled him, shook away everything but the two of them. All his adult life, he'd missed this immersion of his senses, and he was not, not going to let this pass without living every minute and second.

In the moment after their mouths separated, she gasped, a groan of desire that laid waste to his lingering reservations. The breath left his body. Whatever this said about his character, he wanted Portia to come undone. As a point of pride to prove to her she'd been wrong to let them end. He wanted her to fall under his spell, to believe in her soul that no other lover would do but him. He pulled back, just his upper body and not much of that. Enough to kiss the rain from her cheeks and watch her eyes open. Unfocused and half-drunk with the same passion that filled him.

She set her palms on either side of his face and said, so softly the tremor in her words barely registered, "How I've missed you."

Yes. The word roared through him.

This.

He reached blindly past her and found the top of the nearest stable door. He fumbled it open and had just enough of his brain functioning that he thought to snatch a blanket hanging from a peg on the wall and spread it over the straw. Everything at Wordless was at the ready for the viscount to make use of his long neglected estate; clean blanket, clean straw. Thank God.

They dropped onto the blanket in a tangle of limbs and lips and, even, laughter. His lower back hit the blanket, and she was right here, kneeling between his upraised and spread apart knees. Her focus on him sent his heart pounding, and he propped one hand on the blanket and pushed up to loop an arm around the back of her neck and bring her in for another long, carnal kiss.

Outside, the rain beat down on the roof and cascaded onto the flagstones. All that faded away. There was no more cold. No rain. Nothing but the two of them. She offered her mouth. He accepted wholeheartedly.

With his free hand he adjusted their position so she straddled his hips. Kissing her still, he worked his hand underneath her skirts, pushing away damp-to-wet handfuls of that awful pink gown and her underskirts. She gave him the access he wanted.

His fingertips slid along her thighs, then up to cover her sex. Her pubic hair was as sparse as ever, almost nothing there. He pushed a finger between her legs. Slippery wet for him. Her gaze locked with his when his searching fingers slid along her. He knew how to touch her. He'd learned her. Memorized her. And he was better at this now. He was a much better lover than he had been. She set her hands on his shoulders and surrendered to her body.

"I missed you," she said again. "I thought I would die from missing you."

"Good."

She swallowed hard just once, a reaction that echoed through her body as she opened to him. He dropped into a sensual haze. Everything aroused him, from the slide of his fingers on her, the sound of her sigh that turned to a moan, his anticipation of what would come.

While he kissed her, tongue in her mouth, tasting and taking, he found the core of her and that particular spot that would bring on a build to unbearable tension. She groaned when he backed off, and her eyes snapped with frustration. He gave her a smug grin because she knew what he was doing to her and why. He laughed before he licked a trail of raindrops from her cheek and moved his fingers in her. So tight. She tensed, and he waited for her to relax.

"Has there been no one since me?"

Her eyes slowly focused. "I wasn't waiting for you, if that's what you mean."

He pushed his fingers further into her, into that soft, tight heat. "We can argue about that later. Right now—"

"God, Crispin." The words came from her throat in a rush as she bowed toward him, hands pressed on the top of his shoulders, hips rocking into his palm cupping her sex. He watched her, felt her passage clench on his fingers.

There wasn't a damn soul anywhere near so he had the rare, great pleasure of neither one of them having to be in the least discreet. He thought he might have one more chance to pull her from the brink before she came, but her fingers dug into his shoulders, and she left him to fall off the cliff he'd constructed with her, her breath shuddering. He stroked, pressed, and she threw her head back and completely, utterly, with heartrending passion, surrendered to pleasure.

She belonged to him. He felt her tighten around his fingers, and he damn near lost all restraint, he wanted inside with such ferocity. He sailed beyond lust, beyond arousal. Exactly as it had been with them every time before. Despite the words he'd never written to her, he'd bared his soul to her in his letters and kept her close in so doing. He had indulged in a fantastically ironic game of revenge. He'd wanted her to know exactly what she'd given up and to regret that for the rest of her life.

"This is what we're like." The words rasped from his throat while she was still coming down from her climax, her head bowed to his shoulder. "You and I. It's not like this with anyone else. Just us."

While she clung to him, and he stroked away the last spasms of her pleasure, he used his other hand to unfasten his coat and the fall of his breeches and free himself from his clothing. With one last stroke along the folds of her body, he slid his palm to the curve of her backside and brought her up and toward him, and when his cock was at her entrance, she lifted her head and caught her lower lip between her teeth as she answered his upward thrust with the lowering of her hips.

An inarticulate sound burst from him. Heat. Slick dampness. Tight, almost too tight. She didn't relax around him because she'd not done this with anyone but him. He held back his urge to push hard. Slow at the start was good, too.

For a suspended moment, he was immersed in the simple pleasure of having his cock in a woman, but around the edges of that was this flicker of more. They weren't too young this time. This time they were old enough to know there was nothing new in the world and that they did not invent passion, they created it between them, and it was that which was new and rare. He hissed as her body closed and softened around his cock. Nothing existed for him but her and his cock and the feral bliss of their connection.

"Crispin." She grabbed his shoulders, and angled her hips. Her breath stuttered. "My God, Crispin." Her head dropped back and, Lord, she softened around him just enough, and now he thrust the way he wanted, needed to. He leaned in to kiss her exposed throat. So tight around him, she gripped his cock, all of it, and with a shout that was part demand and part plea, he rolled her onto her back and let the imperative of sex take him.

She pushed her hips toward him and drew up her knees, and he shoved her skirts up higher, out of his way. That flicker of *more* stayed with him, and he closed his eyes to deny what that meant. Instead, he found the angles that made her groan with pleasure and the ones that sent him racing to orgasm.

Her body tensed, and he concentrated on bringing her again, the two of them partially on their sides, his hand between them, his mouth at the side of her throat, hard enough to leave a mark, kissing her until she cried out, and he felt the contractions of her passage around him. He remembered everything that had made her moan before, but he was caught up in their desperation, urged on by the sounds she was making, by the roll of her hips against his, the grip of her arms around him.

He planted his hands by her head and pushed up so he could watch her face and leverage the weight of his pelvis with his thrusts into her. More selfish this time, but then she wrapped her legs around his hips and rocked into him, and he didn't feel selfish at all.

His balls tightened, and he thrust into her harder. Hard enough, hard enough. So close and then he was tumbling, soaring toward exquisite pleasure and then falling into it, and he had just enough presence of mind not to come inside her. Barely.

When he returned to his senses, he opened his eyes, but he was still in a sensual stupor and had few thoughts but those that centered around his physical repletion. He drank in her face and the warmth where their bodies still touched. Pelvis to pelvis, her thighs at his hips, his softening member between them.

The rain had stopped while they'd been lost in each other. She wound her arms around his shoulders, and then his head, and pulled him down for a searing kiss. Afterward, when he'd pushed up to get his weight off her, the fierce sadness in her eyes made his heart swell again.

Her fingers brushed his cheek, pushed away the damp. "We ought to go, my lord."

He loved the sound of that honorific, the way the words left her lips soft and intimate and offered him her submission and her possession of him. He needed a few more breaths before he trusted himself to speak, and then she did first.

"Before you catch your death." Her hand lingered at his cheek, and he turned his head to kiss her fingers. She snatched her hand away. "That tickles."

"I don't want to go." He nestled against her. "I'm perfectly warm." He drew her nearer and breathed in the scent of her body, of sex and the damp heat of them both. "I can think of ways for us to stay warm."

"Oh, we'll just live here, then. In the stable."

"It's my stable. We can do what we like here." She didn't know, he thought. She didn't know what this meant to him, how shocking it was to feel he was home after ten years at sea with nights spent dreaming of stripping her naked and burying himself inside her.

She gave him a push, but she was already retreating from him, and he didn't know how to bring her back. "Obstinate as ever, aren't you?"

"I haven't changed."

She looked away. "That's not so."

He dipped his head to her ear, nipped her there and said, "Except, I think my prick is bigger, don't you?"

That made her laugh, and then him, and that was just like them, to be bawdy and find it amusing, as if they were the only lovers ever to speak crudely to each other. She turned her head to his chest, shoulders still shaking. Well. It was a fine joke, wasn't it? He kissed her again and realized it wouldn't take much for him to be ready again.

She pushed at his shoulders. "We should go. It's late."

With a sigh, he pushed away and fumbled to get himself decently back into his breeches. When he'd done that, he helped her arrange her clothes, too, or would have except that she lay on the blanket with her hair beginning to dry and glint with indisputable red, and her pale legs exposed and her lower belly, too. He thought he'd never seen anything more beautiful than her sex. A bit of the old guilt nipped at him, and he embraced that, too. Fucking his friend's sister was wrong, but he couldn't bring himself to care at this moment. Not then and not now.

He set his palm on her thigh, and then on the inside of her thigh. He'd scraped her there during their frantic coupling. When he thought to look at her face, he found her watching him with eyes that killed him. He slid his fingers upward, covered her sex, and, still watching her face, slid a finger inside her, one then two. "I'm no green boy, now," he said. She was getting slicker, and his two fingers moved in her easily. "If we didn't need to get home, I'd prove that beyond your ability to speak."

She pressed her head back because he'd pushed his thumb between her folds and along the flesh there. Her breath caught but she managed to say, "You could try."

"Anything for you, my love. Anything."

"What's this?" She put a hand on his breeches. "Are you rising to the occasion, sir?"

"I think I am."

And she gave him a wicked smile that melted him inside, and made him forget about Magnus and the fact that she was going to be married, and he didn't stop her from unbuttoning the fall of his breeches nor say a word when she took him in hand and drew back his foreskin. "You once liked me very well on my knees."

"Yes." He sat up, then stood and stared into her eyes and understood that this was to be their very last time. "Please."

He buried his fingers in her hair when she took him in her mouth, and he let her bring him that way and all the while he told himself that if she could walk away from this, then by God, so could he.

Afterward, they tidied up as best they could, at last feeling the cold and damp, and they headed for the Grange. The sky hadn't cleared, though it wasn't raining, and the ground was thoroughly soaked. Dozens of tiny puddles lurked in the thick grass and made the footing uncertain. At the stone fence, he lifted her over again and did not put her down as quickly as he should have. He leaned in and kissed her, hard and fast before he released her.

"Don't," she said. "Don't do this."

Since she knew the way, he followed her through the fields. The path was muddier than when he'd tromped through here heading the other way, and the clouds were getting that heavy look while the air turned colder and thicker. They gave up trying to keep themselves out of the muck and just trudged through the field.

He kept a hand around her waist because that was what a gentleman did when he was escorting a lady across treacherous terrain. Before he was quite prepared to return to reality, they were at the Grange. Fat drops of water hit them as they dashed for the front of the house, running now and laughing for no reason other than it seemed right. The very moment they reached the path to the door, the rain became another torrent.

At the door, Portia turned, face to the sky and thrust a fist into the air. "Curse you, god of rain, curse you!"

He fumbled with the door, and when he got the thing open he grabbed Portia's other hand and pulled her inside, they were still laughing.

Until he turned around and saw Mrs. Temple standing in the foyer, a look of utter betrayal on her face.

Chapter Six

WITH FINGERS CLUMSY FROM THE COLD, Portia worked at the buttons of Crispin's greatcoat, so heavy on her shoulders. She didn't dare meet Eleanor's eyes. She couldn't bear to see that wide-eyed hurt again. She wasn't Eleanor's equal, not fit to be in the same room as her.

This time, she'd betrayed more than Crispin and her brother's trust. She'd hurt Eleanor, who did not deserve that, and she'd betrayed Jeremy, the man she was supposed to marry. Again. She wanted to weep with the horror of how badly she'd failed.

Hob appeared at the top of the servant's staircase. He came to a full stop, eyes wide when he saw the condition the two of them were in. Both of them soaked to the skin, her in Crispin's hat and greatcoat, muddy shoes, and water dripping everywhere.

"Hob," Eleanor said in a light voice. God, what a brilliant performance. You'd never guess now, that her sister-in-law thought there was anything the least untoward about this. "Do help Lord Northword with his wet coat."

Hob bowed and said, as he went to Crispin, "I was about to walk out to find thee, Miss."

"As well you didn't. You'd have got drenched, too." She meant to match Eleanor's aplomb and failed miserably at that, too. A shiver cut short her attempt to wipe water out of her face. She'd hardly minded her wet clothes and hair before, but now she was miserable inside and out. She managed to get the greatcoat unbuttoned and off her shoulders. Hob took it from her without a word.

"What on earth possessed you to go outside in weather such as this?" Eleanor's smile was sweet, so sweet.

It was on the tip of her tongue to confess everything. Every horrible impulse, every awful, unworthy thought, and beg for forgiveness. She ought to confess all the ways in which she'd traded a few moments of bliss for her very soul, but Crispin plucked his hat off her head and dropped it on the table by the door and her words went unspoken. "Before you take my coat, Hob, see to sending a maid to help Miss Temple out of her wet things, won't you?"

"Yes, milord."

"That won't be necessary." Eleanor gave a clear, silvery laugh, but Portia knew she'd forever tainted relations with her sister-in-law, and very likely Magnus, too. Eleanor smoothly transferred her attention from Hob to Crispin. "Do take his coat. Lord Northword will catch an ague if he leaves it on."

Crispin lifted a hand. "Well, now, Hob, I can hardly remove my coat in front of ladies, can I? I'll not be so indelicate." On the table, a damp ring formed around the brim of the hat, slowly spreading outward. "I'll need my valet directly, if you'll see to that as well."

"Aye, milord."

Portia could not summon Crispin's cheer nor Eleanor's sweetness. Every glance, every word flayed her to the bone. Eleanor might as well have been there at the stable block, watching Portia fall into sin.

"You were gone so long Magnus was worried." Eleanor picked up Crispin's hat and handed it to Hob. He accepted it with a bow and headed for the stairs.

"We were caught in the rain," Crispin said easily.

"Quite a downpour. We were worried."

"Did you not hear or see how it came down, Mrs. Temple?" He turned part way to her so that half his back faced Portia. He spoke so gently. "Forgive me that, ma'am. I know how intensely you feel everything."

She set her fingertips over her heart. "I do, my lord."

"I know I would have worried had I been in your place and my sister-in-law had gone out in such weather."

"Yes, my lord. Precisely."

"There was nothing we could do but take refuge where we could."

"Which was?"

He spread his hands. Water dripped from his sleeves onto the floor. "As you can well imagine, no place very dry. There was a tree. Not a very big one, I'm afraid. Not so far from the creek at the back of your property."

"A tree."

"Yes. A tree."

It didn't matter what Crispin said, or what excuses he made, or how convincing he was for any of it, Portia knew every word was a lie. Eleanor's expression remained calm and pleasant, but dread curled in the pit of her stomach. That smile lay so heavy on them, around them, between them, that she could not react in any way.

"Thank you, Lord Northword, for going after her."

"You're quite welcome, Mrs. Temple."

"My dear Lord Northword. You ought to change into some dry clothes." Portia felt horrible. Eleanor was a woman incapable of malice and accustomed to thinking the best of everyone, and here they were, deceiving her. "You'll take a chill if you don't."

Crispin set a hand on the back of Portia's shoulder, no longer the man who'd kissed her senseless. Not the man who'd made love to her in a way that obliterated the life she'd built without him. He'd retreated behind a pleasant facade, and she was unbearably aroused by him. "You as well, Portia."

She nodded, but Eleanor detained her with a hand to Portia's arm. Crispin bowed to them and headed for the stairs.

"You've no idea how worried Magnus was for you," Eleanor said.

"We were caught in the rain."

"I do not understand why you would go outside at all when you did not feel well. And to make Lord Northword chase after you." Eleanor's smile faded. "I cannot imagine what people will say when they hear the tale. It's bound to follow you, my dear."

"I was foolish. I'm very sorry for the inconvenience and your worry."

"I do hope you've learned your lesson about acting impetuously."

"I have, thank you."

Eleanor pushed her toward the stairs. "Go on, now. We can't have you catching your death either."

Bridget, the maid she shared with Eleanor, was waiting for her when she entered her bedroom. The young woman clucked at her bedraggled state.

Portia stood where she was, her thoughts no place in particular. She was glad to be ministered to with no need to do anything but move as required to get her wet clothes off. The cold penetrated to her bones. Had that second rain washed away the smell of sex? Lord, she didn't even know if Crispin had come on her clothes or his.

The maid unhooked the last of the fastenings of Portia's gown. "You poor thing. You're soaked to the skin. What happened?"

"Lord Northword and I were caught in the rain." She pulled her arms out of the sleeves of her gown and was immediately caught up in another shiver. "We took refuge under a tree." She fixed an image of the stream in her head, as if doing so would make it true. "By the stream. Near where my brother likes to fish."

"So far from the house, Miss?"

"It rained so hard we were drenched. There was sleet, too." That was true. There would have been sleet by the stream as well.

"And here you went out without a cloak. Goodness, why? Come closer to the fire, Miss."

"Thank you." She shivered again when Bridget stripped her of her petticoats and undergarments. The places where Crispin's early beard had rasped against her skin were livid against her bone-cold skin. The bruise his mouth had left on her throat, the scrape left by his clothes against the inside of her thigh. She'd not felt any of that at the time, but she did now. Her skin contained the residue of his mouth, his hands and his cock, the sigh of his breath. Bridget would surely put the evidence of her deception before Eleanor. Ten years since her fall from grace, and she'd given up body and soul without a thought. She'd tried to love elsewhere. She truly had.

Wiped down, dried off, hair combed out, and her in dry undergarments, she came out of her dumb state when Bridget picked up the pink gown. "I'll be up half the night with this."

"Don't bother." She sank onto an armchair. For the life of her she couldn't think what Crispin had done when he came to passion, other than she was sure he'd not come inside her. "It can wait."

"If I don't launder this right away, it will be ruined for certain."

"If it can't be saved, burn it."

"Oh, it's too pretty for that."

"Keep it, if you like. Whether it can be saved or not." She met the maid's astonished gaze head on and managed a smile. "The color suits you better than it does me."

"That's kind of you. Thank you, Miss." She scooped up the rest of the wet clothes and undergarments then whisked away the gown before leaving Portia alone.

With no one to distract her, her heart crumbled. Part of her soul had vanished when she and Crispin proved unable to make a future together. Today, she'd had him in her arms again, and she wasn't sorry for that. She wasn't. But she'd been left with a newer and more painful reminder of exactly what she'd given up ten years ago.

Chapter Seven

THE BLOODY RAIN HAD STOPPED AGAIN. In Northword's room, with its rear-facing windows, the light shifted with the constant change in the gaps of sky between the clouds. He held the note Hob had just delivered to him. He itched to toss it onto the fire. "No answer, Hob. Thank you."

He left it to his valet to give Hob a coin, which was quickly and discreetly done. The moment the door closed, he crumpled the note—predictably, the sheet was scented—and threw it on the dressing table. It landed half on the portable secretary he'd brought with him and half on the abandoned leather strop. *Meet at his earliest convenience.* The devil he'd be summoned like he was a misbehaving son. Not again.

He yanked on his shirt sleeve. "Are we finished with this nonsense yet?"

"No, milord." His valet was even tempered, thank goodness, since at the moment, Northword wore nothing but a shirt and clean breeches.

"Get on with it."

After that display of impatience and having to endure the arrangement of the rest of his clothes, he fussed more than usual with his appearance. He wanted to strike just the right note of lordly perfection before he went downstairs to face the wife of his closest friend. He was prepared to answer any and all charges laid at his feet. He would not give honor short shrift. Not ten years ago, and not now. He studied his reflection and decided, just this once, that his resemblance to his father was acceptable. His father had been a ruthless, heartless specimen of manhood.

He went downstairs to the parlor, reminding himself that he could not blame the woman for being concerned about Portia. The truth was, he *had* done precisely what one imagined happened when a man ended up alone with a woman. He half expected Magnus to be there waiting to accuse him, too, but he wasn't.

Mrs. Temple was just lifting a dish of tea to her lips when he walked in. She raised her eyes and smiled, and there was no anger in that smile, not the least sign of disapproval. He lifted a hand when she rose. He remembered the expression on his father's face when he had been called to account. His father had not smiled. "Please, don't stand on my account."

"Lord Northword. Thank you for coming downstairs so quickly." Mrs. Temple stood and curtseyed, unnecessarily deep if you asked him. He wasn't the damned Prince Regent. "Tea?"

"Yes, thank you." There was a tray of chevron-shaped shortbread on the table and two plates. The one before her had one of the familiar chevrons on it. The shortbread at Northword House had always been shaped thus.

She poured for him without asking his preference and moments later handed him a cup of tea adulterated with more milk than tea, for God's sake. She gazed at him with that guileless, ravishing smile of hers, and it did absolutely nothing for him.

He took the cup and set it down. He did not care for milk in his tea. Sugar only for him. "Thank you."

"Tea is so much more healthful when one drinks it with milk."

He helped himself to the sugar only to have her tap the table by his tea cup. "My father's physician instructed him to take a cup every morning, prepared just so. Without sugar."

"Indeed?" She meant well. She did. A wisp of steam curled from the surface of his tea cup. He dropped in three lumps and then, in a moment of childish rebellion that was far too satisfying, added two more just to watch her horror. "It's not my habit to take milk with my tea."

She blinked several times, and his immediate instinct was to backtrack. She was not the sort of woman to see nuance in word or deed. "You ought to, my lord. After your adventures in our weather today, extra consideration for your health is in order, don't you agree?"

"I enjoy excellent health."

"Who's to say it will stay that way?" Her hand fluttered around her upper chest. "Why, just today you were caught in a storm and soaked to the skin. I shouldn't be astonished at all if you took ill as a result."

He blinked, took stock of his state and decided he was mildly offended and feeling decidedly manipulated by that wide-eyed look of incipient distress. "Thank you for considering my longevity."

"You're welcome, my lord." She beamed at him, and such was his irritation over tea with milk, he had almost no regret for his ironic tone. Besides, she gave no sign whatever that she'd heard the edge in his reply. "It was no trouble at all. I think you'll find you'll quickly acquire a taste for milk with your tea."

"I dare say you mean I will learn to like a bit of tea with my milk." He laughed and smoothed out the emotion that had sparked his pointed response. He failed, for the bite remained. Was he not better than this? This was not a woman of subtlety, and it was not kind of him to behave so with her.

Her eyebrows drew together and she tipped her head to one side. Portia, he thought, would have laughed out loud. But then again, Portia would have known better then to put milk in his tea. He sipped the concoction, and her smile turned incandescent. "Well?"

Undrinkable swill. He forced a smile, because, after all, he would not hurt her feelings for the world.

"I'm glad you like it." She drank some of her tea. "I don't know what to make of this weather," she said. "It's March, nearly April, yet, goodness. As cold and wet as December."

"Is it?"

"What plans have you for the remainder of the day, my lord?"

He put off the necessity of speech by taking a bite of shortbread. "This and that."

She tilted her head and smiled cheerfully. Beautiful woman, sublimely so. But she was married to Magnus Temple, and in so far as his physical tastes went, he'd never been partial to blonds. At the moment he couldn't conceive of taking any woman besides Portia to bed. If he were to have that choice again. If there were any hope of repairing the break between them. Which there was not.

"I thought I'd walk out with Magnus later. To Up Aubry for a pint." He glanced out the window where there was now not a sign of a rain cloud. "If the weather holds as it looks to be doing. Improves the health, a good brisk walk."

"Oh, dear." She folded her hands on the table. "I'm afraid Mr. Temple is not likely to be back from West Aubry in time for that."

He selected a piece of shortbread before he responded. "I didn't know he meant to go."

"He had parish business to attend to."

"Nevertheless, he should return in ample time."

"It's quite a long ride to West Aubry and back."

"By the road, yes. But he'll have walked. With the weather like this, he shan't be delayed for anything but his business."

"Oh but he did not walk. He rode."

"Why would he ride?" By the road under these conditions, West Aubry was at least two hours distant.

"He would have had to walk through your private lands."

"Yes. And?"

"Enclosed lands. I've told him not to presume upon your good graces when that walk takes him within sight of your house."

He frowned. "He's always done so. Walked past Wordless—"

"Oh, I cannot approve."

"Of what? Magnus taking the shortest route to West Aubry?"

"There are a great many things of which one cannot approve." Her tone of voice gave him an unpleasant shock, for he'd begun to believe he would escape an uncomfortable conversation about him and Portia.

She gave him another ravishing smile. "Forgive me, but your estate, my lord, is Northword Hill. Not Wordless. It's not respectful of anyone to call it that. I've told Mr. Temple he mustn't. Portia, too, though she hardly listens to a word I say."

"Why, when I don't mind?" He put down his half-eaten shortbread. "Call the place what you will, Northword Hill, Wordless, or that 'moldering pile of stones,' your husband has always had leave to walk through the property. Even when my father was alive."

She smiled as if she knew a secret and did not intend to share.

"I've no issues with him or anyone from the Grange continuing to do so."

"It's a matter of what's proper, my lord." She got that lost look again, and it did tug at his heart. He resisted the urge to comfort her. "A man of Mr. Temple's position and station in life, who has dedicated himself to the work of God, cannot be seen by his parishioners to act in any way that is improper." She dabbed at her mouth. How did Portia endure this without going stark raving mad? "That holds true for all his family. All we Temples must be above reproach. His wife and his sister included."

He ate his shortbread without tasting any of it while he marshaled his thoughts and temper. Surely, he thought, she did not mean to be so officiously and stupidly nice about Magnus doing what he had always done, and with his blessing. And surely it was only his guilty conscience that made him think she was working her way toward a condemnation of him being out in the rain with Portia. In the stable block with their clothes undone or tossed up, neither of which facts she could possibly know.

"I think, Mrs. Temple, that your distinction is too fine."

She plucked another chevron of shortbread from the tray and ate it slowly. "When we fail to observe the niceties we court the danger of failing in our larger responsibilities. To God, to ourselves and to others." He could practically hear Magnus speaking through her words. "Does not the Bible tell us to respect our elders and those who are in a position superior to us? As those who are our superiors must be mindful of what is best for those beneath them in rank and consequence."

"I'll grant the inhabitants of Doyle's Grange an easement to cross the estate lands." He shrugged. "I'll write to my solicitor and have it done."

"Until then..."

He was so desperate to put off the looming unpleasantness that he changed the subject with an utter lack of tact or finesse. "I've known Magnus and Portia since I was a boy. We have always been on the best of terms. I should hope you believe there's little I would not do for either of them."

She leaned forward. "Magnus and I are so very grateful for all that you have done for us. He would never ask you for anything on his own, you understand. He is too fine a man for that."

He nodded.

To his astonishment, her eyes filled with tears. "He will not ask you, so I shall."

"Please." He could not help thinking that he'd been maneuvered to a point where he'd agree to almost anything to keep from seeing her dissolve into tears.

"He's worked so long and hard, and for his own beloved sister to thwart him like this." She picked up her napkin and dabbed at her eyes.

"I don't understand."

"This marriage of hers."

"What of it?"

"Mr. Stewart is a fine man. We all adore him." She fisted a hand on the table and looked so distressed he wasn't certain if he should hand her his handkerchief or call for a servant to bring a vinaigrette. "Even if Portia were as madly in love with Mr. Stewart as I am with Mr. Temple, the fact is, her marriage does nothing to secure Magnus's future.

A chill went down his spine, and his heart skipped a beat. "She's not in love with him?"

"Oh, I'm quite sure she has tender feelings for him, my lord." She smiled sadly. "Who would not? He is delightful. But she is not a woman of such pure emotion as I am. Surely, you have noticed this small defect in her."

"I have not."

"She does not feel as I do. Nor love so deeply. I have observed that few people do." She waved a hand. "A marriage between her and Mr. Stewart is of no advantage to Magnus at all."

He floundered, torn in too many directions to make sense of this. He'd come downstairs convinced he would be pressured to marry Portia, that it was only a matter of time before Magnus confronted him, and instead, unless he was badly mistaken, he was being asked to interfere in Portia's engagement. "What is it you would have me do?"

No artist in the world could resist the temptation to paint her smile onto a Madonna. "Convince her to come to London before she ties herself irrevocably to a man who does not suit her. Put the full weight of your approval behind our appearance there with her. Any number of gentlemen of good family would be pleased to marry an attractive woman. You've not noticed that Portia is quite a lovely woman, but I assure you it's so. With the proper gowns and only a little more attention to her appearance, why, she cannot help but make an impression."

As it turned out, he did not need to concoct a reply to that, for she continued talking.

"A pretty woman whose family has the friendship of Lord Northword? Any of them would be men who could do Magnus more good, and suit her much better than Mr. Stewart."

"Have you someone in mind?"

She brightened. "Several candidates, as a matter of fact." She counted off on her fingers, but the names went by in a blur.

"So many?"

"Naturally, there are one or two at the top of my list, my lord. I understand it is a great favor to ask you to introduce suitable men to her, but consider that Magnus might one day be a bishop. Why, he might aspire to York or even to Canterbury. It's not beyond his abilities." She leaned in, intent. "If his sister makes a marriage of no advantage? All I ask is that you make known your approval of her when we are in London. What could be happier for us all?"

Chapter Eight

Ten past midnight

PORTIA DIDN'T MOVE FROM HER CHAIR when someone tapped on her door. With Crispin here, they were keeping later hours and, after all, she wasn't in bed yet. She pulled her shawl tighter around her shoulders, but kept her legs drawn up on the chair. She wore only her chemise and the night wrapper she'd had since she was thirteen. Her hair was still loose even though by now it was dry. One had to expect that a woman who'd taken refuge in her room might not be dressed.

Whoever it was tapped again. In the best case, her visitor was Eleanor. In the worst case, Magnus himself had come to confront her. Either way, the visit could only be about her and Crispin. "Come in."

The curtains weren't drawn. Portia, seated in an armchair halfway between her dresser and the fireplace, continued to stare at the glass. On this clear, cold night with the stars shining bright in the sky, she could just see the moonlit branches of the rowan tree she'd planted. Already, the slender branches looked stronger. Decades from now, her tree would provide shade for whoever lived here. The door opened and cast a slice of light on the windows. Instead of the rowan tree or the stars, she saw a reflection of the door.

With a click, the door closed. She had no need to look, she knew who it was. A moment later, the key turned in the lock. Her skin rippled with awareness during the brief silence that followed that sound. He put his lantern on the table beside the door. "The walls aren't blue any more."

"I decided I liked this better." She stood, but stayed beside her chair, her back to the window now, one hand resting along the top curve of the chair. Out of habit, she thought of all the times Crispin had been here. At night. When he ought not to have been and when the walls had been a pale blue. With them breathless and giddy. She gestured. "Moss. This green is called moss. Darker than the parlor, but green nevertheless and very much underappreciated, I do assure you. Except by me. It seems I overappreciate the color."

He laughed and looked around the room, taking it in. "I like it."

Her fingers dug into the chair. He took up all the space. All the air. "I was expecting Magnus or Eleanor."

"To take you to task, I presume."

She nodded.

"I am the hero of this tale, you know. The knight in shining armor facing down the dragon. Did you not hear your sister-in-law praise me for rescuing you from a storm you were obstinate enough to be out in?" He wandered into the middle of the room and took up even more space. She turned with his progress. "I've already been thanked, so you needn't add yours."

"I was not in need of rescue."

"No?" He looked around again. "Other than the walls, everything's the same."

She made a fist of her hand. "What are you doing here?"

His smile vanished. "She wishes me to join in her efforts to get you to London before you are married."

"Oh. Oh, dear. My apologies for that."

"Shall I?"

She looked down and scratched an eyebrow. "It's awful the way she gets what she wants, isn't it?"

"Thoroughly unsettling."

"Don't abet her in this or any other scheme."

He nodded once and into the growing tension he said, "We should talk. About what happened at Wordless." His voice was so brisk he hardly sounded like the man she knew. His voice turned him into a stranger, into the Viscount Northword, not a man she'd known nearly her entire life. Not the man who'd been her first lover and her most recent one, but a stranger of terrible consequence.

She stared at her hand on the top of the chair and forced herself to uncurl her fingers. "I'm not sure there's much to say."

He walked to her dresser so that she had to turn around to face him. He'd stood exactly there dozens of times before. There was no mistaking him for the seventeen-year-old he'd been. He'd grown into all the promise of his maleness and gained an air of command. Both things suited him. "I think we ought to talk, don't you? Clear the air." He scratched his head. "Of all that."

"Why? I don't regret it."

"Nor I."

She couldn't tell if Crispin was pleased or not and so said nothing.

He continued. "Please be perfectly clear on that point. I don't regret what happened either. Even though it ought not to have happened."

"I don't think men regret such encounters." Force of habit put a lilt in her voice. She wasn't used to being on edge with Crispin, and here, in her room, their old familiarity seemed especially close.

"Is that all it was to you?" Of all the items on her dresser, he picked up one of the few new ones to be found. The porcelain pot no bigger than her fist contained as many crocuses as she could fit in it. A crease appeared between his eyebrows. "An encounter."

"I'm sorry if that's inaccurate." Briefly, she closed her eyes. Her memories of him took on weight, the nights he'd walked here from Wordless under a starlit sky like tonight's. "I don't know what it was to you."

"We'll leave it at that, then." He turned and tilted the pot, watching the play of light over it. He wore a thick gold ring on his first finger, and that, too, was something she did not recognize. In ten years, she'd acquired only two pieces of jewelry: a necklace and a pair of earrings, both a gift from Magnus when she turned twenty-one. Since she'd almost immediately lost one of the earrings, she almost never wore the necklace that matched. "You were not your usual self," he said in his stranger's voice. He looked up. "It would not be absurd to suggest I took advantage. I'll apologize if you need that from me."

"No."

He leaned against the dresser, still holding the pot of crocuses. "Your favorite flower, are they?"

"They've always reminded me of you." Too late, she realized how much that gave away. "They bloom every spring in the field between Northword Hill and the Grange. Every spring when Magnus and I were little, I tried to count them whenever we walked up the hill."

He gave her a sideways look. "I remember."

"There weren't as many then as there are now. The first spring after you left, the hill was covered with crocuses as far as the eye could see." She waved a hand. "Not just a few, but a carpet of them. People came all the way from

Aubry Sock to see them. I told Magnus to paint it for you. Did he not send it on?"

"He did. My wife saw it and thought it lovely." He let out a short breath. "I didn't know it was from you. I had it framed and gave it to her as a gift."

"Did you?"

"You know Magnus. He's a gift for choosing an interesting perspective in whatever he paints or draws. She particularly liked that you could see a part of Wordless. I suppose it's still hanging in her room." Crispin, slouched against her dresser, set the pot back in its place. He watched her under half-lidded eyes. A lock of his hair, that lovely shade that was not quite blond yet not quite brown either, fell in a crescent slash across his forehead. "It's a wonder you don't curse them the way she does."

He meant Eleanor. "Never." She brought her shawl closer around her shoulders and caught the edge of his frown. "Why would I?"

"I don't know." He shrugged and avoided looking directly at her by focusing his gaze just past her ear. "Because I took your virginity on a night like this?"

"Turn about is fair play. After all, I took yours."

That frown of his flashed again. He ought to have smiled at her joke, but he didn't. And this time, he looked her full in the face. "For whatever offense I gave that made you leave me."

She sat on the armchair, just on the edge of the seat, and clutched the padded arm. Her heart turned to ash in her chest while she searched for the words to explain what had happened. "I didn't leave you."

"You didn't come with me." He made a sharp, dismissive gesture. "It was ten years ago. We were practically children. Young and foolish, the both of us, but I have always, always, wanted to tell you that I never wavered." He set his palm on his head and looked away in a gesture she'd seen a thousand times from him. When he did that, he was gathering his words, assembling thoughts, so that when he spoke he said precisely what he meant to say. "It's done. You and I. Over."

"I know." She wanted to go to him, but that would be worse than presumptuous. She wanted so badly to touch him, to tell him she understood his anger and that he should let old hurts go.

"I ought not blame you for youth and inexperience of life, and yet I do." He let out a frustrated breath. "It's nonsense, my doing that. But seeing you again— Sometimes I think we were only yesterday and all my old habits with you come back."

"It's been difficult for me, too."

He pushed away from the dresser and walked to the fireplace. For a while, he stood with his back to her, staring at the line of chimney ornaments on the mantle. He touched a bird's nest he'd given to her when she was eleven. "You still have this."

"I'm sentimental about such things. Magnus is always on about how I won't discard anything. I've collected a box of buttons I'll surely never use. Old grammars and the like. Sketches Magnus did when he was a boy. I kept them all, you know."

He turned, and his eyes were hard as stone. "What happened today should not have. I'm sorry. I hope you'll forgive me."

"There's nothing for me to forgive."

He said, softly, after far too long, "I think about him all the time."

She closed her eyes.

"He'd be nearly ten, if you'd had a boy. I imagine him with your beautiful eyes. My mouth." His voice rasped over her, killing her. "Or a girl with your hair and my smile. She might have had your brother's gifts."

"Don't."

"I don't think I ever told you how I felt, and I ought to have."

She turned her head toward him. "It's not the men who suffer. It's the women who are turned out of the house. Women bear all that burden."

"How could you not trust me? The day you told me you were with child, that night, I lay in my bed at Wordless, and I was glad and at the same time I was afraid of what my father would say when I told him. Afraid of Magnus and what he'd think of me for what I'd done to you. And afraid for you. Terrified for what might happen to you."

She didn't dare open her eyes. She couldn't, didn't, and still the tears came. In those days when she'd been trapped and desperate and unable to tell anyone for fear Magnus would find out, she'd felt as if the poison of Lord Northword's hatred had given the man the power to twist the world into any shape he wished. Crispin's father did not wish for a world where his son married a woman like her, and he had transformed the world until he had what he wanted.

"I knew you were afraid and distraught and that you blamed yourself, as if you'd gotten with child without any help from me. I knew you blamed yourself, but I never told you how much I wanted to marry you and hold our baby in my arms. I thought you understood that. I thought you knew I loved you too much to let that happen to you or our child."

She rested her head on her arm, face down so that she could not see him. "Don't do this to me."

He moved closer. "What, Portia? Do what?" The ice was back in his voice. "You went to that woman without giving me a chance to convince you I would do anything you needed. Anything. My father could threaten me all he liked, and I would not have refused to marry you. You didn't need to save yourself from that fate."

The enormity of her loss hit her again. What might have been, the life they might have had. Words came on the heels of a short, low breath, fast and propelled by the force of all the years she'd kept those words back. She lifted her head and stared at him through a blur of tears.

"Your father told me if I married you, he'd have Magnus expelled from school. He said if you were still a minor he'd have the marriage annulled. He told me if I thought we could wait until Magnus was graduated, that if we did that, Magnus would never have a living anywhere, not for as long as he lived. He told me he'd already personally seen to it that the Royal Academy would never admit him, and he had. He did that to punish me, to make sure I knew he'd stop at nothing. That's why Magnus was rejected. If it weren't for me, he would have been admitted. He ought to have been."

He set both hands to his head this time and stared past her.

"Your father was right about me. And so are you. I didn't love you enough to bring more harm to my brother. I couldn't do that to him when I'd already cost him his dream."

Crispin dropped his hands to his side. She didn't move. The silence ripened. At last, he said, "You ought to have told me."

She leaned sideways against the chair and stared at the window frame past Crispin's shoulders. She didn't want to know if he was looking at her. It would kill her to know. "What difference does it make what I should have done or wish I had? There's only the choice I made. And I am sorry. So sorry to have hurt you. I never wanted that."

"I married someone else, and by the time I understood what an awful mistake I'd made marrying in anger and resentment, it was too late." His voice was bleak, and if there had been a way to blot that out, she would have.

"My wife deserved better. She was a good and decent woman, and she deserved more from her husband than the man she got."

That took her aback enough to look at him. She had always imagined they were happy. Crispin would never have married a woman who wasn't worthy of him. "I'm sorry."

"Don't be."

He made a face when she reacted by reaching to him. Her hand fell back to her lap. "Don't you be either, Crispin Hope. You never wrote of her except in the most tender and respectful ways. I always thought it was plain as anything that you loved her very much indeed."

"Not the way I loved you."

"Of course you didn't." She clenched her hand on her lap. "There isn't only one way to love someone."

He strode to her and did not stop moving until she was trapped between him and the chair. Her heart headed toward her toes. His every look recalled what they'd done today, and though she still felt the aches of their encounter, her body wanted him again. She wanted all the marks of their passion, the imprint of him on her soul rising up and taking shape once again. "Then why do I feel as if nothing's changed with us?"

"The past hasn't changed. It's there in our memories. It won't ever go away."

The silence was uncomfortably long.

"I loved you."

"We can't go back." She wiped at her tears. "My God, can you imagine if we tried? We aren't that couple anymore. I don't know you any more than you do me. Please, let's be friends. Let's keep that."

He stepped back.

Her heart broke again.

Chapter Nine

Two days later

AFTER BREAKFAST THEY WERE ALL SITTING IN THE PARLOR as near to the fire as they dared now that Hob had brought in the morning post. There were letters for everyone. Crispin had several, most of which he put in his pocket, but he read aloud from one in which a friend of his, a man whose name she recognized from reading the *Times,* described with lively detail his days spent hiking in Northumberland.

Magnus sat on a chair idly sketching while Eleanor knit. When Crispin had finished reading his letter and they had exchanged news or excerpts from the other correspondence, Portia cleared her throat and said, "I have happy news."

Eleanor put down her knitting and beamed at her. "I adore happy news, and I should very much like to hear yours."

"Jeremy and I have advanced the date of our wedding."

In the silence that followed, Eleanor drew her eyebrows together. "But the day's been set for weeks now."

"We've decided to be married sooner. Not October, Eleanor, but May."

"May? Next year, do you mean?"

"No. Next month. Nothing fancy. There's no time for anything but the simplest of ceremonies, and we've decided we prefer it that way."

Eleanor's hands stilled. "But May is when we'll be in London. For the end of the season."

"You and Magnus may still go, of course."

"When did you decide this?"

"I wrote to Mr. Stewart just a few days ago." She was aware of Crispin's silence, the way he watched her. "He agreed a May wedding was more convenient than October. I should like it very much, Magnus, if we could be married here at Doyle's Grange on the last Sunday in May. As soon as the last of the banns are called."

Eleanor's hands fluttered. "I've told everyone you're to be married in October. In West Aubry. "

Her stomach folded in on itself. She glanced at her brother, hoping to see in his face confirmation that he supported her in this change. Magnus did not meet Portia's eyes.

Eleanor smiled radiantly. "You see? It's not convenient at all. I assure you, I am happy to be of assistance in bringing your wedding about in a suitable manner. At a suitable and convenient time."

"Jeremy and I are settled on this."

"I excel at managing such matters."

"I'm sure you do."

She leaned close and gave Portia's arm a squeeze. "Your parents would have wanted you to have a lovely wedding, attended by the people you love. You've not had a mother's firm guidance nor been able to see your father's pleasure at seeing you properly married. The way I saw how happy mine were when Magnus and I were married."

Resentment bubbled up even as she told herself that Eleanor only wished for her wedding to be perfect. But she wanted nothing more than to be gone from Doyle's Grange. She did not want to continue an intruder on her brother's new life. She wanted to be away from a world where the Viscount Northword could destroy her peace of mind. "I appreciate that. Truly, I do." Lord, she could feel Crispin's gaze. "But Jeremy and I are in accord that this change in date is for the best."

"You have a sister now, my dear. Wiser and more experienced in such matters. I'll take care of everything. You ought to be married in the church at West Aubry, with your brother presiding. You can't have seen my guest list, the people I've invited for October. Or Mr. Stewart's guests for that matter. I have the list from his mother, you know."

"Have you?"

"With your brother so newly established in his living, you would be very selfish to insist on being married anywhere but in West Aubry. Will you deny his parishioners the sight of their spiritual leader living by example what he preaches to them every Sunday? No, my darling Portia, they deserve to see his sister married in their church, by the man who guides them spiritually."

Magnus cleared his throat. "I think I can as well see my sister married here as at West Aubry."

"But, my dear." She blinked several times.

Portia cast about for anything to stop the tears that threatened. "Magnus is so new to his living, and you have so many expenses just now. The Grange, the work at the vicarage. I don't wish for there to be any fuss. It's not as if I'm a young bride. No, no, Eleanor, I must decline all that, despite your generous offer of assistance. We shall have a small ceremony attended by family only."

Crispin leaned forward, and Portia's stomach hollowed out. His hands had touched her, stroked her, and she wanted to hold the remembered sensations close. "The last Sunday in May, you say?"

"Yes, my lord." Portia wanted to kick him for reminding Eleanor of that. "I know you're to be back in London by then, but it's all settled." She held out a hand and smiled. "I will gladly accept your good wishes."

He did not take her hand or return her smile. "You cannot think for a moment that I would miss your wedding." Just now he reminded her so strongly of his father that she felt an echo of the dread she'd felt when in the presence of the late Lord Northword. "I wouldn't. Not for the world."

She allowed him to see her opinion of that. Magnus got up and put more coal on the fire, a welcome distraction, actually.

Crispin wasn't having any of it. "If I must rearrange a meeting or two, then I shall, and there's an end to it. I will be here. The last Sunday in May."

This, then, was her way out. He'd given her the rope that would save her. "Thank you, my lord. How kind. It will mean a great deal to have you there."

Eleanor gave her a panicked look. "But Portia, the house is so very small. If you're to be married here, where will everyone stay? There's no place suitable for Mr. Stewart and his family to stay in Up Aubry, and Aubry Sock is too far away. As is West Aubry from the Grange. No, the wedding must take place where we can accommodate the people who will insist on being here." Her voice trembled. "Doyle's Grange is lovely. I adore it, but there is so little room for guests—and when it is in this condition… In West Aubry, there's the vicarage and several inns where guests might be made quite comfortable."

Once again, Crispin settled everything. "Your guests are welcome to stay at Wordless. There's plenty of time to open up the house, Mrs. Temple. I am happy to do so."

"Brilliant, Word. And generous. You see?" Magnus said to Eleanor. "It's settled as easily as that."

"Northword Hill is at your complete disposal." Crispin looked to Magnus. "You are not to be out of pocket for this, do I make myself clear? Whatever staff you hire will be employed by me. My valet will be more than happy to assist with the arrangements. I know Mrs. Temple will manage everything beautifully, and I shan't have to worry about a thing. Nor will Portia."

"Thank you, my lord," Portia said. She smiled with pure relief. "That is very kind of you to offer your home."

He waved a hand. "It's the least I can do." Then he gazed at Portia. "I look forward to meeting Mr. Stewart."

Chapter Ten

Three days later

PORTIA STOOD IN FRONT OF THE LAVENDER, scissors in hand. The rowan tree was to her right, leaves no longer drooping, just as Hob had foretold. She broke off one of the forming lavender blossom heads and rolled it between her fingers. Even this early in the season, the scent was lovely. Her heart pinched at the thought that she would not be here to see it in full bloom. Nor any of the rest of the garden.

Jeremy and his mother had arrived several hours ago and after much ado, Mrs. Stewart was resting upstairs. Jeremy, Magnus, and Crispin were ensconced in the back parlor while Eleanor was driving the servants to distraction overseeing preparations for her and Magnus's departure for Brighton. Portia had escaped the chaos at the first opportunity.

Boot heels clicked on the stone steps. Not her sister-in-law, thank God. Too fast to be Magnus. Her brother never walked when he could stroll nor hurried when he could walk. Hob never moved that quickly either. Those footsteps came too quickly for anyone but Crispin.

She turned and saw him striding toward her in his tasseled Hessians and snug breeches. The lawn was muddy from the most recent rain, and he had to slow down, not much, but some, when he left the path to head her direction. When he reached her, she curtseyed and then, from deviltry, added, "Good afternoon, my lord."

He stopped in front of her seconds before she would have been required to move, if only to avoid being run over. He ended up too close. He'd walked out without a hat, which she found absurdly thrilling despite it being obvious he'd come here with his annoyance in tow. She stood her ground. Besides, two steps back, and she'd be standing in the lavender.

"Is that woman somewhere near?" He lifted a warning hand. "You know who and what I mean. Can she see or hear us right now?"

"I don't believe so."

"Then don't curtsey." His mouth thinned. "It's not necessary. Not when it's just the two of us."

"You think not?"

"That hasn't changed." He jammed his hands into his coat pockets. He was splendid in high passion, and it made her sorry for the anger that zinged between them. "She isn't here to cry mock tears and convince us all she mustn't be upset lest she melt away in a puddle of grand emotion."

She crushed the bits of lavender in her free hand and let the bruised and torn pieces fall to the ground between them. "Why are you here?" She waved a hand. "Out here, I mean. Glaring at me as if I've gone into your room and mixed up all your papers. Or poured ink on your best shirts."

His mouth twitched down. "As if you couldn't guess."

"I can't."

He worked his jaw, and she was tempted to take a step back. She didn't though. "What the deuce, Portia?"

"Don't scowl like that." Never mind that he was glaring at her, he was all bluster. Eleanor was inside the house and could not see them. With the side of her thumb, she smoothed away the furrow in his forehead. She had the private pleasure of seeing him struggle to master himself, and it made her feel better, knowing that he might be feeling as to sea as she did. "Did no one tell you your face will freeze in that expression?"

He took her hand and held it. "You can't be serious about this fellow."

She pasted on a smile, but that did nothing for the lurch in her chest. "I like his mother."

"A delightful woman, I grant you that." He'd always been scrupulous in that way, honest even when it would have been easier not to be. "I can't say I find her son equally delightful."

"Stop."

"Your face will freeze like that," he said.

"If it does, at least I won't spend the rest of my life with an ogre's glower."

He burst out in laughter, and she tried not to and failed. "Imp."

"The largest imp there ever was." She curtseyed to him, and she almost, almost, felt as if all was well between them. It wasn't. It never could be, no matter how many times they fell into sin or avoided it.

"Portia." Crispin threw an arm wide. "Fifty if he's a day. I don't care how much you like his mother. What do you mean by this?"

She freed her hand from his and clasped her hands behind her back. She never had liked dealing with what people meant rather than what they were saying and right now Crispin was not saying what he meant. "I don't understand what you're asking. *What do I mean by this?* What do *you* mean?"

"I'm not asking you anything."

"My mistake." She tapped her toe, and even though on the grass her boot made no noise, her irritation with him was plain enough.

"I'm demanding that you explain why you're marrying a man old enough to be your father."

"Sit, Fido," she murmured. "Good dog."

He took a step forward. "Don't make light of this. You don't love him. Don't insult me by telling me you do. I know when a woman's in love."

"I'm sure you do." And that came out too hard and too resentful.

"Mrs. Temple is right. You don't love him."

She set free her hands to break off another stalk of lavender and tap his chest with it. "You're a worse bully than her."

"I've not bullied you since you were ten. You wouldn't stand for that from me." He flexed his fingers then crossed his arms and glared at her. "Do you love him?"

So much was already broken with her life, she did not wish to have it fracture now by telling him things she did not care to admit to herself. Before Crispin arrived, she had been at peace with her decision to marry, indeed, she had been near to desperate to leave Doyle's Grange, and the sooner the better. She reached behind her and broke off another stalk of lavender.

"The truth."

"We've discussed this until it's dead. Exploded."

When she looked at him again, he frowned at her. "No, we haven't. We haven't discussed this at all."

She stared at the crushed lavender on her palm. "Perhaps I don't wish to discuss it. There's nothing can be done."

"Did what happened at Wordless mean nothing to you? Is that what you'll have me believe?"

Guilt slid down her spine, but she ignored it. "Don't tell me what I feel. Or what I ought to do. Or think or decide about anything." She glared at him. "I am capable of making my own decisions, you know. I think I know what will make me happy."

He snorted, and that earned him a glare. "I demand an answer."

His curt words got her back up. "Do you, now?"

Being Crispin, he wasn't concerned with the sort of manners he used with Eleanor. "I do."

"What do you expect me to do about that?" In a fit of pique, she curtseyed. "My lord."

"Stop that. I've told you it's nonsense."

"No, it isn't. It isn't at all. Stop telling me it is."

"Portia." His attention was too much for her just now. That sort of attention. His looking at her the way he had at Wordless. "Please. Do you love him even a little? How am I to bear the thought of you marrying a man you don't love?"

She whirled away from him and the lavender, and walked away from the tree that was her permanent farewell to Doyle's Grange. He followed. Of course he followed. He never knew when to let well enough alone. She let out a breath. "I am weary of all this interference in my life. Yours and Eleanor's. If it continues any longer, I swear to you, I will marry Jeremy tomorrow and you and Eleanor can go to the devil."

"I'm not going anywhere with that woman. Besides, you can't. The banns haven't been read."

She snorted. "Scotland's not far."

His eyes pierced her, and she was sorry she looked because she couldn't forget the feel of him, the rightness of having her arms around him and her heart beating in her chest. He said, "You're too young to be marrying."

She stopped walking and stared at him, incredulous. "What?"

"You heard me."

Laughter bubbled up and for her very life she could not keep it back. He was so ridiculously earnest. She managed to draw in a breath and suppress her mirth long enough to speak. "You ought to be mocked for uttering such an absurdity. Too young? Good heavens, you can't be serious. I'm twenty-seven. Better if you agree with Magnus and remind me at every turn that I am on the verge of too old to be marrying."

"You're not too old." He yanked his hands free of his pockets and gesticulated.

"You shan't find an answer in the air. Nor change my mind, either, not with all the bluster in the world."

"Bluster. I'm not blustering at you. And that isn't what I meant at all. You're too young to be marrying *that* man."

She folded her arms underneath her bosom and gazed at him, tapping one foot on the ground. He stared at her bosom. She looked too, brushing at her bodice. "Have I got something on me?"

He lowered his voice. "Come away with me again. To Wordless. Right now."

"No."

"Why not?"

She pointed at the house. "Because the man I mean to marry is inside."

"It didn't stop you before."

"I was upset. Not in my right mind. That shouldn't have happened. You said so yourself." She closed her eyes a moment and tried to put the ring of truth and conviction into her words. "It was habit. That's all. As you said, it's how we are. That doesn't make it right. It doesn't change anything."

"Meaning?"

"I can't stay here. I won't stay here with all"—she waved a hand—"that. Not even for you."

"For yourself. For God's sake, Portia." He ran his hands over the top of his head, leaving his hair in disarray. "I'll speak frankly, if you don't mind."

"Would you?" she said with full irony. "Just this once."

He threw one arm wide. "I thought the man was going to pull down my britches and kiss my arse."

She took a step away from him. "You don't have to marry him."

"Nor do you."

"Yes, I do."

Crispin opened his mouth to speak and then didn't, then blurted out, "What?"

Chapter Eleven

SHE WATCHED CRISPIN'S EYES GET BIG, and she wasn't sure whether to laugh at him or be insulted when she realized what he was thinking. She put her hands on his chest and gave him a push. Anger was quite useful at times. It kept her from bursting into tears. "Is that what you think of me?"

"No."

"That I'm marrying him because of that?"

He refused to be budged. "Why else would a woman feel she has to marry a man?"

"I am not with child, Crispin Hope." She crossed her arms over her chest.

"I didn't say you were."

"You thought it." Her breath caught at the insult. "Go to hell."

"I'm convinced I shall. Why else would you marry that arse-kissing toady?"

"He's not." She made fists of her hands. "Because I want to."

"He is. Believe me, I have met my share of men like him." He crossed his arms, and he only did it to make himself seem bigger and more powerful. Well, she wasn't about to be cowed by him. "I don't believe you want to marry him. Not ten seconds after I met the man I knew you couldn't possibly be in love with him. You're marrying him because you don't want to be here. There, I've said it."

"You certainly have." She bit off the words.

Crispin seemed to realize he'd spoken out of turn again, for he flushed. "I won't apologize for telling you I don't like him. Someone needs to tell you that you can do better."

Anger boiled up. She was speechless with it. And thank God, for she'd have said words she would surely regret.

He reached for her, but she stepped to the side, and he missed his target. "Don't marry him. You shan't be happy."

She tucked her hands behind her back and cocked her head. "Will you tell me who I ought to marry? Please. I should like to know. There aren't many eligible men here. Men I'd want to marry, and it's been years since any unattached gentleman came to the Grange to ask my brother if an offer would be kindly received." She rocked on her heels. "The blacksmith is handsome enough, I suppose, but he's already got a wife. If you tell me to go to London and find a husband there, I'll never speak to you again. You and Eleanor can dry each others' tears over that."

He took her by the shoulders and stared at her. "I'm serious about this. He's not anything like your equal."

"You are not my father. Nor are you my brother. Nor anyone else with authority over me. How dare you tell me not to marry a decent man?" She twisted away from him. "Under the circumstances, he's the best I can do."

"No, he isn't." He grabbed her upper arm and turned her to face him. "Look at me."

She thwarted him by staring at the sky. Amid the blue, the moon was a pale crescent, washed out by the late winter sun.

"You are a stubborn, stubborn woman. Look at me."

She did and ought not to have because the moment she did all her resentment evaporated.

"I've no authority over you, God knows that's so. But who else will you trust with the truth? Your sister-in-law? Or will you tell Magnus the reason you're marrying a man you don't love?"

"You know I can't." Tears burned in her eyes, and she had to look away to keep him from seeing how close she was to tears. She couldn't. She could not complain to her brother about his wife nor breathe a word about her unhappiness.

"Come here." Crispin tugged on her arm and spread his other arm wide and she walked into his arms where she had always been safe and where all was right with the world. "Tell me. You'll feel better for it, you know you will."

"I've tried to like her. I've tried. And I can't." She rested her forehead on his chest. He smelled good, and his body was warm. "She's empty and shallow, and she loves Magnus, that's obvious to anyone with eyes, but she doesn't love Doyle's Grange." She lifted her head and Crispin used the side of his thumb to wipe away her tears. "I knew there was no hope when she didn't laugh after Magnus told her his ridiculous joke about how it came to be called Doyle's Grange."

"She didn't?"

"No. And that's why I have to marry Jeremy." She gripped the lapels of his coat. "I can't stay here. I can't. I'm not a good enough person for that. I'll go mad if I stay, and if I don't go mad, then one day I'll say something to her I shouldn't, and Magnus must take her side."

Crispin stroked a hand over her head. "But him?" He spoke in a low voice. "The man's not worthy of you."

"You don't know that." She pushed away from him. "I shouldn't have said anything."

He followed her to the very rear of the lawn but needed another step to come even. They were off the path, both of them moving quickly.

She spoke before he'd caught up. "Magnus likes him."

"Magnus tolerates him because he thinks you love the man."

She put out a hand to slow him down. "Oh, do watch where you put your feet. You'll step—"

"What?"

She stopped walking. But Crispin, being a tall man and in the middle of a step, moved those few inches more. She cried out. Too late. His foot came down on the grass. "Look what you've done."

"What? What have I done?" He followed her downward glance with a puzzled expression.

"You've killed it." Tears burned in her eyes and choked off her words until she managed to swallow. "There's little enough beauty here anymore. Eleanor is determined to ruin it all, and now you're destroying what's left for me to enjoy. There's nothing else here I love. Not any more."

"I'm sorry." It was plain he'd no idea what he'd done. None at all.

"You're not." She stared at the crocus that he'd smashed into the dirt, and all she could see was her future if she stayed. She knelt by the flattened plant. "You're not sorry at all. Don't pretend you are. This one's managed to escape her and now you've crushed it, and it's dead."

Crispin crouched across from her and pushed away her hand. He built up a wall of mud and propped the flower on it. "There. Perhaps like the rowan it will recover with some benign neglect."

"It won't." Those were tears thickening her voice, but she met his gaze head on. "If it survives the day, Eleanor will find it, and she'll tell Hob to dig it up. If she doesn't kill it with her own bare hands. That's all she ever does, murder what I love and all the time she makes it impossible to be angry at her."

He frowned at the mud on his gloves. With a hard sigh, he pulled them off and dropped them in his coat pocket. Then, both of them still bent over the plant, he tapped the underside of her chin. "I'm sorry I was clumsy and trod on your flower. I'm sorry Eleanor digs them up." He took her hand and brought her to her feet. "I'm an oaf. I don't watch where I put my feet. And now I've made you unhappy when that's the last thing I meant to do. Listen to me." He grabbed her by the shoulders again, and she looked at him through a blur of tears. "I'll have the groundskeeper plant a hundred of them at Wordless. You can go there every day to see them. She won't be able to ruin them for you there."

Her chest was stuffed full of feelings, and she could not contain them all. "A hundred isn't enough."

"A thousand then." With her hand still in his, he walked them toward the rear of the house.

"It's too late for that, Crispin. I'll soon be living too far away to walk to Wordless."

His mouth thinned. "Then you can bloody well live at Wordless. I don't mind if you do. I'm never there. Why oughtn't you?"

"Because then everyone will think I'm your lover, that's why."

"It wouldn't be true."

Emptiness settled in her belly and made everything familiar and dear seem unfamiliar, from Doyle's Grange to Crispin to her future life. "You've not changed a bit, have you? Still full of grand and impossible ideas. I might as well make my home in the clouds as live at Wordless."

He cupped her face and brushed his thumbs across her cheeks and when he did that and looked at her the way he was now, the world with all its troubles dropped away. When he touched her like that, she believed she could live in a castle in the sky.

"Do you feel that?" he whispered. "Whenever I touch you there's nothing but that heat."

"I cannot live on that."

"He's not your equal."

She blinked several times, but the heat coursing through her stayed. "Of course he is."

"He's not." He dipped his head and for a breathless moment, she thought he meant to kiss her. She could no more deny the passion between them than she could deny herself air. He moved his finger again. "You're cold."

She drew her head back, and his finger slipped away. "Your hands are warm."

"You've made up your mind, haven't you?"

She nodded.

"Nothing will shake your conviction that he's more than he is?"

"He's what I need him to be."

He shook his head. "Don't. It's a mistake. Don't marry just to get away. I, of all people, know what a mistake that is."

She swallowed hard. "I can't stay here. I can't."

"Not even if it's good sense? You're running from a bad situation into a worse one, and it's one you can't take back when the hard light of reason proves your mistake." He kept his voice low. "I promise you, there's nothing worse than to marry where there is no love."

"She's ruined Doyle's Grange for me. Ruined it."

"He's a belly on him and only half a head of hair. No doubt he's losing his hearing." He checked himself and after a glance at the house, lowered his voice. "Do you want to spend the best years of your life shouting at a fat old man who probably never read a novel in his life? And if he did, he'd not think it grand."

While they stood here, the clouds had gotten thicker and darker and the air colder. She grasped his hand and pressed it. "He likes me, with my red hair and despite all my faults."

"Is he marrying a wife or a nurse for his mother?"

"That's uncalled for."

"It's entirely called for."

She recognized that mulish look. "You've never had to do without something you want, let alone something you need."

His eyes widened. "The hell I haven't."

"You? With ten thousand a month and houses all over England? He is a decent man. We understand one another."

"Don't attempt to tell me you love that man. I know what you look like when you're in love."

"It won't be the way you and I were." Her heart cracked open, irreparably broken, and there was just no way to repair the damage she'd done. "Not that kind of love, but then Jeremy and I are not young and foolish or in love for the first time. I dare say we'll get on quite well. I know we shall." She walked away from him. The chickens had been let out and a few of the hens scattered as she and Crispin approached the back gate. "Besides," she said when he was next to her again. "He's no objection to me, not even at my advanced age."

His face emptied of emotion. "Marry me instead."

"You don't want that."

She knew from experience that Crispin, when angry, turned quiet. His gaze was quite capable of freezing one to death with a glance. No doubt he'd learned that from his father. He went silent long enough to tie her stomach in knots. She waited him out and won that contest, for he spoke in a low, tight, voice. "Have you more to say about how I think or feel?"

"You'll always resent me for what happened, for the choice I made. You were steadfast, and I was not."

"I don't blame you. Not for what my father did to you. To us."

"You haven't forgiven me."

"You willfully misunderstand." He touched her arm, and she flinched. "It's not I who hasn't forgiven. It's you."

Her mouth gaped. "I do not blame you. Not for your father, that's hardly your fault, and not for anything else."

"You can't forgive yourself."

She drew in a stuttering breath. "What sort of person would I be if I did?"

"The woman I used to love."

"I'm not that woman. Don't you see? There's no repairing what happened. I'm broken. Nothing will ever fix that."

Chapter Twelve

The following day

NORTHWORD LEANED FORWARD ON THE CHAIR he'd brought next to Magnus's and breathed in the scent of the beer that filled his mug. They were in Magnus's office, sitting on chairs drawn up to the fireplace. It was just after one, and the remains of their luncheon were on the table by the door. That arse-kissing toady Jeremy Stewart had driven his mother, Eleanor, and Portia to Aubry Sock for tea. They weren't expected back for another three hours at least. That left him and Magnus with the house to themselves. They were taking full advantage.

He reached behind him and flipped open the box of cigars on the table. He gave Magnus cigars whenever they saw each other. Northword fished out two and handed one over before he hefted his mug. "Good friends and happy marriages." He did not intend for his toast to extend to Portia and that prick Jeremy Stewart, so when Magnus raised his glass he narrowed the scope of his words. "To you and Eleanor."

While the April sky might be blue, it was bloody cold outside. The nearest window was open a crack to let out the smoke. The office where they sat was on the small side of cozy, with shelves jammed with books, a desk with stacks of pamphlets, papers, a two-day-old *Times,* and a Bible. A trunk with broken trim sat underneath the window. An oak highboy painted red took up half the wall across from the fireplace. The table behind them, close enough for them to use it, was covered with paper. Magnus's doing, that riot of thick, odd-sized sheets of paper.

Charcoal and gum rubber littered the surface, and Crispin had flicked away a pencil that rolled underneath the cigar box. Several of the pages were sketches of the view from various windows of the house or of everyday items: a cup, an apple, a Bible seen from the page edges. Some were of furniture, a view of a window, and more recently, the church in Aubry Sock where

Magnus, naturally, had spent a great deal of time before he had the living in West Aubry. There were a few sketches of him and several of the men and women who lived near Up Aubry. He had a knack for taking a likeness.

Magnus lifted his mug, recently filled from the contents of the earthenware jug he'd brought back from Up Aubry earlier in the day. The tavern there was half the size of this room and comfortably held the entire male population of the village, counting the proprietor and including Crispin. They served a dark and bitter beer that had to be the finest anywhere in England. "To good friends." He winked. He took a long draw on his beer and when he was done, let out a sigh. "Light the bloody thing."

"Impatient sod." He leaned over with a candle for Magnus to use to light his cigar. He lit his when Magnus blew the first puff of smoke in the direction of the open window.

"If the subject should happen to come up, don't mention the cigars to Eleanor."

"Why not?"

Magnus contorted in order to tap the top of the cigar box. "She'll have my head if she finds out about these. Thinks smoking is vile. Ungodly for a man of God."

Crispin didn't reply right away "Are you telling me you aren't permitted to smoke a fine cigar in your own house?"

"Not just my house now." He let out a stream of smoke. "There's always the vicarage in West Aubry, but it's smaller than here. Lovely, make no mistake, but she's taken a fancy to the Grange, Eleanor has. It's here she wants to live."

"If she complains, tell her it was me, and that you tried to dissuade me." He drew on his cigar. When he'd let out the smoke, he said, "Tell her I said I am the bloody Viscount Northword, and I can smoke a cigar anywhere I damned please."

Magnus laughed. "Perhaps I'll not say precisely that. But she'll agree with the sentiment, I tell you that."

"Tell her I refused to save my soul, but that yours remains unsullied."

"That I will." They sat for a bit, contemplating the fire and the warmth and the hint of chill at their backs. "Did Lady Northword mind you smoking?"

"Never. Though to be fair, I never did around her. The way you won't around your wife." He tried for a smoke ring and muffed it. "I don't think less of you for that."

"Your bloody house is big enough you could have a dozen men smoking and no one at the other end would know." Magnus exhaled, then sank a little lower on his chair. "Put another bit of coal on the fire, won't you?"

"Why should I when you're nearer?"

"Because I'm more comfortable than you. Because I'm an old married man now. I need my strength." He put his finger in the stream of smoke leaving his mouth and traced it upward as far as his arm could reach. When he'd settled again on his chair, he examined his cigar. "The last cigar to be smoked at the Grange. What would Doyle say if he were still alive?"

"Arf. Arf."

Magnus's belly shook. "The poor dog froze to death, I hear. For lack of coal on the fire."

"God help us all if the Grange must be renamed 'Doyle and Magnus's Grange.'"

"I'll carve it on my headstone. 'Doyle was a fine dog but Magnus was the better man.'"

"Amen, my friend. Amen." They laughed at that together, and when Crispin was back on his chair, having added half a scuttle of coal to the fire, they smoked in companionable silence. He stretched his legs as close to the grate as he dared. The wind rattled the shutters harder, then died away. "Will it rain soon, do you think?"

Magnus nodded. "They'll be home early, I expect, Portia and Eleanor and the others. Oh, damn." He shot to his feet, wiping at his waistcoat.

"Have you burnt it?" Crispin asked.

"Devil take me if I have. I think so."

"It's good you're a married man." He laughed. "You need looking after."

"So do you." Magnus stared at the spot where hot cigar ash had eaten a hole in the fabric. "Eleanor will have my head." He brushed at his waistcoat before he sat again. "Portia will mend it for me, and not tell Eleanor, either. Solid as a rock, that girl. But then you know that."

"I do."

After several minutes more silence, Crispin put down his cigar and reached for a stack of the papers on the table. He went through them slowly, with the reverence due the pages. As always, he was in awe of Magnus's talent. His art. Magnus Temple was a bloody genius, and here he was, the vicar of West Aubry when he ought to be in London painting for the Royal Academy. What a waste. What a bloody crime. Portia blamed herself for that, when really the blame belonged to his father. And to him. For not foreseeing that his father would threaten not Portia directly but the people she loved. "Why are all these out?"

"Organizing things." Magnus shrugged. "Clearing out the old now that Eleanor's here. I try to do some every few days."

There were several drawings of Eleanor, including one in which she was clearly the inspiration for a Madonna. Crispin came to a portrait of Portia, done a few years ago. So young. His heart hurt to see her. She'd never been a conventional beauty, but he doubted any man would deny her appeal. Spend five minutes with her, and you'd soon be convinced you'd never met a finer woman. In the portrait, done in pen and ink, her head was bowed in concentration. Magnus had drawn just the tops of her hands, enough to show she held a needle. Behind her was the suggestion of the parlor fireplace. One expected she might at any moment lift her head and smile. A wave of lust hit him, pulling him under. He lay the stack of sketches on his lap, the portrait of Portia on top.

She still thought about the baby they'd made, when all these years he'd convinced himself she didn't. How could he blame her for what she'd done as a sixteen year old girl in a desperate situation? His father had all but guaranteed she would carry that burden alone. There were women in her situation who died, and that knowledge chilled him to the marrow. She might have died, and a world without her would have been a barren place.

"My wife's been gone more than a year, now. Nearly two."

"We were sorry to hear that news, Portia and I."

"I was a better man after I was married." Marriage had agreed with him, that was true. Not a perfect union, but not a bad one either. He'd been happy in a calmer way. His wife had been a fine and admirable woman, and he had always hated himself for not loving her as she deserved.

"You'll marry again." Magnus nodded to himself. "You must. Unnatural if you don't."

"That's so." He did not have a son yet, and that must be remedied.

"Have you met anyone who will do?"

He shook his head, but Jesus, the lie of his denial spread ashes across his soul.

"Pity."

"I don't like Stewart."

Magnus took another pull of his beer. "He writes verses. Did he tell you that? No? I expect that's why Portia's set herself on marrying him. The poetry did her in, that's what I think. Lord knows she's never paid any attention to other men, and they've come calling. I know you don't see her like that, but there's a good many men who've wanted to marry her."

He did not move for fear of Magnus seeing more than he ought, but then he wondered if that wasn't a worse way to lie to his best friend than if he plastered on a disbelieving grin. "Is that so?"

"He's not bad, you know. Stewart."

Crispin snorted.

"As a poet." Magnus slunk lower on his chair. "Goes on about cliffs and bluebells flashing with dew. But there's one about a stag I like. Noble antlers and beams of sunrise."

"He's an architect, I thought."

Magnus reached over and tapped the underside of the sketches on Crispin's lap hard enough to make the paper jump. "Only one of his occupations puts money in his pocket."

He slumped on his chair. A poet? The man was a damned poet? "God save us from poets."

"The Lord will strike you dead for that." Magnus grinned and the lines of his face deepened, and it seemed to Crispin there were more now than there had been the last time he'd seen Magnus. "Might take fifty years, though."

He picked up Magnus's portrait of Portia, and something tugged at him as he studied the smiling woman on the page. She was unhappy now, and she did not deserve to be. Not then, and not now. He glanced at Magnus.

The words that came to his lips felt odd and foreign and right. They shook loose from wherever they'd been lodged and flew into the air. "I want to marry Portia."

Magnus choked on his laughter.

He waited until there was silence again and then said, "I will marry Portia."

A furrow appeared in Magnus's forehead. "You mean that."

"With your permission. Of course." He wanted this. He did. No more deception.

Magnus looked at him with his artist's eye, seeing what was there. And what was not. "What makes you say a thing like that?"

He worked through what Magnus had said and the careful way he'd said it and he felt as sick at heart and just as defiant as he had been when he'd said the words to his father. "You won't agree to my marrying her?"

"You're like a brother to me. You know that."

He pushed out of his slouch. He was…affronted. Magnus owed him this. He bloody owed Portia the life she ought to have had. "I feel the same. But that doesn't make Portia my sister."

All trace of Magnus's usual good humor vanished. He leaned forward and set his cigar against the ashtray. "No one could ask for a better friend than you."

He sat up the rest of the way. Magnus was telling him no? The insult pricked him. Dented his pride. More, though, it scared the hell out of him. "Why not?"

"Is it wise?"

"Yes, damn it, it is. Why wouldn't it be?"

Magnus shook his head.

The urge to spear him with a look of blue-blooded incredulity was impossible to resist. "I'd be a better husband to her than that doughty old poet she's going to marry so you and Eleanor can make a life together."

Magnus's eyebrows shot up. "Is that what she told you?"

"Not in so many words, but it's true. If she marries me, she'll want for nothing, you know that. I should think you'd be pushing her my way. Most brothers with unmarried sisters do."

It was Magnus's turn to be insulted. "I'd never. You know that."

"Yes. I do know that. Maybe you should have."

"You and Portia?"

"Why not? Why the bloody hell not, I should like to know?"

"If she'll have you." He rested a hand on Crispin's shoulder. "If she'll have you, you'd have my blessing."

"If she'll have me?" The bottom dropped from his stomach. If Magnus didn't think Portia would marry him, maybe she wouldn't. Maybe he'd never change her mind. "Why do you think she wouldn't if I asked her?"

"I shouldn't say this, but I think she used to be in love with you. After you left, the joy went out of her." He chewed on his lower lip. "I've watched her here, the two of you, and to be honest, whatever there was between you, one-sided as it was, it's long dead. I don't think you're what she needs. Not any more."

Chapter Thirteen

Four days later

HE DIDN'T LIKE THE SILENCE AT ALL. In all the times he'd been at Doyle's Grange, the house had never been this quiet, not when Portia was here. Jesus, what if he was too late? What if while he'd been giving her time, Portia had convinced that ridiculous poet to take her to Gretna Green?

Hob came into the entryway and bowed his head. He wasn't wearing his livery. "Milord." He straightened. "Didn't expect to see thee here."

Out of pure habit, he took off his hat, but rather than hand it over to Hob, he hung it from one of the pegs above the doorway that led to the servants' quarters. "Where is everyone?"

"Gone. Or out."

"I see. Who is out and who is gone?"

"Mr. Stewart. Mrs. Stewart. They've gone."

"And Portia?"

"Out."

"With the Stewarts?"

"With the tree."

"Thank you. I'll just go see her then. I'll announce myself."

"Milord."

He left his hat on the peg and walked outside to the back of the house. She was sitting on the ground by the rowan tree, industriously doing something to the earth around the trunk. Her hands stilled when he had yet another five paces to cover.

"She'll dig them up next spring, but I don't care." With both hands, she tamped down the dirt around the rowan sapling. "I've planted a hundred of them here, and next spring they'll come up, and I'll be the only one who knows it's my name they're saying."

"The crocuses?"

She swiped a hand across her forehead and twisted a bit to look at him. There was a smear of dirt just at the part of her hair. "Yes. Why are you here?"

"Where is Mr. Stewart?"

Her hands fell to her lap. "I sent him away."

"Did you?" He held out his hand, and she put her gloved hand in his and stood.

She glanced away, then back. "He's a decent man, but you're right. He doesn't deserve a wife who will never love him."

He pulled her close and brushed the backs of his fingers across her cheek. "Don't be unhappy. You know I can't bear it."

His bare hand against her warm skin, a touch so light he hardly felt it, except he did. He remembered his mouth over hers and the dizzying wonder of finding her in his embrace again. This contact plunged through his body in the same way. He continued downward, caressing along her jaw, her throat. "I've done nothing but think about you since I left. Every second since I arrived. Before Wordless. After Wordless."

"I as well."

"Every bloody moment of the last ten years and, God willing, every moment of the rest of my life." He brought out his handkerchief and cleaned away the dirt on her forehead.

"Thank you."

"You're welcome." He removed her thick gardening gloves one at a time, and shoved them into his coat pocket. "Please. Hear me out. You're right, too. All along you've been right. We can't change the past, but we don't need to. Everything we need to know about each other we discovered that day at Wordless. If you don't believe me, I'll prove it to you again."

"Prove what?"

"That we are still in love. Despite what happened. Because of what happened. Will you let me show you?"

She tugged on her hand, and he tightened his fingers. "Here?"

"In private, if you don't mind." Her hand clasped in his, he dashed across the lawn to the back door. Inside, they caught their breath, and then headed upstairs, an urgent journey to his room.

Northword closed the door to his room as softly as he could. His fingers were tight around Portia's hand, and he didn't let go even after he turned the key in the lock. Arm straight down, he interlaced his fingers with hers. The palm of his other hand slapped on the wall above her shoulder, taking his weight while he leaned in and kissed her.

Eventually, they left off the frantic kissing and set themselves to an equally frantic removal of each other's clothes. It took some time to remove the layers, to untie knots and unfasten buttons. But they were still young and healthy and far, far wiser about such things than they'd once been.

When she stood in just her shift, he touched her gently, from cheek, to throat, to her collar bone. Her breath hitched when his fingers reached the top swell of her breast. "You see?" he murmured. "That's not changed. The way I react to you. Or you to me."

His palm dropped down, too, touching her breast, curving over her, and with that, the world narrowed to him and Portia and that was precisely right. He allowed himself a smug smile. Again, he brushed just the tip of his finger over her. "Is that good?"

"Yes. Damn you, yes."

"Think how it would feel if you were naked." God, he loved to see her face when she was in passion.

"Beast."

Her name was a sigh on his breath. He kissed her, one hand cupping the back of her neck, the other fully curved over her breast, molding her there so that he could push her breast higher. His tongue flicked out and followed the seam of her lips, and she opened her mouth and for him, it was like falling under her spell all over again.

He pulled away and cupped her face in his hands. She wrapped her fingers around his wrists, but that was all. They stayed like that, touching each other, settling into the familiarity of the contact and this time, there was a sense of the world coming right.

His torso pressed against her as he leaned in and kissed her ear. "I love you, Portia Temple."

He wanted her now and afterward, and that was that. He wanted her in his life, this amazingly lovely creature who kissed with such delicate fever. Portia, who had inhabited his dreams for a decade. Portia, who had become a woman he admired and respected. He drew back before he completely lost control.

"How can you?"

"Because you are brave and strong and when I am with you, I want to see you laugh and smile. Because you would never, ever, ever put milk in my tea and tell me it's good for my health."

She gasped, and her fingers tightened around him. "She makes Magnus drink it that way, too." They laughed together at that and then she draped an arm around the back of his neck, and set the other around his naked waist, fingers angled downward. "She did the same to me once, but I poured it all in the slop bowl. She nearly came to tears. Poor Magnus."

"Poor me. You're not naked yet." He let go of her hand and fumbled at her shift while he kissed her, open mouthed, tongue involved. She kissed him back because Portia never did anything half way. Her shift dropped to the floor with the rest of their clothes.

If Satan himself demanded his soul for this, he'd gladly hand it over.

"I want you in my arms. I want us skin to skin. I want to make you spend and call on God and me. I want your mouth on me, your hands, your thighs around me. I want your eyes glazed with passion for me." He took a step toward her. "I want to hear us both groan when I am inside you."

Northword leaned against her, his cock hard and him halfway to coming because, God save him, Portia's body was soft and curved, and he was going to make love to her until they were witless fools, and she had no choice but to agree they belonged together. She pushed up to kiss him again, and she was so very, very good at setting fire to his blood.

Lust, an unfathomable need, came from deep inside him, and it was everything he'd missed every damned time he'd had sexual relations. It wasn't that he hadn't loved his wife, he had. Or that he hadn't enjoyed other lovers who came to his bed. He had. But not like this. Never. The missing part of his soul clicked into place with her, and he was whole as he had not been since the day his father had engineered their split.

Every shiver of Portia's body, every soft sound to fall on his ears mattered to him because it was her in his arms. Failing to please her would rip him to pieces. He pushed away from her and grabbed her hand while he walked backward to the bed, bringing her along. No half measures. No caution.

Portia laughed and gave him a push. The backs of his legs hit the bed, and he sat on the mattress, splayed out to catch his balance. She stepped between his spread legs and he touched her naked backside or just stared at her breasts.

He drew her to him, hands sliding along her waist, up her back, fingers dancing down the dip of her spine. He took her mouth and she answered with a taking of her own. He cupped her bottom and brought her up until she had her knees on the mattress on either side of his hips. She gripped the top of his shoulders until she had her balance and when she did, he pulled the pins from her hair and kept going until her hair, dark, dark red, curled around his fingers.

"I adore your hair, every curl."

"I'm glad you like brunettes."

"My darling, you are deluded." He took some of her hair in his hand. Light from the window nearest her reflected off her hair, turning even the shadows a rich, dark red. "Your hair is red, and I adore every lock on your head." He slid his fingers beneath her chin and brought her face back to his. "I want you again. I want inside you now." He leaned forward and nipped her lower lip. "Anything you want, if you'll let me do that."

Her smile was everything he loved about Portia. Her smile was bright and bold and for him, and her smile had been living inside him for years. A part of Crispin Hope and a part of the man who had become the Viscount Northword.

"Although, I feel I ought to tell you that I am inclined to be selfish just now." For this slice of time, he was looking not at Portia, but solely at a naked woman whose proportions pleased him inordinately. Wickedly so. He brushed her hair behind her shoulders. In ten years, she'd become a woman. "You're still beautiful, more beautiful and desirable than ever." He put his palm over her mound, slid a finger between, and found slick heat. "That's lovely." He drew in a breath. "You're wet for me."

"Yes."

"Good, because I'm hard for you." Jesus, he wanted those legs around him. He wanted his hips tucked up tight against hers. He swept the back of his hand across her shoulder then down to her breast. "Lovely. That's a fact."

Her nipples peaked, and he swept his fingers across her again. His belly hollowed out. Somewhere in the house, timbers creaked. Outside, rain pattered against the windows. Then harder until it beat on the roof and windows. He held his breath until he was sure the noise was just settlement and the rain, and they weren't about to be interrupted by a furious Hob.

He leaned close, his mouth by her ear. "What I'd like to do isn't decent at all. It's wicked and depraved."

She angled her body against his. "You make it sound delicious. Is it?"

He fit both his hands over her breasts, and she leaned into his palms. He looked his fill of the sight, his hands over her, the flesh he couldn't cover, the way her mouth parted. He pressed his lips to her shoulder; a light kiss while he swept his fingers along the underside of her breast, one, then the other, and the curve of her devastated him. He brushed a finger over her nipple and saw, felt, and reacted to the way she hardened at his touch. "I want my mouth here." His fingertip came to rest at her mons then slid down until his hand cupped her. "And here."

Her eyes opened wide, and she tipped her head to one side, curious. Intrigued. "There?"

"Yes. Precisely there."

She arranged herself on his bed, her hair spread out, and her body open for him. He joined her and slid his hands underneath her bottom. One thing he'd learned was that he loved the taste of a woman. He'd had a mistress before he married, a courtesan who taught him things he hadn't worked out on his own with Portia or some other woman who could never measure up.

Portia gave herself over to his mouth on her, and he made damned sure he didn't bring her too fast. He adored her moans, the tension in her body when she came close, the way her hands touched his head, the tilt of her pelvis toward him. She made him feel like the best lover in the world, and the proof was in the way she came.

For a fraction of time, she went completely still, and in that space he spread her nether lips and licked along the center of her sex. She came apart, holding back none of her pleasure.

"More, Crispin." Her voice shook. "More."

He pulled himself over her, his mouth by her ear. "You have all of me. There's nothing more for me to give." He touched her once and she flinched with unsatisfied passion. "You have everything."

He moved down her body and before long, she devolved into an incoherent cry. He spread his fingers over her belly while she came back to earth and then pulled himself up enough to dip his tongue into her navel. He lifted his head, and when she was looking at him, soft-eyed with pleasure, he thought his heart would burst as past and present emotions warred in him. As they did in her, too.

Northword spread his fingers over her stomach again. He had to work to keep his voice steady and then decided the battle wasn't worth fighting.

"Portia." Her name came in a whisper. "I wanted you to have my child. I still do. I want it enough to beg you for another chance. We were young. You're right about that. But I wanted us. And our child."

"I know. I know. I know."

"Say you'll marry me, Portia. Promise it." He stared at her stomach, fingers sliding, but tipped his head so he could see her face, too. Eyes closed, lips edged with white. "We can have the child we make tonight. Marry me. Please. I'm a better man, a wiser man. I'd be a proper husband to you and a loving father. Magnus knows I want to marry you. He doesn't think you will, but I don't give a damn for his opinion."

"Crispin."

He took her hand and moved over her, one leg across hers. The slide of his skin over hers heated his blood, the very marrow of him, and he pushed her shoulder until she was on her back. She opened herself to him. He pulled himself over her and thrust inside.

She was hot and slick, and he got harder being inside her, and inside, her soft body barely gave. He put his forearms above her shoulders and kept still, giving her time to adjust to him. "I couldn't bear the thought of that man touching you." He drew back his hips and pushed forward. "Nor the thought of you touching him. Nor that you might fall in love with him."

She put her hands on either side of his face and arched her pelvis toward him. "Hush, my love."

He drew back and pushed slowly in again, and it was heaven. Tension sang between them and, for him, it was the certainty that he could do exactly what he wanted, what would please them both, and the fact of her woman's body that sent him into sensual paradise. He stroked in her steadily, and before long he knew he wouldn't last much longer.

He stopped moving and that nearly killed him, holding back all the urges of his body. He took her head between his hands, weight on his forearms. "Marry me." He drew back his hips and pushed forward enough to make his balls go tight. He stopped moving because otherwise he couldn't think. He had to work to marshal his thoughts.

"Marry me because I love you. Marry me because you love me. We'll have children. Us. God, Portia, please. I want what slipped away before. I don't want to live without you. I love you. I've always loved you."

With the last of his wits, the last bit of his coherence, he waited.

She put her hands on either side of his face. "I love you, too, Crispin Hope. I always have."

"Marry me."

She wrapped her legs around his hips and bit his ear lobe once. "Yes, you fool. Yes. Now do this properly. The way you promised me or I shall know you'll never be a proper husband for me."

And so he did.

What Happened at Midnight

COURTNEY MILAN

Chapter One

February 1856, Southampton, England

"You there. Where do you think you're off to? And where is your father?"

Miss Mary Chartley came to a stop in the hall, mere steps from escape. The servants' door was only a few feet away. She silently cursed the board that had let out the telltale creak. Her shoulders ached. Her heart pounded. And behind her eyes, a headache had started, brought on by sleeplessness and unshed—

No. Not tears. She was done with crying.

She gathered her composure and her wits, and turned.

Her father's one-time business partners had started to ransack the house early that morning. She had heard them come in; the constable who had accompanied them had even questioned her briefly. But they'd busied themselves downstairs, leaving her free to do what needed to be done. She had hoped to simply steal out the back door, with nobody aware of her departure.

"Mr. Lawson." She gave the nearest man a quick curtsey. "Mr. Frost." Another dip of her head. Only one of the partners was missing, and she couldn't let herself think about Mr. John Mason. "Good morning."

It was absurd to observe the forms of propriety at a time such as this, but she'd been steeped in proper manners for most of her life. Five years of a very expensive finishing school in Vienna had trained her to smile at these men in pleasant harmony, even while they pawed through her father's things.

Mr. Lawson and Mr. Frost had made a shambles of the office. Her father's carefully-sorted papers had been strewn about the room; books had been pulled from their shelves and left in uneven, teetering piles. They'd wrested the drawers from the desk and splintered the wooden boards into kindling.

Lawson raised his head from the wreckage to contemplate her. "Where is your father?" he asked again.

"She doesn't know anything," Frost said, after giving her a brief, dismissive glance. He was methodically flipping through books, searching for some hidden secret within their pages. "Look at her—dressed for a stroll in the park, as if nothing had changed."

How else she was to dress, Mary did not know. She had walking dresses and riding habits, dinner gowns and morning gowns. But nothing in her wardrobe was marked, "Wear me in the event of disaster." Her hand clenched inside its glove.

Frost tossed the book he held to one side and picked up another. But Mr. Lawson was still looking at her. Staring, really, in a manner that was anything but polite.

Ignore it, and your better manners will soon embarrass him into behaving properly. That was what the etiquette instructor at her finishing school would have advised her.

Ha. The instructor hadn't known Mr. Lawson. He set down his papers and stepped toward her.

Her heart pounded faster. His lips were compressed in anger, but his eyes... She didn't like that unblinking reptilian look in his eyes, nor the slither in his step.

"Where is your father, Mary?"

"Miss Chartley," she corrected gently. "I think we'll all be happier if you call me Miss Chartley, and—"

He grabbed her wrist. "You really don't understand. You stupid creature. 'Miss Chartley' is what I'd call a lady, and in case you haven't discovered it, you no longer fit the description. The sooner you recognize that, the better it will go for you."

Mary yanked her wrist away. She hadn't had time for soul-searching. She certainly hadn't had time to quietly contemplate her new position in the complicated taxonomy of womanhood. All her thoughts since three that morning had been consumed by one thing: getting her trunk and its contents miles away from these men, before they discovered the truth.

"No railway receipt, no record of a hired cab," Frost was saying, shaking his head. "It's as if Chartley simply vanished. And when I find him—"

No question about it. Mary had to get her trunk away from here, and quickly.

But Lawson took hold of her wrist once more, wrenching her arm around her back as if she were a scullery maid caught stealing the silver. "Where is your bleeding father?"

That twisting motion really hurt, sending stars floating across her vision. Aside from the rap of a ruler across her knuckles, nobody had ever touched her in violence.

But it wasn't the pinched face of her etiquette instructor that came to mind. It was the round, frowning visage of her piano master.

Weep later, he would have said in a heavy German accent. *Play now.*

She jutted out her chin. "I don't know." True in at least one respect. She wanted to believe that Papa, who she'd loved so dearly, was in heaven. But if there was any truth to what the curate said, he was likely in hell.

"And what message did he leave you?" His grip tightened on her wrist.

"Nothing." Lying came easier, the more she did it. Her father might have been a cheat and a thief, but he'd loved her and she'd loved him. She would save him this final indignity.

"You're getting tiresome, Mary." Lawson yanked her wrist. She took two stumbling steps toward him before she found her balance. "I don't think you understand what it means that he's abandoned you. If he's gone for good, you're nothing."

Her skin crawled, but she suppressed all hint of a shiver. "I still don't know—"

He wrenched her elbow. "You really don't understand. Why, as your father's closest associate, I'm practically your guardian. And do you know what I do with wayward girls who won't speak to me?"

There was nothing he could do to her anymore. She'd been the one to discover her father's note. She'd found his body. The physical pain was nothing to that. But every second she remained here, being manhandled by them, was another moment where someone might find the trunk she'd lowered out her window.

Her father was an embezzler and a suicide. *Nobody* would help her—nobody except herself. She shut her mouth and tried once again to free her arm.

Lawson pulled his arm back, made a fist—

"Lawson," a new voice said, "what do you think you're doing?"

Lawson straightened, moving away from Mary so quickly that she gasped in relief.

"Aw," Lawson said, "I didn't mean any harm. I was just going to—"

"I have a good idea what you were going to do." With those words, John Mason stepped into her father's office. Mary shut her eyes. She hadn't cried, not even when she'd realized that her father had left her alone with nothing. Not when she'd realized that the future she'd dreamed of was gone forever. It had been easy to bury her fear, her despair, her mourning. Those emotions were too big to believe; her loss too large to comprehend.

Why, then, did the sight of John Mason make her want to weep?

She opened her eyes wide, willing that stupid moisture to evaporate into nothingness.

Across the room, John met her gaze briefly, and then looked away.

He didn't belong with these men; he never had. The other men were both grandfathers; John was scarcely twenty-five. They were dressed in sober, respectable browns and grays, every white starched to points; John's cravat was a bare pretense of a neckcloth, well-laundered but soft. Most of all, the other men were thin and pale from hunching over desks, while John's hours out-of-doors had left him golden-skinned and broad-shouldered.

He hadn't been part of their initial investment scheme. His father and his brother-in-law had been involved. But he'd taken over when his relatives had passed away.

That was how she had met him.

She had always believed his eyes were sweet—large and liquid brown. There had been nothing sweet about them last night, when he'd confronted her father, proof in hand, finger pointing directly at his chest. There was nothing sweet about them now, either. Mary's stomach churned, and she looked away.

"Don't be difficult, boy," Lawson said. "It's your money at stake, too. She knows something. I swear it's so."

"I don't truck with hitting ladies," John responded.

"She's no lady."

John's eyes flicked to Mary, touching her without really seeing her. But he didn't contradict the older man. He simply shrugged. "I don't truck with hitting women, either," he said in a low growl, then spat on the ground.

Don't spit on Papa's carpet, some stupid part of her wanted to say. As if the Turkey carpet mattered. Just one more possession to be sold to make up for his wrongdoings. One more thing for her to leave behind. Still, that disrespect hurt more than John's casual acceptance of her new status.

"Come now," Lawson said. "Given what her father owes us, she's practically a servant. It's not wrong to slap—"

John shoved the other man into the wall of the office. "I mean it, Lawson. That's enough."

She forced herself to concentrate on the hard lines of John's face, so different from the confident smile that he usually gave her when their paths crossed. He made her think of a rocky cliff: impossibly hard, with an unforgiving drop to the crags below.

"Very well," Lawson finally muttered in a sullen sneer. "But one day, you'll regret letting her go. Useless bitch." That last was directed at her.

Mary wouldn't give him the satisfaction of seeing her affected by that epithet. She simply nodded to the two men, as if this were the last round of an exchange of pleasantries, and turned to go.

John set his hand in the curve of her spine and guided her away, down the dark hallway, to the back of the house. He wrenched the servants' door open, and then glanced outside, verifying that nobody was about. Then, and only then, did he turn to her.

"Mary..." He ran one hand through the dark brown of his hair. She'd never heard his voice like this—dark and rumbling like thunder on the horizon. She'd never seen his eyes like this, either. There was a tension in them, worry-lines gathering at the corners. He wasn't quiet because he intended to be gentle with her. It was the quiet of a pot on the verge of boiling over.

"John." She shut her eyes.

"Swear to me that you don't know where he is."

Like everyone else, he was thinking only of her father. But unlike the others, at least he believed her. For now. Mary's thoughts went to her trunk, to the ache in her arms.

"If I had to guess," she told him gravely, "I would say that he went straight to hell. He left me—" All that angry fury raged within her for a moment, startling in its heat. No place to put it now; she had too much to do.

"Did he tell you where the money was?"

"Not a word."

"What are your plans? Is that your trunk over there?" His tone was curiously flat as he spoke to her—not devoid of emotion, but withdrawn, as if he'd turned away from his own feelings.

She hadn't dared to look at the massive steamer trunk where it lay. It had followed her from Southampton to Vienna, and then back for more holidays than she could count. It was large enough to fit all the many components of a lady's wardrobe, and that made it very large indeed. The rope she'd used to lower it was still fastened to one handle; the brass fittings dented where it had banged against the ground when it had gotten away from her. She glanced over, bit her lip, and nodded.

He didn't rush over and open it. Thank God.

"Do you have anywhere to go?"

"My father's second cousin lives in Basingstoke. He'll take me in." The lies came easier now.

"And you have a plan." He nodded. "I wish…" His voice was still flat, but his lips pressed together.

She turned away. "Don't wish. You'll only say something that we'll both regret. After last night, anything more is impossible."

And yet the possibility of that *more* kept intruding on her. Was it so little, then, that they'd had between them? She had liked the look of him, the way that he laughed. He'd liked the look of her. That was all. A few months' acquaintance.

A few kisses, a few conversations—not much, but enough to spark a lifetime of hope. Enough that she'd chosen the possibility of him and family over…

No. She couldn't let herself think that way any longer. Those memories belonged to another woman entirely—Miss Mary Chartley, the daughter of a respected member of the community. She wasn't sure who she was in this skin any longer, but she'd ceased to be that person. No matter what she and John might once have been to one another, it wasn't enough to survive the cataclysm of discovering that her father had taken thousands of pounds from their partnership.

She took off one glove, removed the ring from her finger, and held it out to him.

His flat façade finally cracked. His hand slapped against his trousers, and he turned his head from her. "God damn it."

"Set it against my father's debt."

His jaw worked. It took him a few breaths to regain his composure, but when he turned back, he didn't take the ring from her. "You'll need help getting to the station." Before she knew what was happening, he was reaching for the handle of her trunk.

She couldn't let him touch that. If he tried to lift it, he might wonder what made her luggage so heavy.

"Really, John," she said sharply, stepping in front of him. "I should think you've done enough."

"It doesn't have to be this way."

"Doesn't it? Say you love me, that you would marry me without any fortune, with my father in disgrace. Say your sister would welcome me into the family, knowing that my father stole her son's future."

He met her eyes. She wasn't sure what she saw reflected there. Regret? Anger? "You're right," he finally said. "I can't say anything of the sort. But—"

"I don't love you, either. If I did…" She slipped the ring into his hand. "If I did, surely I could not give you this with my head held high."

If he'd put her in mind of thunder before, that flashing look in his eyes was the lightning, spearing her through in one instant. For one second, she thought he was actually going to grab hold of her. But he didn't move. He didn't even frown. He simply took a deep breath and shoved the ring into his pocket.

"Well, then." Another breath, and he looked away. "Good riddance." His voice dropped low on that last.

It was a good thing her heart had turned to stone, or it might be breaking now. She *hadn't* loved him. She couldn't have. If she'd loved him, she would be weeping now, and she refused to weep. But they would have had a home all of their own. Children. Happiness. Warmth. She would have had John himself, so sweet, so strong, and yet so utterly implacable when betrayed…

She nodded.

He leaned down to her. He didn't put his hands on her and draw her close, as he might once have done. Still, she felt the echo of those prior intimacies on her skin. On her lips, tingling with his nearness.

He was going to kiss her one last time. She'd yearned for his kisses before, but she didn't want one now. She wanted her memories of him to remain unsullied by the last twenty-four hours.

But close as he came, his lips didn't touch hers.

"Mary," he said softly. "My nephew's future depends on the income from this partnership. If I find out that you have lied to me, that you know where your father is and where he hid what he stole…" He raised his eyes to hers. "I will escort you to the gates of hell myself."

Chapter Two

Eighteen months later, Somerset, on the edge of the hills of Exmoor

THE AUGUST SUN BEAT DOWN LIKE THE BREATH OF HELL itself. Fitting, John Mason decided, for the task that lay ahead.

Not, of course, the work that he was supervising now—that was dead easy, watching the digging in four fields so that he might lay drains that had long since ceased to function. No, it was his other, private task that had left him feeling like one of the damned.

Another man would have been happy to see Beauregard approach on horseback. He would have welcomed the respite from the mid-morning sun and the labor.

His host—John supposed that was the proper appellation for the man—had a mare saddled, following behind him.

"Mason," Beauregard said, raising a hand in greeting. "I can't believe you've started work already, and on the first morning, too."

John glanced at the sun—already a good measure above the horizon—and shook his head. "No point in dawdling. I've been in your fields these last five hours. By the time the clock strikes ten, I scarcely consider it morning any longer."

"That's why I have an estate manager." Beauregard grinned. "And friends." He smacked John on the shoulder.

Friends was stretching the truth. Acquaintances, perhaps—and unlikely ones at that. John had dashed off a piece about his experiences with drainage techniques for a farmer's gazette. Beauregard had read it and written to him, asking for help and clarification. Two months of correspondence later, and John had been ready to write the man off as hopeless. That was when a chance mention in a letter had caught his attention.

"I did promise to introduce you to the neighbors," Beauregard said. "I don't expect you to work all day. You're my guest, not a laborer."

John didn't bother correcting the man. Yes, John owned land in Southampton. But he had no illusions about what that meant. There was a lot less *gentleman* in him than there was *farmer*. He wore a thousand hats—veterinarian to his cattle, chemist when it came to soil treatment, mechanic to the plows. Right now, he was posing as Beauregard's personal drainage engineer. He'd inherited a rather soggy piece of land himself, and had developed something of a talent for walking a piece of ground and understanding the underground streams, the seep of water just below the surface, the strange accidents of soil and slope that explained why one field was a swamp and the other a lush meadow.

But all of that was nothing to the role that he'd taken up now—that of investigator on behalf of his seven-year-old nephew, and, if his suspicions proved correct, judge, jury, and executioner, all in one.

"Where are we off to?"

"Doyle's Grange first. That is what you requested, yes? It's not even a mile away. You'll like Sir Walter. He's a capital fellow."

"I'm sure he is," John said. He gave further directions to the men who were working under him, straightened his coat, and then mounted his horse. But as the mare beneath him ambled down the lane to Doyle's Grange, it wasn't Sir Walter—whoever that was—who occupied his thoughts.

He'd looked for Mary Chartley for months after she left, but his efforts had ended in Basingstoke. She'd arrived there via rail; after that, he had only conjecture. She must have met her father, because two days after she'd fled her home, a doctor had issued a death certificate for Mr. Chartley. The parish church records showed that he'd been buried the day after.

Very convenient, that certificate of death. Almost as convenient as the book that Mary had put in the post to Mr. Lawson that same day—her father's secret account book, the one they'd torn the house apart trying to find. The one she'd sworn she knew nothing about. It hadn't shown the details of Mr. Chartley's thefts, but it had contained all the information about the account he'd maintained with a separate London bank. The book itself had noted a few withdrawals, but the balance should still have been intact, at least as of a few months before his embezzlement was discovered.

But the record of those last months had gone missing. Someone—Mary herself, or perhaps her father—had sliced the last four pages from the accounting. When Lawson had his solicitors make a written demand on the bank, the account had yielded a few paltry hundreds of pounds. Not enough to give John's nephew the start he deserved in life. But the accounting had told him one thing: The money was out there. He'd lost it once, when he'd let Mary go. This time, he was going to find it.

John had been looking for Mary Chartley ever since. But he'd found no sign of her—nor of those four missing pages, nor even the eight thousand pounds that should have been waiting in the bank. He'd had no leads at all until Beauregard had mentioned her in passing in one of his letters.

Even Miss Mary Chartley, Lady Patsworth's companion, noticed that the south field has become a swamp this spring.

It could have been some other Mary Chartley. The name wasn't uncommon. But the letter had come two days after the investigator he'd hired had officially declared the search hopeless. It had seemed providential. And so instead of washing his hands of Beauregard and his swampy fields, John had written back.

If it's not too forward, might I suggest that I come and see to their drainage myself? It will be much easier than trying to explain the principles via correspondence.

"There it is," Beauregard said, as they rounded a bend in the road and the trees of the wood gave way to open meadow. "Doyle's Grange."

It was, he was sure, a charming cottage. But John didn't care about the ornamental hedges out front. The gate—if you could call it that—was a mess of grape leaves and such, decoration so overblown that it rendered the fence useless as a barrier. It had no doubt been commissioned by a lazy fellow who preferred tipple to work. Someone had taken care with the flowers; they sprung up in a glorious summer profusion of pinks and reds.

But this was undoubtedly a rich man's country hideaway. There was no kitchen garden to speak of. Still, it was not the plantings that he cared about; it was the scene on the back terrace. The terrace itself was a golden limestone, ringed by a guard rail in the same pattern as the gate. A table was set up in the shade cast by a rowan tree. It was forty yards away—he could make out a white cloth hanging listlessly over the edges of the table and a folding screen set up as a shield against the hot morning sun as best as possible.

Sitting at table were a large man with a graying handlebar mustache and a small, dark-haired woman. No doubt Sir Walter and his wife. Down from them, and farther away, sat a younger woman. Her hair was a burnished gold. She sat, her head held in book-balancing precision. He couldn't make out her features. He didn't need to. God, he even remembered the curve of her spine. A little spark traveled through him.

He'd found her.

The only question, now, was what to do with her. It was a bittersweet triumph. On the one hand, he'd tracked down an unrepentant thief. But seeing the woman he'd planned to spend the rest of his days with struck a peculiar ache in his gut. Matters might have been so different between them. He couldn't think of her without feeling the quiet *what-if* that lay between them still.

Lady Patsworth turned to the younger woman; a few seconds later, Mary stood. Without turning to look at the horsemen coming up the lane, she slipped into the house.

John tamped down his frustration. She'd not get far, not on foot, and it was unlikely that she was expecting him. Still, he felt a bit dazed at the reality. She was here—close enough for him to run her down and ask all the questions that had gnawed at him over these long months.

Why did you lie to me? If you intended to steal the money outright, why did you send back the account book? Is your father dead, or is that another lie?

Was it all just lies between us, or did you ever feel anything?

No, not that last question. No point in even thinking about that.

They arrived at the house and handed their horses off to a groom. A silent, surly maid led them around the side to the back terrace. Mary was still not present. Beauregard made the introductions; John managed to get through them, as silently as possible. Soon, the other two men were discussing the technicalities of drainage—badly and wrongly.

"And so the upper fields drain now," Beauregard was saying, "but as Mason here explains it, the water flows from them into the lower field, leaving me with a fine quantity of mud in the spring. We must reroute—"

The door to the house opened, and Mary stepped out, burdened with a paper fan and a parasol. She stopped dead in her tracks at the sight of John.

He couldn't move, either. It was electrifying to see her this close. It had been that way ever since he first laid eyes on her. She had all the features of classic English beauty—a creamy complexion, rose-pink lips perfectly formed in an expression of surprise, and clear blue eyes. But calling her beauty *classic* didn't capture the essence of her.

She was like a cream-cake with an added hint of lemon. Familiar and comforting in aroma…and yet when one got close enough, one realized that all that sweetness was balanced by something deliciously tart. She had even used to smell of sugared lemon—a clean, fresh scent that made him think of unsullied purity.

It had also made him want to lick her. Everywhere.

She'd seemed so innocent on the surface, but when he peered into her eyes, he'd seen a spark there, a hint of mischief that drew him in. She'd looked on the verge of laughter, and her merriment had spilled out of her all too easily. She'd had an air to her—one that had made him think that she didn't know anything about passion…but that she wanted to learn.

Mary was disarmingly attractive, and he'd wanted her. Badly.

If only he'd known that there was more mischief and less innocence in her. Still, even now, even knowing that everything about her was a sham—that she was a thief and a liar—it made no difference. He still wanted her.

"Dear Lady Patsworth," Mary said into the awkward silence. "I've brought your fan."

"Thank you." Lady Patsworth did not move to take Mary's burdens.

"Miss Chartley. You know Mr. Beauregard from church," Sir Walter said. "This is his friend, Mr. John Mason. But…it looks as if you might already be acquainted."

Mary's face was schooled to careful blankness. She glanced warily at John, and dropped a polite curtsey in his general direction.

"No," John heard himself say. "I've never known her. Not at all."

She didn't grimace at that disavowal. Her expression remained china-doll smooth.

"Mary, dear, if you could move the Japanese partition…" That from Lady Patsworth.

Mary set the fan and parasol on the table and brushed past John. He caught a hint of something like sweet citrus as she passed, and those same old urges welled up in him—to lick her, despite everything. Then she crossed to the other side of the terrace and fiddled with a folding screen constructed from cherrywood and delicate paper. The so-called Japanese screen, John supposed; the paintings on its side were no doubt intended to recall the Far East to men and women who had never traveled farther than Birmingham.

She adjusted the screen to allow a few more inches of shade to fall on Lady Patsworth's side of the table.

Mary's scent hadn't changed, but her eyes had. Once, they'd sparkled. Now, they looked flat. All that hidden mirth that he'd seen in her—it was as if it had been wiped clean and replaced with stark gray slate.

Well. He'd not expected her to *smile* when she was caught. As methodically as she'd gone, she returned, seating herself at the table next to Lady Patsworth.

She'd not said a word in greeting to him.

"What does the fashion column have to say?" she asked, her low tones directed to the lady near her.

Lady Patsworth lifted a monocle and peered at the paper. "It describes a day gown with well-fitted sleeves of sarcenet, embellished at the wrists with cord of silk." Lady Patsworth frowned. "Cord of silk. I have never been fond of cord of silk, and at the wrists?"

"Indeed," Mary said. "It is too shiny."

Too *shiny?*

John glanced over at Mr. Beauregard, but apparently he found nothing strange in this exchange. He'd gone back to talking fields and drainage with Sir Walter, as soon as the introductions had been made.

John made appropriate noises at what he hoped were appropriate times. But apparently, he'd done a poor job of hiding his true interest, because when Beauregard left to ready their horses for their next visit, Sir Walter caught his eye.

"Mr. Mason," he said stiffly. The other man looked him up and down, from head to toe. "By the looks of you, you spend much of your time out of doors."

John gave him a curt nod.

"I hear you're staying at Oak Cottage." Sir Walter's mouth compressed into a thin, squashed line. "That's not even half a mile distant."

Beauregard had offered the tiny outbuilding as a potential shelter rather half-heartedly; John had accepted it with gratitude.

"Mm," John said.

"Beauregard implied you were a gentleman." Sir Walter looked dubious. "You'll excuse me, then, for speaking so directly. You'll understand that a gentleman must protect his own." He paused again and licked his lips. "The ladies of this household are entirely under my protection."

John swallowed. This conversation must have been audible to the women, but neither one so much as glanced in their direction. It was disorienting—as if perhaps this wasn't really happening.

Perhaps he had been looking at Mary over much. She was still beautiful, no matter what he thought of her character.

"I won't hold with any insult to them," Sir Walter continued. "That's why God made milkmaids."

Neither Mary nor Lady Patsworth blinked at this assertion. It was as if their ears were incapable of hearing the men's speech. And perhaps it was just as well, because Sir Walter had not only implied that John was one step from pillaging and raping his way through the household, he'd suggested that he pillage and rape his way through the dairy instead.

No doubt men said odd things at uncomfortable times, without intending all the implications.

"Never you worry," John said gruffly. "I have no interest in ladies."

That got Mary's attention for the first time since she'd returned. Her head jerked up and her eyes met his in shock.

"No interest in—!" Sir Walter repeated. "I—I'll not have such things spoken of in this household."

"Women, yes. *Ladies,* on the other hand…" John spread his hands and examined his fingernails. "They're like mistletoe—pretty enough, if you like pale berries and useless greenery. But just let it take hold, and it will choke the entire tree."

Mary looked away again.

But Sir Walter did not quibble with John's description. He didn't even protest it. Instead, he merely chuckled. "You have an extremely dim view of our ladies. I do allow the expense can be considerable. But I find them quite worthwhile, assuming you can afford to protect them."

"Perhaps," John shrugged. "Or perhaps not. I have no tolerance for parasites."

Sir Walter clasped John's hand. "Then I'll keep my ladies, and you can stay with your milkmaids."

"You do that," John said. He extricated his hand, and hoped that Sir Walter had not noticed his failure to accept the milkmaids.

Aside from that one glance, Mary hadn't so much as looked at him. Her attention was directed far off, her gaze fixed on the purple silhouette of a hill on the horizon.

"A word of warning," John said. "As a farmer, I pull out mistletoe the instant it takes root. And I won't rest until I've cleared it away."

She didn't react to that. But she didn't need to. Mary had always been quick. She had no doubt known she was doomed from the moment she saw him.

Chapter Three

MARY HAD KNOWN SHE WAS DOOMED from the moment she saw him.

Somewhere, someone was laughing at the horrid trick of destiny that had brought John Mason, of all people, to Doyle's Grange. She could almost hear the laughter echoing through the back garden. Sir Walter stood on the terrace, watching John to be sure that he left. Mary stayed, frozen to her chair by a deep despair.

I have no tolerance for parasites.

It was not even as if she could contradict him. She had no defense—certainly not against his hatred, and probably not against any accusation he might level. Lying, thieving, fleeing the scene of a crime... He could have made quite a list of her crimes, and he didn't even know the half of them. The only ray of hope that she had—and it wasn't much—was that he hadn't come with a constable in tow and a warrant for her arrest.

Yet.

Sir Walter frowned and turned back to her. His gaze flicked from Mary to his wife, his eyes narrowed in suspicion.

"You are to have nothing to do with him," he said to Mary after a moment. "You are to see that Lady Patsworth does not, as well."

Normally, she resented his edicts. This one, she welcomed with open arms. "He seems a great brute of a man."

"I dislike his staying at Oak Cottage. So close." He glanced at his wife who sat, arms folded, head bowed over the paper, as if she could not hear the conversation. "Who knows what might happen?"

He spoke as if his wife might accidentally run into Mr. Mason, might just as accidentally have an affair with him—and all that, as easily as she might accidentally stumble and take a fall. If there had ever been any trust in Sir Walter, there was no evidence of it now.

"From what Beauregard says, he'll be here for weeks. If I hear that either of you have spoken with him, have even looked at him in passing..."

"I won't," Mary promised. But deep inside, she wanted to shriek.

He was going to be here for weeks? She was going to have to leave. The only question was how she was to manage such a thing. She had few enough possessions, and Lady Patsworth could do very well without her. The bigger problem was more mundane: She had no money. Without enough to pay for transport and lodging until she could find more work, she'd end up even worse off than she was.

Don't exaggerate, she scolded herself. *You have funds aplenty. You just have to get at them.*

Sir Walter looked murderous. "You stay away from him," he repeated. "In fact, your afternoon walks…"

"I'll walk toward Northword Hill," Mary said swiftly, before he could take that privilege away, too. "Between the two hedges—he'll have no reason to encounter me there."

He considered this. "Very well," he finally said. "For now. But we must think of your safety."

She was beginning to hate that word. That was all she and Lady Patsworth ever heard—of his concern for their safety, their wellbeing, their dignity. It was on those grounds that he barred her from speaking to the other women in the neighborhood when church services were over. He spoke of his wife's delicate health when he refused to allow her brother to visit. To hear him speak, it was always about his solicitude for the two of them—and never about his own twisted jealousies.

"One thing, Sir Walter." Her heart kicked up a beat. "You recall that you'd agreed to hold last year's wages for safekeeping." She swallowed and looked down. "Would it be possible to request that I receive a portion of those funds?"

Sir Walter's frown deepened. "Whatever for?"

"It's so hot these days. I should like to make a summer gown."

He contemplated this. "Peter will be happy to take any orders you have to the store. I'll deduct the necessary funds from your account."

A bolt of linen, obtained by their groom, wouldn't do her any good. "Nonetheless," Mary persisted. "I should like to purchase it myself."

Going into the shops was not allowed. Having money was not allowed.

He sighed and shook his head. "Miss Chartley. When I said I would hold your wages for safekeeping, I took that charge quite seriously. You are in my employ, and you are therefore my responsibility. If I gave you your wages outright, you might squander it on all sorts of fripperies. Trust me, my dear, and allow me to refuse this request. You'll thank me later, when the principal is still intact years from now."

She needed to run. She was *desperate* to run. How could she do so, without a penny to her name? "But—"

"I think we've had enough of this discussion in front of Lady Patsworth," Sir Walter said, reaching over and giving her a pat on her hand. "She is not well and certainly doesn't need to be bombarded with conversation about such vulgar matters. We'll continue this later, if you please." He set his serviette on the table next to his fork and walked inside the house.

Etiquette. Safety. Responsibility. They sounded like such admirable virtues, until Sir Walter got his hands on them.

He didn't look like a monster. He didn't act like one. Mary hadn't even realized he *was* one for months. He'd taken away her money, her freedom, her friends, and it wasn't until she was well and truly leashed, without a penny in her possession, that she'd realized what he'd done. He mouthed all the right words of concern. But the instant Mary's wants diverged from his, he gently, politely quashed all her hopes.

The question of her salary was one of those things. He simply refused to pay her. He would advance funds on her account for gloves or other necessary purchases. He even occasionally gave her a few shillings when they traveled, so she could handle the necessary vails. But he expected her to account for every half-penny, and he always—gently, politely—took them back.

What he was doing was illegal. But what could she do about it when she didn't even have the money to take a cart to the nearest solicitor, fifteen miles away? How could she prosecute him, when she herself might be brought up on charges?

When she'd left Southampton eighteen months ago, she'd known her life had changed. Sir Walter had taught her what that meant. She'd lost all control over her future. She was dependent on the goodwill of the men around her. And if she was to have any say at all over what happened to her...

She couldn't stay, not with John in the vicinity. Yet she couldn't run. Without any money at all, she'd only end up worse off than she was now. She might confide her troubles in Sir Walter, but giving the man an extra weapon to use against her didn't sit well. She wanted to scream. She was helpless, pinned to this house by the slowly shortening leash of her penury.

But then, so was Lady Patsworth. The woman had pointedly ignored Mary's exchange with her husband. She sat, her spine ramrod straight, on the terrace, and studiously read the London paper.

"Lady Patsworth," Mary tried.

"Cord of silk," the woman responded. "Do you think that cord of silk might do, after all?"

"Lady Patsworth, please. Do you think you could ask your husband to pay me my wages?"

Lady Patsworth did not look up from the paper. She did not acknowledge those words, not with so much as a blink of her eye. "Perhaps," she mused, "not in white. A black, or perhaps a gold—that would give it a military look. Very sharp, I think."

Lady Patsworth was not simple, no matter how she acted. She'd simply learned that it was best if she didn't attend to the unpleasant parts of life. As so much of her life was unpleasant, she scarcely attended to anything.

"Or, perhaps, you might be willing to advance me my wages from your own funds."

Lady Patsworth set down her paper. She didn't look at Mary, but she angled her spoon so that the bowl caught the sun, twisting it so it sent bright flashes into the leaves of the trees. "He reads my letters before they are sent," she said quietly. "He hires my servants. He does not let me leave this property. Do you really imagine that he allows me any pin-money? If he did, I would have found some way to get a message to my brother."

Mary swallowed.

"Lady Northword used to make her home here," Lady Patsworth continued. "I once found what I believe to be a piece of her jewelry, hidden between the floorboards. He won't even let me call on her to return it. And when she came by to pay a call, he told her I was indisposed. The most I can hope for is what you just saw—that I might be allowed to sit silent and unresponsive when a neighbor comes to call."

"Surely there is something that can be done."

"No," Lady Patsworth said. "There isn't."

There was no yelling in Sir Walter's household. There was no dramatic posturing, no screaming, no fighting. There was only Sir Walter's indomitable hold.

The worst part was, Mary couldn't even figure out how to voice a complaint. It would not sound so awful, if she told someone about it. He never hit his wife; he'd never touched Mary, and she'd seen enough of the world to be thankful for that. But it would almost have been better if he had struck out. At least then she would have had tangible proof of his character.

She had to leave. She couldn't go. These two facts butted heads with one another, but neither came out the victor.

"Is there not something you can do?" Mary asked in desperation.

But Lady Patsworth had already picked up the paper, folding it back to the fashion page. And that was answer enough.

Mary could do only what Lady Patsworth did: She could endure, and pretend that none of this was happening.

MARY'S AFTERNOON WALK WAS NOT, IT SEEMED, to be a dash for freedom today—just an amble around the boundaries of her cage. Her absence was strictly timed, and the stable grooms were always positioned—Sir Walter said—to prevent her from accidentally intruding on the neighbors' properties and incurring their wrath. Besides, he didn't trust the laborers at Beauregard's farm to treat her with the respect that a well-bred lady deserved. For her own good, she had to be confined.

The end result was the same. She had only a few fields to explore, a small slice of land squeezed between the neighbors' hedges. Her terrain stretched down the hill north of Doyle's Grange, terminating at the creek in back. Forty-five minutes of leisure multiplied by the months that they'd been in residence meant that she knew every inch of that space. She would have no escape today, just a temporary change of prison. Still, she tore out of the house and down the hill, wanting only to get away.

Late summer was the worst season to wander. The path between the hedges had grown over. By now, the thistles were tall enough to scratch her calves under her skirts. As for the nettles… Her arms were bare, and the nettles had grown waist-high. All that rain last May had gone straight into producing tall prickly stalks and stingers, all determined to thwart her temporary flight for freedom—or at least solitude. Her pace slowed to a walk, and then to a few steps at a time.

There was a trick to stinging nettles. If one walked right through them, one would end up red and itching all over. But only the bottoms of the leaves stung. If one were careful, one could take hold of the plant by pushing down on the tops of the leaves, and then very carefully moving it to the side...

"So," a voice said behind her. "I've found you."

The man spoke just as she held the offending plant at maximum distance from herself. Mary let go in surprise; it sprang back into place, slapping its stingers against her bare arm. It felt as if she had been attacked by a half-dozen ants all at once.

She bit her lip and muffled an oath, slapping her gloved hand over her smarting flesh.

"John," she gasped, and then, when she took in his folded arms and disapproving stance, remembered that her actions the last eighteen months had erased any claim she had to intimacy. "Mr. Mason," she corrected herself. "What ever are you doing here?"

He was wearing a long coat and thick, dirt-stained gloves. "I'm walking parallel to the creek," he said. "Seeing how the water drains off the hill." He gave her a pointed glance from head to toe; his gaze lingered impolitely on the exposed expanse of her lower arms. It felt just as rude when he turned his head sharply the other way. "Unlike *some*," he said, with a disdainful emphasis on that latter word, "I've dressed for the terrain."

If she took her coat on a warm summer day, Sir Walter would wonder if she planned a longer journey, and he'd insist on relieving her of her burden. For her health, of course. Always for her health.

She looked up at the clear, blue sky pointedly and then looked back at him. "Really. You're seeing how water drains, when there's not a cloud in sight."

"There's your mistake." His eyes were dark and accusing. "You think I need to see rain to know the lay of the land? I don't. I can see the shape of the hills. I can test the soil. As for the water itself... That patch of snake's head likes the damp, so I can surmise that water collects there, then follows the trail laid by the pink of ragged robin down that slope, where it empties in the soft soil where the meadowsweet grows." He looked at her, and she was quite sure in that moment that he wasn't just talking about wildflowers. "I don't need to stand in a rainstorm to know where to lay the blame. The system is all of one piece."

"I see." She swallowed and looked away.

"So I'll skip the part where I lay out the evidence of your guilt. Where is the money, Mary? Guide me to that, and I'll bother you no more."

She shook her head. "Everything I knew, I've sent on already to Mr. Lawson."

"I have little trust in your words. You swore to me once that you knew nothing—and yet, you had an account book in your possession when you left."

This was the stuff of her nightmares. The accusations. His face, stormcloud angry. He took a step closer to her, looming large, until he seemed to dominate her vision. The slope of the hill above, and the hedgerow to the side, shielded them from all watching eyes. He could do anything—hit her, touch her, kiss her—and she had no way to stop him. Her head spun dizzily and little sparks floated in front of her eyes.

"Please, Mr. Mason."

"You should beg," he said. "Why should I not fetch the magistrate right now?"

She caught her breath. Mention of the magistrate actually calmed her. If his idea of a threat was to wait for a trial, he presented a fluffy daydream in comparison with the visions that woke her sometimes at night. In the grand scheme of things, gaol seemed only slightly worse than the workhouse, and better than a life of prostitution.

"Perhaps I deserve to be in gaol," she said quietly. "But it changes nothing. I can't help you with the money. As for my father, he's dead. I saw him put in the ground myself, and there can be no mistake."

He blinked twice, and shook his head. "Of course you'd say as much," he finally said. "But you have much to gain from the assertion."

"Much to gain!" she cried. She looked around at the only place she could find solitude—a barren, deserted slice of land, inhabited solely by weeds and nettles. Without thinking, she stepped forward and shoved his chest. "Much to gain," she repeated. "Trust in my greed, if you don't believe in my morals. If I had a few thousand pounds to my name, do you believe I'd be here, fetching and carrying for Lady Patsworth?"

He frowned. "Perhaps you're laying low."

"I could *lay low,* so to speak, with greater comfort and more likelihood of success in a hotel in Boston. Or a villa on the Italian coast." She couldn't stop the bitterness from invading her voice. "I could lay low with more than two gowns. With my own servants, instead of lowering myself to do someone else's bidding. Do I look as if I am so much better off than the world that I fled?"

He didn't say anything.

"Ask in Up Aubrey, when you have a chance. Ask them what they think of Mary Chartley. Full of herself, they'll say—attends church and leaves immediately without talking to anyone. Too good to join the other women for a chat. I'm working for a man who doesn't let me leave the property unless I'm guarded. If I had a choice, I would be anywhere but here." She kicked furiously at the nettles.

"Maybe," he said slowly, with a great deal of skepticism. "If your father could cheat his partners, no doubt he could cheat, you too. But even if things have turned out badly for you, I deserve—no, I *demand*—a full accounting. There are thousands of pounds at stake. Do you know what happened to them?"

God. She'd been dreading this moment. She woke up at nights in a cold sweat, thinking of what she'd have to do to account for them.

"I know," she whispered. "But—I can't. John. Please don't make me."

It couldn't be compassion she saw flicker in his eyes. They were long past that. His lips narrowed. "You'll tell me everything. And if there's anything I can recover…"

She tried to look away, but he took hold of her chin, tilting her head up.

He'd touched her almost like this back in Southampton. But then, it had been a prelude to a kiss. His grip was firmer now, and there was no warmth in his eyes, no tenderness—only hard calculation.

"If there's anything I can recover," he repeated, "I will." He let her go.

"I have to get back," she said. "Sir Walter times my walks. He'll come after me in a few minutes. Please don't let him find us together."

But she was only putting off the inevitable. The truth of who she was had caught up with her, and payment was required.

Mr. Lawson had told her she was not a lady, all those months ago. It had taken her months to understand what that meant.

It meant that she saw the darker side of every gentleman. There was no need for politeness, no need to worry about formalities. She could be imprisoned and isolated at whim. Her wages might be stolen; all hope of friendship could be yanked from her. And as bad as all that sounded, Mary knew that she had been lucky thus far.

Her luck had officially run out.

John let go of her. "Go back, then," he said. "But, Mary… We're not through."

Her limbs felt heavy. She was nothing but ice, through and through.

"Yes," she whispered. "I know."

It was better this way. She would be ice, and she would survive.

Chapter Four

THE LITTLE COTTAGE WHERE JOHN WAS STAYING sat halfway up the hill; the window in the front room overlooked the farm. It had been built years ago, for a one-time widowed sister, long since passed away. Beauregard had offered it up as a potential residence during his stay. He'd not meant it seriously—the farm, he said, would have so many more comforts—but John had leaped at the chance. No need to disturb Beauregard in the morning, he'd explained, and besides, this way, he could contemplate the shape of the land from on high.

All good enough excuses, but the real reason he'd opted for the makeshift few rooms up the hill was the solitude he had in the evening.

Tonight, he was too exhausted to talk to anyone. From the morning work supervising the drainage, to the whirlwind tour of the best families within riding distance, he'd been busy for every hour of the day.

And then there had been that afternoon meeting with Mary. That had sucked the life right out of him.

With another early morning ahead of him, he'd prepared for bed. But night had come and sleep had eluded him. After an hour spent staring at the darkened ceiling—tired, but not sleepy—he'd donned loose trousers and gone for a glass of brandy. But the spirits hadn't driven away his cluttered thoughts. They'd only muddled them further.

He hated, absolutely *hated*, that even now, after he'd discovered the truth of Mary's character, she still reminded him of the woman he had intended to wed. It wasn't just her fine, almost fragile, beauty. He'd learned his lesson well enough on that score: Never trust fine appearances.

It wasn't even her scent, compelling though that was, nor the inviting curve of her lips. No; Mary had always been able to set him back on his heels, and today she'd done it again.

Trust in my greed, if you don't believe in my morals.

A few offhand inquiries had borne out her claims. She had only two everyday gowns. She rarely left Doyle's Grange, and when she did, she spoke to no one.

"So it didn't turn out as she expected," he muttered, taking a sip of brandy. "Small surprise that criminal behavior didn't pay." Maybe she'd lied for her father's sake, and he'd abandoned her. Maybe she'd had the money once, but had lost it gambling. He'd been fooled once by her. He'd let her go, so determined to prove by his gentlemanly conduct that he was fair, generous, even though she…

I don't love you.

He took another long gulp of brandy, but the burn that traveled down his throat didn't distract him. He didn't want her. It no longer hurt to remember that he'd fooled himself so badly. So why did it still sting to remember her saying that?

He let out a frustrated, exhausted sigh and took another sip—discovering, in surprise, that he'd reached the end of the tumbler. How was that possible? He'd just refilled it.

The spirits, though, only seemed to increase the weight on his soul—and on his eyelids.

He did believe her. That was the problem. He believed that if she had the partnership's eight thousand pounds, she wouldn't be here. If she was a hardened criminal, she'd have changed her name and fled the country. He'd seen the fraying cuffs of her gown—had even recognized the fabric as a made-over version of one she had used to wear, back in Southampton.

No doubt things had not been easy for her.

"She brought it on herself," he said.

He'd believed it that afternoon. He'd make himself believe it again in the morning. But now…

Right now, half-drunk and completely maudlin, some part of him hoped that she *had* lied to him about at least one thing. He hoped that she had loved him. It was vindictive and cruel of him, but he wished that she'd suffered. That while he'd been back in Southampton, discovering day by day what a fool she'd made of him, she'd missed him. That she still wanted him enough to beg for his forgiveness, all so he could have the pleasure of saying no.

But true anger took energy. He could feel it sapping from his limbs as the night encroached. Sleep was finally catching up with him, and his unquiet thoughts slowly settled into a gentler mode. He set his brandy down and let his wandering imagination take him.

The first time he'd seen her, she'd been sitting at a pianoforte, preparing to play. She hadn't looked at anyone or anything, not even the sheet music in front of her. She had simply sat, seeming so distant and far away.

Then she had begun to play, and John had been utterly lost. It wouldn't have mattered who she was or where she'd come from. He'd heard her play, and that was the end of all rational thought. And so he'd pursued her as assiduously as he'd ever done anything, holding his breath the entire time. He understood machinery and chemicals and germination; all he knew about women was that they giggled when he came near.

But Mary hadn't giggled. She'd smiled. They'd talked. Conversation had led to courtship.

And then one night, he'd handed her down from a carriage and found himself utterly unable to relinquish her fingers. His other hand had stolen about her waist, and he'd pulled her to him until her skirts surrounded his legs. He'd set his lips to her neck, not quite daring to touch her mouth.

But she'd turned her head, letting him kiss her.

They hadn't said anything. They had only breathed in tandem, *wanting*, and he'd known then that he would ask her to marry him—and that she would say yes.

He wasn't good with women, but he'd thought that moment was real. When he found out she'd lied to him…

That space between waking and sleep was slippery. It took the fury that he'd worked so hard to maintain during the day and turned it sideways. He couldn't work himself into a rage. He couldn't sustain any emotion more lasting than regret. Longing and anger twined together, and as usual, he drifted into sleep…and a dream that gave voice to desires he had not fully relinquished. He didn't want just a kiss, but an embrace. He didn't imagine the entwining of their gloved hands, but their bare bodies, skin to skin.

He could almost feel the warmth of her body next to his. But this time, there was no threat of discovery, no need to restrain himself. He didn't need to be angry with *this* version of Mary. She was nothing but a dream, nothing but phantom caresses, haunting kisses.

She was naked, as women in sensual dreams often were. She trailed her hands down his chest to touch his navel, the waistband of his loose trousers. Somehow, his dream shifted to some nondescript bed in a nameless room. In the way of dreams, she straddled him—soft and warm, a welcome weight on top of his hips. He was hard beneath her, hard and desperate.

But for all her brazen nakedness, dream-Mary's touch was hesitant. She didn't grab his member (alas) or take him inside her (double alas). She touched her fingertips to him—lightly, in threes.

It reminded him of watching her play the pianoforte that first time—as if she were finding chords on his body. If only he could listen well enough, he might make out the melody. But his dream was silent…and still too chaste.

"Ah God, Mary," he said. "Put me out of my misery already, and suck my cock."

Speaking shattered the pretense of dreaming. He'd said those words aloud—he could feel his vocal chords vibrating in a way that brought him back to reality.

The moment before he opened his eyes seemed impossibly long. It wasn't some indeterminate bed under him, but the sofa in the front room at Oak Cottage. The night air was still warm around him, disturbed by the soft sounds of wind. And there was someone atop him.

His hands rested on hips. Warm, bare skin met his fingers. Muscles tensed in those hips, and the weight shifted above him.

He fought for consciousness, breaking into wakefulness, and opened his eyes.

"Holy Mother of Christ," he swore, pushing himself up on his elbows.

Because Mary was really here. She *was* naked on top of him. And she'd only hesitated that instant, before her hands went to the drawstring of his trousers, no doubt to implement his last command.

It was her eyes that shocked the last vestiges of drowsiness from him. They were pale and flat, entirely devoid of desire.

He caught her hands at his waist, pulled away from her, and pounded his fist into the cushion of the sofa in sheer sexual frustration. "I swear on Ovid and the Bible. What the *hell* are you doing, Mary?"

You don't have to stop her.

Yes. Yes, he did.

"I'm delivering a full accounting," she said. No tone in her voice. None at all. She removed her hands from his and reached for his trousers once more. "Shall I continue?"

He brushed her hand away. "I was asleep. I didn't mean what I said." But his cock thrummed, putting the lie to his words. "And what do you mean, *a full accounting?* I don't want your...your person." More lies. He tried to concentrate on her face, but he couldn't help but take in all of her—those small, round breasts, so close to his face; the curve of her side in the moonlight. Christ alive.

She raised her chin. "But it won't balance without me. That's what I came here to tell you. Would you like to know where all that money went? It went to a select finishing school in Vienna. It paid for journeys to and fro—for a private companion, and a German tutor, and lessons on the pianoforte from a true master. My father knew I loved playing, and so spared no expense. He stole all that money for me."

God, those words sounded so bitter.

"Ah, Mary." He wasn't sure what to think, what to say.

"All that money, and now the only thing of value that I have is—"

He put his hand over her mouth, but she moved away.

Her chin rose. "I know the way of the world better than I once did. I'm not a lady any longer. Everything about me can be traded. My labor. My time." Her voice faltered, but she drew a deep breath. "My body."

And a very lovely body it was. He didn't mean to keep looking at her, but the faint starlight from the window illuminated everything to her waist. And as for the portions below, hidden in shadow—they were inches from his hands. He could explore them, find out everything that was cloaked by darkness. She'd always smelled of sugared lemon, and this time, if he tasted her, she wouldn't stop him.

Hell, she'd just volunteered for the task. It wouldn't even be *wrong*. Well, maybe only a little wrong.

"Bloody temptation." He pushed himself to his feet, and strode back to the bedchamber. "Stupid, bloody cock," he muttered, giving the offending organ a thump. It made no response. "No morals to speak of." Still rock-hard. Still desperate. Reprimands, clearly, did no good. He yanked a blanket from his bed, and marched back into the front room.

She was sitting up and watching him, her arms crossed over her breasts.

He dumped the blanket over her shoulders, covering up all that luminous, tempting skin. He could still smell her.

"Christ," he muttered, and grabbed a chair from across the room. This he placed a good two feet away from her, and then he sat.

She didn't say anything. Silence enveloped him. Her breath was shallow.

"Calm yourself. I'm not going to accept your offer." Which was a true act of heroism. "I don't hate you that much."

She didn't look at him. She wasn't even really hearing what he said, he realized. "I know it can't make up for what you lost," she was saying. "I'm simply sick, thinking of those thousands of pounds just stuck in my skin with no way to give them back. It wouldn't be enough, but can't you just…take it anyway?"

Couldn't he, though? For a moment, he indulged in a fantasy. He could make it good for her. So good, she'd lose the flat intonation in her voice. She'd smile again, a warm smile that would encompass her eyes. He'd be generous, and she'd be happy, and…

And that was lust talking again, not logic. How exactly would that happen? Because he had a cock made of magic? Unlikely.

Temptation was a bleeding monster.

He sighed and reached forward, wrapping the blanket more firmly about her shoulders. "It would be like trading oranges for moonlight." He tucked one corner about her waist like a belt. "Besides, even if the exchange had made sense, it wasn't my money at risk. It was my nephew's. He's seven years old."

She looked up at that. Their eyes met, and this time, he wasn't even sure what passed between them.

"How awkward," she finally said.

Her hand rested on the cushion next to her. Her fingers moved, making unconscious chords. This time, if he listened, he could almost hear the music—a sonata by Mendelssohn he had once heard her play.

"I can't make this right." Her voice was low.

"Maybe," he suggested, "if you tell me everything that happened…"

"I—" She choked on the remaining words. Her shoulders trembled. Her breathing grew even more ragged, and she pulled her arms around her, swaying from side to side. "It was—"

If this was an act, she had incredible control over her body. Tremors passed through her in waves, too swift to be manufactured. She let out another shaky breath, and looked over at him. "Can't you just…take me," she asked, "so that I no longer have to fear the worst?"

Whatever his body might have preferred, the word *fear* killed the remainder of his desire. "I don't take women to bed who are dreading the experience," he said bitterly.

She lied to you. She stole. She cheated. She's hiding something, and she's using her body to do it.

All quite possibly true. But he hadn't lied to her earlier when he said that he saw systems. And this one—his understanding of Mary—no longer seemed to hang together. It was a mess of discordant notes, of impossibilities and unlikelihoods. It was a tangle of lust and—as he watched her shoulders heave under the weight of his blanket—unfortunate affection, diluted by a good measure of anger.

He didn't know anything any longer.

She had never seemed so impossibly far away as she did at that moment—naked, and two feet away from him. He could have had her body, but Mary herself—whoever she was—had vanished. And for the first time, he realized that this wasn't just about the money. It was about the truth. About the words she'd said that still smarted.

I don't love you.

"Come," he said. "It's late, and we're both rather worked up. Get dressed, and I'll see you back to Doyle's Grange. We'll talk on the morrow. And, Mary…"

She looked up at him.

He held out his hand. "Stop dreading. This is me we're talking about. I should think you'd know me better than this."

Chapter Five

MORNING CAME, AND WITH IT A FULL SLATE OF DUTIES for John. Yesterday's digging had brought a new round of chores, none of them interesting. The tile drains that had been installed in the upper fields years ago were laid too shallow. They'd cracked, and were poorly positioned besides. Supervising their replacement would take weeks. He would have resented the time twenty-four hours ago; now, he suspected he would need every extra day to try to entangle the business of Mary.

As he plodded along the hill, just under the line of trees, he had to wonder how Mary fared on the other side. Had she been caught, returning to the house at the dead of night?

And more importantly...

He took a shovel from one of the men, more than happy to throw himself into physical labor. But the repetitive motion didn't distract him from his thoughts; instead, it focused them, bouncing them off one another in a repeating echo in his head.

Mary's behavior last night had left him with a welter of emotions. Anger. Sadness. Physical lust so powerful that he'd had to take care of himself not once, but twice after she'd left. He'd been so surprised—and so randy—that he'd not had time to consider what her actions meant. But now, with nothing to do but shovel dirt, he considered. And slowly, over the course of the ever-growing ditch, he grew suspicious.

He might think a great many ill things about Mary. But if she'd been the sort to try to cloud his mind by offering up her body, wouldn't she have tried it back in Southampton? He might explain her behavior by calling her an amoral, greedy slut—but if she truly *had* been one, wouldn't she have found it more profitable to throw herself at him eighteen months ago?

If she'd been able to fake that careful, innocent unfurling of passion that they'd begun to explore during their betrothal, she could easily have inveigled him into marriage. He'd been loath to let her go, and so enamored of her that a touch, a kiss, an entreaty would have bought her everything.

But she hadn't even asked. She'd fled to this—a life of demeaning service.

And then there was the matter of her eyes—the way she'd set forth her plan to provide compensation in the form of her person. Nothing about her history—born into a well-to-do family, pampered, showered with affection and cosseted at every turn—would have brought her to his bed in that way.

The girl he had once known wouldn't even have considered offering her body. Not only had she not known such desperation, it wouldn't have crossed her mind to see herself as currency. To see it so much that she'd *begged* him to take her, to free herself of debt.

No. There were no two ways about it. If the Mary he had known—the sweet, sheltered girl who had loved to play the pianoforte—had become this woman, it was because something had happened between now and the time he'd last seen her.

In these last eighteen months, someone had done a grave harm to Mary. His fists clenched around his shovel at the thought; he slammed the tool into the ground with such force that it clanged against the old tile a foot beneath the soil.

Maybe she had brought it on herself.

But he couldn't believe it. Even if she'd lied and cheated and stolen, it wouldn't justify what he'd seen last night.

She'd been willing to offer him her body in exchange for his silence. What threat could he make that would wrest the truth from her? Nothing he would consider doing to her was as bad as what she'd been willing to do to herself. No, if he wanted to have the full truth from her, he wasn't going to get it by yelling and blustering.

"God damn it," he swore.

"Your pardon, sir?" They'd dug far enough to reposition new tile, John realized. And he'd spoken aloud. The laborer who stood next to him was frowning in consternation.

"Ah, nothing." He stared up the hill, at the cottage he couldn't see. "I think, though, that I have…"

Why was he making excuses to this man? The laborer was used to working with Beauregard, who couldn't see fit to bestir himself from his house before nine in the morning.

"I have other things to see to," he said. "Up until we hit that little rise up there—just dig up the old, and lay the new flat. I'll want to look it over, before it's covered again."

A grunt was his only reply.

He didn't need more. He left to wash his hands—and to make his way up the hill to find some answers.

It was a morning precisely like yesterday morning: The sun was hot in the sky, breakfast was spread on the table, and Mary sat in the shade of the rowan.

It all felt fragile and unreal to her, as if her mouth were full of cotton. As if she were encased in a bubble of false, cozy normalcy, and the slightest pinprick would send her crashing down.

"Falls of lace," Lady Patsworth was saying, "thrice gathered over undersleeves of brocaded silk—"

Sir Walter stopped abruptly. "What in blazes is *he* doing here?"

Mary looked up. There was her pinprick—not just one, but a dozen vicious points of cold, pressing into her skin. John Mason was coming up the road; she could see him over the low hedge.

She wasn't sure whether what had happened the previous night had been ill luck or good. In the firm light of day, she wasn't even sure it had really transpired. She remembered the events of the evening as if she'd read them in a story—as if they'd occurred in some strange, distant person's life. Another woman; not her. But John was coming. It had really happened to her.

Ill luck. It had all been ill luck. She had no idea how Sir Walter would take the news that John had to deliver. The truth of what she'd done last night would get her sacked, and no magistrate would listen to her claim for back wages if they heard that sordid tale. Without realizing what she was doing at first, she closed her hand around the silver teaspoon by her plate, hiding it away in her fist, as if she might secret it in the folds of her skirts.

Don't be a fool. Of all the things you are, at least you're not a thief. Not yet.

Sir Walter stood as John came up to the garden gate, and moved to put himself between the table and the intruder.

"Mr. Mason," he said in clipped tones. "How may I be of assistance?"

He was standing in the way. She couldn't see John's face, with Sir Walter standing there. Was he angry? Or did he think that what transpired last night was a mere amusement? She could just imagine that smile she'd once adored creeping up. This time, though, the joke would be on her.

"I noted the good care you took of your ladies yesterday."

If the morning hadn't been so silent, Mary might not have made out John's reply. She concentrated, so as to catch every word.

"I don't know if the women of your household go out walking," he said, "but I'll be directing laborers on the neighboring field for the next few days. You might want to have them turn away from the west, if you would."

Sir Walter rubbed his hand against his head, a gesture that Mary recognized as confusion. She felt similarly dazed. He wasn't going to disclose what had happened?

Stop dreading. He couldn't have meant it, though. Not really.

John continued. "I've heard from Beauregard that you're protective in that regard, so I thought I'd pass along the information."

"Thank you," Sir Walter said. "It was most considerate of you to bring that message."

"We'll be tromping around in the trees near the windbreak until sunset—and possibly after." She still couldn't see him, with the gate and Sir Walter in the way. But he'd said last night that they would *talk*. Clearly this was his way of letting her know when and where. Not a reprieve, then. A temporary cease-fire.

"Sunset is quite late," Sir Walter said.

"I don't believe in wasting good daylight. The sooner I can get my people away from your boundaries, the happier I think we shall all be."

"Indeed," Sir Walter said. "And really—you *are* a good fellow. Better than I gave you credit for at first. My apologies."

"How could you know?" came the reply. "I might have been anyone. One can never be too careful these days. I must take myself off—I've still a good bit left to be done today."

John took a step away—so that Sir Walter stopped occluding him—and Mary got her first good look at him. He looked…tired. His hair was rumpled, and the ends of his cravat had come untucked. But when he met her eyes, they didn't seem implacable, as they had yesterday. They'd softened. "Ladies," he said, "I trust the morning finds you well?"

Mary froze, unsure whether a response would be allowed. Whether she should look away from him, or look at him. But even over this distance, even though she couldn't really see the expression in his eyes, she felt caught up in the net of his gaze. She looked down swiftly.

"Lady Patsworth?" Sir Walter asked. "Do speak."

"Tolerable," the lady returned. "It is dreadfully hot, but the fashion pages are a comfort to me."

John nodded, as if that response made sense. "And you, Miss Chartley?"

Mary's lungs burned. She focused her gaze on the teaspoon that she had not stolen, clenched in her fist.

"Go ahead," Sir Walter said, his eyes flat on her. "You may address him."

John didn't flicker an eyelash at that. But his very lack of reaction gave him away.

You need his permission to speak to me?

She did. It was one of the first rules she'd learned. She wasn't to communicate with anyone outside the household unless she had his explicit approval. For her safety, he said. Always for her safety. He would know who might use her badly. She'd been naked on top of John last night, but today, in the dim light of morning, with him seeing the poor, helpless thing that Sir Walter had made of her, she felt truly exposed. She couldn't win. She couldn't run. She couldn't even draw breath to ask for help.

And now John, of all people, knew.

"As you can see," Mary said to her teaspoon, "I am perfectly well. Sir Walter would never allow anything to happen to me."

Maybe, if she didn't acknowledge the obvious, it wouldn't exist.

But John tipped his hat at Lady Patsworth. "I wish you all continued health," he said. "Sir Walter. Lady Patsworth."

He didn't say her name in farewell. But he caught her eye—just for a second—and he gifted her with a glimmer of a smile.

Her heart came to a halt. For one moment, she felt like the naive, foolish girl she'd once been, giddy simply because a handsome man grinned at her. She felt the weight of all her worries lift, buoyed away temporarily by the curve of his lips.

She hadn't realized how much she'd come to dread everything about her life until she forgot to fear for one second. But then he turned away, and she was left to stare after him, blinking, uncertain of what had just transpired between them.

Chapter Six

It was ten in the evening when John finally saw Mary's slim figure separate itself from the back garden gate.

From there, she picked her way across the meadow, toward the place where he waited in the shadow of the trees. The windbreak wasn't a proper wood—just a section of steep, rocky soil that followed the slope of the hill, one that would have been almost impossible to cultivate.

Maybe that's why nobody had bothered to cut down the little coppice of oaks. It was a wild, stony stretch of land, not quite an acre in size. The trees were stunted by the soil; their lowest branches scarcely topped John's head. The ground underneath his boots was rough with assorted pebbles and carpeted with a thick blanket of granny's nightcap.

Mary looked one way, and then the other, as she approached where he stood.

"Mary," he said softly, as she came to the trees.

Her eyes swiveled in his direction; she frowned, until she made him out.

"Is this going to cause trouble for you, if Sir Walter discovers your absence?"

She paused. Too long; as if she'd heard the question he hadn't asked.

"He doesn't look in on me at night," she said. "He's too busy watching his wife."

There was something ugly there. He'd seen it the first day, even if he hadn't untangled it. Even when all looked well on the surface, something about Sir Walter simply *smelled* wrong. But she held her head high and met his gaze, as if challenging him to ask for particulars.

"Come," he said, holding out his arm. "Walk with me."

She balked.

"We mustn't be seen from the house. Or anywhere else."

"We'll walk amongst the trees," he said. "It's not a lot of space, but we could stroll back and forth."

She didn't say anything. She didn't take his arm. But when he took a tentative step, she matched his pace.

"Go ahead," she said. "Ask your questions. I suppose you deserve answers, if nothing else."

He wanted answers. He didn't think he was going to get them, though. Even if she'd wanted to explain everything, he could see the slight tremor in her shoulders. He could hear the uneasiness in her voice. Last night, he'd asked and she'd choked, unable to even get the words out.

There were, as he saw it, two possibilities. First, she'd been badly hurt—so badly, that she could scarcely bring herself to speak about it. Second, she was lying to him with such brazen deceit that he could trust nothing out of her mouth. In either case, interrogation would get him nothing useful.

"The money is gone," he said slowly. "Spent."

"Yes."

Perhaps it was not so. Perhaps she lied still. But if she did, he was willing to bet that she lied out of fear, not greed. If he wanted the truth, more threats would only heighten her fear.

He shrugged, pretending nonchalance. "Then I don't see the point of asking any further questions."

He'd get his answers by a more indirect route.

A slice of moonlight drifted through the tree limbs, touching her lips with silver. She opened her mouth to speak, then closed it. Opened it again, then shut it once more. "Then why did you insist on seeing me tonight?"

"Today, when I came by, Sir Walter said something that made me think."

"Oh?" Her tone was flat.

"It made me think," he said, "that you might be in need of a friend."

"A friend," she repeated.

"Yes, a friend. You had a good number of them once—you were always with the other young ladies, talking and laughing."

She turned away and strode deeper into the windbreak. "Friends gossip and swap stories," she tossed over her shoulder. "They don't claim friendship just to get the other person to answer questions. If it's all the same to you, I'd rather we not pretend."

He felt a stab of guilt at that, but pressed on.

"We were friends once."

"We were *betrothed*."

"We were *friends,*" he snapped. "We talked of music and books and—" And a future that some part of him still wished they had together. "—And my ambitions," he finished lamely. "Do you want me to beg? I've missed you."

He had only thought to put her at ease, but those words came too easily to be entirely false. "I missed you," he repeated, "and of all the things that most enraged me about your departure, that was the worst—all those moments when I made a note of something I had to tell you, only to remember seconds later that I couldn't any longer."

She looked up at him. "Oh, John," she said, her voice weary. "I am sorry."

Maybe she didn't mean it. Maybe she was just trying to put him off. But no matter how he tried, he wanted to believe she'd meant those three simple words. Her apology caught at his heart.

Stupid, bloody heart.

This wasn't about his feelings. It was about the truth—about convincing her to trust him with the full story. So that if her father had taken everything and abandoned her, John would know where to find his nephew's money. This was about nothing more than that—letting her feel safe enough to finally tell him everything.

"So pretend," he said, more gently than he felt, "that I'm one of your old girlfriends. What would we talk about? Novels? Horses?"

"In Vienna," Mary said, "I would have complained about my piano master. He was a harsh, impossible man. I never could please him; he was constantly heaping abuse on my head. Obviously, that's not a possibility now."

He glanced over at her. "I thought you were happy in Vienna."

"I was. It wasn't…it wasn't *that* kind of abuse, if you catch my meaning. His regular lamentations were more along the lines of, 'Why did God see fit to give you perfect phrasing, and yet not give you the will to practice regularly?' He accepted no excuses, tolerated no errors."

"He sounds difficult." He sounded like John's own father.

"Yes and no. He was furious when I—" Her gaze slid to him, and then returned to center. "When I told him I wasn't coming back," she finished.

Because she'd been caught up in her father's schemes?

The answer came a beat later. No. Because she'd agreed to marry him. He turned and looked at her. Her body was tense, her steps taken gingerly.

He'd heard her play before. He knew precisely how good she was. But he'd never asked himself what it would mean for her to marry a farmer from Southampton. She'd tasted greatness…and she'd chosen him instead.

More lies, or something else?

I don't love you.

He didn't understand anything. He swallowed and looked away. "And in Southampton? What did you talk of with your friends there?"

She snorted. "You. Much of the time."

"*Me?*" The night *was* warm, the air thick around them. He took a deep breath. "You didn't really."

"Oh, but we did. Even before I met you that first time, I'd heard all about you."

"Yes." He looked away. "I suppose. I was rather different from the other fellows. I know that. I was shy around the ladies, and I always had my head in some project or other. Also, my nose isn't straight—"

"We didn't talk about any of that," Mary said, and for the first time since he'd encountered her, a note of humor crept into her voice. "Good heavens, John. Are you blushing?"

"No. Trick of the moonlight." He scrubbed his heated cheeks. "What…uh, what else might there be to talk about?"

"How you saved Mr. Iver's mare, when she was foaling twins. Your proposal to improve the roads at the edge of the city using sawdust and india-rubber. The way you kept badgering all the other farmers to send off for a soil analysis."

"Was that too annoying?"

"The consensus was that you were quite the catch. All the young ladies agreed that in twenty years, you'd be running everything."

Impossible. They'd all giggled at him.

"Are you sure you didn't spend all your time talking about how I set the grain silo on fire?"

"Oh, yes. I heard about that all the time."

"Good. I'd hate to think that everyone represented me as some kind of—"

She actually let out a little laugh. "That's not why we talked about it. Do you happen to recall that while you were working on the firebreak, you removed your shirt?"

"Gah." He set his hand against a tree. "I'll never be able to look any of them in the eye again."

"You look well enough without a shirt." She shook her head. "How odd, that you would see yourself like that. Is that what you think? That you're a little shy with the ladies?"

"Mary, when I first met you, I walked up to you at the end of a brilliant performance and browbeat you about your selection of music."

"That's not how I remember it," she said.

"I couldn't think of anything else to say. I just thought that…"

"That what?"

"That I didn't want to let you disappear," he whispered. "Not without saying something. Anything." The night took in his words, swallowed them up. Crickets called to one another; an owl hooted softly.

"We've come a long road since then," she whispered.

We.

There hadn't been a *we* in months. He wasn't sure there could be again.

"You were right." She swallowed. "I—I do need a friend. Someone to talk to about just this—about people we once knew in common, about things that don't exist for any reason except to lighten my heart. It has been so long."

He should have felt triumphant at that.

"Please," she said, "please, don't tell me that this is friendship if all you want is to hear my answers. I can bear a great many things, but not that. Don't treat me like a real person if you don't really believe it."

He opened his mouth to tell her the truth.

And then he thought of his nephew, of the thousands of pounds that had gone missing. He thought of that moment when she'd handed back his ring and said she didn't love him. He thought of the laugh in her voice just moments before. He didn't know what the truth was. He only knew what he wished it could be.

"God's honest truth," he told her. "I missed you. The money was just an excuse to find you."

And maybe that would be the truth—that he'd loved her and hurt when she left. That he could put aside his hurt and they might take up matters where they'd left off. Maybe it could be the truth.

In all likelihood, it couldn't.

"I must get back soon." But she didn't move away from him.

"Will I see you again here tomorrow?"

"For...for friendship?"

He nodded. Not quite the truth. Not quite a lie. She'd hurt him, and he couldn't let himself forget it, no matter what she smelled like. He couldn't forget the role she'd played in her father's scheme—whatever that had been. But she smiled, and when she did, some tense, hard center deep inside his soul seemed to ease.

"Then yes," she said. "I'd like that. Good-bye, then, for now." She turned to go. But she took only a few steps before she turned around and paced back to him, stopping square in front of him. She lifted her hand to his face, touching his nose ever so lightly. Her fingers brushed his cheek, his lips, as if she were committing the feel of him to memory. He stood in place, not daring to move.

Her touch made full-truth of his half-lies. It made him want to gather her up and pull her close, to forget what she'd done and forgive what she had said. His skin sang with her nearness.

She smiled, a little sadly. "I missed you, too," she whispered.

And then she turned and fled.

MARY'S BREAKFASTS OVER THE NEXT MORNINGS became an increasingly strange affair.

The experience put her in mind of a book she'd read as a small child—her very favorite book, one that her nurse had read to her twice daily, until Mary had been able to recite it alongside her. She'd loved that book so much. But when she read it again at fifteen, she'd been utterly unable to understand the fascination that it had held. The words were still the same; it was she who had altered beyond recognition.

The breakfasts did not change, either, but Mary felt herself shifting, day by day, evening meeting by evening meeting. Sir Walter always read his paper; his wife always perused the fashion page. Tea, crumpets, and preserves were present at all times, alongside the rotating fare of kippers and liver. And yet, somehow, over the course of the week, the tableau altered.

Sir Walter seemed smaller. His wife's discussion of fashion stopped irritating her. The world became less stark, more forgiving.

When Mary was eight, she'd attempted one of her father's books of poetry—dry, dull, inexplicable stuff, she had thought. But at nineteen, the words had captivated her.

That was the difference having a friend made. It didn't change any of the underlying facts. Sir Walter was still a monster. He still held her salary; his wife still retreated into fashion. But Mary no longer dreaded waking on the mornings, and that made everything better.

Today, a few scudding clouds overhead saved her from having to move the screen. Today, she noticed that the roses in the garden, almost past the prime of their bloom, still imparted a faint fragrance to the air. Today she could bear the endless monotony of Lady Patsworth's lengthy commentary…

"An overskirt of black lace," she was saying. "And underneath, pink satin. Black and pink." She frowned. "That seems an unusual combination of color. But appealing, don't you think?"

"It sounds a lovely mix of feminine and strong," Mary agreed.

"What!?"

That shriek of outrage hadn't come from Lady Patsworth. It had come from Sir Walter, who was slamming the paper down in a fury.

Lady Patsworth froze, her eyes wide with terror.

"Not black and pink," she said hastily. "If it's so objectionable. Surely I meant—"

"Is nothing sacred any more?" Sir Walter ripped his section of newsprint in half, and then reached across the table and yanked his wife's section from her hands. He tore that in two as well.

"—I meant pink and *white*," she was saying. "Feminine and virtuous, not feminine and strong. If that will make it better. Please. Don't."

Sir Walter stared wildly at her, and then looked about him. His fists were full of paper; a maid had rushed from the house at his tirade. She drew up a few feet distant, as if unsure how to proceed.

He took a deep breath, and then made a ball of the shreds. "That's it," he announced crisply. "We are done with the paper in the mornings. I am canceling the subscription this very afternoon."

Lady Patsworth swallowed. "But—"

He glared at her. "I won't have my wife exposed to such rubbish." He motioned the maid over and handed her the pieces. "Burn this," he commanded. "Burn it immediately."

She ducked her head and disappeared. After a long moment, Sir Walter followed her into the house.

Lady Patsworth stared after him in stunned silence. "I can't," she whispered. "I can't do this, without something to take my mind…" Her hands were shaking.

Lady Patsworth was not the sort of person who encouraged her companions to share her confidences. She kept her distance.

Still… "Lady Patsworth," Mary said, "is there not something that can be done?"

The other woman shook her head slowly. "That is what it means to be married. There is no escape. Even if I could send word to my brother…what could he do? I'm *married* to Sir Walter. I'm his responsibility, his charge. Legally. And there's nothing anyone else can do about it."

"Can that not be changed? He's not…not faithful, is he?"

They'd never talked of anything so intimate. Lady Patsworth stared straight ahead, and then shook her head.

"So you have cause for divorce."

"Divorce." The other woman said the word viciously. "Who is granted divorces? A handful every decade, and then only to the most wealthy, the most powerful. I have nobody who would even introduce a bill on my behalf in Parliament." She spoke in low, vehement tones. She punctuated the last by spearing a piece of kipper with her fork. But she didn't eat it; she just stabbed it again and again.

"Lady Patsworth."

"Don't try to help," the other woman snapped. "He'll only send you away if you do."

Lady Patsworth's shoulders were rigid, her eyes focused on something far away. She took a deep breath, and then another, and then another. Mary knew all too well what it was like to be trapped, to dread every coming day. She'd been on the verge of breaking when John appeared. If he hadn't come…

"There must be something I can do," she finally said. "Something to make your life bearable."

Lady Patsworth let out another ragged breath. "Yes," she said finally. "You can help me to design my own gowns."

Chapter Seven

"DID I EVER TELL YOU ABOUT THE TIME my mare stopped sleeping?"

Mary had not expected John to start with such a question, when she met him that next night. She wasn't sure what she expected from him any longer. They'd walked. They talked of old times. Sometimes, they touched—glove to glove, glove to sleeve. It was welcoming, to be able to forget for a few minutes every day what waited for her back at Doyle's Grange.

"I thought of it," he said, "because this is the fifth night when we've foregone sleep, and I was wondering if the effect on humans would be much like it was on horses."

"I don't understand," Mary said. "Aren't horses always sleeping? Every time I walk by one, it seems to be dozing off on its feet."

"That's just napping," he said, with a wave of his free hand. "Horses sleep curled up on the ground, too. Like dogs. They don't need much sleep, but they do need some. I first noticed something was wrong because she had a scrape on her front fetlock. The next morning, another."

"Poor thing."

"And then there was her personality. She was always a placid, sweet thing. But she began to shy from shadows. I thought the stable manager was abusing her, actually. So that night, I silently climbed into the hayloft to observe."

"And?"

He guided her around a tree, keeping her in the shade of its branches. "I stayed up half the night watching for my hapless employee, nursing my wrath. And what I saw was this: around two in the morning, she started to collapse."

"With nobody there?"

"With nobody there," he confirmed. "She fell where she was standing, striking her fetlock against the stable floor. Then she scrambled to her feet. Precisely as if she had nodded off while on watch duty."

"Oh, goodness. But why did she not just sleep?"

"That took a little longer to determine. You see, I had just built a windmill to pump water from the south field. The noise it made was different, and it was frightening her. She was waiting for whatever was making those odd creaking sounds to catch up to her and devour her."

Mary gave a little laugh. "I'm sorry. That shouldn't be funny."

"I moved her to a pasture where she couldn't hear the carnivorous windmill, and she was good as new after that. So I understand the dangers of not sleeping. You risk your knees—*and* your dignity. Tell me if your knees suffer, will you?"

She laughed again.

"There," he said, "Now that's what I like to hear. You have the most beautiful laugh, Mary."

She pulled away. "Save your compliments for your horses." But she was smiling.

Deep inside, she knew that she was only setting herself up for a fall. He would leave. He would remember that he hadn't really forgiven her. And having tasted friendship once again, having remembered how sweet it was to trust someone else, it would be all the more bitter to have it wrested away. But even knowing that she was being foolish—knowing that this would end, and she would be hurt—she couldn't make herself push him away.

She'd been right. She'd missed him—missed the life she had once had—too much to be anything other than very foolish when it came to him.

"So," Mary said, as lightly as she could manage, "why did you build a windmill?" As she spoke, she rested her hand against his arm.

He started walking. "I was sixteen," he said. "And my father had given me a piece of land."

"A gift?"

"A threat." He sighed, and turned his head to look out over the valley. "He didn't want me to think so much about farming. There was no money in land anymore, he said. We had some wealth remaining, and he was throwing it all into investment—*that*, he said was where all the money lay. But I kept coming to him with my head in the clouds, spouting ragged bits of advice I was learning from books and farmers' magazines. He was sick to death of my hopeful burbling, and so he told me that I could make all the changes I wanted on the farm, if only I could do one thing."

Next to her, he smiled in memory. It was a deep, dark smile, one that drew her in.

"He gave me a piece of land where all the water for miles drained. What wasn't fen in the plot was taken up by bulrushes. And he told me if I could make a crop of rye grow there, I could do as I wished, instead of going into business."

"Didn't you want to go into business?"

He shrugged. "Not particularly. It seemed to involve a great deal of sitting around and talking to others. Rather dull, actually. I've always liked working with my hands. I gather he gave me that plot of land to beat my misplaced ambitions out of me. To give me an impossible task, just so I could fail at it."

When he'd been sixteen, she would have just started in Vienna. She'd been full of hopes about her playing—that she'd become so brilliant that she might play anywhere, despite the unfortunate deficiency of her sex. They'd both taken on impossible tasks. But he'd succeeded at his.

"I didn't believe them," John said. "Not even when all the available choices failed. Tile drains, laid at reasonable intervals, simply covered in water. There was too much mud to manage a proper drainage canal. It took me two years to convince myself that no passive draining scheme would serve. And even then, I wouldn't give up. That's when I began to consider an active scheme. I ordered architectural drawings from the Netherlands, from drainage windmills in Kent."

"And so you built a windmill and showed them all."

"It wasn't that easy," he said. "I built it, and it didn't work. It took me another six months to work out the details. By that time, my father…"

"Was he urging you to give up, to move on?"

There was a long pause. "No," John said softly. "But I remember the moment when I finally got the machinery in the tower to work right. It looked right. I examined it from every angle, and it matched the specifications I had. I took it apart and put it back together three times, and still the bloody thing wouldn't work. I was beginning to lose the light, and the oil lamp was not bright enough to show intricate detail. I had told myself I was going to finish that day. And that's how I figured it out—because I was too stubborn to leave. It got so dark I couldn't see—so I heard it instead. Just a faint grinding. Enough for me to realize the wood pump rod wasn't seated properly. It was so close to straight I couldn't see that it was off. But I could hear it. I fixed it in the dark, and the next morning, when I came to look at the results, my reservoir was filling and my land was drying."

"What did your father have to say to that?"

"As I recall, what he said was, 'What are you showing me all this mud for? Haven't you got seed to sow?'" John quoted. "He wasn't much for talking. But after that he said no more of my going into business and leaving the farm to others to manage."

"How horrid."

"No. It just wasn't his way to give praise. Not to my face. After he passed away, though, I heard that he'd crowed about it to all of his friends."

That put Mary in mind of her piano master. But thinking of Herr Rieger only made her sad. Maybe that's what she'd liked about John, when first they met—that automatic understanding of what it was to take on an impossible, years-long task. She'd met him long after he'd built his windmill. At that point, there had only been talk of all the things he'd done—and no hint of how difficult they might have been. The other girls had spoken of him in hushed tones, as if he were some sort of magician, and a handsome one at that.

But he was real—real and warm. And he wasn't with any of those other girls. He was here in the dark with her, holding her arm, losing sleep to talk with her at night. He'd achieved so much on his own. And what had she done?

Once, that question might have made her throw up her hands in despair. But perhaps it was because she was so close to him. Perhaps it was because they'd resumed their friendship, and the world no longer seemed as impossibly frightening as it once had been.

Crickets sounded again, thin and reedy in the night.

Perhaps, she had given up hope too easily. She'd let Sir Walter take everything from her without a fight. Maybe she didn't need to be devastated when John left. Maybe she was strong enough not only to face her world, but to change it.

Herr Rieger came to mind again, his mouth narrowed to a flat, white line. *Not right,* the image of him barked in her head. *Try again. This time, slow—once your fingers know the way of it, you can speed it up.*

"I was wondering," she said quietly. "Could you perhaps do me a favor?"

"What is it?"

A little step. She'd play it slowly at first. Once she knew the way of it…

"A paper," Mary said. "Bring me a newspaper."

IT WAS NOT UNTIL NOON THREE DAYS LATER that Mary had a chance to reveal her bounty. Lady Patsworth was sewing; her husband had left the two women alone to answer letters. He sat in the next room over, close enough to hear, but hidden by the door. It was as good a chance as either of them would ever get. The front room, papered in a delicate pink and gold, gleamed in the morning sun.

"Now," Lady Patsworth was saying, "white ruffs might seem too much like livery, but—"

Mary adjusted her skirts, rescuing the paper from its place in her petticoats. She slid it into Lady Patsworth's sewing basket and gestured for the woman to continue. But Lady Patsworth had stopped talking. She looked at the paper; she looked at Mary. She reached out and touched it with the edge of her fingertips, as if she were afraid it might reach up and bite her.

And then she gave Mary a brilliant smile.

Keep talking, Mary mouthed, tilting her head toward the door behind which Sir Walter sat.

Lady Patsworth glanced in her husband's direction, and then picked up the paper.

"Of course," she said loudly, "now that I'm designing my own gowns—"

She stopped again as she unfolded the pages. Sir Walter always read the news of the world, while handing the middle page of fashion and gossip to his wife. But she was staring at the front page—not the fashion column.

"Now that I'm designing my own," Lady Patsworth said more quietly, "I can do…anything I want?" Her voice raised in a question.

"Of course you can," Mary soothed her.

Lady Patsworth's hands were shaking. She turned the paper around.

Mary hadn't had the chance to look at it yet. When John had given it over last night, it had been too dark to make out letters. If she'd tried to read it herself in daylight hours, she would have risked losing her contraband. So this was the first time that she'd seen the headline.

Queen Grants Royal Assent to Matrimonial Causes Act.

Mary drifted over, skimming paragraphs, trying to take it all in. No wonder Sir Walter had canceled his subscription. The gossip pages wouldn't have been safe any longer. The new bill had created a civil court to hear cases of divorce, allowing anyone to bring suit. Anyone—not just those with access to Parliament. And when that court came into existence…oh, the gossip that the paper would print.

Mary raised her eyes to Lady Patsworth. The woman was staring at the words in confusion.

Mary tilted her head, reminding the other woman that her husband was near. "What sort of *gown* do you think you will make first?"

Lady Patsworth was staring at the black ink before her.

"I don't think…" Her fingers plucked uselessly at the pages. "That is to say…" She let out a breath and shook her head. "I believe I will make the same sorts of gowns that I always have. Nothing has changed, really."

How many years had Lady Patsworth suffered under her husband's rule? More than Mary knew. She knew that the other woman hated his restrictions—but maybe, after all this time, she'd forgotten how to live without them.

"I think you should make a riding habit," Mary said. "With divided skirts, so you might be able to challenge anyone to race—and dash away quickly, so that they might never catch you."

The other woman's eyes widened at those words. She stole another glance in the direction of her husband. "I…I couldn't. I haven't the slightest notion how to cut the cloth."

It wasn't *right*. The last few days, talking with John in friendship…they'd been a real balm for Mary. But John would leave, and when he did, Mary would find herself all the more aware of the bars that made up her cage. This was her chance to prove that she could *do* something besides wait to be released.

"Let me sketch you how it is done," she said, reaching for a pencil. She wrote in tiny letters in the margin of the paper.

Would your brother help you?

Lady Patsworth bit her lip and took the pencil from her. *But how am I to get word to him? Even if he came—he did two years ago—Sir W will simply not let him on the property.*

"With the right riding habit," Mary said, "you might even take a horse over an obstacle. Just jump over it if it gets in your way."

He has a pistol, Lady Patsworth wrote. *I'm afraid he'll use it.*

They stared at those words, and then Lady Patsworth turned away. "It's a silly project." She sniffed. "I don't ride, I'm afraid. I haven't since I was a girl. No sense in countenancing such waste."

There must be some way to change matters, Mary wrote. Her hands were shaking. If Lady Patsworth could break free, Mary might as well.

But the other woman shook her head vehemently.

"Make an evening gown, then," Mary suggested. "One you might wear to an elegant party at a neighbor's house."

"Alas," Lady Patsworth said coldly. "My health does not permit such excursions."

We could make it happen, Mary wrote.

Lady Patsworth looked at those words for a very long time before reaching for the pencil. *How?*

Mary let out a breath of relief.

I have an idea.

Chapter Eight

"I NEED TO TELL YOU SOMETHING."

John had been meeting Mary for a half hour or so every night for more than a week, now. It was easy to be patient, to pretend to be her friend. It was easy to fall into their old camaraderie—so easy that most of the time he forgot that he was pretending. In fact, he'd stopped probing after the first days. He had time, he told himself, and it would go better if she trusted him…and he was enjoying himself.

He only remembered that he was lying to her at moments like this—when she looked at him with her eyes round and solemn, and he recalled that she had secrets he wanted to uncover.

There was a luster to her eyes, something more than the reflection of starlight. There was something about the way she looked at him that made his chest feel tight.

"I need another favor," she said. "Two favors, this time, and rather larger. But in order for my requests to make any sense, you have to understand who—what—Sir Walter is."

One confidence was good. It might lead to another, after all, the one that he truly desired. But that didn't explain the warmth that filled him at the thought of her trust, the smile that he felt come onto his face.

"He's an ass," John said simply. "That much I can tell. But I'm sure you have specifics."

"He has not let his wife be in company for six years. Not to go to church; not to visit the shops. The last time her brother came to see her, Sir Walter threw him off the property and threatened to shoot him if he returned."

"What is his reasoning?"

Mary shook her head. "Does it matter? His reasoning is flawed. He says he wants to keep her safe. I think he's afraid that she will be as unfaithful as he has been."

It matched what little he'd seen of the man. Mary's voice was scornful, but when he looked down, her hand was a little unsteady on his sleeve.

He set his own hand over hers, holding it in place. "And what has Sir Walter done to you?" His voice went low. And angry—how angry he felt in that moment.

"He withholds my salary," Mary said. "I have no money—literally not a penny. I'm not allowed to speak to anyone. I live in fear that he'll discover that I'm climbing out my window to talk with you at night. If he sends me away, I will have nothing, absolutely nothing. He made my world this small." She held up her thumb and forefinger, indicating. "And I made myself fit into that space."

He pressed her fingers into his arm. "I could strike him."

"Don't be too angry with him. I did it to myself," she said. "I let him make me small. I *believed* him at first, when he said he knew what was best for my welfare. I gave up everything, because—"

She was shaking. His hand on hers was no longer enough; he reached and put his arm around her, pulling her close. She had always fit against him so well; she did so again, her body molding to his. The skin of her arms had broken out in gooseflesh, even on this warm night. So he held her and said nothing, held her until she grew warm.

"I let him," she whispered in his ear, "because I thought I deserved it for what I had done."

Here was the other half of the confession—the one he had waited for so patiently. So why didn't he feel any triumph?

"Nobody deserves that," he responded.

"I thought I did." She took a deep breath. "You see, when I left Southampton, I went to Basingstoke. I had only a little money, and so much I needed to do. I asked the maids at the inn if there was a doctor who might help me with a private problem for the least amount of money. The maid I talked to suggested Dr. Clemmons. I should have known what I was asking for."

John felt curiously calm, despite the words she was saying. As if all his emotion was just beyond his reach. "What did you need a doctor for?"

She looked into his lapels. "To falsify a certificate of death."

His sense of calm grew. It was always thus when he became angry. He'd been right. She *had* been lying to him. Her father wasn't dead; the money was still there. He should have been delighted to know there was something to recover, but all he felt was that ugly sense of betrayal.

His hands were still on her, gripping just a little too tightly. "You told me that your father was dead. That you'd watched him buried with your own eyes."

"The fact of his death was not false."

He took a breath of relief.

She looked up at him. "The day on the certificate and the cause, though, were lies. My father died in Southampton two days prior. I had to find a doctor willing to certify a lie, and Dr. Clemmons was that man."

"Two days prior in Southampton? But that's when we were last together. Why did you not tell us then that your father had passed away?"

"Because he killed himself." Her voice shook. "He killed himself, and I found his body, and all I could think at the time was that if I somehow managed to get him a proper burial on hallowed ground, if I kept everyone from finding out—that maybe, maybe everything would not be ruined."

"Oh, Mary," he breathed. All his anger turned to cold ash. He didn't let go of her, though. He couldn't.

"And so I went to Dr. Clemmons. The only problem was that I didn't have enough money to convince him to perjure himself on my behalf."

Her breath was coming faster. And she was holding on to him, too, her grip even stronger than his.

"Did he help you?"

"He offered." She put her forehead against his chest. "He offered to help, despite my lack of money. All I had to do was help him in return. It was such a little thing he asked for. It wouldn't even risk pregnancy, he said."

Oh, God. Had he been angry at her? He couldn't even remember it, not in the rush of emotions that followed. Fury at the doctor, whoever Clemmons was. Anger at himself, for letting her go out into the world alone. But mostly, he felt sorrow that she'd discovered how vicious the world could be—and that he hadn't been there to make it right.

He'd wondered how she had learned to think of her body as currency. Now he knew.

Mary drew another ragged breath. "He had pushed me to my knees and was undoing his buttons when I told him that I would tell the magistrate. I would spill the whole sordid story: I'd tell about my father's suicide, and how he'd tried to take advantage of a distraught young lady. So I struck a new bargain—he could keep his reputation and not risk punishment, and in exchange, I'd have that certificate issued as I asked."

"Thank God," John said.

"And do you know why I did it?" she continued. "Not because I would have balked at that exchange, for the chance at my father's eternal rest. I wasn't above making the trade. It was because I knew that once he found he could obtain that sort of concession from me, he would not stop. He'd require more from me—more and more. There was no truth in his bargain. I didn't stop because I refused to sell my body." Her voice shook. "I stopped because I didn't trust him to keep his word."

"Shh." He stroked her hair.

"And so I told myself I deserved what Sir Walter was doing to me. I was practically a whore, and the fact that he didn't use me as one gave him the right to do everything else."

"You don't still believe that." He set his hand against her hair, caressing the soft silk.

"No. But I've been so afraid—so angry with myself, with *everyone*."

"You should be," he said bitterly. "You should be angry with me, not yourself. I let you walk away from me in a fit of pique. I didn't think what it might mean to you. And there you were, with…" He paused, the ramifications of what she had told him spilling through him. If her father had died in Southampton, and been buried in Basingstoke…

He stopped and remembered that great big steamer trunk that Mary had taken with her. At the time, he'd assumed it had been filled with clothing—petticoats and corsets and crinolines and gowns would have easily filled the available space.

"You hid your father's body in your trunk," he said.

"Yes." Her emotion was beginning to leak out in ragged, rapid gasps of breath. "I had to. I couldn't let everyone think he was a suicide on top of being a thief. At the time, I could think only of his reputation."

"Oh, Mary." There had been lies from her—of course there had been. But they'd come from pain and loyalty, not from deceit.

"He'd done so much for me—I thought that I could do just one thing for him. He wrote his final note explaining why he'd taken his life in the account book where he'd documented his thefts. I could see that he had done it for me—to give me a chance that no other girl in Southampton had, to buy me gowns, to give me lessons, to make the world right for me. He'd done it all for me."

"He wrote the note in the account book," John said slowly. "That's why you took it, when first you left?"

"Yes. I didn't even realize what else was in the volume, until a few days later." She sniffled. "I suppose I should have checked, but it was not my most rational hour."

"And that's why, when you sent it back, two pages had been sliced from the middle. You didn't want anyone to find his note."

She nodded.

He'd wanted the truth. It was this: There was no money left to recover. Mary hadn't stolen it. He'd lied to her, accused her, and threatened her, when her crime had been having too loyal a heart. He had his arms around her now in false pretenses. He'd only pretended to be her friend, but she'd been his in truth. Everything he'd accused her of doing to him, he had done to her.

And the hell of it was he wouldn't have taken his arms from her in that moment. Not even if it would have meant the return of every missing guinea.

"It took me months to grow angry with him," Mary was saying. "I never asked him to steal for me. I didn't need vastly expensive pianoforte lessons in Vienna. It wasn't even originally my idea—it was his. He said he did it for me, but he didn't. He did it for himself." Her whole body trembled against his. "That's all everyone ever does—they hurt me, claiming it's for my benefit. My safety. My wellbeing. And it's all lies. It wasn't for me at all."

His arms were still around her. She hadn't pushed him away. And she was the woman he could have held for the rest of his life. She'd been changed by what had happened to her, but she'd not been destroyed by it. He could scarcely see her, flush against him, but he could feel the strength of her.

"I'm so sorry," John said, leaning into her. "I'm sorry I—"

"Oh," she said in surprise, looking up at him. "I didn't mean everyone. I didn't mean you."

Her eyes were so bright. Her body was so warm. He was looking down at her, their faces mere inches apart.

"You were a little nasty in the beginning," she said, "but at least you always told me the truth."

He should have told her right then. But he didn't. Instead, he slid his hand around her neck. He wanted her. He wanted the woman who stood before him now. He adored her bravery in the face of monsters. He wanted to believe that the light in her eyes reflected the truth of him, not the partial truths he'd given her. He wished this were clean and uncomplicated.

But it was messy and complex. And warm, like the intermingling of their breath. And no matter how hard he tried, he couldn't keep himself from leaning over her, his lips brushing hers in a brief prelude.

She wrapped her arms around his shoulders, and he let out a gasp of air against her lips—a single, desirous exhalation, before he took her mouth. No more shyness between them—just that heated storm of a kiss. There was no lightning in the air, no thunder on the horizon. But there should have been. The atmosphere seemed charged and humid, as if some great bolt of electricity were about to arc up from the ground, starting right between them.

The entire valley—dark and shrouded in night—seemed to fold itself into their kiss. His hands slid down her back, pulling her close; her lips were soft and yet so demanding on his. He wanted her, every inch of her. The crickets about them seemed to chirp an entire symphony, accompanied only by the distant sound of frogs.

If only the world could shrink to those things—heat and want—and expel the ragged past between them.

He pulled away from her. "Do you remember the first time I saw you? Your father had us all to dinner. And before we went in, you played the pianoforte. All the other men—barbarians, I was sure—talked through your performance. I could only think that it was the most extraordinary thing I'd ever heard."

"I remember." She took a breath. "I haven't played in so long."

"You were playing some variations."

"The Goldberg variations," she confirmed. "By Bach."

"And after, I went up to you and demanded that you tell me what the point of a variation was—taking the same piece of music and altering it over and over, instead of creating something new. Do you remember what you said?"

She frowned. "Something like, 'Why limit yourself to one melody, when the music is big enough to lend itself to endless possibilities?'"

"That's what I think when I see you now," he said. "I don't understand most of what you're saying, except that it makes me angry on your behalf. I can't compress you into a few words, no matter how I try. I feel like I'm listening to endless variations on a theme of Mary. And I love what I hear."

Her breath caught. "John." She didn't say anything else. She just held him, and when he kissed her, she melted into him again. Kiss after melting kiss—months of dreams and longings, all coming to life. He could make this right, somehow. He could make it up to her. They might have each other after all.

As for everything else? He'd make things right with his sister. He'd find some way to compensate his nephew for the loss. It didn't matter how impossible it seemed that their families could reconcile; it was more impossible that he would give her up.

"I've missed you," he murmured. "God, I missed you."

She nestled against him, so right against him that he couldn't imagine ever letting her go again.

Maybe…

"You mentioned a favor," he said. "At the beginning. I had almost forgotten it. About Sir Walter?"

She looked up, blinking in surprise. "Yes," she said. "I…I became distracted. We are going to destroy Sir Walter. You and I."

She fumbled in her skirt pocket and pulled out a tiny twist of brown paper. This she undid, revealing a piece of jewelry. It glinted in the moonlight as she held it up. "And we're going to use this."

Chapter Nine

JOHN DIDN'T THINK HE WAS THE SORT to be easily overawed, but Northword Hill was by far the most intimidating home he had ever entered. The entry was all mirrors and marble and a vast candelabra that sparkled overhead; the murals on the walls had the rich look of old wealth. Even the corridor that he was led down, when he'd handed over his card and a brief description of his business, was lined with paintings done by a single hand—a beautiful woman, playing the role of a Madonna; a still-life with candlelight on fruit so vivid that he couldn't believe it was flat paint.

He caught a glimpse of a pianoforte edged in gold through one door, and a library, well stocked with volumes, through another, before he was ushered into a parlor.

"Mr. John Mason," the footman intoned, bowing, and then taking up watchful residence at the door.

The lady of the estate sat in a seat, the arms carved with delicate patterns. For all that he towered over her while she was seated, he had the impression that she might have been on a throne, looking down on him.

"Lady Northword," John said, bowing his head.

He had heard that Lady Northword was elderly. But the woman who inclined her head to him looked only old enough to command respect. There was still more auburn in her hair than grey, and she wore it half up, the rest a mass of tangling curls.

"Mr. John Mason," she repeated. "Please sit." She waited until he had done so before she continued. "Northword told me about you the other day. You're the fellow who's come all the way from Southampton to work on Beauregard's fields."

"Yes, my lady. That's right."

"That's quite kind of you," she said. "The rest of us have been hearing about his swamp for some time now." Her eyes focused on him. Nothing rheumy or unclear about her, despite her age. "Beauregard says that you asked for no compensation. I find that passing strange."

He ducked his head. "Not so strange, my lady. I had other reasons to visit the district."

"Had you, now." She contemplated him, as if wondering how villainous his reasons were. "And now you've come all the way from Beauregard's farm to see me."

"Yes, my lady." His hand played over the metal in his pocket.

"Passing strange," she repeated.

"Not so strange," he said. "You're the only one I can give this to." He opened his hand.

In that moment, faced with Lady Northword's regal demeanor, the plan suddenly felt foolish. Some tenant might have lost the earring in the decades since Lady Northword had resided at Doyle's Grange. And even if it had belonged to her, what did a viscountess care about a twist of gold and a bit of peridot? She likely had far finer pieces to adorn her—including the pearls at her ears now.

But her eyes widened and she stood up half out of her chair, reaching for the metal.

"Mr. Mason," she said, her voice growing temporarily raspy, "how extraordinary." Her fingers touched the earring, pressing it into his palm. "I had never thought to see this again. I lost it so long ago—before my marriage, even."

She took it gently from him. John said nothing as she peered at it, lost in a long ago time.

Finally, she looked up. "My brother Magnus gave me this for my twenty-first birthday. He passed away just a few years ago." Her fist closed around the jewelry, and she pulled it close to her chest. "Where did you find it? How did you know it was mine?"

"Lady Patsworth found it at Doyle's Grange."

She frowned. "But if she found it, why were you tasked to return it?"

"She is not allowed to pay any calls." John was unsure how much else he would have to say to convince the woman.

But Lady Northword leaned forward, her eyes narrowing. "Ah."

She'd been a viscountess and the leading lady of this region for nearly half a century. What Lady Northword would have seen in that time, John could only begin to guess. She was no fool, that was for certain. She inclined her head to look out the windows in the direction of her one-time home.

"All is not well at Doyle's Grange," she said softly.

"No, my lady." He drew a deep breath. "Lady Patsworth sends this to you with her regards, and her most desperate plea for your assistance. She would have brought it herself, were it allowed. She needs you."

Lady Northword looked still to Doyle's Grange, unmoving, as if caught in the grip of some long-ago memory. "Nobody should be imprisoned like that. What must be done?" she asked.

"Invite her to dinner," John said. "She needs to get away from her husband's domain. You'll have to make the invitation in person…"

He trailed off, realizing he was giving commands to a viscountess. But she simply raised an eyebrow, and motioned him to continue.

"And you'll have to insist that she come—no excuses allowed. If her husband complains, insist that Beauregard and I have seen her strong and well. You own Doyle's Grange, do you not? And as nobility, you and your husband are the only ones in the area that Sir Walter cannot truly refuse—if you insist. Insist, and we'll manage the rest."

Her eyebrow rose even higher. "We? That is you and…Lady Patsworth?"

He met her eyes straight on. "Lady Patsworth has a companion. We were once engaged." He frowned. "In fact, as the engagement was never officially broken off, we are still betrothed."

She sat back in her chair and gave him a curiously pleased grin.

"You see," he repeated. "There's nothing strange about it."

"Consider it done," she said. She raised the piece of jewelry in the air. "And give Lady Patsworth my compliments, if you please."

Mary did not often mourn the loss of her gowns. But a week after she and John had made their plans, as she dressed for the dinner party, she wished she still had one of her finest. Her blue silk, for instance. She was, after all, preparing for battle. The right gown could serve as both sword and shield.

She'd contemplated her Sunday best, but the dove-gray gown had no pockets. If everything went well tonight, she might never return to this room. And if she was going to be restricted to the contents of her pockets, she wanted those pockets to be as large as possible.

The practical took most of the space available: a comb, a toothbrush, a sliver of hard soap, and a small hand towel—she'd learned in her last desperate flight from home that a lady should never be without a towel.

Aside from that...

She'd been carting around the damning pages she'd sliced from her father's account book for too long. She couldn't leave them here to be discovered by Sir Walter; after all she'd gone through to keep her father's secret, there was no point betraying his shame to her worst enemy.

But she didn't want to keep those words near her heart any longer. His note had all the sentimental value of a bludgeon. It was time to let the words go.

Sighing, she lit a candle and fed the pages into the flame. But as the edge blackened and smoked, her eye was caught by the numbers on the reverse of his final message—not blank, of course; it was an account book. She'd seen those numbers a hundred times without thinking about what they meant.

The last entries were not surprising or strange. But they'd never before set in motion the cascade of possibilities that rushed through her now. She'd been so used to seeing those words as a chain, holding her in place, that she'd not recognized that they could be something else entirely. She'd seen only what her father had taken—those thousands of pounds, spent on her behalf. She hadn't thought about what he'd left behind.

The paper caught fire right at that moment, a thin lick of orange darting up. Mary dropped it on the desk and beat her fist into the flame, smothering it before it could consume the future she'd glimpsed.

She brushed away ash and the charred edges of cracked paper before unfolding the pages and surveying the damage.

The numbers were still there, unburnt.

When John talked of thousands of pounds missing, she'd thought of the money her father had spent. But the way he spoke, he made it sound as if nothing had remained. Her father had taken thousands, but he'd husbanded his ill-gotten gains. The other partners should have recovered quite a bit.

If John thought they hadn't...

Mary reached out and picked up the paper again. She folded it—this time, not for the words he'd written in front, but for the ones she'd never thought about on the back. And then, for the first time in a long while, she laughed.

Now she was ready to take on Sir Walter.

Chapter Ten

BY THE TIME THE DINNER GUESTS ADJOURNED to the back room, Mary felt too wracked by her nerves to speak. She'd scarcely touched her food; she hadn't dared look at Lady Patsworth, lest her questioning gaze give everything away to her husband.

The closer they came to success, the sicker Mary felt. Luckily, as a mere companion, there was no need for her to join in the conversation. She let it swirl around her, and she waited.

The salon was grandly appointed. The walls were a mix of moss-green and gold, clever carved moldings around the edge telling a story about a nymph and a harp. Windows looked out over the night-shrouded valley, dotted by little flashes of lamplight where there were settlements.

Easier to look out the window than to focus on what stood before it: a pianoforte. That would be Mary's contribution this evening. She'd never been nervous about performing before. This crowd—just Lord and Lady Northword, John, the Beauregards, Sir Walter and his wife, and two other families—would hardly have flustered her a few years ago. Then again, she'd never had a performance this important.

"Miss Chartley," the viscountess said, "you keep looking at the pianoforte. Do you play?"

It had begun. The evening was so carefully scripted; Mary had only to do her part, and the rest of it would happen.

"A little," Mary said, looking down.

"A little?" John, a few feet away, made a sound of disbelief. "That's balderdash, if you'll excuse the expression. Miss Chartley is utterly brilliant."

"A bit of exaggeration, I'm afraid." Mary put her head down in a pretense of modesty.

"But…" Sir Walter looked up, frowning. "Mr. Mason, I thought you didn't know Miss Chartley. How would you know that she plays?"

John met Mary's eyes and gave her a melting look; Mary looked away. They'd decided it would do best to have Mary pretend embarrassment—to have Sir Walter believe that she'd been caught out in misbehavior. Mary didn't have to pretend at all; a slight pink flush rose on her cheeks unbidden.

"Well," John said, "I had to find out."

Sir Walter let out a soft hiss. "But you…"

Mary looked up. It wasn't difficult to meet John's eyes. And she wasn't pretending when everyone else in the room seemed to fall away. There was only his smile, only the light dancing in his eyes.

"Hmph," Sir Walter said. He gave her a dark look, one that said, *Don't you dare speak to that man*.

"Well, Miss Chartley, perhaps you could play for us a little." Lady Northword spoke as if she hadn't seen that interchange.

"Of course." Mary blushed and glanced at John again. "And perhaps, Mr. Mason, you might turn my pages."

"Miss Chartley," Sir Walter whispered in harsh tones. "This behavior is most unbecoming!"

But Mary stood anyway and moved to the instrument. Sir Walter glared as she thumbed through the available music. His arms were folded across his chest; his chin promised retribution.

John came to stand by her. His simple presence assured her that she was not alone. He didn't touch her. He didn't say anything as she flipped, unseeing, through sheets of music. He was just *there*, steady and honest and trustworthy.

It wasn't hard for Mary to turn to John and give him the largest, most scintillating smile she could muster. She was *supposed* to be doing it to rivet Sir Walter's attention. But she had only to look at the man who'd kissed her every night for the last week, and she felt herself burst into bloom. It wasn't just a smile she gave him; it was her heart, writ large across her face. Her nervousness faded. Her breath eased. The whole room seemed to fade to an indistinct blur—everything except him. He was the only solid thing in a shifting world.

"You know," he said, leaning down and whispering in her ear. "There's one flaw with this plan. I don't know how I will turn your pages. I can't read music."

"Don't worry," she murmured back. "I'll play from memory. Just count to twenty-five and turn, and nobody will be the wiser."

She took out a sheaf of music and set it in front of her, and set her hands on the keys.

It had been so long since she'd touched an instrument. She had worried that she might have forgotten how. But the ivory, cool under her fingers, woke memories that went deeper than a few years' hiatus. Her muscles still knew what to do. The first sprightly notes came out precise and clear, exactly as she remembered them.

She had always loved Beethoven's *Diabelli* variations, in part because the individual pieces were so…various. They were not minor alterations in key and structure, but complete transformations. Chords were taken from one variation and built into a new melody in the next. The notes of the original waltz were still present, if you knew what to listen for—they were just given an entirely different meaning. It was music tied to a common heart, but made without limitation.

Her fingers faltered at first. But the joy of a variation was that it was all too easy to cover a mistake. Those first missteps, she converted into alterations of her own—little ones, at first, and then trills that she added on purpose.

Herr Rieger had told her—and Mary suspected the tale was apocryphal—that Beethoven had composed the music on a dare from a friend: Take the most mediocre waltz you can find, someone had taunted the composer, and see if you can make it magnificent.

That's what Beethoven had done, thirty-three times over.

She glanced up at John, standing behind her, and smiled again. She'd had her run of mediocre waltzes. Now it was time to make what she had—what they had—magnificent. The music didn't carry her; she carried it, from chord to breathless chord, from variation to variation.

She didn't do all of them. She hadn't the time, or the strength in her fingers. But she played until her fingers began to ache with the unaccustomed exercise. She played long enough to see Lady Northword tap Lady Patsworth on the shoulder out of the corner of her vision. She played with John's hand hovering mere inches from her shoulder and Sir Walter glaring at her, promising dire retribution.

When her hands began to falter, she skipped to the final variation and ended.

The handful of guests clapped vigorously—all but Sir Walter. The applause died into a moment of silence. Then the windows rattled, and the house shook with the booming roll of real thunder. Even the weather itself applauded her. Mary smiled and ducked her head.

"Miss Chartley," said Lady Northword. "Mr. Mason was right. You are more than proficient. You are magnificent. I see that I shall have to ask you to visit far more often."

"Unfortunately," Sir Walter said, "that will not be possible. You see, my wife…" He stopped and looked about him, and abruptly shot to his feet. "Where is my wife?"

There was a moment of absolute silence—the kind of moment that performers dreamed of. Mary was not yet off the stage. She stood, collecting the piano music into some semblance of order.

"Why," Lady Northword said, "she is talking with her brother."

"Her brother." Sir Walter took a step toward the door. "Why is her brother here?"

The back door to the salon opened. "Because I am leaving with him," Lady Patsworth said.

There was a long pause. "Leaving," Sir Walter said. "On a visit? Think of your health, my dear."

"Leaving. For good."

Those words settled in the room.

"Come now." Sir Walter was beginning to turn red in the face, but his words were still smooth. "You're overset. Surely there's no need to draw these people into whatever trifle it is that has you angered." He drew in a deep breath, and addressed the rest of the crowd. "My wife—she's not well, you see. If she were, surely she would know how absurd it is to suggest that she might leave her lawfully wedded husband. There's no need to involve these people, Lady Patsworth. You know what a magistrate will say." He took a step toward her and held out his hand.

Lady Patsworth did not shrink. In fact, she stepped up to him and set her finger against his chest. "And I was so sure you'd seen the paper. A week ago, the Queen gave her assent to the new Matrimonial Causes act. Come next January, I will testify before all of England about every milkmaid that you've taken. I'll tell the world how you kept me prisoner in my own home. How you sent my brother away at gunpoint, telling him I never wanted to speak with him." Her voice was as smooth as his. "I don't need Parliament to grant me a divorce. I am free, and you can't hold me any longer."

"I still have that gun," Sir Walter growled.

"Mary threw it in the well," Lady Patsworth returned. "Yesterday evening." She smiled grimly. "You remember, don't you? I had a spasm, and you had to take me to my room. For my health."

Sir Walter did not say anything. His gaze flicked from his wife to her brother, and then across Lord and Lady Northword to settle on Mary.

"You," he said. "You arranged this. You sent for her brother."

Mary didn't shrink from him. "Yes. I did."

"You're sacked."

"Yes, sir," she said. "I'll be having my back wages, then."

He cast her a sullen glance. "What back wages?"

"That would be the sixty pounds you owe her," Lady Patsworth said. "If I've heard you say it once, I've heard you say it a hundred times, how you were keeping the money safe."

"And paying me interest on the principle," Mary added. "That *is* what people do when they hold your money, is it not?"

While Sir Walter was sputtering, Lord Northword came up behind him. "As it happens, I can advance you the amount you need right now," he said quietly. "Around here, we don't like to see employees used badly." He looked round at the other landowners, who were watching in confusion. "Do we, gentlemen?"

Sir Walter looked around, his nostrils flaring, as his neighbors shook their heads.

Lord Northword set his hand on Sir Walter's shoulder. "So we won't have to see it," he said jovially. "You'll come with me and write me a note, and I'll give Miss Chartley her money immediately. Now, if you please."

For a moment, it looked as if Sir Walter would actually strike Lord Northword. But he looked around—at the other guests, at the footmen in the corner, at John Mason not so far away. He remembered that Northword was a viscount and his landlord, and he was a mere Sir.

His hands curled in frustration, but he left with the other man.

THERE WAS QUITE A BIT OF CONFUSION in the thirty minutes that followed Sir Walter's exposure, and John's work was not yet done.

No matter how Sir Walter grimaced and gesticulated, he could not change matters. He'd been exposed on all fronts—and coward that he was, he hadn't the ability to bluster himself into disagreeing with Lord Northword. Northword sent for a secretary, who arrived very slowly, and was told he should write out a note of promise to cover Mary's wages. They disappeared to a back room to sign the thing.

John took the time to bundle Lady Patsworth and her brother onto horses, sending them on their way before Sir Walter had the chance to stop them.

Thunder rumbled overhead, and the horses rolled their eyes uneasily.

"West Aubrey is fifteen minutes on horseback across the fields. You should just make the evening train. Leave the horses at the Wayfarer's Pigeon."

Lady Patsworth nodded. "But won't he know we're going to West Aubrey?"

"Of course he will." John smiled. "But we'll be putting the carriage out in the next five minutes. Your husband will think you're going by road—and that's a two-hour journey. Let him chase after that. By the time he realizes you're not there, you'll be en route to London."

"Thank you." She took his hand. "And thank Mary, when you have the chance."

"Off with you now." He didn't bother to watch them go.

It was going to be a hellish ride for them. Thunder rumbled again, and he felt a drop of rain against his cheek. It took another five minutes to get the carriage on the road—and not a moment too soon. No sooner had it turned the bend, than Sir Walter raced out into the night.

"Wait!" he called, running after the conveyance. "Stop!"

Of course, it did nothing of the sort. He followed it as long as he could—about twenty yards, before he doubled over, trying to catch his breath. He caught sight of John just as he stood and turned.

"It's no use," he sneered. "It might take me half an hour to fetch a horse from my own stables, but I'll catch them on the road. And then we'll see about that so-called divorce."

"Don't go out, Sir Walter," John suggested. "It's beginning to rain."

"Ha," was his only reply. The man set his hat on his head and turned to jog back in the direction of his own stables.

John withdrew into the entry. Lord Northword was standing there, watching Sir Walter go.

"A better man, I think, would not be so amused at the futile nature of Sir Walter's quest," John said.

"You're wrong," Lord Northword said. "I'm old enough to be confident that I'm at least as good as you, and I think it's damned funny."

John grinned, and then turned around. "Where's Ma—Miss Chartley?"

"With Lady Northword."

He nodded, but at that moment Lady Northword came into the entry. "No, she's not. I thought she was with you."

A beat of panic entered John's breast. Sir Walter hadn't taken her—he knew that; he'd just seen the man. Wherever she was, she was safe.

But Lady Northword was already inquiring of a passing footman, who went to seek news. The man came back. "She left, my lady. Not five minutes past."

Thunder boomed again. There was no rain—not yet—but there would be. Mary was out there? What was she doing? She would not have returned to Doyle's Grange and Sir Walter.

"She said, what with the rain coming on, she had better get started to Up Aubrey, where she could get a room in the Lost Sock."

They hadn't talked about what she would do afterward. He'd assumed, what with the kisses—all those kisses—and the walks hand-in-hand, that she was contemplating a future with him. Why would she set off on her own at a time like this?

John looked out the window. A flash of lightning illuminated the valley, briefly capturing a glimpse of high summer grasses, waving furiously in the wind of the oncoming storm.

"You'd better go after her," Lady Northword said. "Bring her back—Miss Chartley can surely stay here until her future has been settled. If she's going to walk half an hour to West Aubrey, she'll be soaked."

"The stables are dry," Lord Northword added. "Deserted, too, at this time of night. If you wanted to take her somewhere."

He got a discreet elbow in his side from his lady. "Don't be inhospitable, darling. She's very welcome here."

"I had no such intentions. I have very fond memories of the stab—"

He was interrupted by a less discreet elbow. "Pay no attention to him," his wife said. "In fact, please forget that he ever spoke."

The impression John got in that moment was not something he'd ever wanted to think about. Lord and Lady Northword, kissing in the stables? He shook his head to clear it of that image.

"Even if there is somewhere else closer, somewhere dry," Lady Northword said, "you can be assured that I'll be willing to say that she spent the night here. Nobody will dare gainsay me."

Another drop landed on his head. The air was heavy with unspent rain. John nodded, but he scarcely heard their words. It was impossible to dwell on Mary's reputation. She was out there alone—and soon it would be cold and wet.

"Thank you," he said. "Thank you both, for everything." He tipped his hat at them, retrieved his coat, and set off across the field.

Chapter Eleven

MARY WAS FREE.

Just two weeks ago, the thought of getting sacked had filled her with dread. But now, she could walk away from Sir Walter and not only remain standing, but feel that she'd had the better of him.

Months had passed while she told herself she wasn't a lady any more, that she scarcely deserved common courtesy. And yet being a lady had not brought Lady Patsworth any real respect. A thousand rules of etiquette, drummed into her head—and in the end, it was her piano lessons that she'd drawn on.

She could remember Herr Rieger standing over her and scowling. *Why did you stop playing?*

Because I made a mistake.

Don't stop. Never stop. They'll never respect you if you stop and cry like a girl.

But—

He'd frowned at her and made a motion with his hand. *Weep later. Play now.*

Mary had pushed all her emotions away—grief, anger, guilt. But she'd not realized that she'd condemned herself to avoid the good ones, too. Pride. Happiness. Love. She deserved to experience those as well.

She'd stopped for too long. But now she was free, free to take a running start once again. The sharp smell of the oncoming storm only made her feel giddier.

Giddy was the least of the things that she felt. Relief, that things had not been so bad as they could have been. Pride, in a job well done. And a subtle sense of satisfaction—one that she would never have found if she'd stayed a genteel young lady all her life. She would have married John and disappeared into being his wife, putting all her own dreams away just to be with him.

Once, that had seemed worth the price.

But now, she was no sheltered lady who needed to be protected from the world. No; the big bad world needed protection from *her*. Bad things had happened to her, yes, but she had prevailed.

She felt daring with her victory. A bubble of laughter rose up in her.

On the horizon, summer thunder rumbled. It was dark enough that she could only tell there were clouds by the lack of stars. She'd left with scarcely a hand towel to her name. She should have been frightened. Instead, she felt recklessness rise up in her. She was free. She was *free*. She had bills folded in one skirt-pocket, a towel in the other, and her entire future ahead of her.

Nothing could stop her.

Mary knew it was an illusion, just as she knew that the heavy, humid heat that hung around her was about to give way to cold rain. Sixty pounds was no real security—just enough money to get her into trouble, and not enough to buy her way out. But it wasn't the money that made her heart sing. It was the proof she'd received: that she could trust to her own competence. That, ultimately, she had been the instrument of her own deliverance.

Tomorrow would be enough time for reality. When dawn came, she'd take stock of her resources, make decisions for the future.

But tonight…

Lightning sparked on the horizon, a great blinding tree of electricity stretching from the clouds to the skies. Mary held her breath at the wonder of it all, and counted. Five, six, seven—on the count of eight, thunder growled around her. The very ground rumbled beneath her feet, and the air shivered with the power of the storm. Her hairs stood on edge.

Ladies did not run off into storms. But then, ladies didn't sneak out of their windows and kiss gentlemen, no matter how handsome that gentleman was. She was damned glad not to be a lady any longer.

Tonight felt wild—a night that belonged to some other woman. Tonight, she would celebrate the rediscovery of herself. It seemed a night for dancing barefoot across the fields, or, perhaps, for making her way to the village a few miles distant for some good brandy.

Lightning flashed again, illuminating the stone wall along the road, half a mile in the distance. Sharp stones had been set at an angle in the mortar on top; they made a jagged row of teeth, stretching off into the distance. Darkness returned as swiftly as it had fled; then thunder rumbled. A droplet of water landed on her nose.

Rain was coming, and soon. If the lightning came any closer, it wouldn't do to be standing out in the field. Luckily, she had a destination in mind, and one that was just beyond the curve of the hill.

"Mary!" someone called behind her. She turned around. The figure was still far behind her, but she recognized him.

John. Precisely the man she'd been hoping to find.

"Mary," he said. "You've got to come in from this, before the storm starts in earnest."

It was a night for wildness, a night for celebration. It was a night for pagan acts, for leaving behind all that held her back. She didn't just want John; she yearned for him, with an ache that went all the way through to her heart.

He wasn't just the man she loved, the one she'd once agreed to marry. He was everything that had been wrested from her—her innocence, her childhood, her foolish belief that so long as she was *good* that nothing bad could transpire. He was the only thing that joined the person she was now—this reckless, uncageable creature—with the quiet girl she had once been.

And she had, after all, wanted to celebrate.

He caught up to her. He was carrying a shawl, which he dumped unceremoniously over her shoulders—as if he hadn't realized how hot it was.

"Mary," he repeated. "Thank God I found you. You've no idea how worried I have been these last ten minutes."

Lightning flashed again, searing all sight of him from her eyes. She waited for the reverberation of thunder. Another solitary raindrop found her cheek, then another. Then the thunder came, booming around them.

"Worry?" she asked. "Why were you worried? I've never been better."

Mary let the shawl slip down her shoulders.

"Come," he said, "we've got to get you back to Northword Hill."

But it was too late. The fall of droplets had become a light patter around them.

"No, John," she said, and it felt as if her voice came from very far away.

She had stopped hoping to be granted her heart's desire. She was going to start taking it now.

"No?" He picked up the edge of the shawl, looped it around her elbows, and wiped the raindrops from her face.

"No," she said quietly, raising her hand to his jaw. "I have been looking forward to this part of the evening for the past week. I didn't get tossed out of my employer's house with nowhere to go but your arms just so that I could return chastely to the viscount's home. You're taking me to bed."

Lightning slashed down, illuminating his silhouette. He seemed so still—looking at her as if he'd no notion what to say in response. And then the rain truly began, pelting into them. He grabbed her hand—too tight, too close—and together, they ran to Oak Cottage.

BY THE TIME JOHN BROUGHT MARY BACK TO OAK COTTAGE, she was soaked through. He could feel her trembling all the way through the shawl he'd put around her. But despite her shivers, there was something about her that heated him more than any of their kisses.

It wasn't just the way she removed the soaking-wet shawl, or how she turned to him and undid the buttons of his coat. It wasn't just the physical thrill of seeing her bodice cling to her skin. After she took off his hat and set it on a hook, she found a clean, dry cloth and wiped the droplets from his face—slowly, tenderly. Their breaths made little white puffs of air in the entry.

"You know," she said, her voice low, "I'm never going to get dry with my wet things on."

He swallowed. She turned her back to him. Her gown laced from her neck down to the base of her spine, ending just below the swell of her petticoats. From that angle, she presented a most appealing picture.

"I need your help to remove them," she continued.

She was right. He held his breath and undid her laces. The rain had hardened the strings to tight knots, and his fingers fumbled against her back—again and again, until he loosened her laces enough for her to take the fabric off.

As she moved to do so, he turned away. "I'll make a fire."

It was cold, but not so cold that they needed a regular blaze. Instead, he made a small coal-fire in the grate, just enough to cast a little red illumination in the room.

But Mary hadn't wrapped herself in one of the towels that he'd brought in. "John," she said, crooking a finger at him.

He swallowed. "Yes?"

"I'm soaked through. All the way to my drawers."

That brought to mind white linen clasping soft thighs. He groaned and leaned against the wall as she undid the buttons holding her petticoat in place.

"I—I'll go in the other room," he offered half-heartedly.

"Don't you dare. I'll need you for my corset laces."

She let her petticoat fall to the floor. "Here," she said, lifting her hair and turning to him. If it had been a trial to undo her gown, unlacing her corset was torture. The fire cast scant light; he could only find her laces by feel. First, the smoothness of her shoulders—then the stiffened fabric of her corset. He found her corset-laces and followed them down to where they'd been tied in a secure bow. These laces, slightly drier, didn't stick; he managed to undo the knots fairly easily. But then he peeled the fabric from her body. What little light there was in the room seemed to fall on her breasts, wet and peaked under her shift.

"Christ." He couldn't look away. Not from her. Not from this. His own wet clothing seemed suddenly too hot.

She took the edge of her shift in her hands.

John took a step back. "God, Mary. It's like you're—"

"Like I'm trying to seduce you?" she said, her voice rich as cream.

"Trying to torment me."

"Oh, no," she said, her voice cool. "I have no wish to torment you." She lifted her shift above her knees, high enough to pull her drawers down. All that creamy white fabric, fresh from her legs. His mouth went dry. He wanted her—wanted her so badly he could hardly speak. And then she pulled her shift over her head. His brain simply ceased to function, to do anything except to desire. He wanted to taste, to touch, to smell. He wanted to take, to possess. He wanted her so much his fists clenched with the effort of standing still.

The darkness only seemed to make her more alluring—to show the silhouette of her nearly-naked form in flashes, enough to taunt him with her proximity and yet whisper that if he wanted to know all of her, he'd have to discover her curves not with his eyes but with his hands.

He fought for rationality.

"There's no need to rush this. I can wait—" He swallowed as she sidled up to him "—a little." A very little.

"Are you saying that you don't want to do this?"

He took her hand and guided it to his crotch, setting her palm against the wet fabric—and his hard member underneath. "I want this."

He'd expected her eyes to widen in shock. But she didn't leap back. Instead, she grew very still for a moment, not moving, as if she were just understanding what she had discovered. Then she traced her fingers gently down the length of him. He let out a hiss. Another stroke. Then another.

He set his hand over hers. "Mary," he said, with the last ounce of decency that he possessed, "I don't want you to do this because you believe you owe it to me for the role I played. I never want that."

She tipped her head down, and her wet hair tickled his chest. Then she drew her hand from under his, running it up, up, past the seam of his trousers. She hooked his shirt with one finger and then pulled the fabric over his head.

"Don't be ridiculous, John," she said when she'd pulled the sleeves away from his wrists. "If we waited until we were married, you'd own the right to use my body. Now, I can say no."

She ran her hand down his bare chest, brushing his nipple. He gasped.

"And I can say yes," she whispered. "Not as a trade, not in compensation. Not because you deserve me."

"Why, then?"

"Because I deserve you." Her hand slid to the waistband of his trousers, and she gave a little laugh. "But you're going to have to help me from here, because I'm not sure what to do next."

"This," he said, and took her face in his hands and kissed her. He'd learned her mouth, her taste, over the last days. But he hadn't learned the feel of her skin, clammy at first against his, and then warming gradually. Her nipples were hard buds. Her hips pressed against the wet fabric of his trousers. He ran his hand down her body, cupping her breast.

She let out a sigh. "It's almost as if..."

"As if I loved you?" he whispered.

She nodded; he could feel her head move against his chest.

"There's a reason for that." His arms came around her, drawing her in. Pulling her close to his heart. He leaned down and pressed his lips to her neck, and for a few moments they swayed together in tandem.

"How can you be so warm," she asked, "when you're still in your wet clothing?"

"Blood flow." Indeed. His blood was flowing with great vigor. He should go to the other room, before his blood left him unable to do the right thing.

Instead, he ran his hands back up her ribs, chasing the remainder of the chill from her skin. He could scarcely see her in the dark, so he discovered her with his fingers—the arc of one hip; the swell of a breast. And she busied herself with him—first undoing his trousers, and then sliding them down. Her hands brushed his thighs, then slid up to touch his hard cock. Her fingers were tentative, so light that he gasped to keep from laughing.

"So warm," she repeated.

"Let me make you warmer."

He leaned down and caught the nub of her nipple between his lips. She heated soon enough under his inspection, her pebbled skin smoothing but her nipple staying hard to his touch. She let out a breath and arched against him.

"Blood flow," he repeated. "I think you could use more of it."

He'd wanted to taste her for so long. She smelled of sugar and citrus, but she tasted of cool rain and woman. He started with little nibbles at her breast. Then he licked his way to the hollow of her throat. A few kisses there, and she threw her head back and relaxed into his embrace.

He wasn't sure when, in the midst of her caresses and his exploration, they made their way to the bedchamber, or when he set her down on his covers. He wasn't even sure at what point she spread herself naked before him.

But he did vaguely recognize the moment when they passed from mere naked caresses into the act of intimacy: when he spread her legs, fell to the floor in front of her, and set his mouth on her sex. She tasted as good as he'd always imagined—sweet and sensual all at once. He parted her folds with his hands and took her more fully, exploring every bit of her, listening to the ebb and flow of her breath as he did.

The rhythm of her breathing altered as he touched her between her legs. And when it did, he licked where his fingers played, again and again, tasting her until her fists clenched in his hair and her hips arched into his face.

He could taste her pleasure, could feel the waves of her orgasm build up, waiting to break through.

"Yes," she said in a high drawn out cry. "John—don't stop. Don't st

He didn't. He took her over the crest, until her pleas lost all coherence, until they became cries of pleasure. It was the sweetest of sounds—that, and the slow return of rhythm to her breathing after.

She set her hands on his shoulders. "Don't stop," she said, and by the way she pulled at him, he knew she wasn't referring to what he might do with his tongue. "Don't stop."

There was nothing she could have asked him at that moment that he would have denied her. He slid on top of her. Her body was slicked with sweat, still shaking with pleasure. She shifted beneath him. He was so far into want that he was almost beyond thought. He pushed inside.

Tight. So tight. So *good*. And slick from the work he'd done already—she was beyond ready. She tensed only momentarily at his intrusion.

He stopped. "Does it hurt?"

"Only a little. But it also feels so, so right."

"And this?" He gave an experimental thrust.

"*Yes,*" she said. "Again."

"As you command." He kissed her throat and then thrust again.

"Yes," she whispered.

More encouragement than that he did not need. He let loose all his pent-up desire. The complexities of reality dissolved around them. He fit right where he was. Nothing mattered but that she was there, and she was his.

Her legs locked around him, drawing him in. And he took—took it all, the warmth of her body, the pleasure she gave him, the entirety of Mary beneath him.

"Christ," he swore. She was his. She was *his*. And then, with his crises upon him, he knew the truth. No. He was *hers*. He came hard, feeling it om head to toe, every last thrust overwhelming him.

Their hands were joined. Their breathing rose and fell together. For a ent, they were one.

n her breath caught. She moved; he disengaged, and like that, they one any longer, but two.

ns," she said. "That was…"

? Extraordinary? Perfect?

e said roughly, "was something we need to do again. Often. Maybe soon."

t a little laugh.

e suggested, "in five minutes."

She shifted underneath him. "Mmmm. Maybe. In a day."

"Then perhaps we can figure out how to marry between now and then." He folded his arms around her. "Marry me. I can't imagine sharing my life with anyone other than you."

She sighed next to him. "There's so much I need to say, so much I want to talk to you about. But we've come to a true understanding. I think—"

"Oh, bloody Christ," he said aloud, remembering everything.

She stopped. "What? What is it? Did you forget something?"

"Yes," he said bitterly. "I did." He sat up, reaching for a shirt. "I forgot to tell you that I am, in fact, a complete ass."

"I think I would have noticed, if you were." She sounded puzzled. But her fingers found his hand. "Come, John. After everything I've told you, surely you don't fear this."

He took a deep breath. "Do you recall when I said I wanted to be your friend? At the time, I intended nothing of the sort. I just wanted to make you feel comfortable enough to tell the truth." He set his head in his hands. "I lied to you. Worse." He couldn't stop himself. "I told you I was doing something for your benefit, when in truth I was doing it for me."

She didn't say anything. But he could feel her in the dark, bringing her knees up and hugging them for comfort. "That's quite a bit to take in." Her voice had lost the rough, pleased warmth of a few minutes ago. Her tone was cool. He could feel her withdrawing from him.

"I hurt you," he said. "I never meant to."

But that wasn't true either. There'd been a time when he was so angry, that he hadn't cared if his actions had hurt her. He tried again.

"I love you," he said. "That's not a lie. I should have said something before, but…well, I didn't."

It sounded wrong to his own ears.

"I can hardly hold it against you," she said slowly. "I was not alwa honest with you."

I don't love you. It still smarted that she'd been able to say that. That sh walked away once. He blew out his breath. "Do you mean about your fa or when you told me you didn't love me?"

There was a long pause. "I lied to you about my father," she said th

"Did you love me? Did you say you didn't at the end just to m leave you alone?" He wouldn't shout. He *wouldn't*. "Did you love me?"

"I don't know! At the time, I didn't even know who I was, or how I would survive. The last thing I could think about was whether I loved you."

"And what of your piano-playing? Why did you never mention that you'd given up the possibility of playing professionally, when you agreed to marry me?"

She shifted against him. "I might have. But I came home because I had a choice to make. There was the world my etiquette instructor described, a polite place where men and women quietly fell in love and had families. And then there was the harsh, solitary life my piano master showed me. I talked to a few truly dedicated female musicians, and they had nothing—no children, no sweethearts. Their only friends were their fellow musicians. I loved music, but it couldn't be my whole life. I didn't just want you. I wanted a normal, quiet life. I wanted to be just like the other girls."

"Is that what you want now? To be normal like the other girls?"

Her fingers drifted down his chest. "No." The word was soft, but he could feel her resolve filling her. "I couldn't fit in. And I no longer wish to do so."

So. That was that.

"This is," she said quietly, "perhaps not the best time to tell you that I have business elsewhere tomorrow?"

"Elsewhere? Where elsewhere?"

"London. I'll have to rise early to catch the train."

He swore. "I've three days yet before I can finish my work at Beauregard's. I suppose I can put it off—"

"I don't want you to come with me," she said, just as quietly. But her words had a gentle finality to them.

He pushed away from her. "Tell me, then. Tell me you don't love me. Tell me you can live without me. Don't leave me here to wonder for another few months if you'll be my wife."

The rain was still coming down hard, the wind driving it in gusts against the window.

"Dear," she said softly. "John, I intend to be so much more than your wife."

"More than my—"

Her hand sought his. "We can have so much more than that. You'll see," she said coaxingly.

"I only want the same chances you had." She reached out for his hand. "I want your quiet confidence. You set yourself impossible tasks and you solve them. By yourself. There's…there's one thing I need to put right. I want you to let me go, so I can do it. No—I *need* to know that you will let me go."

He wanted to refuse, to deny her. He wanted to pin her in place. But Sir Walter had put her in a cage for long enough. All he could do was watch her leave.

He felt hoarse, and he hadn't even been shouting. "You'll come back, after?"

Her only answer was to kiss his cheek—sweetly, not passionately, and to move away.

"Oh, no," he said. "I'll let you go—but not like that, Mary. Not like that." He set his hand on her shoulder and gently, oh so gently, turned her toward him.

I love you. He kissed the words into her lips. Her chin. Her neck.

I love you. The tip of her breast brushed his hands; her sigh of acceptance nearly undid him.

I love you. I love you. I love you.

Caress after caress bore those words. He swallowed the emotions he felt and gave them back to her as kisses. And perhaps she heard what he meant, because she stretched out beneath him. Her eyes were shut, her hair strewn across the pillow. She threw her head back, and the long column of her throat begged for his kisses.

I love you.

He kissed the hollow in her neck, the point of her chin. But when he made to kiss her lips, she turned away from him. He was losing her, and he had no way to hold on.

"I wish you every happiness," he whispered.

Even without me.

But he didn't say that last. He didn't dare.

Chapter Twelve

It took days before John finished the drainage work on Beauregard's farm and headed home. He felt bruised and weary. Even though his nightly walks had come to an end when Mary left, he had found himself unable to sleep. She had money this time. She would be well, wouldn't she?

Still, he vowed that if he didn't hear from her when he arrived back in Southampton, he would search her out, and this time, he wouldn't stop until he found her.

But there was no rest to be had when he arrived back at home. His sister met him at the railway station even though he hadn't given her any word about the precise day of his arrival.

"John," she said, waving madly at him from the platform.

"Elizabeth." He managed not to groan her name in greeting.

Don't ask me how it went.

"So," she said. There was a gleam in her eye—the kind of sisterly gleam that suggested that somehow, she was going to make his life miserable. "How did it all go?"

"Hmm," he said, warily.

"Never mind." She spoke swiftly. She always spoke swiftly. "There will be time for you to tell me everything later, and besides, I can already guess how went. I was sure you would be coming in today. Come now; we haven't ch time."

"Time for what?" he asked in befuddlement, but she was already ing away in front of him, gesturing to her waiting carriage.

followed after, feeling more than a little confused. A footman relieved is pair of valises and stored them in the boot. He had no choice but za in the carriage. But instead of setting off in the direction of his iver turned and headed toward the center of town.

ll me," she said, giving him a shake of her head. "When you saw , it took you three minutes to lose all hint of sternness and to ain."

. It took days, in fact."

ount it days too long."

an aggravated breath of air. "Yes, well. You've got the right of

She wagged her finger at him, but there was no real exasperation in the gesture.

"I asked her to marry me," he said. "And if I can find her, she might still say yes."

"*Might* say yes!" Eliza rolled her eyes. "You mean to tell me that you couldn't even get her to agree to that? Good God, John."

"I thought she'd had enough of people ordering her about."

His sister met his eyes, and she shook her head again. "In any event, I did say that there would be time for all that later. We've urgent business in town. I need you."

He sat up straighter. "What do you need me for?"

"I need you to be male," she said. "If you're not in the room, nobody will take us seriously. If they insist on talking to you, as they always do, direct them back to me, as I know what is going on."

"Are we talking to your banker again?" he asked dubiously.

"Something like that," she said, with a dismissive wave of her hand. "Ah, here we are!"

Her carriage drew up in front of a public house.

He'd been traveling by rail for the better part of the day, and it was already six in the evening. The sun was still out, but he was nonetheless exhausted. He was *not* in the mood for a beer and a friendly chat. But Eliza had always put him in mind of a tropical cyclone. If she touched land in the vicinity, one couldn't say no to her. She wouldn't even understand what the word meant.

She let him hand her out of the carriage, and then marched into the building. Apparently, they were expected; the proprietor took one look at the two of them, bowed, and escorted them to a back room.

"Who is here, so far?" Eliza asked.

"Just the lady who was here when you left earlier, ma'am."

"Good," Eliza said. And she swept into the room as the man opened door.

John followed. He took two steps into the private chamber, stopping completely. He hadn't known what to expect—he'd suppose he was here to act as mediator in some dispute with Eliza's neighbor smooth the way for Eliza with the banker.

But Mary was sitting at the table in front of him. She was wearing gown—a blue satin that brought out the gray of her eyes. He simpl unable to say anything. Unable to even step forward and take her in his arms. All he could do was *want,* and that more deeply than he had ever done.

Eliza swept up to her, as if finding her here after an absence of a year and a half was hardly a surprise, and kissed her on the cheek.

Mary's pale hair was bound up into a pretty little chignon, complete with curls; she returned Eliza's kiss, and then looked over at John. And then, little minx, she winked at him.

"You," he said stupidly. "Do you know how I've worried about you?"

Her eyes sparkled in response. *Sparkled* was the wrong word for it. Sparkling made him think of candlelight glinting off silver—all shine, no depth. Her eyes put him in mind of moonlight reflecting off a deep lake. All that brilliant luster, reflected from untold deeps.

"Miss Chartley has been telling me quite the tale," his sister said.

"She's right," John said swiftly. "I believe her implicitly. Because she's right. And because it's logical—because it's the only explanation that makes sense of the available evidence. I'm not merely saying that because I—"

Because I want to get her in bed. Because I have to have her in my life. Because I can't bear to have her leave me again.

Beside him, Eliza shook her head. "Goodness," she said. "Could you babble any more, John?"

Mary smiled more broadly, and something in the vicinity of his chest acked. His heart, maybe, or his lungs. All his internal organs. He reached to take her hand.

Eliza smacked his wrist with her fan so hard that it stung. "Behave lf, John," she admonished. "Spare my nerves and save your lovemaking n I am not present. As I was saying, Miss Chartley has told me g." She gave a sniff.

recisely *everything,* I hope." If she had, Eliza might well have n rather lower than his hand.

o me for five minutes," his sister said. "Five minutes. This is are to sit quietly, act like a hulking male, and observe." She air at the head of the table, and John sat.

im a sharp nod.

hn said, "I know it appears that my sister is browbeating me. can stand up to her. It's just easier to let her think she's for the things that don't matter."

Eliza stuck out her tongue at him. "Fiddlesticks. You listen to me because I'm right. I always am."

John thumbed his nose at her; she smiled back cordially.

"There," Eliza said, turning to Mary. "That is how one handles him. You can thank me for the lesson later."

Mary shook her head and smiled. "Perhaps, but I think I'd prefer less sisterly methods."

The two women held each others' gazes for a long moment. And that was when John realized there was no tension in their exchange. Mary's father had stolen Eliza's son's inheritance. Eliza should have been on the verge of tearing her hair out, or screaming imprecations. Instead, the two were sitting at a table together and exchanging meaningful glances.

Something had happened. His sister and the love of his life were in league with one another. And that made him feel... Befuddled. Amazed. Delighted. And very, very afraid. He'd wondered how to convince Eliza to be polite; now he was yearning to be a part of whatever it was they had planned.

Eliza sniffed. "We've distracted ourselves. The substance of the matter, John, is that Miss Chartley has brought the most unimaginable—"

But she didn't get to finish her sentence. The door opened behind them, and two men entered the room.

It had been a few months since John had last seen Mr. Frost and Mr. Lawson, the other partners. They swept in.

"Mr. Mason. Mrs. Tallant." That last with a nod in the direction of his sister, but they scarcely glanced at the women sitting at the table.

John stood and shook their hands; behind their backs, Eliza made a face.

"What's this all about?" Lawson asked. "You'd think, Mason, that you might give us more than twenty-four hours before calling an urgent meeting."

John glanced at his sister and Mary, but they both sat at the table, looking on with silent interest. Apparently, the introductions were to be left to him. If only he knew what he was introducing.

"Thank you for coming on such short notice," he improvised. "We've just received some, uh, some information." Safe enough. "We thought it would be of interest to you gentlemen."

"This is about the partnership, yes?" Lawson sighed, and brushed past him to pull out a seat from the table. "Don't tell me you've managed to track down Chartley's bitch of a daughter." He sat—and only then realized that the women sitting at the table were not, as he'd supposed, Mrs. Elizabeth Tallant and a servant, but Mrs. Tallant and…

He sat back and coughed heavily.

"Yes," Mary said calmly. "Mr. Mason did find—how did you put it?—Chartley's bitch of a daughter."

Lawson flinched at her wording. But John knew that light in her eyes. It was the way she'd looked when she'd given him Lady Northword's earring. If ever she'd directed that look at him, he'd have run screaming for his life.

"As it turns out, gentlemen, I had something in my possession that I believe will shed some light on a few things." She undid a clasp on a large brown envelope and pulled out a few pages—frayed along the folds, well-inked, and charred on the edges.

"These are the pages that were missing from my father's account book," she said. "As the book I sent earlier documented, some eight thousand pounds were taken over a period of four years. This shows the final withdrawals from the account where my father kept them: around two thousand pounds. Leaving a balance, on the day of his death, of five thousand, nine hundred and sixty-seven guineas."

John's heart began to pound. They'd told him the account had eight hundred pounds in it—eight *hundred,* not almost six thousand.

Lawson, who hadn't seated himself, snorted dismissively. "Surely you aren't trusting to the accounting of a thief—and a document held by a liar."

"No," Mary said calmly. "He doesn't need to trust me." She passed over another sheet of paper. "This is a copy of the account balances and withdrawals, certified by Mr. Waring, the bank director. According to this, the balance—which precisely matches my father's figures, once one accounts for the interest that was paid in—was withdrawn two weeks after my father's death, by Mr. Frost on behalf of the partnership."

Silence. She was beautiful in her triumph, so beautiful. John held his breath, waiting to see what Frost would say to that accusation.

"Lies," Frost breathed.

Lawson didn't move.

"And this," Mary continued, "is an accounting of what was done with those funds. They were rolled over into a new account on behalf of the partnership again. Don't you find it odd, Mr. Mason, that the partnership has had an entire new account, and that neither you nor your sister were told about it? It's nice to know that the partnership has finally begun to prosper.

Over the last year, they've managed a thirty-five percent profit. Extremely handsome."

John took the pages and ruffled through them. "Thirty-five percent profit, it seems, *after* the distributions made to Frost and Lawson. More than that before." The silence stretched.

"How did you get this?" Lawson's voice was hoarse.

Now, John supposed, was the time for him to start being—how had his sister put it?—a hulking male. He leaned over the table and fixed the men with a glare. "Did you think you would get away with this forever?"

"An oversight," Frost said, coughing into his fist. "Purely an oversight, I assure you—the paperwork must have been, ah…misplaced. There will be no more mishaps like this, now that you've brought the matter to our attention."

"No," John said. "There won't."

Eliza hadn't spoken the entire time. But she raised her chin now and glared at the gentlemen. "You lot should be convicted and beaten about the square," she said passionately. "I can only think about how I've worried this last year. An *oversight*. It was nothing of the kind. You saw your chance to make a profit after a sad bit of business, and you took it. At my son's expense. I will see you publicly brought down."

"Now, now, Mrs. Tallant."

John could have told the man that condescending conciliation would only make matters worse.

Eliza stood, slapping her gloves against the table. "Don't you take that tone with me, sir. You stole from a widow and a seven-year-old child. You ought to be ashamed of yourselves."

"No need to make a fuss," Frost said. "It's been a dreadful ordeal. I think this all demonstrates that it's more than past time to liquidate the partnership and divide the proceeds—taking into account, of course, the amounts that we have already—I mean, that have already been paid to some parties. To the third owed to you, Mrs. Tallant, I should like to put in an additional five hundred pounds—for your trouble."

"And from mine," Lawson added hastily.

"You think you can buy me off with mere money, when I've scarcely been able to concentrate? When I couldn't even eat, for wondering what would become of my son?"

Now John knew that Elizabeth was acting. The day his sister stopped eating would be an alarming day indeed.

"Seven hundred pounds," Frost said uneasily, glancing at his partner, who nodded.

"I won't have my father's—my husband's—memory so despoiled," she said. "Their spirits cry out for *vengeance,* not compensation!"

"A thousand pounds from each of us," Lawson said, looking green. "And that little strip of land near your husband's house—the one he always wanted to buy? I'll give you that, too." He licked his lips. "And that will leave Frost and I far the worse off."

"Come now," John said to Elizabeth, "don't you think a thousand pounds each is enough to pay for their sins? After all, it was only a little embezzlement."

"My nerves," Elizabeth moaned, which nearly set him off laughing. His sister had nerves of steel. "I can't be sure. What…oh, John, what do you think that this means? I don't think I can sort it out myself. Perhaps we ought to call the constable, and have him figure out the best way to proceed."

"Twelve hundred each," Lawson said immediately, while Frost nodded vigorously beside him.

Eliza sniffed.

"We're dreadfully sorry," Frost put in. "More sorry than you can know." He licked his lips, looking calculating rather than sorry. "And if you're looking for revenge, do think about what this will mean to the both of us. After our deductions, we'll take just two thousand pounds apiece—when we put in that much five years ago. We'll barely be getting out with our capital intact."

Mary stirred on the other side of the table. "Really, Frost. How do you figure that? As I do the math, the partnership owns seventy-five hundred in assets, and there have been three thousand, five hundred in unauthorized deductions."

Mr. Frost was only just beginning to frown. But John already knew where Mary was headed.

"Plus the proceeds of last year's sale," John continued on. "Don't forget those."

"Divided four ways," Mary said, "and you'll be taking a lot less than two thousand pounds a piece."

"Four ways!" Lawson said. "You can't mean to suggest…"

"It is not a suggestion," Mary said. "You're forgetting—how did you put it? Yes. You're forgetting about Chartley's bitch of a daughter. You thought you'd be safe from accusations of theft if you lodged the account in the name of the partnership. How do you suppose I got the bank to provide me with such detailed information? My father was never removed as partner, and I inherited his share on his death. The bank gave my solicitor the accounting because I am legally part owner." She set her hands flat on the table. "Legally speaking," she said, "you stole from me, too."

"Yes," Mr. Lawson said, his voice beginning to shake. "Divided four ways. Of course. And you'll accept, ah, an equal share." He looked almost green.

Perhaps this was what the ladies had been waiting for—for these two criminals to offer them everything. They exchanged glances.

"Shall we accept?" Eliza said. "They certainly could not offer us any more."

"That's true," Mary said. "And yet something in me revolts at the prospect. It doesn't seem right, if we let them go and they then proceed to do some other unsuspecting folks out of their fair share by unscrupulous means."

Mr. Lawson and Mr. Frost stood at once, looking about the room in terror.

Mary brushed off her hands. "After all, the court will divide the proceeds. I'm sure it will do a fair job of it—and I don't ask for more than fairness."

"John," Eliza said, "do poke your head outside the door and see if the constables have arrived yet."

John stood and opened the door. "Ah," he said. "What a coincidence. Here they are."

THE NEXT HALF-HOUR SEEMED TO PASS IN A WHIRL. John made angry, accusatory noises when the constables entered the room, and Lawson and Frost were brought in on charges of theft and fraud. Eliza watched them go with a nod of sharp self-satisfaction. When they'd been conveyed to prison for the evening, Eliza offered her arm to Mary.

John watched in horror. "Wait," he said. "Where are you two going?"

Eliza turned and cast him a glance over her shoulder. "I'm taking her home with me," she said, as if he should have guessed this. "If you should like to come to supper, you're invited."

"But—"

"Come, Mary," Eliza said.

But Mary didn't move. She was looking at him—simply looking, but her eyes glistened.

"You can't go with him," Eliza said, rolling her eyes. "Everyone will see you, and they will all talk. There will be enough talk to get over as it is."

"Eliza," John said, "that's enough. I'll take her to wherever it is that she's staying."

"With me."

"Good. Then it's scarcely a mile. We'll walk. In public. Nothing untoward about that."

"But—"

John folded his arms and looked at her. He simply looked—and she sighed, shaking her head, and stalked away.

That left the room at the public house empty except for the two of them. It was hardly private. They could hear the other guests in the main room, and the maids went past the door every few minutes. Still, for the moment, they were free from prying eyes. John walked up to Mary. He didn't know what to say. She was here in Southampton…but then, she'd had business with Frost and Lawson. Perhaps she'd come only for that.

She was looking up at him, her eyes so clear and guileless that he didn't know what to make of her.

And then, she stood on her tiptoes, set her hands on his shoulders, and kissed him so hard that he staggered back a pace and had to reach out a hand to steady himself against a wall. One breath to get his wits; the other to regain his balance, and a third to kiss her back as she deserved.

"Thank God," he murmured against her lips. "I don't know what I would have done without you. Promise you'll let me make you into a respectable married lady."

"No," she said passionately, still kissing him. "Never."

"Mary." He pulled away from her, but she was smiling. She didn't look as if she were refusing to marry him, and so he held out a hand to her.

She placed her fingers against his palm. "Not a lady," she said. "A lady wouldn't have gone to London and discovered the circumstances of the money. A lady doesn't plot to help women get divorces. A lady doesn't force her employer to pay wages by enlisting the help of a viscountess. I'll never be a lady." She smiled, and squeezed his hand. "I think…I rather think I'm something better."

He pulled on her hand. "And the rest of it?"

"I'm afraid I won't help you with the respectable part, either. There was my precipitate departure from town. With Frost and Lawson going to trial, the details of my father's embezzlement will come to light. And if that isn't bad enough, before you arrived, I inquired at the public assembly hall. They've officially asked me to play the pianoforte. And"—This last came out quite defiantly—"They're going to pay me two guineas a month."

"I see." But he didn't. He was even more puzzled.

"I'm officially going to be paid for my labor. And I don't intend to limit myself to playing at assemblies. That's just a start. Respectable married ladies do not do such things, and so I refuse to be a respectable married lady."

She hadn't let go of him.

"I see," he said again, with perhaps a little more understanding this time. "But that leaves *married*. What of that?"

"I will never be just your wife."

"Why would you, when you have so much more you could be?"

He'd wanted her the moment he saw her. But the way he felt now, he was beyond want. She wouldn't just be a beautiful possession to trot out to prove his luck to other fellows. Mary was more than a pretty picture to hang upon the wall and gaze at lovingly.

She was going to do amazing things. And he was going to help her do them.

"There's only one way to be respectable." She leaned her head against him. "But there are so, so many ways to be married. I think we'll find a thousand variations on a theme of marriage, John. All of them magnificent. I love you. I love you. I love you."

He kissed her, long and slow. And because that wasn't enough, he kissed her a second time, and a third, and more, until he lost count of all their kisses, until a maid came into the room to clear away the dishes and gasped out loud at the sight.

And just to be sure that they'd caused a scandal, he kissed her again.

Epilogue

Forty years later, on the road to Doyle's Grange

THE EXMOOR HILLS SHIMMERED ON THE HORIZON, indistinct in the morning haze.

It had not been so much of a struggle to climb the hill to Doyle's Grange all those years ago. Now, Mary could feel the strain in her back, her hips. Nothing uncommon, just age taking its usual toll. But then, what age took, age returned. There was no need to hurry now. Doyle's Grange wasn't going anywhere, and they had all the time they wished to explore. She stopped at the rise just before the path dipped into the windbreak and turned to look around.

John squeezed her hand in his. "I'm not going too fast for you, am I?"

"No. Just my back again."

They'd walked more than a mile from the railway station, but she hadn't really felt the exercise until they'd reached the hill.

"That's a shame." He set his arm around her waist and pressed his fingers into the small of her back. After all these years, he didn't need to ask where it hurt. He simple rubbed his thumb in a circle right where the tension had gathered, pushing lightly until the gathered pain began to dissipate.

"That's nice," she said. "It's quiet here."

In comparison, it was. There were no trolley cars, no sellers hawking oranges or flowers. There was only a farmer plowing a field off in the distance and a kestrel circling overhead. It was louder than it once had been—there'd been an actual stand of cabs waiting at West Aubrey—but still quiet.

"Quiet is nice." John smiled. "For now. It'll be loud enough, once we're in Vienna."

"It's different. Not the way I remember it."

She didn't remember it being so *bright*, for one. The spring air had only a hint of a bite to it. It was too quiet here, too quiet at home. Caroline,

George, and Jacob were long since out of the house. Even Caroline's children were off at school. Aside from a few last students, Mary had too little to do. So when John had suggested that they retrace their most important moments together as a second honeymoon, she'd jumped at the chance.

"Ready?" he asked.

Maybe he was asking about her back. Or maybe...

This, the first portion of their journey, was the only part she'd fretted over. Doyle's Grange brought to mind a darker time, one she'd been glad to leave behind her. She feared that visiting this place again would bring back all those long-settled memories. But she shrugged and started up the hill again.

She wasn't sure what she'd expected to see when she came through the trees. Doyle's Grange was the same—and yet so different. Someone had planted a hedge of shiny green leaves between the house and the lane. The drab front shrubberies had been torn out and replaced with beds of dark soil, sprouting the green beginnings of spring flowers. And in the meadows that surrounded the property, growing amidst the new grass, were crocuses—thousands of them.

And then she heard a sound—a shriek; not one of horror or pain, but a child's excited squeal.

"You can't catch me!" someone taunted. Another shriek, and the taunter tore into view, dashing across the road and into the tall grass across the way.

"Hyacinth!" came the return shriek, from far off. "You had better hide well."

She and John exchanged amused looks.

"Well," Mary said with a sigh, "you were right, after all."

"About what?"

"I've got forty good years behind me. *This*—" she waved her hand at the cottage "—this is nothing in comparison. I'm bigger than it now."

He smiled. "You always were."

This place wasn't a box, to hold her worst memories. It was only a bright, sunlit house—a place of happiness for a new generation.

And the last forty years had brought quite a bit of happiness. From here, they'd go on to London. With the money Mary had recovered from the partnership, they'd spent a few months of their first winters there. She had played in salons, enough to get her name out. From London, they'd move on to Vienna. She'd never played at the grandest halls—living in Vienna only during the winters, when the farm was quiet, had restricted her choices—but she was the only musician she knew whose husband never missed a performance.

There had been no professional reason to visit Paris, which made those few weeks in 1870 all the more memorable. She was looking forward to seeing that new tower they'd erected. After a week *there,* they had passage on a steamer to Boston—that was where John had displayed his new, more efficient water turbine, the one that had truly secured their future.

It had been a good life.

She took his hand again, and together, they started down the hill. Halfway to the station, though, she heard a noise—a faint little whimper, so high-pitched that she almost didn't hear it.

"What's that?" she said.

John shrugged. "What?"

She listened, turning her head to one side. "That noise—there it is again."

"I don't hear anything."

Mary shrugged this off. Likely, the noise was too high for his ears. He couldn't hear half the notes on the upper register of her piano anymore. She turned to the side of the road and rustled through the early summer foliage of the hedge.

"I knew I heard something!" she said, leaning down and moving branches aside.

"What is it?" He had come up behind her.

It was a dirty burlap sack, the end tied in a knot. Under the fabric, something moved.

"Oh, no." Mindless of the branches that snagged her sleeves, she reached in. Her fingers closed around the edge, barely gripping, and then yanked the burden high—eliciting a high-pitched *yip* from the residents of the sack. She sank to the ground. Her fingers tore into the knot, her hands shaking.

And when the sack was opened—

"Oh, John." She'd scraped her arms rescuing the bag. But she could scarcely feel those scratches for the feeling that almost overwhelmed her. The bag contained two tiny puppies—tawny all over, barely palm-sized, their eyes still creased closed.

"Oh little ones," she crooned. "Who would do this to you? We'll have to get you something to eat. John?"

He was looking at her with a small smile on his face.

Maybe another man would remind her of the expensive hotel that awaited them in Vienna, or the long voyage to America that would follow. Another man might have mentioned that puppies needed to be trained, or he might have made noises about needing his sleep at night.

John simply smiled. "Well. I guess it's not going to be quiet any longer."

Mary hugged the puppies to her and stood. She had forty good years behind her—a life that anyone would be lucky to live. Was it selfish to be glad that it still felt like the beginning?

"I wonder who's at Beauregard's farm now?" he said. "I think they'll have milk."

John put his arm around her and she snuggled up against him.

"I think," she said, "I'm going to need another forty years of you."

A Dance in Moonlight

SHERRY THOMAS

Chapter One

Summer 1896, Somerset, a few miles south of the Exmoor hills

THE WOMAN WAS BACK.

Ralston Fitzwilliam had seen her once before, two days ago. He had been on the tail-end of a fourteen mile walk, up and down hills so gentle they were barely bumps in the ground, across rain-swollen streams, and alongside green, sheep-dotted pastures.

Given that dark rain clouds, so low he could almost touch them, had crowded the sky from horizon to horizon, he should have gone straight home to Stanton House, set at his disposal by the Duke of Perrin for the few weeks a year Ralston spent in England. But the walk had not been sufficiently tiring for a man who wanted his limbs aching and his mind blank, so he had traversed Beauregard's farm and headed up the slope at the top of which sat Viscount Northword's country seat.

Only to have the rain come down hard halfway uphill. He veered toward Doyle's Grange, a smaller property of the Northword estate. It was vacant at present, and he could take shelter under its ivy-covered portico without being fussed over and lectured about the foolishness of being abroad in such weather, without even an umbrella. As he approached the garden gate behind the house, she had appeared on the garden path, a young widow all in black.

She was beautiful—tall, regal, her hair as dark as the beads of jet that trimmed her hat. But what had truly caught his eye was the story of her life that had been written on her otherwise exquisite face.

It had not been the easiest of lives. There was an air of fragility to her—not an inborn timidity, but the residual fear of someone who had been burnt by the vagaries of fate.

He recognized himself—as he had been for many years, and perhaps even as he was now.

She hurried into the house without noticing him. But he thought of her as he waited out the rain beneath the eaves of the garden shed, for the entirety of his walk home, and when he extinguished his light at night.

He called on Doyle's Grange the next day, but the front gate was locked, the house shut tight.

And now here she was again, a lovely, somber silhouette in the waning light of a summer evening, stepping down from a hansom cab, a satchel in hand. His heart leaped until he realized that the hansom cab, parked on the country lane before the blooming rhododendron hedge, did not leave. It was waiting for her to come out from the house and would ferry her elsewhere.

He hesitated. But before long, he found himself slipping into the front gate and walking up the drive. A movement of an upstairs curtain caught his eye—he had been sighted. Under the portico, as he raised his hand toward the bell pull, the door flung open, and she launched herself into his arms.

He was over six feet in height and sturdy of build. But she was at least five foot nine and no skeleton. He stumbled back a step.

Before he could quite recover from his surprise, she gripped his face and kissed him.

He'd kissed women to whom he hadn't been properly introduced, but never before he'd uttered so much as a greeting. She was ravenous, almost barbarous, as if she wanted to level him to the ground and lay waste to him.

The next moment her kiss turned tender. Now she was kissing her beloved, thought to be lost on the battlefield, but found alive and well, needing only to be cared for and cherished. Her fingers, which had been digging hard into the sides of his head, relaxed. Her body fitted itself to his. And he, who'd until now been largely stunned, wondering how to disentangle himself without giving offense, was suddenly caught in the kiss.

She smelled of roses. Not the smothering scent he'd encountered at times, as if he'd been stuffed inside a perfume bottle, but light and fresh, like a single petal held beneath the nostrils. Her cheek beneath his hand was wondrously soft. And her body was all velvet—her mourning gown was made of the stuff—plush, smooth, sensational.

"Oh, Fitz," she murmured, her arms banding tighter about him. "My darling Fitz."

His nickname at school had been Bosh—he liked to roll his eyes and say "bosh" when his mates sprouted nonsense. But he supposed one could call him Fitz, short for Fitzwilliam. Which raised the question, who was she?

Where had he met her before that she considered their acquaintance to merit such a passionate kiss at this reunion? And if indeed they knew each other so well, how was it that he did not have the least recollection of her?

But that was for later. For now, he pulled her closer and kissed her back.

ISABELLE ENGLEWOOD ALMOST COULD NOT WITHSTAND the wild burst of joy in her heart. Her Fitz, her beautiful, beloved Fitz. He had realized his mistake and returned to her at last.

He smelled wonderful—but different, of cedar and bergamot, with the faintest underpinning of oriental spices. And he was more substantial than she remembered—good, she preferred a little more meat on his bones. And how she loved the way he kissed her, with a gentleness that nevertheless scorched.

Since her return to England, he'd been reticent to be physically close to her. But not anymore. Now he was unhesitating. Now he was hungry.

As was she. She'd been dreaming of this moment. It had been more than eighteen months since she'd lain with a man, more than a decade since she understood that she wanted to wake up next to him every morning of her life.

She broke the kiss when she could no longer breathe. Locking her fingers together behind his neck, she rested her head against his shoulder and panted, all the while pressing kisses into his cheek and jaw.

At last he was hers to have and to hold. To love and to cherish. Tears welled in her eyes, but she did not care; it had been far too long since she'd wept tears of happiness.

Happiness, what an alien sensation.

She nibbled him just above his collar, and the sound that emerged from his throat was full of suppressed desire. And his body—she could feel his *un*suppressed desire against her, making her giddy even as a tear escaped the corner of her eye.

She smiled. And giggled—she loved being dizzy with hope.

"Let's go inside," she said, reaching up to touch his hair. "But let me dismiss the cabbie first, before he begins to wonder what…"

She forgot what else she was about to say. The hair beneath her finger was brown, with perhaps the slightest reddish tint. Fitz's hair was not brown; it was black, like her own. Not to mention when she last saw him, this very morning, his hair had been at least two inches shorter.

Dazed, she looked up into his eyes. "What happened to your—"

The eyes that gazed back at her were green. *Green.* A man could conceivably dye his hair—or put on a wig. But how did he change the color of his eyes?

She leaped back from him. "You are not Fitz. Who are you?"

A SIMPLE CASE OF MISTAKEN IDENTITY.

Which would have been rather funny, a woman kissing the wrong man, if she did not look so shattered.

She stared at him as if he were a piece of art for which she'd bartered all her worldly possessions, only to realize that he was but a forgery, an inferior copy of what she truly wanted. She blinked furiously, then, forgetting—or perhaps no longer caring—that she'd asked for his identity, she turned her back to him and reached for the door of the house.

"Mrs. Englewood," he blurted out.

He'd spoken to the estate agent who had overseen the letting of Doyle's Grange. He knew her name. He knew that she was the mother of two young children. He knew that she had lost her husband, a cavalry officer, in India.

"My apologies, Mrs. Englewood. I did not mean to…disrupt your evening. My name is Fitzwilliam and I live nearby. I was informed that you have taken Doyle's Grange and hoped to make your acquaintance."

The breath she took was audible. Stiffly, she turned her head enough to look at him. "I should apologize to you, Mr. Fitzwilliam. The mistake and the responsibility were both mine."

For years, whenever he'd sought company, he'd made sure he singled out those who were carefree and lighthearted. Or at least, those who were as *determined* to be carefree and lighthearted as he, so that all his social interactions were characterized by a resolute cheerfulness. He did not quite understand why Mrs. Englewood, who made no effort to be jaunty and breezy, and whose pain was as unmistakable as her mourning gown, should exert such a pull upon him.

But he could not look away from her, this woman who did not hide her heartbreak. Who had perhaps never considered concealing her desolation beneath a frenzy of merrymaking.

"Clearly I have come at an inconvenient time," he said, staring at her sharp profile. "I shall wish you a good evening and take my leave. But will you allow me to call on you again, perhaps next week?"

She bit her lower lip. "You are very kind, sir. But I will not be here next week. In fact, I plan to never come back again."

Then he would never know her story. The thud of dismay he felt was out of all proportion with their negligible acquaintance. "But I understand you have signed a lease for an entire year."

"So I have." She briefly closed her eyes, as if the mention of the lease caused her actual pain. "But the lease only stipulates payment, not my presence."

"I hope I have not contributed to—"

"No. No, indeed, sir. My mind was made up this morning. I came back to retrieve a personal belonging, that is all."

Her hand opened and closed. It was obvious she wanted to be far from him, far from this house. He should be gentlemanly and understanding. Should immediately make himself scarce.

But he did not want to make himself scarce. He wanted to know what had made her kiss him with such devotion—and what made her unable to even look at him anymore. "If I may be so forward, Mrs. Englewood, did you change your mind, however momentarily, when you thought I was someone else?"

She jerked, as if he had slapped her, and turned away. "Good evening, Mr. Fitzwilliam."

He'd already overstepped the bounds; what did it matter if he were to say something even more hugely inappropriate? "If it pleases you, Mrs. Englewood, you are more than welcome to call me Fitz."

ISABELLE SPUN AROUND, HER THROAT BURNING WITH ANGER. But at the sight of Mr. Fitzwilliam, she forgot what she was about to say. Even knowing that he was not Fitz, that he was but a stranger who bore an uncanny resemblance to the man she loved, it took a superhuman effort not to once more throw herself into his arms.

She turned her face to the side. It was easier when she didn't look at him directly. "You do not know who Fitz is or what he means to me. Nor do you have the least idea how cruelly fate has already mocked me. To you I am but a chance for a dalliance, the possibility of one night's pleasure—my acceptance would mean little to you, my refusal even less. So no, it does not please me to call you Fitz, as dear a name as I have ever known. And I would be forever grateful if I am never to see you again."

She waited a few heartbeats for him to leave. When he did not, she reached for the door.

"I do have some idea how cruelly fate has mocked you, Mrs. Englewood—your anguish is writ plain on your face," came his answer, in a deep, slightly gravelly voice that thankfully did not sound like Fitz's at all. "I won't deny that I also find you beautiful and that my thoughts may have occasionally turned amorous. But I am far more interested in your story than in your body, if that is what offends you."

Wasn't it enough she had already *lived* her life? She had no interest in recounting her sorry tale to anyone, least of all a man she was constantly on the verge of mistaking for Fitz.

"Goodbye, Mr. Fitzwilliam."

She entered the house and shut the door firmly in his face. Then she sagged against the doorframe, her face numb with pain. She understood in her very marrow that life was cruel. This, however, was cruelty beyond even what she could endure.

She had lost Fitz the first time when she was eighteen, tears streaming down her face, watching him marry an heiress he barely knew, because a distant cousin's death had saddled him with a title and a bankrupt estate. She had lost him a second time only hours ago, when he'd told her that he could not see himself living in this charming house with her, because he had, after eight years of marriage, fallen deeply in love with his heiress wife.

And now she had to lose him a third time when God saw fit to set in her path a man who looked almost exactly like him but—

Something struck her with the force of a thunderbolt: God had seen fit to set in her path *a man who looked almost exactly like Fitz.*

And she had been too stupid to understand what a gift it was.

Cursing herself, she lifted her skirts, ran up the stairs, and skidded to a stop before the sitting room window. Mr. Fitzwilliam had not yet vacated the property, but he was near the gate, passing through the long shadows cast by a line of pine trees.

Night was falling. She could not tell the exact color of his hair, except that it was darkish and noticeably longer than Fitz's, which she did not mind. Fitz possessed a beautiful bone structure that would have carried off longer hair with poetic ease—but he never had because he was old-fashioned that way, always preferring his hair trimmed short.

Mr. Fitzwilliam reached up to pluck a pine needle. His motion was easy and graceful, like Fitz's. His height was almost identical to Fitz's. And though in her arms he'd felt more substantial, viewed as a whole he was far from bulky: wide shoulders, trim waist, and long limbs.

As if sensing her gaze, he glanced up over his shoulder. Her heart roared in her chest. Fitz, her dear, dear Fitz who had lingered beneath her window all those years ago, waiting for a glimpse of her, except he would pretend to be examining something in the garden, as if her mother's rather scraggly rosebushes could sustain the interest of a young man with no particular fondness for horticulture.

How she'd loved holding herself flat against the wall and spying on him, to count how many times he looked up from his supposed botanical study to scan her window. Seven, eight, nine. She usually rewarded him after the tenth time by opening her window, leaning out, and calling his name.

Before she quite knew what she was doing, she opened the window, leaned out, and shouted, "Wait! Wait!"

Chapter Two

RALSTON COULD ALMOST HEAR THE POUNDING of his heart in his ears.

She ran toward him, stopping bare inches away, her breaths audibly uneven in the quiet country twilight. Soon it would be too dark to make out her features, but for now her eyes shone with a wild, almost ferocious light. "Mr. Fitzwilliam, are you married?"

He blinked. "No, I am not."

"Are you promised to anyone, explicitly or implicitly?"

"No."

She exhaled, as if in relief, only to tense again the next moment. He tensed too, a long breath held. He could not predict in what direction her questions were headed. Or perhaps he could and he was not quite ready for it yet.

She looked down. In the last remaining rays of the day, her lashes cast shadows over her cheeks. She licked her lips. And suddenly he thought of their kiss, the heat and urgency of it, the willingness of her body against his.

"You said I was welcome to call you Fitz, Mr. Fitzwilliam," she said, her gaze somewhere to the left of him. "I can't do any such thing, unless—unless you agree to pass for him."

Somehow he managed not to exclaim aloud, though shock jolted through him. "Do I look that much like him?"

"The resemblance is uncanny, except for your coloring and your voice. If you remain silent and stay away from strong light, it would require no effort at all for me to believe that you are him."

"I see," he said slowly.

He'd expected something, but this was far beyond what he could have imagined.

She still did not look at him directly. "If you are willing to assume the role, then come back here at ten o'clock. I'll leave the front door unlocked. I'm sure you can find your way to my room."

Had she been a different woman, had the occasion been trivial and frivolous, he might have agreed, in exchange for a new, interesting experience. But reducing himself to a jointed dummy for her to pose and fondle when he wished to… He didn't know exactly what he wanted, but it was not becoming a mindless substitution.

"If you are against the idea"—her voice caught—"you have but to walk away and I will never trouble you again. If not, you have also but to walk away—and dismiss the hansom cab on your way out. I've already paid the cabbie for the wait."

Ralston could just see the very rear of the hansom cab from where he stood. He should bow, walk out of the gate, and go home, leaving her to deal with the cabbie and her mad desires.

And never see her again.

Silence escalated. Her fingers clasped tightly together. She stole a peek at him, then glanced away just as quickly, almost as if she could not bear the sight of him.

The cabbie's horse snorted. A breeze rustled the pine needles overhead. Somewhere deeper in the gardens, a bird took flight, the flapping of its wings startling her.

"Before I can consider your request, Mrs. Englewood," he heard himself say, "I need to ask you a few questions in return."

Mr. Fitzwilliam's first question Isabelle could guess. "Fitz is the man I would have married, had he not inherited a bankrupt earldom that required him to marry an heiress instead."

His brow lifted slightly. "You speak of Earl Fitzhugh?"

The dissonance of Fitz's face and another man's voice still flummoxed her, even more so when that voice brought up his name. "Do you know him?"

"Not personally. But I'd heard talk—his seat is not that far from here."

Doyle's Grange's proximity to Henley Park, Fitz's estate, had been one of the reasons she'd chosen the place.

"It must have been a number of years since Lord Fitzhugh married his heiress," Mr. Fitzwilliam went on. "Does it still matter so much to you?"

She took a deep breath to steady herself. "I came back from India not long ago. Fitz and his wife had always lived in a platonic marriage. So when he and I met again, for the first time in eight years, we decided that we would pick up our old dreams where they had fallen apart."

How she missed those first sweet moments of their reunion, when everything—the sun, the moon, entire constellations—had appeared not only possible, plausible, or probable, but absolutely, staggeringly certain.

Ironclad.

But soon Fitz's conviction had begun to waver. He never said anything to the effect, but she'd sensed, increasingly, that his mind was not so much on her as on the girl he'd married most unwillingly eight years ago. During Isabelle's long absence, he and his wife had grown close—much too close.

It was stupid to sign the lease for Doyle's Grange without first having his firm agreement, but as Isabelle's vision of happiness slid from her grasp, she'd needed to do something. And securing the house had felt like a solid something.

She wanted desperately to believe that Fitz would be utterly charmed by the rhododendron hedge, the gate with its whimsical wrought-iron carvings, and the garden full of blooming pinks and delphiniums. And when he roamed the bright and comfortable rooms of the house, he would instantly feel at home—the home they would have made together, had life not intervened eight years ago.

But as he walked through Doyle's Grange this morning, he had regarded the property not with the dreaminess of a man about to embark on a new chapter in life, but with the solemn ruefulness of one coming to the conclusion that he had been reading the wrong book altogether.

Can you picture yourself here? she'd asked, holding on to one last shred of hope.

I'm sorry, Isabelle, but I picture myself elsewhere, he had answered gently, but his words had been daggers in her lungs.

The corners of her lips had quivered. *You mean you'd like to look at a different house?*

No, I picture myself at Henley Park.

Henley Park was the estate he had inherited, the albatross around his neck that had destroyed their happiness. *That hovel?* Her voice had risen with her despair. *I never told you but I went to see it before you married. It was a horrible place.*

It was. But it isn't anymore.

He'd taken her to see Henley Park, an undeniably beautiful place, radiant with hope and vibrancy. They'd spoken not a word on the state of his marriage, but Isabelle had felt all too clearly the devotion and nurturing that had been imprinted upon every square inch of the soil.

She could have made a scene. She could have demanded, with a tantrum to end all tantrums, that he honor his promise to her. Instead, she'd wished him well through her tears and bid him goodbye, too proud to debase herself when she had been told that she was no longer needed.

She forced herself to speak past the raw pain in her heart, to finish answering Mr. Fitzwilliam's question. "Until this morning, I had believed—and hoped—that Fitz and I would indeed put those dreams to fulfillment. So yes, he still matters."

And he would always, always matter.

Mr. Fitzwilliam was silent and still. She could no longer distinguish his individual features in the encroaching darkness. He was but a silhouette of a man, upon whom she could project all her starkest needs.

He bowed and walked away.

HE HAD DONE AS SHE'D SPECIFIED, leaving without a word to make his decision known to her by dismissing the cabbie. Or not.

But already she felt rejected. And with it, a sense of utter incredulity.

What had come over her?

He might have been forward, but not mad. She, on the other hand, had proved herself completely barmy. He would take himself home without a backward glance, revisiting her antics only to amuse his gentlemen friends the next time they were deep in their cups.

Slowly she made her way back into the house, her legs heavy, her heart heavier, her head spinning with mortification.

In the upstairs sitting room, she lit the lamp and located her great-great-great-grandmother's miniature portrait. Two days ago, she'd come through the house to make sure everything was perfect and to set the portrait on the mantel of the sitting room. Great-Gran Cumberland had also been an Isabelle, a woman both terribly wild and terribly lucky. Among her descendants, it was said, in every generation there would be a girl as wild and as lucky as she.

Isabelle had always hoped she would be that girl of her generation. But while she'd had wildness aplenty in her younger days, luck had been elusive.

But that, she was promised, would change once her mother's cousin, Mrs. Tinsdale, passed down to her Great-Gran Cumberland's miniature portrait, as reliable a talisman against the woes of fortune as anything the family had known in a century. Why, on the day Mrs. Tinsdale received the portrait, the physicians had advised her to make funeral arrangements for both her sons. But within a week, they'd miraculously recovered and went on to produce a total of nine grandchildren for Mrs. Tinsdale.

But the talisman had not proved effective for Isabelle. And in coming back for it—she'd already boarded a train that would take her from London to her sister's place in Aberdeen, Scotland when she remembered that she'd left it behind at Doyle's Grange—she'd only added humiliation to her heartache.

Had she been younger she might have thrown the miniature portrait into a fire. But this older, sadder Isabelle wrapped it carefully and put it into her satchel. It might yet change someone else's luck someday, when the woman most needed it.

And now there was nothing else left to do in this house. It was time to take herself to the hansom cab, then onto the next train going back to London. In the morning she would start for Aberdeen, where her children were having a riotous good time with their cousins. Perhaps in time, some of their fresh joy in life would rub off a little on her.

She wiped the tears that gathered anew at the corners of her eyes, lifted the satchel—and stopped before she'd taken a single step.

The sound of a carriage moving.

There was no other carriage within hearing range except her hansom cab.

She rushed to the window and threw it open. In the light of its own lantern, the hansom cab rolled away, picking up speed as it went.

Mr. Fitzwilliam would be calling at ten o'clock.

For a long minute she couldn't breathe, let alone move. Then it occurred to her she needed to get ready. She lugged the satchel to the bedroom she'd have shared with Fitz and pawed frantically through its contents, while having not the least idea what she might be looking for.

After a while, it dawned on her that she was about to embark on her first ever affair. With a man she'd spoken to for all of five minutes, whose Christian name she did not even know.

She gave a wild little laugh, smacked her hand against her forehead, and went on with turning her satchel inside out.

Chapter Three

THE LAST TIME RALSTON APPROACHED A LADY'S HOUSE at night, feeling as if he had been turned upside down, he had been twenty-one. That, too, had been an illicit visit: He'd climbed up to her window and knocked, hoping she was alone.

From time to time he still saw her face in his dreams, her smile wide with surprise and pleasure. They'd giggled madly—and kept telling each other to shush while laughing. It was a wonder he hadn't lost his grip and plummeted into the boxwood hedge below.

It was odd to think of her so openly. He'd become used to the opposite, to snipping his thoughts in the bud, rarely allowing full, uninterrupted recollections.

Perhaps it was the effect of Mrs. Englewood's naked pain and undisguised yearning. Perhaps it was simply the result of walking past the same door year after year without ever glancing its way. One of those days he was bound to fling it open, to come face to face with—what had Mrs. Englewood called it?

Old dreams that had fallen apart.

And here he was, about to help create an illusion that Mrs. Englewood's old dreams *hadn't* fallen apart.

EVERY MINUTE CRAWLED—it had been ages since Isabelle had eaten the sandwiches she'd brought with her and changed into somewhat more appropriate attire for seduction. A wonder her restless pacing hadn't worn the carpet threadbare down the center.

The front door of the house opened. Her hand went to her throat. Now she would hear his footsteps coming up the stairs and approaching in the passage.

But that did not happen. After the front door closed, all became quiet. Straining her ears, she heard him moving below quietly, as if he were looking into each one of the rooms below.

Her pulse sped. What if—what if it was not Mr. Fitzwilliam, but a thief, grinning from ear to ear at the bounty of this unlocked, undefended house? And what if this thief were to see her in only her nightgown and dressing robe?

Now the footsteps ascended the stairs. Now they came swift and resolute. Her chest tightened. A glance toward the fireplace showed no sign of a poker, so she gripped the silver hairbrush her mother had given her when she became a bride—it wasn't much of a weapon but it would still give a man a nasty bump on the head.

As the man neared the door, she realized that he carried a handcandle: its light swayed upon the wall. He extinguished the light and knocked on her door.

Not a criminal then, only Mr. Fitzwilliam, who had remembered her requirement for dim light. She panted in relief, only to have her heartbeat race for a different reason altogether.

She set down the hairbrush and hoped her voice would hold. "Come in."

She'd left a lamp in a far corner of the room, the wick trimmed so short it was practically drowning in lamp oil. In this gauzy, barely-there light, the man before her bore such an uncanny resemblance to her erstwhile sweetheart that she could not quite suppress a gasp.

Fitz, her heart cried.

Just this one night. This one bittersweet night, so that she could look back as an old woman, when she had forgotten everything else, and remember what it was like to have her beloved in her arms.

Her palm hurt. She realized that she was clutching Great-Gran Cumberland's miniature portrait and the frame was digging into her skin. She let go of it and beckoned him to approach her.

He did, but he did not fall upon her, as she'd meant him too. Instead, he reached past her for the miniature portrait and studied it. Then he studied *her* face.

They did not look much alike, she and Great-Gran Cumberland, except for the pitch black hair they shared—and even that was hardly discernible, as Great-Gran Cumberland's coiffure, done up in the style of Madame Pompadour, had been enthusiastically powdered.

"She is an ancestress from six, seven generations ago," she offered, made uneasy by the silence. Silence, to her, manifested grief. Or unhappiness. Or the distance of two lovers drifting apart. "Each of her four husbands cherished her. Her eleven children all survived her. On her seventy-fifth birthday, she had what she declared to be the best meal of her life at the dinner her favorite granddaughter threw in her honor, then she retired to bed and, with truffles and a forty-year-old claret in her stomach, passed away in her sleep."

He nodded.

It didn't feel terribly odd to speak of Great-Gran Cumberland—she had yet to tell Fitz about the latter. In her younger days, when she'd believed herself invulnerable, tales of Great-Gran had been just that, stories about a woman who lived in a different century. Then she'd had no need for anyone else's luck; now she put her faith in legends and relics, no longer quite trusting her own ability to navigate life's bitter seas.

He returned the miniature portrait to its place. Belatedly she noticed that in his other hand, he held a bottle of wine by its neck, two wineglasses, and a corkscrew.

Several times since her return she'd suggested to Fitz that they could have something more potent than tea or coffee, but he'd always turned her down, leaving her to recall wistfully those occasions years and years ago when he'd come to visit, and all the young people in the house would sneak out at night. They'd always had a bottle of something and a handful of thimbles. Hidden behind a high hedge, they'd pass around thimbles of the night's tipple, tittering all the while, drunk as much on youth and the first taste of freedom as on port, sack, or champagne.

He set down the wine on the nightstand and extended a glass toward her. Their fingers brushed as she took the glass from him. A harsh heat sizzled along her nerve endings, but he did not seize on the moment or even remark upon it. Instead, his attention turned back to the bottle and he removed the cork with an audible pop.

He poured. The wine landed with a beautiful sound, nectar on glass. She took a sip; the claret flowed over her tongue, cool, delicious, leaving a trail of reassuring warmth in its wake. "Good idea," she said. "The wine."

He poured for himself, casting her a glance as he did so. Now she began to feel odd, carrying on this monologue, even though it was by her request that he remained silent.

"Nice claret," she went on, unable to stop herself.

He turned the bottle so she could read the label. "Château Haut-Brion. I see from your pride that it is probably the Mona Lisa of wines. But I can't tell the difference between a French red and an Italian one, let alone distinguish the parcel of land that produced a wine by the taste of it. All I know is that I like the conviviality a little wine brings."

He drank from his glass and waited for her to speak more. She stared a moment at his almost unbearably familiar face, mesmerized, before her mind seized on the length of his hair to remind her that no, he was but a stranger.

"My—my late husband was a conscientious officer, always stern before his men. But every evening at dinner, after half a glass of wine, he'd begin to smile. After an entire glass of wine, he'd tell me the jokes he'd heard from the other officers. And on rare days when he allowed himself a second glass, he might even imitate his horse, a gorgeous bay stallion who ran like the wind, but had the habit of breaking wind loudly at the most inopportune moments."

She could not quite believe what she had said. But oh, how she'd loved those two-glasses-of-wine evenings. Lawrence had mastered a marvelous parody of himself, and when he would copy the noises that issued from his horse's hindquarter, she almost invariably dropped her fork laughing.

After a moment of surprise, Mr. Fitzwilliam smiled. She had the sensation that he relaxed somewhat. Of course he must have been on guard: This had to be the most outlandish situation in which he'd ever found himself.

His increasing ease made her unclench a bit—she hadn't quite grasped how tense she'd been, caught between her desire to make love to Fitz and her—thankfully—still quite sane awareness that no matter how much Mr. Fitzwilliam looked like Fitz, he remained another man entirely.

Mr. Fitzwilliam indicated a chair by the fireplace.

"Of course. How inconsiderate of me. Please have a seat."

He settled himself in the chair and raised his glass to her.

She reciprocated the gesture. "How did you know I'd like some wine?"

He lifted a brow. He had a livelier face than Fitz. The small gesture conveyed a wealth of meaning, not the least of which was an even-tempered awareness of the ludicrous demands that had been placed on his person.

She reddened. "Please forgive me. Of course you may speak. I don't know what came over me earlier."

"I'd like to say I have that effect on women," he answered, smiling slightly. "But I don't—not these particular effects, in any case."

There was no mockery in his voice, but something that was the audible equivalent of a friendly nod. It put her further at ease—he hadn't taken her mad request too seriously. Or at least, he'd treated her moment of insanity for what it was and did not consider her permanently batty.

"And to answer your question, I had no idea whether you would like wine, but I was fairly certain I would like some."

"To gird yourself?"

He hesitated a moment. "In a way."

It was unnerving to keep looking at his face, so she lowered her gaze a few inches. But it was almost as disconcerting to contemplate the width of his shoulders, the length of his arms, and the casual way he held his wineglass, the stem dangling between his fingers.

She noticed for the first time that his waistcoat was scarlet—Fitz never wore such flamboyant colors. And he slouched to a degree, whereas Fitz's back would have been straighter than a yardstick.

The man who looked exactly like Fitz might not remotely resemble him in temperament or inclinations.

"I am curious, Mrs. Englewood," he said, "how would your life have been different had Lord Fitzhugh not inherited his title?"

"Other than the fact that today I might still believe myself fortune's darling? Probably not very much. Fitz had wanted to be a cavalry officer. The man I married was also a cavalry officer."

"Does this mean I am not your first replacement for Lord Fitzhugh?"

Her nerves pulled taut. But he did not sound peevish, only genuinely curious.

"It might look that way, but I never *set out* to marry a different cavalry officer. When Fitz married his heiress, I was cast adrift. My mother and my sister convinced me to not let life go by, to at least go to London and see what other choices I might have. That London Season led me to Captain Englewood."

She smiled a little the memory of meeting her Lawrence for the first time, of the way his eyes had followed her the entire night. "It wasn't until I'd accepted his suit that my sister asked me whether I was trying to duplicate the life I would have led with Fitz. I broke down and cried myself to sleep.

The next day I woke up and vowed to never think of Fitz again for as long as Captain Englewood and I both lived."

"Not an easy promise to keep."

"No. At the beginning of our marriage, whenever Captain Englewood did something that I didn't like, I would instantly wonder how different things would have been with Fitz—how I would have never experienced a single moment of annoyance or dissatisfaction. But I'm proud to say I pushed those thoughts away quite diligently and did my best to love Captain Englewood for himself, rather than as a second choice when my first was no longer available.

"It became easier after a while. He was a good, devoted husband. We had two lovely children. I enjoyed life in the cantonment and made friends with the other officers' wives. It wasn't the life I'd planned for, but it wasn't bad at all. In fact, I was feeling quite fortunate and grateful, when Captain Englewood and I both caught a tropical fever."

She stopped for a moment, unable to help the tremor in her voice. Mr. Fitzwilliam gazed at her steadily, as if in encouragement. She took a deep breath and went on.

"He was the hardiest man alive, never a cold, never a toothache, never even an upset stomach. Soon he seemed to be on the mend, while I took a turn for the worse. In what I thought would be my last moment of clarity, before I descended into delirium, I told him how thankful I was that he came into my life when he did, how much I adored him and our children, and how I wished I could grow old with him and together welcome our grandchildren into the world."

Mr. Fitzwilliam sat straighter. She clutched her wineglass with both hands. "I woke up two days later, weak as a newborn, and so confused I barely knew where I was or even who I was. When I did remember, I said a long prayer of thanksgiving—I was alive, I was well, the life that I had painstakingly rebuilt had remained intact. Only to then be told—"

Tears spilled down her cheeks. He was instantly before her, holding out a snow-white handkerchief. "Thank you," she murmured, accepting the handkerchief and hastily dabbing her tears away. "I'm sorry."

"Be glad you can cry. There are those can only sit dry-eyed with pain burning in their hearts."

Was he speaking of himself? She wanted to ask but didn't know how. "I'm sorry," she repeated herself. "I have been going on and on about myself. Please understand I am only belatedly trying to appear halfway sane."

"I never doubted your sanity—what we do in moments of heartbreak isn't always rational or explicable," he answered, his voice as gentle as it was authoritative.

She couldn't remember the last time she felt so grateful. Impulsively she reached out and touched his hand. "Thank you, sir."

He rested their combined hands against his chest. The lapel of his jacket was warm and soft upon her skin. Then he let go and returned to his seat. "So you grieve for Captain Englewood, you wonder what would happen to yourself, and you remember your old sweetheart. Except he is no longer your sweetheart."

"Then you appeared out of nowhere, and I thought my prayers had been heard." Memories of their kiss tumbled back. The firmness of his hand at the small of her back, the scratch of the beginning of stubbles upon her cheeks, the sounds of enjoyment that he made as she pressed wantonly into him. She cleared her throat. "Well, you know the rest."

"Not everything." Mr. Fitzwilliam tilted his head. "If you don't mind, Mrs. Englewood, did you really intend to take me to bed?"

Her face warmed, but his tone was not the least bit judgmental, as if he were inquiring into nothing more controversial than whether she had intended to offer him a box of chocolates.

"I had convinced myself of it at one point."

He smiled. "Until I appeared in person, you mean."

She couldn't help reciprocating some of his amusement. In hindsight it *was* funny, what had transpired this night. "I couldn't delude myself as much as I thought I would."

"You have done very well tonight: Instead of a lover you'd be ashamed of in the morning, you now have a friend."

Did she? Her stomach fluttered at the bond friendship suggested, that he would not be a transient figure in her life, here tonight, gone tomorrow. But she did not dare let herself hope too much. "Isn't it premature to pronounce yourself one of my intimates, sir? I know nothing of *you*."

He shook his head. "That is patently incorrect, Mrs. Englewood. You know I am one, eminently good natured, and two, gentlemanly enough to not take advantage of a damsel in distress."

She was amazed now that he had come at all. *He didn't want you to be all alone, tonight of all nights,* the thought dropped into her head. It was like being given a thick blanket and a hot cup of mulled wine, when she'd expected to shiver by herself in a corner for a long, long time.

Not quite knowing what to say, she turned to making fun of herself. "I doubt you were ever thinking of taking advantage of me. Quite the opposite, I dare say. You probably brought the wine so you could use the bottle to smack me on the head, should you need to get away from my frenzied grasp."

The corner of his lips lifted. "Believe me, if I were that worried I wouldn't have come."

There was nothing blatant to his expression, just that of a strapping young man being confidently unafraid. Yet she felt a shock of warmth in her abdomen, an understanding that had she propositioned him under less questionable circumstances, now she would be beneath him.

Naked.

She poured the rest of her wine down her throat.

Chapter Four

MRS. ENGLEWOOD SET THE GLASS ASIDE, and exhaled from parted lips. Those lips were quite red, her breath just noticeably uneven. The sight and the barely audible sound of it made Ralston's body tighten rather pleasurably. He shifted in his chair.

She, on the edge of the bed, sat straighter, as if better posture would cut the sudden tension in the room. But it only drew his attention to her beautiful neck, above the collar of her nightgown and the lapels of her dressing robe—then down to her bare feet on the carpet, the most substantial evidence that she had indeed meant to take him to bed, for a lady's feet were never bared except in the most intimate of circumstances.

She arched one foot, her instep high and shapely. He had a vision of himself holding that foot, holding both her feet, in fact, one in each hand, drawing them apart—

He rose before his thoughts could get away from him and replenished her glass. She murmured a "Thank you," as her toes delved rather deeply into the fibers of the carpet. The strain in the tendons of her foot made him tighten further. He pulled in a deep breath as he sat down again, trying not to dwell on unprofitable notions.

She needed a friend, not a lover.

"Do you remember what you said to me when we first met—that you are interested in my story?" she asked, returning his attention to the conversation.

"Yes?"

"Why are you interested in a story that you could already tell was full of torment, as writ large on my face?"

Because I recognized your grief, he wanted to answer, *as if it were my old friend, too.*

But he could not quite bring himself to say it, so he shrugged.

"I see," she said, narrowing her eyes slightly. "Do you know now, Captain Englewood sometimes came home aching from a day in the saddle—and wanting to be fussed over. But he could never tolerate the sound of himself complaining, so his devoted wife had to deduce where and how much he hurt and then pamper him accordingly."

She was more perceptive than he had given her credit for. "Are you suggesting, Mrs. Englewood, that I have the appearance of a man staggering across the threshold, groaning?"

"No, I am suggesting that you have the appearance of an otherwise stoic man who is perhaps ill-served by his stoicism. And now allow me to be like that fictional detective—what is his name?"

"Sherlock Holmes."

"Indeed, I will be Mr. Holmes and divine the story of your life. And if I am right, you have but to take a sip of your wine."

"And you, will you drink when you are wrong?"

"I shall take the liberty to imbibe either way—it is an excellent night to be tipsy, perhaps even outright intoxicated."

As if to underscore her point, she drank from her glass, then focused her attention on him. He did not fail to notice the quick blinking of her eyes, which happened almost every time she looked full-on at him—she still had to make an effort to untangle him from her Fitz. It was an odd feeling: whether anyone cared for his face or not, he'd never been consistently mistaken for someone else. Particularly not in such a manner as to yank the beholder's emotions left and right, for he could see them on her face: confusion, a flicker of involuntary hope, then resignation, the three bundled now in such a tight package that they were but one fleet shadow upon her face, chased away the next moment by a conscious resolve on her part to appear normal and unaffected.

She touched the rim of her glass to her chin. "The color of your complexion indicates that you have been abroad a great deal in hot, sunny places."

He took a sip. "Good, but a low hanging fruit. What else can you guess?"

"You have been to India."

He obliged with another sip. "That fruit was so low it had already landed on the grass and been pecked over by all the birds of the orchard."

"North Africa, too."

"Slightly less low hanging. Logical deduction, or lucky guess?"

"Somewhere in between. Let's see. You are not a member of the diplomatic corps—these gentlemen do not go out in the sun much."

"Indeed I am not."

"And you are not a soldier. I have been around a great number of those; I can tell one from a furlong away."

"Not a soldier."

She blew out a breath. "It is the end of low-hanging fruits as we know them. Now I must actually climb the tree—or shake the branches awfully hard. Do you happen to be an adventurer?"

"No."

"I have no other ready guesses. What are you then?"

"I am a cartographer."

She sucked in a breath. "All the mapmakers I have met are secretly spies."

"Not surprising, given that mapmakers who pass through military cantonments are likely in the employ of the empire. But mapmaking also has legitimate civilian uses. No construction of roads, railroads, and canals can proceed until those in charge have the most accurate maps possible."

"I don't doubt that, but what are you?"

"Not a spy," he answered honestly. "Though I will admit, on certain expeditions the local embassy has been known to insert one or two gentlemen as 'observers'. Those gentlemen, I imagine, are indeed spies—or at least better trained in covert arts than I."

"I'm surprised the spymasters didn't exert greater pressure on you to swell their ranks. They are not always scrupulous in their recruitment methods."

"I am lucky: I can name myself the Duke of Perrin's heir."

Her eyes widened. Most ladies, upon learning that he was in line to inherit a title, glowed with greater interest. Her reaction, however, was all alarm. "Are you? I hope you will be one of the more fortunate peers who will not need to marry an heiress to keep a roof over your head."

"Thankfully, the Perrin estate has always been in excellent repair—not to mention the current duchess is a very wealthy woman."

She exhaled and raised her wineglass. "A toast then: to becoming a duke without becoming a pauper."

Wine seemed to affect her swiftly. Her cheeks were already flushed, a flirtatious shade of pink, like that of a woman freshly pleasured. "A toast," he echoed and drank deeply.

No one ever said being a gentleman didn't have its costs.

"So…" She twirled the stem of her wineglass. "Have you been overseas so diligently to avoid the scheming mamas?"

She winked at him. All of a sudden he saw her as the girl she must have been once, bursting with vitality and thirst for life, ready to make her mark on the world.

Abruptly her expression turned somber. "No, no, what was I saying? Of course you haven't been running away from the matchmakers. You have been running from something else altogether—that which you could not bring yourself to speak of earlier."

HE DID NOT SAY ANYTHING. He didn't know whether he wouldn't or couldn't.

This time, it was Mrs. Englewood who rose, lifted the wine bottle by its neck, and refilled his glass. The hem of her dressing robe brushed against his trousers as she sat down in the chair next to his.

"As a rule I don't pry," she said, her voice quiet and solemn. "But I don't believe you came here to *not* speak of it. So if you will forgive me, whom did you lose?"

He breathed hard. To calm himself, perhaps—or to hungrily inhale her faint scent of fresh rose petals.

"Is it a lady?" she asked, her instinct unerring.

It was a long time, or at least it seemed so, before he could nod.

"What is her name?"

Now he had no choice but to speak. "Charlotte," he said, his voice sounding almost rusty. "Her name was Charlotte Fitzwilliam."

She flinched a little at his use of the past tense. "Your wife?"

"Yes."

"Were you married long?"

He shook his head. "Three months."

Two of them absolutely glorious, the last filled with despair and denial. He'd remained by her bedside almost every minute of the day, holding her hand, trying to keep himself together, unable to comprehend the possibility that he might become a widower at twenty-two.

"When she died, I refused to let her body be prepared for burial. I had to be forcibly removed, shouting at the top of my lungs that putting her into a coffin would suffocate her and I would never allow it."

He looked at Mrs. Englewood and attempted to smile. "So you see, your action can never compare to mine, when it comes to grief-driven irrationality."

Her eyes glimmered—her tears were again gathering. She rested her hand on his cheek. "I'm so sorry this happened to you."

He placed his hand over hers. And now that he started speaking, he couldn't shut up. "Do you know what I regret? Mrs. Fitzwilliam wanted to visit the Faroe Islands during our honeymoon. She'd read all about their misty greenery and those brightly painted houses against a gray Atlantic. But we married in October. I told her the weather would be harsh so late in the year and promised to take her the next summer."

But Charlotte had not lived to see the next summer. "I went myself—it was an almost eerily beautiful place. I should have taken her that October, so she'd have had her heart's wish."

Seven years had passed, but that regret had remained as constant as the sea.

Mrs. Englewood cupped his face with both hands. "No."

He stared at her, not sure what she meant.

She gazed into his eyes, her own swimming with unshed tears. "I cannot speak for Mrs. Fitzwilliam, but I don't believe she minded the Faroe Islands. I have always wanted to go to Mykonos and Captain Englewood had promised me he would take me there someday. He died before we could go and I would have gladly given up all chances of ever visiting Mykonos if it would have saved my husband—or just kept him on this earth for a few more hours, to say a proper goodbye.

"So if Mrs. Fitzwilliam had any regrets, it would be that the rest of her life was too short to spend with you—because *that* was her heart's desire, not the Faroe Islands, and not anything else."

Tears slipped down her cheeks. The strangest feeling overtook him. It was a few seconds before he realized that he had a lump in his throat.

"You did say a proper goodbye to him," he told her. "He went to his rest knowing that he had the love of his wife and children. It would have been more than good enough for me."

Her lips parted in a slow smile, even as another drop of tear made its way down her cheek. "Thank you."

He touched his thumb to her cheek, wiping away her tears. Then, to his shock, he realized she was doing the same to him: The tears that had eluded him all these years were falling freely.

And through his tears, she was as beautiful as a dream.

Almost without thinking, he pulled her to him and kissed her.

IT WAS A SWEET KISS, ALMOST LIKE A WHISPERED "THANK YOU" in the ear, a squeeze of the hand, or an umbrella held out in a downpour.

Sweet and brief.

When they pulled apart, Mr. Fitzwilliam did not apologize or explain himself—he had done exactly what he meant to, it seemed, and no words were needed. For a few seconds, they existed in perfect camaraderie, her hand on his cheek, and his hand on hers, two friends who had shared the most intimate details of the heart.

And she did not mistake him for Fitz in the least.

Then all the norms of etiquette and decorum began pressing in. Isabelle dropped her hand and drew back into her seat. He, too, looked as if he was at a loss for words.

She cast around for something to say, "Do you carry a picture of Mrs. Fitzwilliam with you, by some chance?"

He pulled out his pocket watch. It had a hidden compartment that held a small photograph of a pretty, demure-looking young lady. In return, she opened the locket she wore around her neck to show him a photograph of her entire family, taken six months before she became widowed.

"Was Mrs. Fitzwilliam as decorous as her image would like me to believe?"

"Ha! Mrs. Fitzwilliam lived to belie her image. Magnificent mustache on Captain Englewood, by the way."

She smiled. "Ridiculously so, isn't it? I stepped on his foot twice the first time we danced because I kept staring at the mustache."

Dear Lawrence had grown so conscious of it that he'd shaved off the moustache entirely before he came to call on her the next day and she had not recognized him without it.

"Are you sure you are not blaming this magnificent moustache for your own clumsiness? Perhaps you are naturally mistake-prone."

"I will have you know, sir, that I am light-footed and graceful, and never has a more elegant figure graced a dance floor." She rested her head against the back of the chair and sighed. "I miss dancing. It has been so long since I last danced."

She missed the crowd, the excitement, the sensation of being young.

He rose from his chair. "Then let us dance."

She sat up straight. "Here?"

The room was not large, and there were too many pieces of furniture.

"There is a terrace in the back. Come, the moon is rising."

Dancing, the two of them pressed together. She had not forgotten what he felt like in a heated embrace: a big, strong man, fully aroused. She was hot in the back of her throat—and everywhere else too, it seemed.

"What about music?"

"I will provide the music," he said, gathering the bottle and the wineglasses. "But do take a wrapper. It will be chilly outside."

"Won't we be seen?"

"One would have to be standing directly at the gate, peering in. It is late enough that no one respectable would be out walking and anyone driving would be unable to see out the window."

He held out his hand. She placed her fingers in his, but she still hesitated. "Do *you* miss dancing, Mr. Fitzwilliam?"

"I miss—I miss not forcing myself to have a good time." He smiled ruefully. "Does that make any sense?"

It made perfect sense: Only a man who had disguised his heartache with gaiety would have found anything remarkable in her naked pain.

"Then let us dance," she said, rising.

THE TERRACE, ISABELLE HAD BEEN TOLD BY THE ESTATE AGENT, had been refurbished with limestone quarried from the Mendip Hills. Low guard rails of wrought iron, with motifs of vine and grapes, surrounded the terrace. A short flight of stairs—only two steps—led down to the rear garden where an unusually large rowan tree stood, its leaves glistening in the moonlight.

It was the sort of tree upon the branches of which young lovers stole kisses, then later carved their initials into the bark to commemorate the sweetness of first love. She smiled a little, remembering an enormous oak at home, under which her sister and the young man she would eventually marry used to sit on a picnic blanket and read aloud to each other from a book of poetry.

Mr. Fitzwilliam hummed a few opening bars of *The Blue Danube*, then swept her into the first turn. She sucked in a breath at the sensation: She felt almost...weightless.

As a girl she'd burned with excitement at being alive, but then she'd changed. Throughout her marriage, she'd dreaded any news of unrest and upheaval—she wanted her husband to be a peacetime soldier and only a peacetime soldier. Instead of exploring the streets of India, she'd stayed behind the walls of the cantonment. And even there, the earlier version of herself would have wanted to be a leader of society, organizing functions and events, taking the newly arriving ladies under her wings. But she never did much more than what civility and reciprocity demanded, preferring to only look after her own family.

Fitz's wife had once reminded her that all had not been lost, that she had gone on to have a devoted husband and two beautiful children. Isabelle had answered flatly that it had not been the same. That nothing could approach the perfect, unmarred happiness she'd known with Fitz.

It had not been a verdict on her husband or her marriage, but on the person she had become, one who approached life and joy, especially joy, with fear, always afraid that moments of lightness and laughter were but prepayment for some future devastation. It had been one of the reasons she'd latched on so tightly to the idea of making a life with Fitz, because she wanted to return to her old self, the one who lived and loved with zest and abandon, and she'd believed him the only possible path back.

Yet here she was, dancing as if she were flying.

"You are right," said Mr. Fitzwilliam in her ear. "You *are* wonderfully nimble on your feet."

She shivered from the nearness of his lips. She was alive, as she hadn't been for very long. What a terrifying yet enthralling feeling—electric, like the sensation of his breath brushing her skin. She inhaled his scent, spice and musk against the woodsy freshness of the night air.

Moonlight cast the shifting shadows of the rowan tree upon his person. His hand was warm at the small of her back. Her motion and a cool breeze lifted the edges of the short mantle she'd put on over her dressing robe, making her feel as if she'd truly sprouted wings.

They spun in ever wider, ever faster circles. She felt dizzy, an effervescent dizziness, as if she'd been indulging in champagne. On impulse, she threw her head back. The entire sky seemed to revolve around them, the stars streaks of faint gold.

The sound of laughter, she was surprised to realize, was her own, giddy and clear upon the night air.

They danced until Mrs. Englewood begged, giggling, to sit down, citing her spinning head. Ralston guided her to a swing seat set deeper in the garden. She collapsed into it, still giggling.

He emptied the remainder of the wine into their glasses and sat down next to her.

"Oh, dear," she said as she accepted her glass, "I am about to turn into a sot."

She smiled widely as she drank. "Such good wine." Now she beamed at him. "*Such* good company."

It was an extraordinarily trusting look. His pulse raced. He wanted to kiss her wine-sweet lips and revel in the taste of her fire. But he only sat down next to her. "Are you warm enough?"

She snuggled closer to him. "Now I am."

"You *are* tipsy."

"Maybe not so much tipsy as a little lightheaded and very lighthearted." She sighed, a sound of plain contentment.

He placed his arm around her shoulders, careful not to touch her otherwise. She burrowed a little more into his person, her hair tickling his neck and ear. More than tickling, actually. The sensations she evoked shot directly toward the middle of his person. He swallowed and kept still.

"Did the missus also enjoy dancing?" she asked.

"The missus would have been the first to inform you that she possessed two left feet. She was, however, an excellent tennis player and regularly had the gentlemen begging for mercy."

"Did you play a great deal of tennis together?"

"No, I counted myself among those gentlemen who begged for mercy."

Mrs. Englewood set a hand on his elbow, to keep herself steady while she pulled away to look into his face. Such eyes she had, pools of luminosity even when there was barely enough light to see.

"If she didn't like to dance, and you were less than accomplished at lawn tennis, then how did you two woo each other?"

"I drew maps for her."

"What kind of maps?"

"She always enjoyed stories, especially folk tales, fairy tales, and the sort—anything with a talking animal was dear and near to her heart. So instead of writing love letters, I made a detailed map of Alice's Wonderland."

She clapped. "How fun."

And now she gripped onto the back of the swing for balance. He rather wished she would brace against him again.

"Was that the only map you ever made for her?"

He had to remind himself that the eagerness in her voice was not for him, but for a good, entertaining story. "For our honeymoon I drew a large map of a forest, crisscrossed with footpaths. Little Red Riding Hood's grandmother's house was in section H5, if memory serves. The gingerbread house in which Hansel and Gretel almost met their doom in B11. The seven dwarfs and their cottage were to be found in P2—so on and so forth."

She laid a hand against her heart. "That is so, so charming. Do you still have it?"

"No, it was buried with the missus."

Some of the light went out of her eyes. She closed them briefly and laid her head down on his shoulder again. "Did you feel at the time that you could never bear to see it again?"

"Yes, but now I wish I still had it. She doesn't need it anymore, but I am beginning to forget the exact phrasing of some of the comments that she'd written in the margins of the map. I thought the words would be seared on my mind forever, but time blurs memories, even those I hadn't believed would ever fade."

She ran her hand through his hair, a gesture of sympathy and affection. He just stopped himself from taking her hand and pressing a kiss into the center of her palm.

"Tell me about Mrs. Fitzwilliam's comments. It will help you remember them better for the future."

"Ah..." He had never spoken to anyone about the map and particularly not the comments, holding them in the innermost sanctuary of his heart.

"I am so sorry. What was I thinking? I was a newlywed once myself. Dare I assume her comments were quite naughty?"

He felt his cheeks warming. "Quite."

"I'll tell you a secret: During my honeymoon I wrote a limerick. I did it on the train as Captain Englewood and I left Rome, that beautiful city we never ventured out of our hotel to see."

Now he was warm everywhere. "I will not ask you what you were so busy doing in your hotel."

"And you will be wise not to." She tittered. "My goodness, I *am* drunk. I am not the most close-lipped of women but I assure you I do not go about on a regular basis disclosing how I allocated my time during my honeymoon."

"Well, then, since you are already drunk, recite me that unforgettable masterpiece of yours."

"Well, bear in mind that I *adored* making love."

He sucked in a breath at a huge influx of lust.

"Not to mention I found it wonderfully calming afterwards," she went on. "I always felt invulnerable in the aftermath of the pleasure. My bridegroom was quite happy with how much I welcomed, indeed, demanded his advances."

He wished she would demand *his* advances.

She cleared her throat. "*There was once a young lady from Bembley, who learned to love married life quickly. Not again, her husband groaned; Yes again, our young lady moaned. So once more unto the breach, well and truly.*"

He burst out laughing. "My God! Did you share this with your husband?"

"I did—in the dining car, and he spat out his coffee. Years later he would still lean over to me and whisper, *Once more unto the breach,* especially when we were at some interminable ceremony." She laid her hand in his; he wrapped his fingers around hers. "It was times like those that I felt happiest, knowing that I was the only person who could understand the joke."

And now he, too, understood the secret joke. It had been so long since he felt such closeness, not only to another person, but to everything inside himself that had once made him relish the arrival of each new day.

"Do you still want to know what Mrs. Fitzwilliam wrote on the map?"

She sat up and gazed at him. "*Of course.*"

He still needed a few moments to overcome his residual shyness. "About the gingerbread house she said, *This is the house I earned by allowing my bridegroom to have his way with me on a desk.*"

She snorted with laughter. "Is that so? You would only draw part of the map if she agreed to a certain marital deed?"

"No, I would have drawn the map for nothing. But it was more fun that way." He smiled back. "Much more fun."

"What, may I ask, did she have to do for the dwarfs' cottage?"

"Take a turn in our hotel room—after I had disrobed her."

"Oh, my. Newlywed love games indeed." She sighed. "Oh, to be a newlywed again."

And then, after a moment of silence. "Or even better, to be an old married woman, thumping her cane on the floor of the parlor, because her husband is making them late for church again."

"I am always late for church," he said impulsively.

She brushed her hand through his hair again. "And how fortunate the lady who would be thumping her cane at you someday, my dear Mr. Fitzwilliam."

"WILL YOU COME BACK AND BRING YOUR CHILDREN HERE?"

Isabelle opened her eyes, surprised that she'd almost fallen asleep. "I haven't thought about it yet."

When Fitz had decided that his future lay elsewhere, she'd been sure she never wanted to set foot in Doyle's Grange again. But now the place held good memories. Wonderful memories.

"What is next for you then?"

"Back to my sister's place in Aberdeen. My children are still with her and I miss them."

"Bring them here. Winters are harsh in Scotland."

"Aberdeen's is milder than one would expect for a city so far north, or so my sister assures me."

"Still, it will be cold and dreary. Bring them here. They will thank you."

But if she were to set up household at Doyle's Grange, soon her entire family would come by to visit. There would be calls on the neighbors, afternoon tea parties, and dinners to make sure that she was surrounded by kind people. And when they saw Mr. Fitzwilliam, after picking their jaws up from the floor, they would immediately assume that she'd decided to come back to Doyle's Grange because she wanted to be close to Fitz's lookalike.

It would be impossible to make them see otherwise. And should word get back to Fitz, she would die of mortification, to have him believe that she wanted to hold on to him so badly anyone who looked like him would do.

And it would be a tremendous insult to Mr. Fitzwilliam too, to have everyone assume he was but a replica of Fitz, when nothing could be further from the truth.

"Let me think about it," she murmured, the wine and the lateness of the hour making her drowsy again.

"Yes, think about it," he said softly.

When Mrs. Englewood's breaths had become soft and even, he lifted her into his arms.

"Careful, old widower," she mumbled, her words slow and sleepy.

"Ha," he countered. "This grandpa still has a spring in his step."

He carried her into the house, up the stairs, and back into her bedroom. She thanked him indistinctly as he set her down on the bed. He took off her slippers, straightened the hem of her nightgown, and covered her with a blanket.

She sighed softly and slept on.

Light from the oil lamp still flickered. Her hair had tumbled loose in the course of the evening. Now midnight black strands of it streaked across the pillow.

But as he looked closer, he realized that not every strand of her hair was the same vibrant raven hue. His dear Mrs. Englewood had a few white hairs that gleamed silver in the lamplight.

He wondered if premature graying ran in her family. If by the time she was forty, she would have a head of snow-white hair.

He wanted to see it. He wanted to be the one to brush her hair and jokingly count her last few remaining black strands. And then to kiss her upon her silver head.

"Come back," he murmured. "And soon."

Chapter Five

IN THE MORNING, IT TOOK ISABELLE A MINUTE to realize where she was.

She yawned, sat up, and walked about. The house was empty, Mr. Fitzwilliam nowhere to be seen. And he was thorough in removing the evidence of his presence: The wine bottle, wine glasses and corkscrew had all been removed, as well as his hand candle. Even that consulting detective, Mr. Sherlock Holmes, would be hard pressed to conclude that anyone other than Isabelle had been in the house the previous night.

What of their rapport? Had it too wilted in the harsh light of the day? The next time she saw Mr. Fitzwilliam, if she ever did, would she be obliged to pretend that theirs was the most incidental of acquaintances, rather than the sublime friendship it had been, however briefly?

She sat on the swing seat for a few minutes, gazing at the rowan. Its season of flowering had passed; now hundreds of clusters of berries hung from the branches, some still pale gold, others already turning a riotous red.

Slowly she returned to the house. Just as slowly, she made her way upstairs. But as she reentered the bedroom to gather her belongings, she saw an envelope addressed to her on the nightstand. She snatched it up and tore the seal.

My Dear Mrs. Englewood,
I hope you have slept well. And I hope now that you have awakened, you still think upon last night with as much wonder and fondness as I do. If not, allow me to assure you that I will have exited Doyle's Grange with the utmost care and will not speak a word of our friendship to anyone.

But if you do not regret our hours together, I shall be delighted to hear from you, as frequently as you'd care to write, and follow your progress through the sometimes treacherous shoals of life.

Your devoted servant,
Ralston Fitzwilliam

P.S. You may post your letters to Stanton House, Up Aubry, and they will reach me anywhere.

P.P.S. As an inducement, I dangle before you the late Mrs. Fitzwilliam's comment on Little Red Riding Hood's grandmother's cottage.

She touched his letter to her cheek and smiled. So it *was* reciprocal, this camaraderie of theirs, and not a figment of her imagination.

She hummed those most famous bars of *The Blue Danube*, twirled about the room, and began packing.

TWENTY MILES AWAY, AT THE MANOR IN HENLEY PARK, Lord Fitzhugh, Fitz to his friends, gazed down on his sleeping wife, who, presently, without opening her eyes, reached up and rubbed the palm of her hand against his stubbles.

"You haven't gone for your ride?" she murmured.

He loved the sight of her unbound hair. For so long he'd only seen her hair properly coiffed. The sensuality of her hair—of her person—was still a revelation. "I can't tear myself away from you."

She was trying not to smile too widely, holding on to her bottom lip with her teeth. "Exactly what an old married lady wants to hear from her husband when she wakes up in the morning."

She was only twenty-four years of age. And although they'd been married since she was sixteen, they had not consummated their marriage until recently. The consummation had made a difference, naturally. But the real difference had been made through almost eight years of affection, friendship, and common purpose.

He had loved her long before he realized he had also fallen in love in with her.

Now she opened her eyes and regarded him teasingly. "Get up, sir. You are the master of this house, sir. Duties await."

He was a most dutiful man, but on the first day of the rest of their lives, he was not about to let drainage, roofing, or factory reports get in the way. "And duties can wait a little longer."

She twirled a strand of her hair and peered at him from beneath her eyelashes. "Oh, so you mean it is time for *marital* duties again?"

"It is always time for marital duties around here," he teased her back, enjoying the flush in her cheeks. "But actually, my dear, I propose to whisk you away on holiday—a proper honeymoon."

Her eyes widened. "Really? Where?"

"Shall we go back to Italy?" They'd once had a lovely, if platonic holiday on Lake Como.

"We should. But we can't afford to be gone that long—the Season isn't finished and we still have to chaperone your sister."

"In that case, how about a quick jaunt to the Lake District?" They'd spent several weeks there after their wedding, but they'd been strangers with almost nothing to say to each other. "This time I will be a most solicitous bridegroom."

She wrapped her arms about him. "Yes, I adore the idea."

Then, after a moment, "I only wish Mrs. Englewood can be as happy as we are."

Another woman would little concern herself with the happiness of a rival who almost made away with her husband, but Millie, he knew, had always felt guilty for the pain she had caused Isabelle, even though she herself had never had a say in the selection of her bridegroom.

"Hastings has promised to write her every other day. I cabled her sister yesterday, asking her to keep me informed of Mrs. Englewood's welfare." He wanted the very same, a sunny future for Isabelle, but there wasn't much more he could do now without making an intrusive nuisance of himself.

Millie sighed softly. "In that case, let me begin packing."

"Later," he said, pulling away the sheets that covered her person. "Marital duties first."

"Yes, of course." She wrapped one leg about his middle. "Marital duties always come first."

My Dear Mr. Fitzwilliam,

I was not so drunk last night as to wake up this morning with rue and self-loathing. In fact, though the sight of the bright sun streaming into the house reminded me anew of the hopes I'd nurtured as little as twenty-four hours ago, I am in far less despair than I could have believed as little as twelve hours ago.

I am grateful for your kindness and friendship, sir. And I can only hope that I will not flood your desk too liberally with missives. For in my relentless need to hold on to everything old, I have forgotten the joy of making new friends. And a friend of your caliber—I could live another fifty years and encounter none finer.

Yours,

Isabelle Englewood

P.S. I anxiously await the disclosure of Mrs. Fitzwilliam's very private message.

P.P.S. Am about to detrain in Aberdeen. The thought of holding my children in my arms again warms me. You, sir, I hold firmly in my affection and my esteem.

P.P.P.S. I would have posted this from the rail station itself, but I was met by my sister and our five children—what joy! In addition, the sight of my twin nieces made me realize that I still had a few more words to write. Namely that except for the very first time I met them, I have never mistaken the twins for each other. Despite their almost disorienting resemblance, each girl is resolutely her own person.

My Dear Mrs. Englewood,

I take pleasure in your reunion with your children. And I rejoice in your compliment. It is decided then: We are friends and nothing shall stand in the way of our friendship.

Your mysterious comings and goings have become a topic of much interest in the vicinity. I have disavowed any knowledge of your schedule or your intentions. Not as easy a feat as I first imagined: I was interrogated by Mrs. Beauregard, proprietress of the farm next to Doyle's Grange who saw me out of her window, making my way to my house, when she got up for a glass of water in the middle of the night. Rest assured, however, I divulged nothing. On the other hand, now I have a reputation for sleepwalking. All in your honor, lady!

I hope you find Scotland fair and the company of all the children bracing.

Your devoted servant,

Ralston Fitzwilliam

P.S. Thank you for your reassurance that I am not a mere stand-in for Lord Fitzhugh. Allow me to assure you in return that I have never been made to feel as one. Even when you didn't know who I was, you knew very well who I wasn't.

P.P.S. Mrs. Fitzwilliam, bless her memory, wrote, "My own Big Bad Wolf ate me—and I dare say I liked it."

My Dear Mr. Fitzwilliam,

Scotland is indeed fair, though we are shortly departing for the Lake District—my sister had made plans before my return to the country. The company of all the children is beyond bracing. Hyacinth, my daughter, is a most mischievous girl. My sister loves to point out how similar she is to me as a child. I look at her and marvel that I was ever so rowdy and fearless.

My sister worries that losing Fitz again is too heavy a blow for me. I will not pretend it does not hurt, but part of me wonders if it isn't a blessing in disguise, a failure that forces me to look forward to see what the future holds, rather than backward, trying to recreate a past that never was.

In my original plans, by now the children and I would be at Doyle's Grange, and not tagging along to the Lake District, where Fitz and his wife had honeymooned years ago. My sister had offered to change the destination, but I told her it did not matter—and I did not feel myself to be lying outright. Lying somewhat, but not lying outright.

Yours truly,
Isabelle Englewood

P.S. Country gossip is delightful. A sleepwalking gentleman? Can a sleepdancing one be far behind?

P.P.S. I have yet to tell anyone about you, lest they think I have made you up out of whole cloth. Do reply, dear friend, and reassure me again that you are not imaginary.

P.P.P.S. I made a mistake of sitting down to read your letter with a cup of tea. When I reached Mrs. Fitzwilliam's comment—well, let's just say that the entire letter is tea-stained and I very nearly killed myself laughing. What I pity she and I never met. We'd have been such a pair of mischief-makers.

P.P.P.P.S. I know my curiosity is unseemly, yet I must ask, were there only three locations on that map? Or were there more that you have not divulged yet?

My Dear Mrs. Englewood,

You are hereby assured that I am not imaginary, but very much real—and deeply curious about where in the Lake District you are headed.

I write to you from a hill overlooking Mrs. Fitzwilliam's final resting place in Dorset. I visit the area every time I return to England, walking through the village, and perhaps venturing as far as the gate of the churchyard. But today marks the first time since her interment that I have touched her tombstone with my own hand, and traced the letters and numbers that mark her all-too-brief life.

And wept as I was never able to, all those years ago, at the sight of her casket being lowered into the ground.

Now I sit here, upon this familiar hill, overcome by an entirely unfamiliar lightness of being, as if I am closer to the clouds than to the ground.

Thank you, once again.

Your devoted servant,

Ralston Fitzwilliam

P.S. On the map you would have also found the house in which Goldilocks becomes an intruder.

P.P.S. Mrs. Fitzwilliam would have enjoyed your friendship enormously. That her words have made someone spew tea years after her passing is no doubt delighting her in the hereafter.

"Why are you caressing that letter?" asked Louise, Isabelle's sister.

Isabelle stilled abruptly. Was that what she had been doing, stroking Mr. Fitzwilliam's words? She set down the letter. "Hastings wrote again."

It was not a lie. Hastings *had* written again—he was Fitz's best friend and was no doubt writing at the latter's behest.

"But that is not Lord Hastings's letter, is it?" said Louise, ever astute.

Isabelle considered the question and realized that she had no desire to lie to Louise, or even to fudge her answer. She *wanted* to talk about her wonderful friend.

"The letter is from Mr. Fitzwilliam, my neighbor at Doyle's Grange."

"A very enthusiastic neighbor," pronounced Louise, "considering that his letters arrive with the regularity of sunrises."

"I encouraged it."

Louise chewed her toast contemplatively. "And is Mr. Fitzwilliam the reason you are not as distressed by Fitz's decision as I was afraid you might be?"

"Yes." A lovely, clean answer for all the lovely, unmistakable feelings inside her.

Louise's mouth was wide with both surprise and joy. "Isabelle. Oh, Isabelle."

Isabelle felt a similar warmth welling inside her—and a great relief, like stepping on solid ground after days on a choppy sea. Now Louise no longer needed to worry about her. "Don't say anything to Fitz yet. I know you have been writing to him."

"No, no, my lips are sealed. Now tell me more about your Mr. Fitzwilliam."

But before Isabelle could say anything, Louise frowned, as if remembering something. "He doesn't go by Fitz, does he?"

Isabelle's pleasure faded. She had not even brought up the resemblance, and already Louise wondered whether her preference for Mr. Fitzwilliam had something to do with Fitz. "No, he does not. And what do you wish to know about him?"

MY DEAR MR. FITZWILLIAM,
    We shall be staying at the Lakehead Hotel in Ambleside.
    I cannot take credit for your lightness of being, but sometimes I feel as if I share in it.
    I was drafted into a game of hide-and-seek yesterday afternoon. But I was not an unwilling participant and it was quite good fun hiding under a bed with my daughter, trying not to giggle audibly when her cousin's feet appeared right before our eyes.
    After we'd been spotted, Hyacinth leaned into me and said, "I like it when you laugh, Mama, even if Victoria also heard you."
    A lightness-of-being moment, without a doubt.
    Yours truly,
    Isabelle Englewood
    P.S. I hesitate to say this, for fear of how preposterous it would sound. But I wish I had been there with you at the churchyard. Not by Mrs. Fitzwilliam's headstone—I would not dream of such an intrusion into your privacy—but by the gate, perhaps, for when you came out.
    P.P.S. I cannot wait to learn Mrs. Fitzwilliam's remarks concerning the Three Bears' house.
    P.P.P.S. You are no longer a secret. I have confessed to my sister that my well-traveled, well-connected neighbor from Somerset has been heroically lifting my spirits. I have even described you as handsome—"at least as handsome as Fitz" might have been my exact words. Whether out of prudence or cowardice, however, I have not mentioned The Resemblance. But now, having lied by omission, I fear I might have made that particular subject more difficult for the future.
    I hope not.

Chapter Six

"Mama, can you find me a submarine boat?" asked Hyacinth.

Isabelle and her children were on a knoll just behind their hotel in Ambleside. Louise, worn out by a long hike in the hills, was taking a nap, as was her son. Her twin daughters were in their room, having a tea party with their dolls. Hyacinth had managed only a quarter hour of the doll's tea party before she clamored to be taken outside, and Alexander, her devoted shadow, had followed along.

"That might not be easy, my love," answered Isabelle, stretching out her hand from underneath her parasol. It was much easier to be a black-swathed widow in England than it had been in the sweltering heat of the Subcontinent. The heavy silks didn't weigh her down as much; the skirts, just as narrow as before, somehow allowed her to move more freely.

Or perhaps the spring in her step had nothing to do with the bracing air of the North Atlantic and everything to do with her reawakened optimism. For too long her goal had been to protect herself against further pain and loss, and it had made her definition of happiness smaller and smaller. But now she felt as if she'd ripped off her blindfold to stand blinking in the sun, marveling at the size of the world and all the colors and shapes she had forgotten.

"Why can't it be easy?" Hyacinth wanted to know.

Indeed, why couldn't it be? Happiness had never been about the absence of pain and loss. It was like the sun—one had but to draw aside the curtains and push open the shutters and it would always, always be there.

She laughed at herself inwardly when she realized that Hyacinth was still speaking of the acquisition of a submarine boat. "Well, quite a few inventors, I grant you, are working on submarine boats, but most of them are commissioned by the military. You are not planning to make war on someone, are you, my love?"

"No, I just want to see some fish at the bottom of this mere," said the girl, her eyes glistening. She scanned the lake, blue in the light of the afternoon. "And see if there is an underwater tunnel that will lead me to the open sea, so I can battle a giant squid."

Isabelle smiled. She'd been reading *Twenty Thousand Leagues Under The Sea* to Hyacinth and Alexander at bedtime. The girl's imagination was in ferment.

"But you might be hurt by the giant squid," Alexander piped up. "Or you might hurt the giant squid."

If ever there was a child who didn't want anyone—or any creature—to get hurt, it was Alexander. Isabelle ruffled his hair. "The ocean is big. Hyacinth could motor about for years without running into a giant squid."

"Or I could my first week," said Hyacinth, a dreamy look on her face. "Will you come with me, Mama?"

"I will require you to surface at least once a day so I can have some fresh air. And you must always have a supply of tea and biscuits. If you can manage both, I will come with you."

The topic was entirely fictional, yet Isabelle felt a stirring of her old spirit of adventure.

"What about me?" asked Alexander nervously. "I don't want to go inside a submarine boat."

Small, airless places had always made Alexander anxious, and sometimes downright lightheaded. "Of course you won't need to go into a submarine boat. You can come along on a regular steamer. You do enjoy those, do you not? I can spend one day on the steamer with you and the next in the submarine boat with Hyacinth."

This compromise was apparently satisfactory to Alexander. "Can I be the captain of the steamer? Then I can make sure Hyacinth doesn't get lost."

"And I will make sure your ship doesn't get attacked by giant squids," Hyacinth reciprocated gallantly. "And we can take turns going ashore to get Mama her tea and biscuits if we run out."

Isabelle placed her hand over her heart and kissed each child in turn. "That is very, very kind of both of you."

How fortunate she was, to be in the midst of so much good will and good hope.

"Look, it's Uncle Fitz," shouted Hyacinth.

Isabelle's mind went blank. "What?"

"Over there," Alexander affirmed. "It *is* him. Shall we go speak to him?"

Hyacinth was already running toward the man coming up the slope toward them. As soon as Isabelle had a good look at him she broke into a wide smile. No, it was not Fitz, but Mr. Fitzwilliam. And she felt like a child being presented with a surprise cake richly slathered in chocolate buttercream, ready to jump up and down for joy.

Instead she sprinted after Hyacinth. "Silly girl." She took the girl's hand and reduced her pace. "Walk, don't run. That is not Uncle Fitz. That is our neighbor in Somerset, Mr. Fitzwilliam. And you will make a most provocative impression if you were to rush up to him hollering at the top of your lungs."

"But that is Uncle Fitz. That has to be."

"I know why you think that, my love—I made the same mistake too, when I first met him. But don't you remember, Uncle Fitz's hair is black. Look, Mr. Fitzwilliam's hair is much lighter in color."

Alexander caught up to them. "Did you know Uncle Fitz was coming, Mama?"

"That is not Uncle Fitz. That is Mr. Fitzwilliam." Hyacinth boasted of her new knowledge. "See, he doesn't have black hair."

"All right, children. Behave when you are presented."

Now if Isabelle could only make sure that she herself behaved. She must remember not to wrap both her arms around him as part of her greeting.

That she managed, but it was impossible not to beam from ear to ear, for he too, did exactly that, his eyes shining with pleasure. "Mrs. Englewood, I hope you have been well."

Ever since she'd received his previous letter, she'd entertained herself imagining this: That his question on where she would be staying in the Lake District had not been an idle one, that he would be arriving at just such a gloriously unexpected moment.

And he didn't even pretend it was a coincidence!

"I have been very well indeed, sir. And I have not eloquence enough to tell you how glad I am to see you." It was only after another tremendous smile at him that she remembered her children were still waiting patiently—or impatiently, in Hyacinth's case—to be presented. "May I introduce my daughter Hyacinth and my son Alexander. Children, this is Mr. Fitzwilliam."

He shook hands with the children. "Miss Englewood, enchanted. Master Alexander, a pleasure."

They stared at him openly, still astonished that he was not Fitz. Isabelle smiled again—in fact, she might never stop smiling.

The next moment, a very different emotion buffeted her, one much closer to tears. It was impossible to overstate how many times she had read his letters, particularly the one on his visit to Mrs. Fitzwilliam's grave—and how she always came away with a sense of wonder, renewal, and hope.

"When did you arrive?" she asked, trying not to be too emotional in public.

His smile changed into something slightly more solemn, not melancholy, only pensive—he had sensed her change in mood. "About an hour ago."

"Are you staying at the Lakehead?" She wanted him to be near—as near as possible.

"No, I'm staying at the Governor, a little closer to High Street."

"We've passed it," said Hyacinth. "It has a big sign."

Isabelle shook her head. The girl would never be the sort of the child who was only seen and not heard.

But he did not mind. "Indeed," he answered. "The sign makes it easy to find."

The Governor was not far from the Lakehead. In the evening, after her well-exercised children had been put to bed...

She mustn't let her imagination get away from her altogether. Yes, he had kissed her before, but the first time she'd all but forced herself on him, and the second time he had been in the grasp of a great many emotions, with lust for her person probably quite low on the list.

But even if his friendship did not carry a component of physical interest, she was still beyond thrilled to see him, her friend who had turned what would certainly have been one of the worst nights of her life into one of the best, the memories of which brightened every hour of her day.

"Now, children, Mama needs to speak to Mr. Fitzwilliam." For a long, long time, she hoped. "Hyacinth, would you take yourself and Alexander to Miss Burlingame?"

"Yes, Mama," said Hyacinth. She curtsied prettily to Mr. Fitzwilliam, then, Alexander in hand, skipped away to find their governess.

Isabelle made sure her children entered the hotel as they were bid. When they had disappeared from view, she turned toward Mr. Fitzwilliam. The westerly sun caught a few glimmers of red in his hair; his waistcoat was as vivid a shade of blue as the lake. And his eyes, oh his eyes, they looked upon her with such interest and fondness—she warmed all over. "I see you have not suffered from my absence," she murmured.

He offered her his arm, his gaze lingering on her face. "That is because you have not been absent a day from my life, my dear Mrs. Englewood. Not even an hour."

MILLIE, LADY FITZHUGH, STARED AT THE HOTEL before which the carriage had come to a stop. "My goodness, is this where we spent our wedding night?"

In separate rooms, with a seemingly unbridgeable chasm between them.

"Yes, it is," said her husband, taking her hand in his. "A terrible night for you, wasn't it?"

It had not been easy for her, but she'd been prepared since birth for a loveless marriage. He, on the other hand, had to give up the girl he loved madly almost without warning, not to mention the career in the army he'd planned for himself. All for duty—and a crumbling house. "It was worse for you."

He shook his head. "Getting drunk and smashing mirrors in my room? I cringe at the memory. And let's not even mention my conduct the rest of the honeymoon."

The carriage door opened. He alit and handed her down, his fingers warm upon hers. "However," he said, leaning down so that his lips just brushed her ear, "I am going to make it up to you by being the world's most devoted husband."

She cleared her throat—when he spoke into her ear like this, it never failed to send a torrent of heat surging along her nerves. "More devoted than you have been elsewhere in the Lake District, sir? How is that possible?"

"Oh, you will see, my dear Millie, you will see."

She was quite ready to "see," but she had also learned, in the short weeks since their marriage was first consummated, that sometimes it was even better to wait a little, to delay their next embrace by just long enough so that they were both breathless for it. "Maybe. But in the meanwhile, I must have a turn about the garden."

"Anything you want, Lady Fitz." He smiled as if to himself, and she only heated further.

The garden was to the side and the back of the hotel, full of late-flowering clematis in bursts of fuchsia and purple. "The sundial is still here," she noticed.

"And that's the bench you were sitting on, when I woke up the next day and looked out of the win—"

He blinked. She looked in the direction of his gaze and could not believe her eyes. Mrs. Englewood! She sat on a low stone wall halfway up the green, gentle slope behind the hotel, twirling her black lace parasol in what could only be described as a flirtatious manner.

Next to her, a man sat with his back to them. He spoke; Mrs. Englewood burst into laughter. Millie had never seen Mrs. Englewood except either in a state of grim apprehension or in tears. In laughter her loveliness was almost shocking. Then, even more shocking: She lifted her gloved hand and briefly touched the man's cheek.

Fitz pulled Millie behind a hedge.

"Who is that man?" whispered Millie, still trying to see around the edge of the tall hedge.

"I don't know," Fitz whispered back. "But this is the most thrilling view I've had in days—other than that of your lovely person undressed, of course."

She could not agree more. The ease and intimacy of Mrs. Englewood's gesture was hardly that of a woman still pining for another. "We had best make ourselves scarce, don't you think? Should we find a different hotel?"

Fitz's lips again brushed her ear. "Or we can go to our rooms and not come out again until it is time for us to leave."

This time, she did not need to be persuaded twice.

"Do you know now, this is the first time we've exchanged pleasantries," said Ralston.

They'd shared their views on the weather, the hotels, and the lakes. The clouds above were as white and soft as spring lambs, the scent of summer grass perfumed the breeze, and the stones of the low wall radiated a gentle warmth beneath his hands—the perfect time and place for a bit of leisurely small talk.

"What? We spoke of nothing of substance for an entire quarter hour?" She grinned. "The waste. The horror."

It had not been that long since he first saw her in the rain, an almost wraith-like figure in a shroud of a mourning gown. Her gown was still black, but now it was trimmed with bands of lavender at the cuffs and on the hem—she was transitioning from secondary mourning to half mourning. The lavender was muted, grayish. But to his eyes it was a burst of color almost as brilliant as a sunset sky.

And her face—so much fear and sorrow had been etched in her features. But not when she smiled. When she smiled, as she did now, there was only brightness, clarity, and warmth.

"I hope I haven't come at an inconvenient time," he said impulsively. "But I couldn't wait any longer to see you."

"Good," she said, meeting his gaze. "If you didn't come, I'd have been sorely disappointed."

He loved her candidness. There was never any coquetry to her, any pretense. In fact, the entire positioning of her person—the angle of her torso, the tilt of her head, the placement of her hand right next to his—implied a physical eagerness that made him as randy as a sixteen-year-old boy. He imagined her slipping into his hotel room at night, wearing nothing but a smile. He imagined kissing her everywhere. He imagined her as ravenous as she had been on her honeymoon.

Abruptly she scrambled off the low wall on which they'd been sitting. He started. Surely she had not heard his lustful thoughts.

"Don't look behind you, but my sister is standing at her window." Her voice was low and taut. "She has seen us."

Mrs. Montrose—Mrs. Englewood's letters to him always came from the Montrose residence—must have waved. Mrs. Englewood waved back with a tense-jawed smile.

Ralston had made sure that Mrs. Montrose was not in sight before he approached Mrs. Englewood, believing that she should be the one to decide when to present him. But now he wondered whether it wouldn't have been better to have done the opposite—once Mrs. Montrose had seen him, then she would no longer need to worry about what Mrs. Montrose's reaction would be. She would know.

"Should I absent myself?" His preference was otherwise but he did not want to make the situation more taxing for her.

She half-grimaced, her grip tightening on her parasol. "You have no idea how much I would like to say, 'This is my dear, dear friend, Mr. Fitzwilliam.' But I haven't prepared her at all and it would be too much of a shock."

He remembered how *she* had reacted to him. "I understand," he said, meaning every word.

She closed her gloved hand over his, her eyes wide and deep with gratitude. "Thank you for being so kind. Let me talk to her. I promise I will present you no later than tomorrow."

He had not expected such an emphatic pledge. Perhaps at the back of his mind there had been a small fear that she might want to keep him hidden and never publicly acknowledged, for at her reassurance he suddenly felt as light as one of the clouds floating overhead. "I will wait for your word, then."

She took a deep breath and, with her sister as witness, set her hands on his shoulders and kissed him on his cheek.

LOUISE WAS ALREADY PACING IN THE SITTING ROOM of Isabelle's suite, her skirts rustling with the agitation of her gait. "Is that Mr. Fitzwilliam? Is he here to visit the lakes or to visit you?" she demanded almost before Isabelle had closed the door behind herself.

Trust Louise to waste no time on the preliminaries.

"He is here to visit me," said Isabelle. *That* still gave her little starbursts inside.

"Then why didn't you invite him for tea? I should meet him, if he has traveled hundreds of miles to woo you."

Isabelle crossed the room. Her window overlooked the front of the hotel; the hills stretched green and glossy into the distance. "There is something about Mr. Fitzwilliam you don't know."

"What is it?"

She had meant to idly toy with an edge of the curtain, only to find that she had to unclench her fingers from around a handful of fabric. If her brother thought her mad, perhaps she wouldn't mind so much. But Louise had always been her champion, her shoulder to cry on. "He bears a great resemblance to Fitz."

Dead silence. Then, "No, Isabelle. No. Please tell me it isn't true."

Her heart sank. She swiveled her head a few degrees from side to side, trying to loosen the tension in her neck, before she closed the window and turned around—there was certainly no turning back from this point. "You have twins, Louise. You know that a superficial resemblance is just that, a superficial resemblance."

"No." The jut to Louise's jaw only made Isabelle's heart plummet further. She recognized that expression—Louise was digging in and not even a steam locomotive would make her budge. "Victoria and Cordelia are both my children. Your situation is not remotely analogous. Imagine if your son was taken away from you. Then you accidentally came upon another child who looks exactly like him and brought him home to raise as your own. How would that look?"

Desperate, that was how it would look.

"And this isn't fair to Mr. Fitzwilliam either," Louise went on inexorably. "You wouldn't have been interested in him at all if he didn't look like Fitz."

"I will admit that on the day we met, I would not have given Mr. Fitzwilliam a second glance had he not looked like Fitz. But—"

"See, you admit it yourself."

Elder siblings—sometimes they were wonderful; sometimes they conveniently forgot that she was no longer twelve. "Let me finish, Louise. It took me no time to begin to see Mr. Fitzwilliam for himself. He has led an entirely different life from Fitz and is an entirely different person. I like him for who he is, not whom he resembles."

Louise looked at her as if she were a child trying to deny having stolen a sweet, with that very same piece of confection still in her mouth. "No, Isabelle, that is wishful thinking on your part. Maybe you don't mind him for who he is, but make no mistake, you want him because of whom he resembles."

This was exactly what she'd been afraid of, being buried beneath Louise's anxious concerns with no way of changing the latter's mind. "That is not true. That is simply not true," she could only repeat.

Louise clasped a hand on Isabelle's arm. "I'm sorry, Isabelle. I should have realized something was amiss when you didn't return home bawling. I know what I say hurts you now and will hurt you for some time to come, but you can't simply substitute a lookalike for Fitz."

"I am *not!*" But how could she make Louise understand? How could she make anyone understand?

And the worst part, she now realized, was that she and Fitz had never known the kind of intimacy she shared with Mr. Fitzwilliam. They had been children, deeply in love but also deeply limited in what they knew of life. Theirs had been a connection of unbridled youth and untested hope, like aluminum, shiny, but easily dented. The bond between her and Mr.

Fitzwilliam had been forged from far stronger materials, a steel that had been tried by fire.

"Isabelle—"

"Please, Louise, don't say anything else." Her head was beginning to pound. "I will ask Mr. Fitzwilliam to call on us tomorrow. You will be able to see for yourself what he is and who he isn't."

"That is not a good idea. The meeting will make him believe he is more accepted by the family than he is."

"Then you will pass judgment on a man without ever meeting him?"

"I am not passing judgment on him, Isabelle. I am questioning *your* motives."

She'd always enjoyed Louise's bluntness, but now she felt bludgeoned. "I have no motives here beyond those of friendship and fondness."

Louise pinched the bridge of her nose, as if she too, had been ground down by their quarrel. "This will not end well, Isabelle. Even if I were to believe every word you say, can you imagine what Mr. Fitzwilliam will do when he meets the man to whom he bears a great resemblance? Remember, the one you cannot have?"

Isabelle had thought her insides already wound tight enough, but Louise's question gave them another wrenching twist. "That Mr. Fitzwilliam must decide when the time comes. For now, all I can tell you is that he has earned my affection and my esteem."

Louise gazed at her a long time, shaking her head all the while. "I hope you are right, Isabelle. For your sake, I really hope so."

Chapter Seven

MRS. ENGLEWOOD DID SLIP INTO RALSTON'S HOTEL ROOM that night, but she was fully clothed and wearing the furthest thing from a smile.

He closed the door, followed her to the middle of the room, and set his hand on the small of her back. The silk of her gown was smooth and warm under his palm; the scent of rose petals wafted subtly from her skin. "No luck, I take it?"

She scowled. "None whatsoever. She was even opposed to meeting you, because she did not approve of our friendship."

This surprised him, though it did not manage to completely distract him from his desire to pluck the small, black evening toque from her head and bury his face in her lustrous hair. "That bad?"

She clamped her fingers over her temples. "I overrode her on that particular point and you are expected tomorrow morning at half past ten. There is nothing I can tell her to change her mind, so I hope that you in person would make a difference."

Now he felt slightly ashamed to be so entranced by her charms, when lovemaking was nowhere on her distressed mind. "I don't know whether I will make any difference, but I will attempt to be both sincere and charming."

She made a noise at the back of her throat, a low growl of frustration.

He turned her around and wrapped his arms about her. "Allow me to apologize for my troublesome face."

She sagged against him. Her reply, however, was emphatic. "Never apologize for your face. If you had a different face, we wouldn't be the friends we are today—and I would not change that for anything."

Her words flowed deep into his heart, a cascade of lyrical warmth. "It will all be fine," he murmured, his voice thick with gratitude. "Perhaps not tomorrow, perhaps not next week. But everything will be all rght."

She sighed. Her hand settled on his sleeve and he forgot what else he was about to say. The cambric of his shirt was lightweight, hardly a barrier to the warmth and pressure of her fingers.

Her fingers spread. Then, without warning, they tightened on his forearm. She clasped him as if she could not bear to let go, her breaths shallow and ragged.

He, on the other hand, could not breathe at all, caught in the urgency of her gesture. He stared at her still gloved hand, imagining the strain in her knuckles, her fingertips white from the force she exerted. Gradually her grip eased, but the tension inside him only escalated. He wanted that jolt of pressure from her again, that involuntary expression of need.

He set his hand on her wrist. She stiffened, but as he did nothing, only held her wrist loosely, she slowly relaxed again.

He opened the hook-and-eye closure on her cuff and slid his fingers beneath the black silk of her mourning gown. Her skin was wondrously soft. His breaths came back in gulps.

All of a sudden her fingers were in his hair, her mouth fastened to his, parting his lips and seeking his tongue. He heard a small moan from himself. Yes, this was what he had hoped would happen, when he came to the Lake District: a sweet friendship made even sweeter by the pleasures of the flesh.

He tilted his head to kiss her more closely, more completely. Little whimpers escaped her throat. She spread her hands against his back, running her fingers over his shoulder blades and the channel of his spine. His body pulsed with arousal.

She already had his jacket off his shoulders before he began to reciprocate the disrobing. He did not hurry, but relished the feel of each fastener popping apart, the sensation of his knuckles sliding against the soft, almost airy nainsook of her corset cover while he divided the stiff silk of her dress. She did not stand idle, but continued to strip him of his clothes, and applied her lips to every new square inch of skin she exposed.

Those dropped kisses were slightly moist, and scorched him wherever they landed. He kissed her on the mouth as he roughly pushed her dress to the floor. Now there was no more patience. He yanked her corset cover over her head and all but tore her corset in half.

"I knew I employed a sponge tonight for a reason," she panted.

"My God. Do you mean to tell me this is all premeditated?" The thought of her inserting the sponge while anticipating his lovemaking made him almost painfully hard.

"Precisely. So you had better make my efforts worthwhile."

He pushed her to the edge of his bed; she pulled him into it. He kissed her—her throat, her collarbone, her shoulders—while she pushed his trousers, first with her fingers, then with her foot, off his person. Her hand dug into his bottom. He took her nipple into his mouth. The feel of her, all glorious skin and impatient desire; the taste of her, milky and wholesome; the sound of her, a sonata of unabashed moans.

"Yes, more," she cried, as he licked her nipple with the underside of his tongue. "Yes, more," she cried, as his hand arrived at the seam between her thighs. "Yes, more," she cried again, as his fingers parted her damp folds and penetrated deep inside.

He thought he would never heard sounds lovelier than an infinite loop of those two syllables. But then he licked her where his fingers had been, long, slow strokes, and this time, she made only beautifully incoherent noises, too far gone for words.

Her first climax came quickly, an undulating shudder that started at the center of her body and propagated everywhere else. Her second climax came even quicker, with barely a pause for her to catch her breath. After that her climaxes blurred into a continuum, her nipples hard, her body writhing, the entire room ricocheting with the throaty moans of her pleasure.

When he entered her at last, she quivered, peaking anew. Then she pushed him onto his back and climbed atop him, her long legs spread wide, her hair tumbling free, her flesh gripping his in a way that made him throw his head back in amazement. And when she tossed her hair over her shoulders, and teased him by playing with her breasts, the sight of her slender fingers upon those rosy nipples drove him completely over the edge, his release fevered and endless.

OH, HOW SHE'D MISSED IT, the euphoria of lovemaking, the bone-melting relaxation following the quakes and tremors.

"My God, Isabelle," he murmured against her cheek. "Now I can see why you wrote that limerick. But I don't believe Captain Englewood ever groaned when you wanted to be pleasured again. In his place I'd have been ecstatic."

She giggled. "No, he never quite groaned. Though he was rather shocked in the beginning—he'd been led to believe that genteelly raised young ladies only participated passively in such animal acts."

"I love being ravished by you."

"Then you've made the right friend, Ralston."

"I have made an amazing friend, Isabelle."

Such a sense of ease permeated her, not just from his compliment, but from his presence and the combined optimism their togetherness generated. She kissed him on his jaw. He turned his head, kissed her on the corner of her mouth, and brought a strand of her disheveled hair to his lips.

"You have some white hair."

"Had my first one when I was sixteen. I'm going to turn grey early in life, like my mother did."

"You will be the most gorgeous silver-haired lady in all of Britain."

That she would be silver-haired by the time she was forty had never bothered her. But now, for the very first time, the thought excited her. She slid her fingers along his arm, meaning to interlace her fingers with his.

"I want to brush your white hair someday," he continued.

She stilled. Her hair wouldn't be completely white for almost another decade and a half. Either he was suggesting a very long affair or…

"Don't let your sister stop you—if that's what you are worried about."

He'd misinterpreted her silence. As much as she wanted him to be accepted—indeed, embraced—by Louise and the rest of her family, it was no longer her family's opposition that had her fretting. She knew now what she was up against; she was prepared to dig in and hold her own ground. Not to mention she was both of age and financially independent: She wanted their approval but she did not need it.

"My family can huff and puff, but they will come around eventually."

"Then what are you worried about?"

She exhaled, not quite ready to face that eventuality. "You."

"Me?" He sounded surprised, even amused.

It hadn't mattered at all when she'd propositioned him at Doyle's Grange. Even when they became long-distance friends it hadn't been a pressing concern. But now that he'd come for her, now that they were lovers—lovers who hoped to remain lovers for a long time—the problem could no longer be skirted.

She pushed herself up on her hands and gazed into eyes that were the color of a mossy pond. "Everyone would think, as my sister does, that I am using you as a substitute for Fitz, a replica I happened to find when I couldn't have the original. You would hate it."

He shook his head firmly. "Not as much as I would hate it if you were to let such a trivial reason stand in the way of much happiness."

She did not plan to let her fear stand in the way of anything—she had no wish to ever again allow fear to be the guiding force in her life. But it did not mean she could not have legitimate concerns. "What would happen when you and Fitz run into each other?"

He smoothed her hair. "I dare say I would find it a laugh. Then I would thank him for choosing otherwise, so that you and I could meet as we did."

He sounded so confident, so certain, it seemed almost churlish not to believe him. "Are you really sure about that?"

He pulled her toward him, his gaze upon her, and whispered against her lips. "More sure than I am of anything else in my life."

WHEN RALSTON ARRIVED AT THE LAKEHEAD THE NEXT MORNING, he was shown into the sitting room of Isabelle's suite. The room was furnished in the lightest of colors: An ivory chaise, chairs upholstered in buttery hues, and creamy wallpaper—the use of such pristine shades made possible by the hotel's distance from the sooty air of the cities. Isabelle, seated in a straight-back chair, was the somber focus in the midst of so much delicate brightness.

The wait for his arrival had not been easy: Her hands were clutched together, her jaw tight. But before he could direct a reassuring smile at her, a sharp gasp erupted from a different part of the room. He turned to see a dark-haired woman of about thirty coming out of her chair, agape.

"Louise, may I present Mr. Fitzwilliam? Mr. Fitzwilliam, my sister, Mrs. Montrose."

They shook hands, Mrs. Montrose's hand limp and unresponsive in his. To his inquiry concerning the agreeableness of her stay in the Lake District, her answer was a few mumbled, indistinct syllables.

"I understand you reside in Aberdeen," he said, making small talk. "I passed through years ago, when I was still at university."

"Yes, I suppose," she murmured, her shock-widened eyes never leaving his.

A sense of unease crept over him. He had expected a strong reaction, but not an extreme one. "And Mrs. Englewood tells me Mr. Montrose is a barrister."

Isabelle had also informed him that her sister had to wait a number of years to marry, as Mr. Montrose had come from a family in trade, rather than country gentry, like theirs.

"Yes, I suppose," was again Mrs. Montrose's response.

Nonplussed, he turned to Isabelle. He might be the one needing *her* reassurance now. "And how do you do, Mrs. Englewood?"

"Very well, thank you." Despite her obvious nerves, she smiled a little. "One might even say I am in an enviable state of being."

He couldn't help smiling back. "And Miss Englewood and young Master Alexander?"

"They are on the water, rowing with Miss Burlingame. Alexander will be in heaven; Hyacinth will wish herself in a submarine boat instead, crawling along the bottom of the lake."

A hotel attendant brought in a tray of tea. Isabelle offered him a seat and busied herself pouring tea for everyone. The moment he had a cup in hand, Mrs. Montrose said, "I trust we've beat about the bushes quite enough?"

She had, it seemed, recovered from her shock. Isabelle's lips flattened. Ralston set down his tea and rose to stand next to her chair—Mrs. Montrose was no doubt acting out of concern, but she was still distressing her sister.

"This is madness, Isabelle." Mrs. Montrose's displeasure was palpable. "Until Mr. Fitzwilliam walked in, I had thought you meant he shared a general resemblance to Fitz: hair color, eye color, build, and so on. But this is worse. This is so much worse than anything I could have imagined. Does this poor man have any idea? Have you not shown him any photographs?"

"I don't carry a photograph of Fitz with me everywhere I go," said Isabelle defensively. "Not anymore, in any case."

"Mrs. Montrose, please do not speak of me as if I am no longer present," said Ralston. "And please do not attribute any exploitation to Mrs. Englewood's part. I was given to understand, the moment we met, that I am Lord Fitzhugh's spitting image. Our friendship developed not because of it, but in spite of it."

Mrs. Montrose glanced Isabelle's way, and back at him. "I was also given to understand, sir, though not as soon as I should have been, that you resembled Lord Fitzhugh. But being told is not the same thing as witnessing with my own eyes. I can only imagine, by your nonchalance, that you have yet to meet Lord Fitzhugh?"

"Indeed I have not."

"I have, sir, many times. And I cannot look upon you without thinking of him in the most visceral manner possible."

Her vehemence took him by surprise. Isabelle chair scraped against the floor as she shot out of it. He set his hand on her elbow a moment before turning back to Mrs. Montrose. "I understand you have twins, Mrs. Montrose. I have cousins who are twins. I do not mistake my cousins and I am sure you do not mistake your own children."

"Oh, drat it. Why do the two of you insist on using twins for an analogy? How many times do I have to explain that it is not the same?" Mrs. Montrose stalked to the window. "I can have quadruplets who look exactly like each other and they can all be my children. But Isabelle can only love one man. You are so sure, Mr. Fitzwilliam, that—"

Something below caught her attention. "My goodness gracious," she whispered.

"What is it?" asked Isabelle immediately.

"It's Fitz—and his wife. They look like they are about to leave."

"What?" Isabelle rushed to the window. "Are you—"

She fell silent. Slowly, carefully, she turned her head and glanced at Ralston. It must be Lord Fitzhugh then. Ralston hesitated, but the next moment he was standing before the window, acutely aware of the two women's attention on him.

Outside the hotel there was more than one party leaving. Porters rushed about with portmanteaus and steamer trunks. Ladies in their bright summer dresses waited in small clusters. A group of gentlemen, a father and his two grown sons, by the looks of it, were engaged in an animated discussion.

There was no sign of anyone who looked remotely like him.

Then his gaze landed on...himself.

It was as if he stood before a mirror, with his reflection acting independently of him. The real him clutched at the windowsill, dumbfounded, while his reflection leaned down and spoke into the ear of a petite, pretty brunette, who laughed behind her fan.

But this is worse. This is so much worse than anything I could have imagined, echoed Mrs. Montrose's words in his head.

Lord and Lady Fitzhugh climbed into a carriage and drove off, leaving Ralston with a strange hollowness in his chest. He turned away from the window, only to catch sight of himself in a mirror on the wall.

I cannot look upon you without thinking of him in the most visceral manner possible.

Dear God, he could not look upon himself without thinking of Lord Fitzhugh in the most visceral manner possible.

"Mr. Fitzwilliam. Mr. Fitzwilliam," came an urgent voice. "*Ralston.*"

He looked blankly at Isabelle.

She was pale and hesitant. "Are you all right?"

No, he was not all right. How could he be? He was but an almost exact replica of a man who was now in love with another woman.

He shook his head to clear it, but it was no use. "Please excuse me, ladies, I'm afraid I must take leave of you. I'm—I'm—"

He gave up trying to think of an excuse, bowed, and walked out of the room.

Chapter Eight

HE LEFT WITHOUT A BACKWARD GLANCE—and with all too swift a gait, as if he would have gladly broken into a sprint had the road outside not teemed with chattering tourists.

Isabelle remained at the window until he disappeared from sight—then she remained some more, rooted in place by disbelief.

"I'm sorry," said Louise, her arm around Isabelle's shoulders. "Will you allow me to apologize?"

Isabelle bit her lower lip. "He walked out on his own two feet. It wasn't your fault."

"No, I want to apologize for earlier, when I said that you were using him as a copy for what you couldn't have."

Isabelle laughed. It was either laughing, or crying. "What changed your mind?"

"If Fitz was the one you still wanted, when we were all at the window, you would have been looking at *him*. But you had eyes only for Mr. Fitzwilliam. So I was wrong to tell you that you didn't know your own mind. Forgive me."

"What's there to forgive?" Louise only wanted her to not make a mistake she'd regret. And as much as her stubborness had frustrated Isabelle, she could not resent her for it. "You should have seen yourself, like a mother tigress, growling in protectiveness."

"Mr. Fitzwilliam was protective of you too. He didn't like it when I was too hard on you."

Isabelle did not reply. Was it only yesterday that she'd thought happiness as simple a matter as throwing open a window to see the sun outside? The curtains of the window before her were open, the shutters drawn back, the sky beyond wide and blue. But she could not see the sun, only the shadow it cast of the hotel.

The next moment she squared her shoulders. No, she would not be so pessimistic. She could not see the sun because her window faced west, and it would be hours before the sun's path took it within view. In the meanwhile, light drenched the surrounding hills, reflected from the windows of every passing carriage, and shimmered upon the waters of Windermere.

"He will come back," said Louise earnestly. "It's just the shock. Once it wears off he will remember that even twins who resemble each other most fiercely are still separate persons."

Isabelle snorted. "Since when did you subscribe to the twins analogy?"

"Once I saw how you looked at him."

She'd looked at him as the man who had promised to brush her hair when it would have turned all white. But he, he hadn't looked at her at all. Had all but run away.

In the distance she could make out a boy in a sailor suit and a girl in a reddish frock walking alongside a young woman in a brown tailormade—her children, returning from their excursion on the water with their governess. They looked chatty, all three of them, smiling and gesticulating. Hyacinth and Alexander would reach the hotel bursting with discoveries to share.

And she would have to be sure not to cry in front of them. She never had, not even on the day of Lawrence's funeral. She must not begin now.

"He will be back," Louise said, patting her on the shoulder. "I promise you he will be back."

Isabelle blinked back her tears. "I'd better order a tray for the children. Mr. Fitzwilliam will do as he pleases, but my children must eat when they are hungry."

RALSTON WALKED. WATER, HILLS, TREE-SHADED PATHS, pink-cheeked tourists returning from their morning hike—everything was a blur to the roiling unrest within. At some point, vaguely realizing the day might not be long enough for him to go all the way around Windermere, he turned around, took the ferry he'd passed on his way, and crossed the ribbon-like lake at its midpoint.

His thoughts kept dragging him back to the kiss beneath the portico of Doyle's Grange. The memory of it had always both amused and aroused him. Now, however, he truly understood for the very first time that her need and fervor had been for someone else.

A man cast from the exact same mold as he, but another man nevertheless.

And what of their lovemaking the night before? Her voluptuous climaxes had filled him with both gratitude and pride. But whom had she been embracing, really, when she'd cried out in her moments of pleasure?

At the village nearest the ferry landing, his tongue parched, his head light with hunger, he bought a sandwich and a canteen of water. He ate sitting by himself, staring at the table before him. When he was done, he resumed his walk, despite the protestation of his feet against shoes only meant for the drawing room.

He was no longer famished, or thirsty, but he was tired. He welcomed the fatigue; he welcomed even more the weary quiet of his mind. No more thoughts, no more memories, just a blessed blankness as he pushed himself forward, while leaves rustled overhead and birds sang in the distance.

Isabelle's hands around his face, her eyes brimming with tears. So if Mrs. Fitzwilliam had any regrets, *she told him, her voice urgent,* it would be that the rest of her life was too short to spend with you—because *that* was her heart's desire, not the Faroe Islands, and not anything else.

The vividness of the recollection stunned him. He could almost believe himself in the midst of it, her fingers warm and strong upon his cheeks.

Isabelle running her hand through his hair, her eyes full of sympathy and affection. Tell me about Mrs. Fitzwilliam's comments. It will help you remember them better for the future.

He'd barely stopped himself from taking her hand and pressing a kiss to the center of her palm.

Careful, old widower, *Isabelle mumbling, as he carried her back up to her room.*

And he had gloried in his strength, his ability to take care of her when she most needed it.

These were not interactions she could have had while pretending he was Lord Fitzhugh. Of course not. Little of their entire history, beyond that first kiss, had been about her erstwhile sweetheart.

And when they'd made love, what had they been discussing until the moment they gave in to their desire? The fact that his face was going to cause them much trouble, but that she wouldn't change a thing, because if he didn't resemble Fitz, they would not have become friends.

Or lovers. Lovers who should still be together years from now, when her hair had turned white.

He stopped altogether in his tracks, his heart pounding with dismay. What a fool he had been, rushing out like that. What a bigger fool he had been, to ever doubt her sincerity and honesty. And it made him the biggest fool of all to have put miles upon miles between them, so that even after he came to his senses, he was still far away from her.

Too far away.

He swore and began to run.

As it turned out, he didn't need to run all the way back to Ambleside. At the next jetty he came across there was a small steamboat for hire. He leaped on board, waving all the currency he had on hand.

He returned to his own hotel room first and ordered a bottle of the hotel's best claret—his groveling would have a better chance of being heard if it was accompanied by a glass of good wine. He also asked for a bouquet of flowers—it would have been better had he gathered the flowers himself, but a man could not both run in panic and think of flowers at the same time.

As he waited for everything to be delivered, he changed into clean clothes, opened his window, and froze. In the gardens behind the Governor, between a bed of white lilies and a sizable cluster of purple acanthus, stood none other than Lord Fitzhugh and his wife, thoroughly engrossed in each other.

This time, Ralston did not feel as if he were looking at his own reflection. Of course Lord Fitzhugh was a different man. Ralston would never look so at Lady Fitzhugh. That kind of tenderness he saved only for his Isabelle.

He ran out of the door, almost knocking over the porter who had come to deliver the wine and the flowers.

As there was no way to soften the jolt, he didn't try to, but simply came to a stop behind the Fitzhughs. "Lord Fitzhugh, Lady Fitzhugh."

The Fitzhughs turned around, gaped at him, looked at each other, then gaped at him some more. Lord Fitzhugh was the first to recover his composure. "May I—ah—be of help, sir?"

"My name is Fitzwilliam, my lord. I live not far from Doyle's Grange—I am Mrs. Englewood's neighbor."

Lady Fitzhugh's jaw dropped. "You wouldn't be the gentleman we saw speaking to her yesterday afternoon, would you, behind the Lakehead?"

"I was indeed. Mrs. Englewood and I met the last time she was at Doyle's Grange." Judging by the Fitzhughs' expressions, they understood exactly the context of Mrs. Englewood's prior visit to Doyle's Grange. "The way I look, you will not be surprised that I caught her attention."

"No, indeed," said Lady Fitzhugh, glancing from Ralston to her husband and back.

"To make a long story short, her sister is not in favor of her spending too much time with someone who looks like a replacement. She thinks Isa—Mrs. Englewood is courting future heartache. So this morning Mrs. Englewood arranged for me to meet Mrs. Montrose in person, hoping that I might be able to better persuade the latter."

"Mrs. Montrose was shocked, I take it?" said Lord Fitzhugh.

"She was, but that was nothing—I don't mind Mrs. Montrose. But then I happened to see you and Lady Fitzhugh leaving the Lakehead."

Lady Fitzhugh's hand came up over her heart. "My goodness. We thought it would be a good idea to change hotels, to not disturb Mrs. Englewood with our presence. We did not mean to cause any trouble."

"No, please don't blame yourselves," Ralston hastened to reassure her. "You are not in the least responsible for how I acted."

"I hope you did not suspect Mrs. Englewood of actually using you as a substitute," said Lord Fitzhugh. "She is incapable of that kind of pretense. In fact, she is incapable of any kind of pretense."

"I am afraid I forgot that entirely when I left in a blaze of theatrics. And now—" He glanced in the direction of the Lakehead, his heart constricting with the disappointment he must have caused her.

"Courage, Mr. Fitzwilliam," said Lord Fitzhugh. "The course of true love never did run smooth."

Ralston exhaled. "Then may I ask a favor, sir? May I ask that you come with me, just for a few minutes, so that Mrs. Englewood can see that I have made peace with our resemblance? Your presence would make for a better testimony than my words alone."

Lord Fitzhugh studied him for a few seconds, then smiled. "It will be my great pleasure, sir."

ISABELLE STARED AT THE BOTTLE OF CLARET as she trailed her fingers over the bouquet of white lilies and purple acanthus that had been delivered at the same time. They could have come from no one else. Did this mean—she didn't dare let herself complete the thought.

The sun had begun its descent to the horizon. A golden light suffused the sitting room. She lifted the bottle to the light, turning it this way and that, and watched it sparkle.

A knock came at her door. Her heart raced. Ralston. What would he say to her? What would she say to him?

In the end, she said something she could not have predicted. "Fitz!"

He smiled. "Isabelle."

She smiled back at him. Dear, old Fitz. She hadn't been entirely certain before, but now, face to face, she realized they would always remain friends. "Come in. Shall I ring for some—"

Fitz had not come alone. Next to him stood—

"Mr. Fitzwilliam," she said stiffly.

"Mrs. Englewood," he returned a soft greeting.

An apologetic one.

Part of her was inwardly running about and screaming at his reappearance; another part of her saw red. She narrowed her eyes, but stepped back and let them in.

"Is Lady Fitzhugh well?" she asked Fitz, ignoring Ralston, while at the same time being acutely aware of his windswept hair and sun-reddened cheeks—he had been outside all this time.

"She is very well. She sends her regards." Fitz watched them with restrained amusement.

Ralston hadn't taken his eyes off her since his return—her anger was beginning to be perforated by a rising giddiness. She continued to ignore him. "I don't think I've ever told you this, Fitz, but my children demolished the honey from Lady Fitzhugh's lavender fields."

"She will be delighted to hear that—and you have just assured Hyacinth and Alexander each of a lifetime supply of lavender honey."

"They will be gorging themselves silly." She touched her hand to his elbow. "Will you stay a while? Louise is at her bath. I'm sure she would like to see you too."

"And I her. Lady Fitzhugh and I will gladly call on her tomorrow, but for now—" He glanced at Ralston. "For now Mr. Fitzwilliam would probably like a few minutes of your time. He sought me out, hoping to show you that he is more than comfortable in my presence and most certainly does not see himself as a stand-in of any sort, for anyone."

"Well, it took him long enough," she said testily.

Fitz returned a pat on her elbow. "I will see myself out. Lady Fitz is waiting with bated breath to learn how Mr. Fitzwilliam's apology turns out."

"If you leave now, then you will not know how the apology turns out."

"It is a rare and superior man who not only admits his mistakes but seeks actively to make amends. I have every confidence that Mr. Fitzwilliam's apology will go over very well."

"Hmm," said Isabelle.

Fitz laughed softly, kissed her on the cheek, and shook Ralston's hand. "I shall come bearing jars of honey, next time I call on Doyle's Grange."

"CAPITAL FELLOW," SAID RALSTON.

Before Isabelle could glare at him, the door opened and in came Louise. *Her* glare was far more awe-inspiring: If Isabelle could throw daggers with a look, then Louise launched broad swords with hers.

"What are you doing here, Mr. Fitzwilliam?" she demanded.

"I've come to apologize for my conduct earlier today. And I hope for your forgiveness, Mrs. Montrose—and Mrs. Englewood's," he said, not sheepishly, but gracefully, with both humility and dignity.

Louise, however, seemed to take no notice of his remarkable demeanor. "And why should I forgive you? You led my sister to believe that you cared for her. Then, at the least appearance of an obstacle, you ran away, not only injuring her, but humiliating her before her family."

Isabelle opened her mouth to protest. Surely, there was no need to go so far in castigating him.

"I agree that my actions were deplorable. There is no excuse. But if you would allow me to give a *reason*, then it is this: I love Mrs. Englewood. I love her to the depth and breadth of my soul."

Isabelle sucked in a breath.

"But whereas earlier I'd thought my affection returned in full," he went on, "the sight of Lord Fitzhugh filled me with doubts."

"You insult my sister with your doubts."

"Louise—" Isabelle protested.

Louise held up a hand. "My sister, who is not only beautiful, but candid and loyal. And you treated her as if she were a liar and manipulator."

"That is not true, Mrs. Montrose. I never thought for a moment that she exploited *me*. What I did wonder was whether she had deceived herself. But of course she hadn't. She had been honest both with me and with herself."

He was still speaking to Louise, but he looked directly at Isabelle. "I know I have made a hash of things. I know I deserve any punishment she deigns to mete out. But I also know that I love her more than ever, that my doubts, when vanquished, only strengthened my faith in her."

The beauty and utter conviction of his words made her dizzy.

Even Louise's voice softened, though her next question was no less pointed. "Pretty words. But every Tom, Dick and Harry will still think that you are a replacement for Fitz—and some of them will tell you so to your face. What will you do then?"

"Take my own advice and chortle. It doesn't matter what anyone else thinks, as long as Mrs. Englewood and I know the truth of our hearts."

"I don't know about—"

"That's enough, Louise," Isabelle said quietly. "Mr. Fitzwilliam made a mistake. He has apologized. I am more than pleased to accept his apology—let us not harp on him anymore."

Her sister not only did not object, she smiled. "Good. I was beginning to run out of shrewish things to say. No, no, don't look so surprised, Isabelle. Mr. Fitzwilliam deserved a good dressing down, but he also deserves credit for an apology properly done. I gave him the dressing down, you come to his defense, and now all is well."

Isabelle was still agog as Louise hugged her. "I will expect Mr. Fitzwilliam to join us for dinner tonight." Louise lowered her voice. "But afterwards, I will once again pretend not to notice that you have slipped out."

"Is it true you have accepted my apology?" asked Ralston when they were alone, scarcely able to believe it.

"Didn't I already say I did?" She gave him a look that was exasperated, but also half smiling.

He closed the distance between them and took hold of her hands. "I love you, Isabelle. And my heart's desire is to spend the rest of my life with you. Tell me what I need to do to achieve that good fortune."

"Well, hmm. I will need a cube of ice from the glaciers at the heart of Antarctica, a mountain of sand from the Great Victoria Desert, teeth of a piranha from the center of the Amazon, and the braided tail of a unicorn."

He loved the light that had returned to her eyes. The entire room glowed with the afternoon sun, but she glowed most of all. "When it comes to the unicorn tail, do you have a preference as to the color?"

The corners of her lips quivered. "White would be good enough."

"But that's so common. Are you sure that for your hand, I don't need to bag a rainbow-colored unicorn tail instead?"

This time she couldn't quite suppress her smile. "I love you too," she said softly. "And yes, I will marry you."

No one would ever convince him that he didn't levitate an inch or so off the floor at that moment. He wrapped his arms around her and kissed her with all the joy in his soul.

"Mama, will you come and have tea with us?" came Hyacinth's voice from the other side of the door.

They pulled apart, breathless, and giggled at each other.

"There are egg mayonnaise sandwiches, Mama," added Alexander. "You like egg mayonnaise sandwiches."

"Will you be all right until after dinner?" Isabelle asked softly, smoothing a finger over Ralston's brow. "You are most welcome to join us for tea, if you'd like."

"I will be delighted to join you for tea, darling," he answered in all honesty. Every moment with her was a thrill.

"Well, then." She gave him a quick kiss, then walked to the door, opening it wide. "Look, children, look who is back."

Epilogue

HYACINTH AND ALEXANDER'S LAUGHTER, as they chased each other in the gardens, rose up to the open windows. They adored Doyle's Grange and could not wait to make the acquaintance of Lord Northword's grandchildren and some of the younger children from Beauregard's Farm.

Upstairs there were boxes and more boxes. As Ralston helped put up Isabelle's photographs on the mantel of the sitting room, he suddenly remembered her ancestress. "Where is that miniature portrait of yours, darling?"

"I sent it to a cousin of mine—she just gave birth to a sickly baby and needs the luck more than I do."

"So the portrait is supposed to bring good luck?"

"Of course." She kissed him on his lips as she passed him, headed for yet another box. "That was the belonging I had come back to Doyle's Grange to retrieve. And it led me directly to you."

He knelt down next to her at the new box, which contained framed photographs of Hyacinth and Alexander at various points in their young lives. Together they cooed over the pictures, which were adorable indeed.

She was on her way to the mantel with a handful of the photographs when she stopped and looked back at him. "By the way, you never did let me know what Mrs. Fitzwilliam said about the Three Bears' house."

"Ah, that." He smiled a little at the memory. "She wrote, 'Once in a while Goldilocks finds something just right. So have I, by the way.'"

"How interesting." Isabelle beamed at him. "I would say that also describes exactly how *I* feel about you."

With a framed photograph in each hand, he rose and stole a kiss from her. "And I shall only love you more when you are a silver-haired lady, stomping your cane about how I will make you late for church again."

About Carolyn Jewel

CAROLYN JEWEL WAS BORN ON A MOONLESS NIGHT. That darkness was seared into her soul and she became an award winning author of historical and paranormal romance. She has a very dusty car and a Master's degree in English that proves useful at the oddest times. An avid fan of fine chocolate, finer heroines, Bollywood films, and heroism in all forms, she has three cats and a dog. Also a son. One of the cats is his.

Visit her on the web at http://www.carolynjewel.com, on Facebook at http://www.facebook.com/CarolynJewelAuthor, on twitter at http://www.twitter.com/cjewel.

Awesome people sign up for her newsletter. She sends one out 3 or 4 times a year, depending on how fast she's writing.

Other Books by Carolyn Jewel

Historical Romance

Reforming the Scoundrels Series
 1. *Not Wicked Enough*
 2. *Not Proper Enough*

Other historical romances
 Scandal, 2010 RITA finalist, Best Regency
 Indiscreet, 2010 winner, Booksellers Best, Best Short Historical
 Moonlight, a short story
 Lord Ruin
 The Spare
 Stolen Love
 Passion's Song

Paranormal Romance

My Immortals Series
 1. *My Wicked Enemy*
 2. *My Forbidden Desire,* 2010 RITA finalist, Paranormal
 3. *My Immortal Assassin*
 4. *My Dangerous Pleasure*
 4½. *Free Fall,* a novella

The Crimson City Series
 A Darker Crimson, Crimson City Series, Book 4
 DX, A Crimson City novella

About Courtney Milan

COURTNEY MILAN IS A *New York Times* and a *USA Today* bestselling author. Her books have received starred reviews in *Publishers Weekly* and *Booklist*. She's twice been a RITA® finalist, and her second book was chosen as a *Publishers Weekly* Best Book of 2010. Courtney lives in the Rocky Mountains with her husband, a medium-sized dog, and an attack cat. She's working on a garden, an older house, and her next book.

Want to know when Courtney's next book comes out? Sign up for her new release e-mail list at http://www.courtneymilan.com, follow her on twitter at @courtneymilan, or like her on Facebook at http://www.facebook.com/CourtneyMilanAuthor.

Other Books by Courtney Milan

The Brothers Sinister Series
½. *The Governess Affair* (available now)
1. *The Duchess War* (October 2012)
2. *The Heiress Effect* (2013)
3. *The Countess Conspiracy* (2013)

"The Lady Always Wins,"
in *Three Weddings and a Murder*

The Turner Series
1. *Unveiled*
1½. *Unlocked*
2. *Unclaimed*
3. *Unraveled*

The Carhart Series
½. "This Wicked Gift," in *The Heart of Christmas*
1. *Proof by Seduction*
2. *Trial by Desire*

About Sherry Thomas

Sherry Thomas burst onto the scene with *Private Arrangements,* a *Publishers Weekly* Best Book of 2008. Her sophomore book, *Delicious,* is a *Library Journal* Best Romance of 2008. Her next two books, *Not Quite a Husband* and *His at Night,* are back-to-back winners of Romance Writers of America's prestigious RITA® Award for Best Historical Romance in 2010 and 2011. Lisa Kleypas calls her "the most powerfully original historical romance author working today."

And by the way, English is Sherry's second language.

To keep in the loop about Sherry's upcoming books, sign up for her new release e-mail list at http://www.sherrythomas.com. You can like her on Facebook at http://www.facebook.com/authorsherrtythomas, or find her on twitter at @sherrythomas.

Other Books by Sherry Thomas

The Fitzhugh Trilogy
  1. *Beguiling the Beauty*
  2. *Ravishing the Heiress*
  2½. *A Dance in Moonlight*
  3. *Tempting the Bride*

Lightly Related Historical Romances
  Private Arrangements
  Delicious
  Not Quite a Husband
  His at Night

Printed in Great Britain
by Amazon.co.uk, Ltd.,
Marston Gate.